EAST END ANGELS

Meet The East End Angels, the newest members of Station Seventy-Five's ambulance crew

Strong-willed **Winnie** loves being part of the crew at Station Seventy-Five but her parents are less than happy. When a tragedy hits too close to home she finds herself wondering if she's cut out for this life after all. Former housemaid **Bella** was forced to leave the place she loved and is finally starting to build a new life but it seems she may have to start all over again. East-Ender **Frankie's** sense of loyalty keeps her tied to home so it's not easy for her to stay focused at work. These three very different women soon realise they'll need each other if they're to get through the days ahead.

EAST END ANGELS

EAST END ANGELS

by

Rosie Hendry

Magna Large Print Books
Long Preston, North Yorkshire,
BD23 4ND, England.

British Library Cataloguing in Publication Data.

A catalogue record of this book is
available from the British Library

ISBN   978-0-7505-4569-3

First published in Great Britain in 2017 by Sphere

Published in Large Print 2018 by arrangement with
Little, Brown Book Group

Magna Large Print is an imprint of Library Magna Books Ltd.

Printed and bound in Great Britain by
T.J. (International) Ltd., Cornwall, PL28 8RW

For my Dad,
who taught me so much.

'Oh! I have slipped the surly bonds of Earth
And danced the skies on laughter-silvered wings.'

John Gillespie Magee (1922-1941)

Chapter One

London, August 1940

Stella Franklin brought the car to a smooth halt and risked a quick glance at the pail of water standing on the floor beside the examiner's seat. She was relieved to see that although the surface was rocking slightly, none of the water had slopped out and it was still as full as when they'd set off.

'If you'd like to switch off the engine, Miss Franklin; we don't want to waste a drop of precious petrol, do we?' The examiner spoke without looking at her as he started to write on the form attached to his clipboard.

Stella did as she was told and the sound of the engine died away. The quiet that replaced it seemed all the more pronounced as she waited for the verdict. Had she passed or not? She was desperate to know and had to clamp her mouth shut to stop herself from blurting out the question. She must be patient and wait, listening to the sound of the examiner's pen nib scratching against the paper while her heart thumped so fast and hard inside her chest that it felt like it was trying to batter its way out.

'So, Miss Franklin,' the examiner finally said, snapping the lid back on his pen and tucking it safely into the inside pocket of his tweed jacket. 'You wish to be an ambulance driver?'

She nodded. 'Yes, I do.'

Was he about to fail her? She'd tried so hard, being extra careful changing gear, slowing down smoothly, making sure the car made no sudden jerky movements to spill any of the precious water, which was supposed to test the gentleness of the drive, replicating how an injured patient would be jolted around.

'I understand you've completed all your other training, first aid and anti-gas precautions and such?' The examiner paused and then smiled at her. 'Well I'm pleased to say that you've now passed your driving test.'

'I've passed?' Stella wanted to throw her arms around him in delight, but managed to rein herself in.

'Indeed you have. You drove extremely well. Of course you'll need further practice once you've been assigned to your station, to familiarise yourself with driving ambulances, but I've no doubt you'll make a fine driver.'

Stella beamed at him. 'Thank you very much.'

The examiner opened the car door and eased himself out, then picked up the pail of water, taking care not to spill any. 'Good luck to you, Miss Franklin. If Hitler turns his sights on London, we'll need drivers like you.'

Stella sat still for a moment and watched him walk away, letting the knowledge that she'd done it sink in, the delight it gave her fizzing and coursing through her body, warming her to her very core. Not many girls from Stepney ever got the chance to learn to drive, and there'd been plenty who'd questioned the sanity of what she was doing when she already had a steady job at the garment factory with regular money and hours, and where she knew everyone and they knew her. But spending the war sewing uniforms wasn't for Stella, so she'd grabbed the opportunity to do something beyond the boundaries of the life that had been mapped out for her. She'd often seen the women from the London Auxiliary Ambulance Service driving around and had admired their daring, and now ... she looked at her reflection in the rear-view mirror and smiled, her blue eyes sparkling with happiness ... she was going to be one of them.

Auxiliary Ambulance Station 75 was a short raven's flight away from the Tower of London, tucked away in flat-topped mews garages opposite a crescent of grand terraced houses. Ambulances were now kept where luxurious cars once parked, and the chauffeurs and their families had long since moved out of the flats above the garages to make way for the ambulance crews.

Walking through the wide arched passageway leading into the crescent, Stella saw that the garage doors were flung wide open, with ambulances and cars lined up inside ready for action, and her heart skipped with happiness at the thought that she was finally here, finally about to start the job that she'd dreamed of for months. She took a deep breath to try and still the fluttering nerves in her stomach, and walked towards the garages, hoping that she'd find someone there who could direct her to the station officer, to whom she'd been told to report.

As she passed the bonnet of the nearest grey-painted ambulance, a jet of icy-cold water hit her squarely in the stomach, making her gasp with shock.

'Got you!' a plummy voice shouted as a tall woman with honey-blonde hair and pillar-box-red lipstick sprang up from where she'd been hiding around the side of the ambulance, the hose of a stirrup pump clasped firmly in her hands. At the sight of Stella, standing there dripping, the front of her once-neat best blouse and skirt soaked through, with a darkened patch spreading by the moment, the woman's face blanched white and her grey eyes opened wide with horror. 'Oh my goodness, I'm so terribly sorry! I thought you were Sparky.'

She dropped the hose and hurried towards Stella, examining the wet patch, which was seeping and dripping downwards, its icy-cold fingers chilling Stella's skin.

'Are you all right?'

Stella nodded, momentarily lost for words – she'd often dreamed about her first day as an ambulance driver, but she had never imagined it would be like this.

'You must be the new girl. Station Officer Steele said you were starting sometime today, and look what I've done to you. A fine welcome I've given you. I really am most terribly sorry.' The woman held out her hand and smiled warmly. 'I'm Winnie.'

Stella shook the offered hand. 'Stella Franklin.'

'I'm pleased to meet you, even if I have soaked you to the skin,' Winnie said. 'So what shall we call you then?' She paused for a moment, her

16

head tilted to one side. 'I know, how about Frankie? What do you think?'

'But...' Stella began.

'I should explain, no one goes by their first name here. You're either known by your surname or a nickname. My real name's Margot Churchill, which has earned me the name Winnie, like dear old Winston. I much prefer Winnie to Margot, it's so much less stuffy.' She studied Stella's face. 'You know, I think Frankie sounds rather lovely, and it suits you; it's a friendly sort of name, don't you think?'

Stella considered the idea for a moment. A new name for a new job. She smiled back at Winnie. 'Yes, I like it. Frankie it is.'

'Splendid. Come on then, Frankie, let me help you get cleaned up and dried off. I...' Winnie stopped talking as the sound of loud, cheerful whistling drifted towards them. They both turned around and saw a man walking in through the arched passageway with a newspaper tucked under his arm. 'Oh no, that really is Sparky. Come on, quick. If he sees what I've done to you, I'll never live it down.'

Winnie linked her arm through Frankie's and hurried her towards a door at the side of the garages where a flight of stairs led to the upper floor. 'This way. All the staff rooms are up here.'

'Who's Sparky?' Frankie asked, following Winnie up the stairs.

'My nemesis!' Winnie laughed. 'He's a driver, and good fun really. I was only trying to get him back for soaking me with the stirrup pump last week.'

'Tell me if you're goin' to do it again so I can keep out of the way,' Frankie said. 'It's quite a shock when you ain't expecting it.'

Winnie put her hand on Frankie's arm. 'I am sorry, truly I am, but I can see you're a jolly good sport and I hope you won't hold it against me?'

'Of course not.' Frankie smiled. It wasn't the best start to her job here, but Winnie was so genuinely sorry she'd already forgiven her. 'Can you show me where to find the station officer? I was told to report to her.'

'Yes, of course, but we need to get you changed into some dry clothes first. In here.' Winnie opened a door and ushered Frankie inside, quickly following her and closing the door behind them. 'Our station officer doesn't always see the funny side of us playing around with stirrup pumps,' she said in a hushed tone. 'So if you don't mind, it's best we don't say anything about what happened to you.'

'Don't worry, I won't.'

'Thank you.' Winnie smiled and squeezed Frankie's arm. 'Right, so this delightful room is the ladies' changing room. If you wait here a moment, I'll go and find Bella; she's terribly organised and is bound to have some spare clothes that you can borrow while yours dry out.'

Left on her own, Frankie looked around the room. Hanging on pegs on the wall were a number of the familiar black steel helmets with the letter 'A' painted in white on the front. She couldn't resist taking one down and trying it on in front of the mirror to see how it looked, looping the strap under her chin so it sat securely on

18

her auburn hair, which she'd secured out of the way in a knot at the nape of her neck. Staring at her reflection, turning this way and that, she thought she almost looked the part.

The sound of the door opening made her jump, and she spun around as Winnie walked in, followed by a shorter woman with dark curly hair who was carrying a pile of folded clothes in her arms.

Frankie's cheeks grew warm and she hastily removed the steel helmet and replaced it on its peg. 'I 'ope you don't mind. I couldn't resist trying one on.'

'Not at all.' Winnie laughed. 'You'll be wearing one for real soon enough. This is Bella. She's got a spare pair of dungarees and a blouse that you can borrow.'

'I'm Stella Franklin ... Frankie.' Stella held out her hand.

Bella shook it firmly, her lively brown eyes warm and welcoming. 'Peggy Belmont, otherwise known as "Bella". I'm sorry you got caught up in one of Winnie's daft pranks on your first day here. We're not all as childish as she is.' She handed Frankie the pile of clothes. 'These should do till your own clothes dry.'

'Thank you, I appreciate you helpin' me out.'

'You're welcome.' Bella smiled at her, her cheeks dimpling prettily, then turned to Winnie. 'You really want to watch yourself, Winnie, or you're going to get yourself in big trouble with the boss one of these days. It could have been Station Officer Steele walking out there.'

Winnie clasped her face in her hands. 'I know,

I know. I'm most awfully sorry about soaking Frankie; I wouldn't dream of doing that to her on purpose ... or to you, Bella, I just wanted to get Sparky back for giving me such a horrid drenching last week.'

'And no doubt you will.' Bella grinned. 'Only next time you try, please warn us first so we can keep well out of the way.'

Station Officer Steele reminded Frankie of a headmistress. She spoke in a firm, no-nonsense manner and her shrewd brown eyes behind her owlish horn-rimmed spectacles had a way of looking at you that made you feel as if she knew everything about you. Frankie understood exactly why Winnie hadn't wanted her boss to know that she'd soaked her with the stirrup pump.

'You'll need to spend a week working as an attendant before we can send you out as a driver; it'll give you a chance to learn how we do things and become familiar with the routines,' Station Officer Steele explained. 'I'm going to put you with Winnie to start with; I'm sure she'll look after you and show you the ropes, providing of course that she doesn't continue to use stirrup pumps for anything other than their intended purpose...' She paused, her arched eyebrows slightly raised as she looked at Winnie, who had a tinge of pink creeping across her creamy skin. 'There is very little that goes on here that I don't know about, Miss Churchill, so let's just stick to the rules, shall we? It's best for everyone's sakes. There may well come a time when stirrup pumps are all that stands between us and the station burning down, and

20

should that time arrive, we'll need them in perfect working order and not damaged from any misuse. I hope we're in agreement there?'

'Yes, of course, Station Officer Steele,' Winnie said. 'I'm sorry.'

'Jolly good.' Station Officer Steele nodded and turned her attention back to Frankie. 'Driving an ambulance is rather different to a car and you'll need to get used to handling them before we let you loose on any patients. I'll ask Sparky to take you out on driving practice this week. The more experience you can get, the better.'

Bella appeared in the office doorway with another bundle of clothes in her arms. 'Here's your uniform, Frankie, such as it is: one regulation coat, one cap with optional ear flaps and a steel helmet,' she said, handing them over. 'Any chance of us ever getting a proper uniform like the Auxiliary Fire Service?'

'Not at the moment,' Station Officer Steele replied. 'Though it would be jolly useful so we wouldn't have to wear our own clothes. Now, Bella, while Frankie's working with Winnie, I'm going to put you with a new driver who's being transferred to us from another station this week.' She picked up a piece of paper from one of the neat piles on her desk and glanced at it. 'A William McCartney; he's an excellent driver by all accounts. Do your best to help him settle in, won't you?'

Bella nodded. 'Yes, of course.'

'Who'll be Frankie's attendant when she becomes a driver?' Winnie asked.

'I'll make that decision when the time comes,'

Station Officer Steele said. 'In the meantime–'The ringing of the telephone interrupted her and she immediately picked it up. 'Yes, yes.' She grabbed a pen and paper and started writing rapidly.

Frankie looked over at Winnie, who mouthed back, 'It's a call-out.'

Replacing the receiver, Station Officer Steele turned to them. 'This one's for you, Winnie. Frankie, you can go with her; you may as well start getting some experience right away.'

'You find out where we're going and I'll meet you at the ambulance,' Winnie instructed Frankie, before rushing out of the door.

A heady surge of panic laced with adrenalin raced through Frankie; she hadn't expected to go out so soon.

'Take this.' Station Officer Steele handed her the slip of paper she'd written on. 'It's the address of the incident. Off you go then, and good luck.'

'Come on.' Bella grabbed Frankie's arm and pulled her out of the door. 'The driver always goes off first and starts the engine; it's the attendant's job to find out where the incident is and then get down to the ambulance as quick as they can,' she explained over her shoulder as they ran down the stairs. 'Everything in the ambulance is already prepared and ready to go.'

Outside, Winnie was waiting with the engine running and the passenger door wide open.

'Where are we going?' she asked as Frankie climbed inside, still clinging on to the bits of uniform that Bella had given her.

'Good luck,' Bella said, shutting the passenger

door for her.

Frankie glanced at the neat copperplate handwriting on the slip of paper. 'Twenty-four Carlisle Street. Do you know where that is?'

'Of course.' Winnie put the ambulance into gear and they were off.

Frankie looked back at Bella, who waved at her. She smiled and waved back, trying hard to quell the nerves that were knotting tightly around her stomach. This was what she'd dreamed of doing for months, and now that it was happening for real, it was a potent mixture of anxiety and excitement.

Winnie drove through the high-arched passageway linking the terraced houses and the garages and out onto the road, where she turned left, making the ambulance sway slightly.

She glanced at Frankie. 'Are you all right?'

'Yes, I'm fine, just a bit surprised. I didn't expect to go out on a call quite so soon.'

'We never know when it's going to happen or where we're going to be sent; it's all part of the excitement, or the worry, however one looks at it. Keeps us on our toes.' She glanced at Frankie again and smiled. 'Don't worry, you'll soon get used to it. I absolutely love it. I'd rather be doing this than any other sort of war work. The idea of being in the WAAF or the ATS and having constant orders barked at me, being bossed around every moment of the day, having to march up and down, yes sirring and no sirring – it would drive me absolutely crazy.' She laughed. 'Though I suspect they wouldn't be very happy with me either. It's really not my sort of thing at all; it

23

would remind me too much of school.'

'Oh, I liked school,' Frankie said.

'You wouldn't have liked mine. It felt like a prison to me after India; there were so many rules and things that had to be done in certain ways, uncomfortable uniform, horrible food...' Winnie braked gently as they approached a junction and, checking it was clear, turned right.

'Why were you in India?'

'I was born there. I didn't set foot in England until I was eleven years old, when my parents decided it was high time I was educated like an English young lady.' Winnie sighed. 'So they sent me here to be educated like my older brothers before me. I hated boarding school.'

'I suppose at least you got to go back to India in the holidays.'

'Good gracious, no. My parents didn't allow that.' She paused. 'I've never been back to India since and I still miss it terribly. I wish I could go back to see my darling ayah again.'

'Ayah?'

'My nursemaid, Sita. She looked after my brothers and me from the time we were born; she was like a mother to us. Leaving her was awful...'

'You must 'ave missed your parents, too.'

Winnie shook her head. 'No, not really. We only used to see them once a day anyway. After I came here to school I didn't see them for five years, not until they left India and came home to live.'

Frankie stared at Winnie, shocked at what the other girl had told her. Winnie's upbringing was so different from anything she'd ever heard of. Where Frankie came from, mothers looked after their own children and would never send them away for years on end, even if they could afford it.

'So you 'ad to stay at school all the time, then, even in the 'olidays?'

'Thankfully, no!' Winnie laughed. 'That would have been the end of me. My salvation came in the form of my godmother, darling Connie. My brothers and I stayed with her here in London every holiday. I live with her now, in fact.'

She slowed the ambulance down and turned into a side street. 'This is it, Carlisle Street.' She came to a halt near where a policeman was waiting for them, parking close to the pavement and turning off the engine. 'What have you got for us?' she asked, leaning out of the open window.

'A dead body, I'm afraid. Young man fell out of that window onto the railings.' The policeman pointed up at a third-floor window. 'Didn't stand a chance. We 'aven't moved the body, thought it best to wait.' He cleared his throat. 'It's not a pretty sight, so we've covered him up as best we can...' He nodded to where another policeman stood guard beside a blanket-shrouded form on the iron railings in front of the house.

'Righto, we'll get a stretcher out and be with you in a moment.' Winnie turned to Frankie. 'There's nothing anyone can do for the poor chap now, so there's no rush to get to the hospital with this case. Ready?'

Frankie nodded, although she felt anything but ready. She hadn't for one moment thought they were going to collect a dead body – she'd never seen one before. All sorts of scenarios had run

25

through her mind after the call had come in, from broken bones to a woman in labour, but not this. But then, why not? It was all part of what an ambulance crew had to deal with, she reminded herself as she got out of the ambulance and went round to the back, where Winnie had already opened the doors.

'All set?' Winnie took hold of one end of the stretcher.

'Yes, ready when you are.' Frankie did her best to smile and look calm, but her heart was racing inside her.

This might be her first time, but she would be fine, she told herself as they walked towards the policeman; and she was as they put the stretcher down and she took off the folded blankets and laid them to the side, but the moment the policeman removed the cover shrouding the young man, Frankie's resolve crumbled. The sight of the body skewered on the iron railings, with a spreading pool of dark-red blood congealing on the pavement underneath, shocked her to her core. She suddenly started to shake. Try as she might, she couldn't stop. She bit down on her bottom lip and tried to ignore the loud sound of her own blood whooshing rapidly in her head.

'It's going to be a job getting 'im off there,' the policeman said. 'If we lift 'im up slowly, we should be able to ease 'im off the spikes.' He took hold of the young man's shoulders while the other policeman held his legs. 'Ready, three, two, one.'

Winnie glanced at Frankie as the two policemen began to struggle with the body, which clearly wasn't going to come off as smoothly as they'd thought.

'Frankie! Are you all right? You've gone very pale.'

Frankie swallowed hard. 'I've not seen a dead–'

Winnie swiftly took her arm and spun her around so that they faced the other way. 'Go and sit in the ambulance and we'll deal with this. It won't take long.'

'But–'

'I absolutely insist,' Winnie said firmly. 'Off you go.'

Frankie nodded her thanks and fled back to the safety of the ambulance, where she sat looking down at her hands clamped firmly together in her lap, her knuckles standing out in a pale-pink blur through her tears. She dared not glance up to watch Winnie and the policemen removing the body, because she was scared of what might happen if she did. An odd mixture of relief, anger and disappointment was flooding through her – this was her first job and she'd failed miserably. What use was an ambulance driver who couldn't cope with the sight of a dead body?

It was only a few short minutes before the back door of the ambulance slammed shut and Winnie climbed into the driver's seat beside her.

'How are you?' she asked kindly.

'I'm sorry, I–' Frankie began.

Winnie laid a hand on her arm. 'No need to be sorry. You've had a nasty shock, Frankie – it happens to us all. I've known people keel over in a faint or be sick their first time, and you didn't do either of those. You'll get used to it.'

'But what if I don't?'

'I know you will. You won't give up easily; I have every confidence in you. The first one is always the hardest, and you've just had one of the worst first ones I've seen, extremely messy and awkward. I can assure you that most of our work's not as bad as that.'

'I've done all the first-aid training but I ain't seen nothing like that poor man.' Frankie shuddered. 'What an 'orrible way to die.'

'It would have been quick, if that's any consolation.' Winnie started the engine. 'Let's get him to the mortuary and they'll tidy him up.'

'Will you tell Station Officer Steele?' Frankie asked, fearing what would happen when she found out. She couldn't imagine the stern woman taking the news of such feeble behaviour well.

Winnie looked at her and smiled. 'Of course not. Remember, we don't always tell her what goes on, only what she needs to know. It's for her own good – and especially ours!'

'She knew about you squirting me with the stirrup pump,' Frankie reminded her.

'I know, but I suspect she saw that from upstairs. She likes to keep an eye on things and watches out of the window. It was just bad luck she saw me.' Winnie checked her mirror and then pulled out into the road. 'But fear not, she wasn't here to see what happened, so she'll never know, will she?'

'You've survived your first day at Station 75 then,' Bella said.

'Just about,' Frankie said. She and Bella were walking down the street together after their shift had ended and they'd waved Winnie off on her bicycle in the opposite direction.

'We're not that bad to work with, are we?'

'No, you've all been very kind and welcoming.' Everyone at Station 75 was fine, Frankie thought; the problem was *her*. She couldn't shake off the worry that she wasn't up to doing the job she so desperately wanted to do. Winnie had kept her word and not told anyone back at the station what had happened on the call-out, so no one else knew that she'd failed, but what good was an ambulance driver who turned into a trembling wreck at the sight of a dead body? 'But...'

'But what?' Bella asked gently.

'I 'ad a problem at the incident,' Frankie blurted out. 'Winnie 'ad to help me out.'

'What happened?'

'I couldn't do it.' Frankie's voice wobbled. 'I...'

Bella put a hand on her arm and steered her over to the side of the pavement, out of the way of other people. 'Listen, you were sent to the worst first incident I've ever heard of.'

'But the sight of the body... I just turned to jelly, and Winnie made me go and sit in the ambulance while she dealt with it,' Frankie confessed, her eyes stinging with tears. 'I was completely useless.'

'You'd have to be made of stone not to be upset by what you saw, especially as it was the first time you've seen a dead body.' Bella patted Frankie's arm. 'I would probably have been sick on the spot if it had happened on my first call-out.'

Frankie shrugged. 'Winnie said she ain't going to tell anyone and that I'll be all right next time.'

'And she's right. It's no one else's business what happened; as long as the poor man was taken to

29

the mortuary, that's all that matters.' Bella smiled, her brown eyes warm and kind. 'We look out for each other at Station 75, help each other out when things are hard. You had a nasty start, Frankie, but I promise you not all incidents are like that one.'

Frankie nodded and managed a smile. 'I 'ope so, otherwise I'll be back sewing uniforms for the rest of the war.'

'I'm sure that won't happen.' Bella put her arm through Frankie's and they started to walk again.

'I 'ope you're right. And thanks for lending me these clothes today; I'll make sure they're washed and bring them back to you.'

'You need to get yourself something to wear that you don't mind getting dirty; this isn't the cleanest of jobs,' Bella said. 'Dungarees are perfect for working on the ambulances, comfy and tough and I don't worry if they get messed up. You should buy yourself some.'

'I'll make some,' Frankie said. 'I've got my grandmother's Singer sewing machine; it shouldn't take me long. I've had plenty of practice working at the factory.' She knew far more about making clothes than she did about driving an ambulance, so if the worst did happen and she found herself thrown out of the ambulance service, at least she'd be able to get another job sewing in one of the many East End garment factories. The thought should have cheered her up, but it didn't, because in her heart she didn't want that to happen; she wanted to stay in the ambulance service. It was up to her to prove that she could do it.

''Ow'd you get on today?' Josie from number 5

called out to Frankie as she turned into Matlock Street. Josie was standing on a chair cleaning her front window, her meaty arms moving furiously to remove any specks of dirt that dared sully her criss-cross-taped glass. 'I 'eard you was startin' your new job.'

'Fine, I went out on a call.' Frankie kept walking, resisting the urge to be polite and stop to chat as she normally would, because that would give Josie the chance to probe her with more questions, and she couldn't risk revealing any hint of what had happened. Everyone in the street knew that she was starting at Station 75 today; it would have spread up and down amongst the neighbours, because in Stepney, everyone knew each other's business, the good and the bad.

Frankie didn't want anyone to know how she'd failed miserably on her first day. Despite both Winnie and Bella's reassurances, a great heavy cloud of doubt still hung over her, and all she could do was desperately hope that she'd be better prepared for future incidents, whatever they might be. If not... She didn't want to think about what would happen if she couldn't do the job.

'They don't 'ang around before putting you to work. I know where to come now if I need medical 'elp,' Josie called after her loudly.

Frankie waved back at her, knowing that she meant well, and kept walking towards the far end of the cobbled street, where she could see a game of cricket being played between the two rows of terraced houses. It was good to see the children enjoying themselves, filling the street with the sound of fun and laughter. She'd missed them

31

during the quiet weeks and months after many of them had been evacuated at the start of the war, but when none of the feared bombing had materialised, they'd gradually trickled home again.

They'd piled up gas-mask boxes to make the wickets, and Frankie recognised the familiar fair-haired figure standing in front of one of them, his bat poised for action. He looked up and saw her just as the ball was bowled towards him, but instead of hitting it, he dodged out of the way and raced towards her.

'Stella, you're back! I bin looking out for you. Did you drive an ambulance?'

Frankie smiled at ten-year-old Stanley, who, since coming to live with her and her grandparents after his mother's death four years ago, had become like a brother to her.

'Not today, though I did go out in one. I've got to practise driving them for a bit first before they let me out in one all by myself.'

'Stanley, are you playing or what?' one of the other children shouted.

'Go on, finish yer game and I'll tell you all about it later on,' Frankie said, squeezing his shoulder.

'Promise?'

'Cross my 'eart.' Frankie made a cross sign over her chest.

Stanley grinned and ran back to take up his place by the wicket again.

Frankie stood and watched the game for a few minutes, glad to see how happy and relaxed he was now, so different from the child she and her grandfather had fetched home last autumn. Stanley had been one of the unlucky ones, evacuated to stay with an older couple who had no desire to have a child in their house, only the billet money that came with him. They'd made poor Stanley's life a misery, and it had been several months before Frankie and her grandfather found out what was going on. They'd gone straight there to fetch him home again. Home was where Frankie could watch over him, care for him and make sure that no one else hurt him.

She couldn't put it off any longer; she took a deep breath and walked the last few paces to number 25 Matlock Street, the house she'd lived in all her life, but which over the past year had grown to feel more like a battle zone than a home. It wasn't the house that had changed, just one person in it. Ivy might officially have been her step-grandmother, but the woman didn't possess a single caring bone in her body, nothing to make her deserve that title, so Frankie always called her by her name. It was an appropriate one: just like the plant, Ivy had found herself a good home and was clinging on tightly to keep it.

Closing the front door quietly behind her, Frankie walked down the hall towards the kitchen at the back of the house, a room that had always been the beating heart of their home, full of warmth and laughter, the smells of delicious cooking, and her grandmother's love. She stopped, blinking away sudden tears. If her beloved grandmother had been here, Frankie would have been able to talk to her about today, tell her the truth about what had happened, and she'd have understood and known how to help her. But Gran was gone, taken too soon by a heart attack, and replaced by a two-faced impostor who'd wormed her way into their home pretending she was something she wasn't and changed it for the worse.

She took a deep breath, mentally bracing herself for what was to come as she stepped through the doorway and saw Ivy lounging in her usual armchair, her feet up, an empty cup by her side and *Picture Post* open on her lap, *Workers' Playtime* blaring out of the wireless set.

'Gawd! You made me jump. Whatcha doing creepin' about like that?' Ivy snapped, her voice gravelly from all the cigarettes she smoked.

'I wasn't creepin'.' Frankie walked over to the table and felt the teapot; it was stone cold.

'You can make me another cup while you're at it. And I ain't had time to do no tea for tonight either, so if you want somethin'...'

Frankie sighed as she lit the gas and put the kettle on to boil, watching the flames lick around the bottom of it. This was nothing new. Ivy was the laziest woman she knew, and if it wasn't for Frankie, the family would often have gone hungry or had to eat fish and chips or go to the pie and mash shop night after night. Even on top of working long hours sewing at the factory, she'd usually been the one to cook a meal when she got home.

It hadn't been like that to start with. When Ivy had first wheedled her way into the family, not long after Frankie's grandmother had died, she'd been kind and neighbourly, doing everything she could to help them, charming Grandad with her cooking and by taking care of Stanley.

Barely a respectable year after Gran had died,

Ivy had her claws sunk so deeply into Grandad that he'd married her. It was a surprising match – she was fifteen years his junior, a peroxide blonde with scarlet lips, and a complete contrast to Frankie's grandmother – but she seemed to make Grandad happy again, and it looked like being the perfect arrangement: a wife for him and a mother figure for Stanley. For the first few months she had kept up the act, looking after the house, cooking and caring for Stanley, but then the mask had started to slip.

'There's a bit of rabbit I got from the butcher's, you could cook that,' she said now. 'Killed my feet queuing for that, it did.'

Frankie knew all about how Ivy queued for food. She sent Stanley to wait and left him standing there until she came swanning in at the end to do the actual buying. She never stood for hours waiting for anything herself.

'Dig up some carrots and spuds from the garden and it'll make a nice stew,' Ivy added. 'Your grandfather will be 'ungry after his shift and Stanley's been out playin' all day – didn't even come in for 'is dinner.'

Frankie closed her eyes. Ivy was no fool: she knew Frankie wouldn't let Stanley and her grandfather go hungry.

The kettle whistled. Frankie turned off the gas and poured the hot water onto the already used tea leaves lying damply in the bottom of the pot, eking out every last drop of flavour from them before they used fresh ones.

'So did yer drive an ambulance then?' Ivy asked.

'No, I've got to practise first. They're different to cars.'

Ivy laughed cruelly. 'So even after all that training you done, you ain't a proper driver yet. Serves you right for getting so 'igh and mighty and above yourself, goin' off and leaving a perfectly good job at the factory.' She sniffed. 'It was good enough for me when I worked there. Course I had to leave when Reg and I married so I could devote myself to being a proper wife and looking after 'im.' She patted her hair and puffed out her ample chest. 'He didn't want me to work, he believes a wife's place is in the 'ome. But *you...*' she sneered, an ugly look on her face, 'you think you're better than anyone else, getting fancy ideas about drivin'. Who d'you think you are?'

Her eyes suddenly narrowed. 'There's somethin' different... What on earth are you wearing them for?' She pointed to Bella's dungarees. 'Where'd they come from?'

'I borrowed them, they're better to work in.' Frankie wasn't going to tell her the real reason or Ivy would twist it and use it against her. 'I'm going to make myself a pair.'

Ivy laughed, the throaty sound cruel and mocking. 'Well you ain't goin' to win no fashion parade in them, that's for sure. You look a right drab mess.'

Ignoring the woman's taunts, Frankie went into the scullery and out through the back door into the garden, her hands bunched into fists at her sides. She knew what Ivy was up to: she was trying to goad her into an argument, throwing out her nasty barbed comments to start another row. But as much as Frankie wanted to fight back, she wasn't going to this time. She knew that Ivy wanted her gone. It was as if she viewed her step-granddaughter as a rival and was trying her hardest to get Frankie to leave home. But Frankie was going nowhere. Not while she had her grandfather and Stanley to look out for. She needed to stay to protect them.

She feared that Ivy might already have turned her malice towards them; she couldn't be sure as she wasn't there to watch over them all the time, but certainly her grandfather didn't seem the same happy man he was when he'd married Ivy. Unless Frankie witnessed Ivy's vindictiveness for herself, she wouldn't know what was going on, because the woman chose her moments and hid her behaviour from those she didn't want to see it.

Frankie found the garden fork and set about digging up some potatoes and carrots. Grandad had turned most of the garden into a vegetable plot, fitting in as much as he could, even sowing lettuces in the soil covering the Anderson shelter. Everything he grew helped to eke out their meagre rations, along with the eggs they got from the six hens they kept in a run at the bottom of the garden.

Carefully pushing the fork into the soil, she pressed down on it with her foot and loosened the clods, unearthing pale potatoes that she gathered up into a basket. She was brushing the soil off some carrots when she heard the back door open behind her. She spun around, expecting another barrage of comments from Ivy, but it was her grandfather who appeared.

'Ivy said you were out 'ere. How'd you get on?' He strode over to her, looking smart and tall in his police uniform.

'Good.' Frankie put the carrots in the basket. 'Once I've got some practice driving an ambulance, I'll be allowed out by myself.'

Grandad nodded and smiled at her, his blue eyes kind. 'You'll soon get the 'ang of it.'

'Shouldn't you be on the beat?'

'I was just passin' and couldn't resist dropping in to see if you were 'ome.' He reached out and patted her shoulder. 'I'm proud of you, and I know your father would have been too if he were 'ere to see it. He always 'ad a fancy to learn to drive one day.' He paused, and sighed. 'Only he never got the chance in the end.'

The unexpected mention of her father surprised Frankie. Her grandparents had never talked about him much, so she'd always loved it when from time to time they'd let something slip out and she'd learnt little snippets about him that she squirrelled away in her memory to treasure.

Her father had been killed in the final months of the Great War, before Frankie was born, and all she had of him was a photograph and a few memories gleaned from her grandparents. She understood why they hadn't talked about him much; the Great War had dealt them a cruel blow, taking not only her father but both of his brothers too. Now she grabbed the chance to ask more. 'What about my mother? Did she want to learn to drive?'

Grandad shrugged. 'I don't know.'

Frankie knew hardly anything about her mother. She'd died in the Spanish flu epidemic when Frankie had been just a few months old, and her grandparents had taken her in and brought her up. Her mother hadn't come from around here and had no family of her own, so there hadn't been anyone left to ask about her. She would always remain a mystery to Frankie, just a face in a photograph beside her husband.

Winnie loved riding her bicycle home through the streets of London after she'd finished her shifts at Station 75, delighting in taking different routes through the city and passing by magnificent buildings like St Paul's on her way.

Reaching her godmother's home in Bedford Place, Bloomsbury, she carried her bicycle down the steps to the basement and went inside, planning a long soak in the bath to make the most of those precious five inches of hot water before spending a pleasant evening with Connie.

'Oh Winnie, you're back,' Connie said, emerging from the sitting room just as Winnie was about to go upstairs. 'There's a telephone message for you from your mother.'

Winnie's happy mood instantly evaporated; the news that her mother had telephoned could only mean one thing: something was required of her. She turned to face her godmother, trying hard to paint a neutral expression on her face. 'What did she say?'

'She expects you to join her for supper at the Dorchester at half past seven.'

Expects, Winnie thought: that summed her

mother up perfectly. She never asked or invited, just issued her commands and expected everyone else to jump to it and comply with them.

Connie's blue eyes met Winnie's and she smiled sympathetically. 'That's what she said.'

'Thank you.' Winnie turned and trudged up the stairs, her lightness and happiness of a few moments ago replaced by a heavy dread of the evening ahead. A soak in a hot bath would be like harbouring in a calm port before going out to face the stormy evening ahead.

Winnie was early. She waited outside the Dorchester, not wanting to go in before she absolutely had to, but not daring to be late, as tardiness was her mother's pet hate. Whatever the reason for the summons this evening, she didn't want to taint the occasion with lateness before it had even begun. At precisely twenty-five minutes past seven, she entered the restaurant and was guided to the table where her mother was already sitting, dressed in a pre-war dove-grey suit, her hat perfectly positioned on her immaculately styled ash-blonde hair, her back poker-straight as she cast her icy blue gaze around at her fellow diners.

'Ah, there you are, Margot.' She glanced at her watch to satisfy herself that she hadn't been kept waiting.

The use of her first name startled Winnie; she was now so used to going by her nickname, which even Connie had loved and quickly adopted, that she wondered for a moment who her mother was talking to, but the superior tone quickly filtered down into her subconscious, stirring countless

40

memories of other times when her name had been uttered with an air of exasperation or disappointment.

'Hello, Mother.' She bent down and lightly kissed the proffered powdered cheek, the smell of Chanel No. 5 instantly taking her back to having to do the same thing as a child at the end of each evening's brief visit to her parents, after which she'd be whisked away to bed by Sita, her nursemaid, so that her mother could resume her life without the responsibility of personally caring for her children. Those few minutes had been Winnie's least favourite part of the day. She was relieved to be distracted from the memory by the maitre d' pulling the chair out for her to sit down. She smiled at him and he bowed his head before leaving to deal with other diners.

'I didn't know you were coming up to London,' she said once they were alone.

'I had a meeting this afternoon and thought I'd stay over and have supper with my only daughter.' Her mother paused briefly, smoothing imaginary creases out of her immaculate fine-wool skirt. 'Tell me, how is your work?'

Winnie was instantly suspicious. Her mother never normally wanted to know anything about her job; as far as she and Winnie's father were concerned, she was merely playing at being an ambulance driver – it wasn't serious work worthy of their time. They'd done everything they could to discourage her from joining the ambulance service, ignoring the fact that at twenty-two years old she was legally responsible for herself and knew what she wanted to do. It had only been

Connie's intervention that had finally put a halt to their opposition, at least for the time being.

'It's going wonderfully well. The station's superbly organised and we're doing a good, useful job.'

'But you can't be terribly busy – there hasn't been any of the expected bombing, with hundreds of casualties to deal with,' her mother said smoothly. 'As you expected there to be, as I recall.'

Winnie was stunned by her mother quoting the actual words that she'd used herself in her battle to convince her parents that becoming an ambulance driver was a worthwhile contribution to the war effort. She gave herself a mental shake. She shouldn't have expected anything less; her mother had an annoying ability to store away information ready to bring out and use to her advantage at a later date. Despite what her parents thought, Winnie was proud of what she did; it wasn't always easy and she prided herself on doing a good job.

'Indeed, we haven't had bombing casualties yet, but all that could change any day, according to the whims of Herr Hitler. If and when it happens, we're prepared for it. In the meantime, we're being kept busy doing general work taking patients to hospital.' Hoping that would satisfy her mother, Winnie changed the subject. 'How's Father?'

'He's well; terribly busy, of course, at the War Office. We all have to do our bit. I've been asked to chair another committee, and one doesn't like to say no, as it would set a bad example, though goodness knows where I shall find the time. Of course...' Her mother stopped and her face switched to a surprised expression, closely fol-

lowed by a welcoming smile as she looked past
Winnie's shoulder. 'Why, it's Charles! What a
lovely coincidence.'

Winnie turned around and her heart plummeted
at the sight of Charles Hulme striding towards
them, grinning all over his shiny round face. What
was he doing here? What were the chances of him
being in the same place, at the same time, as her
and her mother? She'd been set up, she realised.
This was what this supper was really all about: her
mother putting Winnie once again in an awkward
situation with a man she loathed. Would she never
give up and accept that her daughter was where
she wanted to be, doing what she loved, and marriage to the dull, pompous Charles Hulme would
never, *ever* happen?

'Charles, how lovely to see you.' Winnie's mother
fluttered ridiculously, like a schoolgirl with a
crush, laughing as Charles kissed her hand. 'Are
you dining alone?'

'Alas, yes.' He shot a look at Winnie, and she
had to do her best not to physically squirm when
he took her hand in his sweaty paw. 'Margot, you
look as charmingly divine as ever.'

'Charles.' Winnie nodded at him. It took all her
willpower not to snatch her hand back and wipe
it clean with her napkin.

'Well we can't have that. I'll have them set
another place and you must join us; I simply
won't hear otherwise.' Winnie's mother waved a
waiter over and issued her command for another
place to be laid and a chair brought.

Taking a deep breath, Winnie braced herself for
a tedious evening ahead. All she wanted to do was

tell them what she really thought and get out of there as fast as possible, but she'd been brought up to behave impeccably in polite society and so would have to waste her evening tolerating an obnoxious man whom her parents thought the perfect match for her. It showed how little they knew or understood her.

'I wondered how soon you'd be able to get away.' Connie's voice called from the sitting room after Winnie had let herself in the front door. 'Come and have a drink, I dare say you could do with one.'

Winnie flung herself down on the sofa, sighing loudly as Connie poured her a small glass of brandy from her emergency supply. 'Thank you.' She smiled gratefully as she took the glass. Sipping the amber liquid, she leaned back against the sofa and enjoyed the warmth the brandy spread within her as it went down.

'Was it awful?' Connie asked, sitting down beside her.

'Yes. It was a set-up with that pompous fool Charles Hulme. Mother pretended it was a happy coincidence that he was dining alone in the same place and at the same time as us, and we simply had to invite him to join us. I spent the whole evening fending off a two-pronged attack, with them trying to convince me that I should leave the ambulance service and become a Wren, or alternatively simply give in to the inevitable and marry Charles as both his and my parents wish.' She threw the last of the brandy down in one gulp.

'Are you going to?' Connie asked, her mouth

twitching with suppressed laughter.

'Of course not... That way madness lies.'

'Good. That's exactly what I would expect of my darling goddaughter.' Connie took Winnie's hand and squeezed it, her blue eyes smiling gently. 'You and I are cut from the same cloth; we're individuals who do what we want to do and will not bow down to the inevitable family pressures.'

'Look where that got you.' Winnie giggled.

Connie threw back her head and laughed, making her blonde bob swing wildly about her face. 'Precisely, and I'd not have it any other way.'

Winnie sighed. 'I just wish Mother would respect that I have opinions of my own and accept the choices I make in my life. I'm a grown woman and I know what I do and don't want.'

'And that doesn't include the delightful Charles?'

'Never.'

Bella was used to sleeping in attics. This attic room was by far the nicest she'd ever had, painted a cheerful primrose yellow, with a colourful patchwork cover on the bed, a washstand, a chest of drawers with a mirror on top, a bookcase, and a little table and chair under the window. She especially loved it because it had been chosen by her, and wasn't merely where she slept because the room went with her job. Those rooms always had the most basic, meagre furnishings and were a harsh contrast with the lavish ones in which her employers slept. Unlike those others before, this attic room was her own; she didn't have to share it with anyone, and that was bliss.

45

Sitting at the little table under the window, Bella was reading one of the books she'd borrowed from the public library on her way home that afternoon. A gentle tapping on the door pulled her out of the book and she left it open on the table and went to see who was there.

'I've brought you a hot drink, dear.' Mrs Taylor, her landlady, held out a steaming mug of cocoa. 'Thought you might like one before you turn in for the night.'

'Thank you.' Bella took the mug from her. 'It's very kind of you. You spoil us lodgers.' There were two other girls living in the house; they both worked night shifts in a munitions factory, so Bella didn't see much of them.

Mrs Taylor swatted away the idea with her hand. 'Nonsense. I love looking after you girls. I think of it as my contribution to the war effort.' She smiled, her brown eyes crinkling at the corners. 'Are you on early shift again tomorrow?'

'Yes, starting at half past seven, but we'll be rotating shifts again soon, then I won't start till half past three in the afternoon and finish at half past eleven at night.'

'Make sure you let me know when you do so I can have your food sorted out for you. Goodnight, then.'

'Goodnight.' Bella smiled to herself as she closed her door. She'd been so lucky to find a landlady like Mrs Taylor, who was more like a mother to her and the other girls. Until she came to live here, it had been a long time since anyone had looked after her.

Sitting back down at the table, she picked up

her book again and started to read, soaking in the words and learning as much as she could to prepare herself for her future, because the war wouldn't last forever, and when it was over, she was determined that she wasn't going back to what she had been before.

Bella woke with a start. The eerie wail of the air-raid siren had broken into her beautiful dream. She'd been at home, her real home, with her father, mother and brother, and she'd felt so happy... She wanted to hold on to that feeling, enjoy it for a few more precious moments, but it was quickly snuffed out by the surge of adrenalin that started to course through her as the mournful sound continued to rise and fall.

Throwing back the covers, she felt for her clothes in the darkness and pulled them on, then hurried over to the window and carefully pulled the blackout curtain open a crack and peered outside. She could see the beams of searchlights probing the night for enemy planes; they looked strangely lovely as they wove hypnotically to and fro in the pitch-black sky over Bethnal Green. She wanted to stop and stare, but she mustn't, so she dropped the curtain and grabbed her small torch from the chest of drawers, using it to light her way down the stairs to the first-floor landing.

'Oh Bella, thank goodness.' Mrs Taylor stood waiting for her, dressed in her coat, her handbag in her hands and her grey hair in curlers.

'Come on, we need to get to the cupboard.' Bella took hold of the older woman's elbow and gently guided her towards the stairs.

'Do you think we're going to be bombed?' Mrs Taylor asked in a shaky voice as they made their way down.

'It could be another false alarm, but it's best to take cover.' Bella opened the under-stairs cupboard door and ushered Mrs Taylor inside, where she slumped down on the chair they'd managed to squeeze inside for her because her arthritic knees wouldn't put up with sitting on cushions on the floor like her young lodgers.

Bella followed her in and closed the door.

'All we need to do is light the candle and we'll be as right as rain.' She propped her torch up on the shelf, where they'd left a candle and matches in readiness. She struck a match and the flare of light lit up the confined space, casting their shadows on the walls and highlighting the looping strands of cobwebs high up under the top stairs. 'There we are.' Satisfied that the candle was alight, she blew out the match and settled down on a cushion. 'We're as snug as bugs in a rug in here.'

'What time is it?' Mrs Taylor asked.

Bella looked at her watch. 'Five past three.'

'And you're due at work at half past seven; what if this is still going on then? You can't go out in it,' Mrs Taylor fretted.

'I'm sure it will all be over long before then. It's probably a false alarm and the only damage done will be to our sleep.'

'And my nerves.' Mrs Taylor sighed. 'I'm glad you're here. I'd hate to be in here on my own.'

Bella reached up and patted the older woman's gnarled, veiny hand. Her landlady was normally such a cheerful, happy woman, it was awful to see her so on edge and afraid. 'We'll be all right, just–'

She broke off as the sickening noise of a muffled crump, closely followed by another, and another, shattered the peace of their sheltered cocoon.

'They've come!' Mrs Taylor shrieked, grasping Bella's hand in both of hers and squeezing it tight. 'They're bombing us.'

'We're safe in here,' Bella said, trying to re-assure herself as much as her landlady, because if a bomb fell directly on them, would they stand a chance in that little space under the stairs? Until now, they hadn't had to rely on it for their safety, because London hadn't been bombed. All they could do was sit tight and hope for the best.

Chapter Two

Station Officer Violet Steele stood by the open staffroom window looking down at the activity in the cobbled area in front of the garages. It was a little after eight o'clock on a warm late summer's day, the morning after the bombers had dropped their deadly weapons, leaving people dead, injured and homeless.

'Cup of tea?'

She turned around at the sound of Sparky's voice and smiled at him as he held out a steaming mug of tea.

'Thank you.' She took the mug, cradling it in her hands. The day might be warm, but her

49

whole body felt cold to her core. It wasn't the disturbed sleep that was upsetting her; it was the dreadful sense that the war had finally come to London with all its terrible might. 'Is everybody accounted for who should be here?'

'Yes, all in safe and sound, probably a bit tired from being woken up by the air-raid sirens, but nothin' they can't cope with, I'm sure, though they're all a bit quieter than usual.' Sparky took a sip of his tea as they both looked down at the work going on below, where the crews were preparing their ambulances for the shift.

Winnie was cleaning the bonnet of her vehicle, while Frankie was up the ladder leaning against its side, washing the roof. Other crews were doing similar jobs, or checking engines or tyres, everyone making sure the ambulances were clean and ready to go.

Jones the elder and Jones the younger, two sisters who were a similar age to Station Officer Steele and worked at Station 75 as volunteers, suddenly started to sing one of their favourite Gilbert and Sullivan songs as they washed their ambulance.

'Trust them to try and cheer things up,' Sparky said, smiling at the pair, who always looked on the bright side and were a tonic to the station.

Station Officer Steele did her best to smile, but last night's events had left her feeling deeply sad that the innocent people of London were now in the front line and as open to attack as any soldier. She sighed and took a long drink of tea.

'You all right?' Sparky asked.

She mentally reined her thoughts in. She had a

50

job to do, and after the events of last night, it was even more important that it was carried out properly.

'Yes, of course.' She turned to him and smiled. 'I'd like you to take Frankie out for some practice in an ambulance once they've finished their preparations. And after that, you can give Bella another driving lesson.'

Sparky shook his head. 'She'll never be ready to pass her drivin' test; she's too nervous of other traffic. It's a waste of time.'

'On the contrary, I'm sure she'll pass one day, but only if you,' Station Officer Steele arched her eyebrows as she looked at Sparky, 'keep taking her out so she can practise.'

'You're the boss.'

'Indeed I am.' She took another sip of tea, and returned her attention to what was happening outside. Hooky, who worked as an attendant, had knocked over a full pail of water, soaking her shoes and sending her hopping around, moaning and fussing, which made the other crew members laugh. Station Officer Steele watched with interest as Frankie went to help her. Hooky wasn't a popular member of the Station 75 crew because she was more interested in making friends with people she considered to be the right sort, rather than being friendly with everyone and joining in to work as a team, and had a habit of rubbing her colleagues up the wrong way.

Clearly Frankie had a good, kind heart, though perhaps she was too gentle for this job. Purely by chance, Station Officer Steele had heard about what had happened yesterday: how Frankie hadn't been able to deal with the young man speared on the railings. It put a question mark over her ability to do her job; was she capable of being an ambulance driver? If last night's air raid was a taste of things to come, could she be relied on to go out and help people hurt or worse in a bombing raid?

Station Officer Steele sighed. Sometimes being the boss was a heavy weight to bear. She wouldn't have doubted Frankie's capability if she hadn't run into one of the constables who'd been at the incident yesterday, who had enquired how the new crew member was, hoping she'd recovered from the shocking sight. When she'd asked him what he meant, the whole story had come out.

Not that she blamed the poor girl; it must have been a horrible sight, and particularly bad for a first call-out, but Station Officer Steele feared her crews would have worse things to deal with if last night proved to be the start of a new phase of the war. Could she have a crew member who couldn't do her job properly when the time came? The simple answer was no. She was going to have to watch Frankie carefully, make sure she came up to scratch, otherwise she'd be out. There was no room at Station 75 for people who couldn't do what was needed.

'Take it steady,' Sparky said.

Frankie gently turned the steering wheel and felt the back of the ambulance sway first to the right, then to the left, before the vehicle gradually settled into its normal rocking rhythm as she straightened up and drove along the road. The way the back moved around wasn't so much of a problem now as when they'd first set out; she just needed to remember to take corners slowly, drive smoothly and focus on getting used to handling a much wider and taller vehicle.

'That's it, you're getting the 'ang of it now.' Sparky looked across and smiled at her. 'We'll soon make an ambulance driver of you.'

'I 'ope so.' Frankie smiled back at him before quickly returning her gaze to the road.

Sparky yawned loudly. 'Oh dearie me! I didn't get much sleep last night after the siren went. We were in a street shelter and it was pandemonium, babies cryin', people talkin' and singin', not much chance for a bit of shut-eye.'

'We went in our Anderson shelter.' Frankie dropped down a gear as they came up behind a slow-moving lorry that had pulled out from St Katharine Docks with a heavy load of sacks on the back.

'Wish we 'ad room for a shelter in our back yard,' Sparky said. 'Wouldn't 'ave to put up with noise from other people then.'

'We're lucky we've got the room.' Although one member of the family wasn't grateful for it, Frankie thought. Stanley had been fine, treating their nighttime flit to the shelter as an adventure. He'd wanted to look out of the door for enemy planes, but she'd stopped him and he'd soon settled down, snuggling up in one of the bunk beds that Grandad had built in there and falling asleep until the all-clear had sounded. Thankfully he'd missed Ivy's constant moaning. She'd made such a fuss, going on and on about how she hated being stuck in a metal box in the ground, grumbling about how uncomfortable she was, how she was missing her beauty sleep, and threatening to go back into the house. Not once did she spare a thought for her husband, who'd gone out to see if he could help. Worrying about her grandfather out there in the middle of an air raid had kept Frankie awake for most of the night. 'Do you think they'll come back again tonight?' she asked now.

'I 'ope not. But I reckon old Churchill won't let it go. He'll retaliate. An eye for an eye.'

Frankie sighed. 'Then they'll retaliate back at us.'

'And we'll do it right back again,' Sparky said. 'You've got to stand up to them or they'll be all over us like they did to Holland and France. We don't want them marchin' down our streets tellin' us what we can and can't do. That's what Hitler wants.'

Frankie shuddered at the thought of the threatened German invasion that was hanging over the whole country. After what had happened at Dunkirk, it seemed like a matter of *when*, not if – the country was hanging on by its fingernails. For now, the battle was going on above them. She glanced up at the sky, where a series of white trails looped and criss-crossed over the blue, marking the path of the small planes that were hurtling through the air doing their utmost to knock out the enemy.

'Go left 'ere and we'll 'ead back to the station. I've got to give Bella a driving lesson after this,' Sparky said. 'I'll need a cup of tea before I can brave it, though.'

'Is she practising driving an ambulance too?' Frankie asked.

'Good God, no! Bella has enough trouble managing a car.'

Winnie needed to concentrate. She'd promised Connie a pair of knitted socks to put in one of the Red Cross parcels that her godmother helped to pack, and she was determined to keep her word. All the preparation work on the vehicles had been done and every ambulance or car was ready to go, so now some crew members were having a break while they waited for a call-out.

'Are you going to join us in a game?' Jones the elder asked as Winnie carried a deckchair out from the back of the garage. 'We're going to play chase the lady.' She shuffled the pack of cards expertly in her hands.

'Not this time, I'm afraid. I need to work on my knitting,' Winnie explained. 'I'd better sit over there on my own to make myself get on with it. I easily lose concentration if there are other things going on.'

'Fair enough,' Jones the younger said. 'We can get a bit loud playing.'

'Speak for yourself,' her sister said as she started to deal out the cards.

Winnie left them to their game. Choosing a sunny spot further around the courtyard, she unfolded the deckchair and settled herself into it. Then she took her knitting out of her bag and set to work, trying hard not to drop a stitch as she went round and round on the thin double-pointed needles.

Connie had taught her how to knit and she was doing her best to make a good job of the socks, but it was a challenge. Winnie wasn't blessed with a great deal of patience, and making socks needed plenty, so it was as much a test of character as it was of her limited knitting skills. She was trying her hardest to keep that in mind as she selected the next stitch and wove the wool between the crossed needles, then lifted off the old stitch and made a new one before going on to the next.

Her thoughts drifted as she knitted. She'd meant to take Frankie down to the station's allotment in the dry moat at the Tower of London to get her to help with the weeding, but Frankie was upstairs in the common room, poring over a map to familiarise herself with all the streets around here. Now that the street signs had been taken down in case of an invasion, every driver had to know how to find their way round without them.

Bella wasn't here either – she was out on one of her dreaded driving lessons with Sparky – so Winnie had no distractions. This was the perfect time to give her patience a chance to develop. Or not, she thought as she dropped another stitch and had to carefully coax it back onto the needle before it could run a ladder down through the previous rounds of knitting.

'...And this is Winnie.'

Winnie looked up at the sound of her name and saw Station Officer Steele and a man she hadn't seen before walking towards her.

'Winnie, this is William McCartney.' The station officer indicated the tall man with dark blond hair standing beside her. 'He's just joined us from another ambulance station.'

The man held out his hand. 'I'm Mac. Pleased to meet you, Winnie.' His voice had a warm burr to it, very different to the local London accent.

Shaking his hand, Winnie couldn't help noticing what an unusual colour his eyes were, a dark blue shot through with streaks of amber. 'Welcome to Station 75.'

'Will you introduce him to Bella when she gets back from her driving lesson? She's going to be working as Mac's attendant to start with. And one last thing, please avoid soaking our latest crew member with a stirrup pump, if you possibly can.' Station Officer Steele raised her eyebrows and smiled at Winnie before turning her attention back to Mac. 'Do ask Winnie if there's anything you need to know about the station; she'll look after you.' Then she nodded, turned on her well-polished lace-up shoes and headed back inside.

'What was that about the stirrup pump?' Mac asked.

Winnie frowned. 'I'm afraid I accidentally soaked Frankie with a stirrup pump yesterday, just seconds after she arrived for her first day here. It was a complete accident, I assure you, and not intended for her at all...'

Mac grinned. 'That's quite a welcome.'

'Please don't joke about it. I felt absolutely awful, but Frankie was a good sport about it and forgave me. Anyway, the upshot of it is that we're not supposed to use stirrup pumps for anything other than their intended purpose. Water fights are now strictly forbidden.'

57

'Pity. In my last post we were stationed next door to an Auxiliary Fire Service crew, and we had quite a few water fights with them, stirrup pumps at the ready.'

'Sadly you won't be able to do that here. Why don't you grab yourself a deckchair out of the garages and come and sit down by me, and you can ask me anything you need to know while I knit. I must keep going or I'll never get the socks finished.'

Mac fetched a deckchair and set it up near Winnie, then sat down, stretching his long legs out in front of him.

'Where are you from?' Winnie asked. 'You don't sound local.'

'No, I'm not. I'm from Gloucestershire. I only came to London to join the ambulance service.'

'Where were you stationed before?'

'In the West End.'

'That patch must be much grander than ours. We get sent out to a real mixture of places from here, sometimes into the City but more likely down to the docks or the East End. I rather like it.' She paused while she rescued another dropped stitch. 'You never know where you're going to go or what you'll find. Didn't you like being in the West End, then?'

'The place was fine, it was just some of the people.' He paused, and a flash of unhappiness passed over his face. 'They didn't like working with a conscientious objector.'

Winnie stopped knitting and stared at him. 'You're a conscientious objector?'

Mac nodded.

'I've never met a conscientious objector before.' Putting her knitting down on her lap, Winnie leaned forward, elbows on her knees and her chin cupped in the palms of her hands. 'Do you mind me asking why you've chosen to be one?'

'The simple answer is because I couldn't kill another man. I knew that if I complied with my call-up papers there was every chance I'd be expected to do just that, and I can't. I had to follow what I believe. I wasn't against helping with the war effort like some COs, so when I got my conditional exemption I joined the ambulance service.'

Winnie put her head on one side, considering what he'd just told her. 'I think it takes a great deal of courage to stand up for what you believe in. You know, I'm not sure if I could kill someone if it came to it either.' She paused. 'What happened at your last station?'

Mac shook his head and waved his hand as if swatting away something unpleasant. 'It's past. Let's just say some people made it difficult for me to do my work properly, so I asked for a transfer. I'm not a coward; I just can't kill.'

'I suppose some people find it hard to see men refusing to join up, especially if they have family members off fighting or who've been injured or killed.'

'I know.'

Winnie smiled. 'Well I certainly won't hold it against you. I've got two brothers doing their bit; one's a Spitfire pilot and the other's pushing paper around for the government. If either of them had registered as a CO I'd have supported them.' Although whether her parents would have was another matter, she thought.

'Thank you.' Mac smiled, his face lighting up and his blue eyes crinkling at the corners.

The sound of a car driving in through the archway made them look round.

'Watch out, Bella's back.' Winnie quickly tucked her legs in under her deckchair. 'Mind your toes.'

The car came to a jerking stalled stop in the middle of the cobbled area, and seconds later a white-faced Sparky and a flushed Bella got out.

'It's best if I park it in the garage,' Sparky said, walking round to the driver's door.

Bella nodded and hurried over to where Winnie and Mac were sitting.

'I'm still shaking. Look!' She held up her hands, which had a definite tremor to them. 'I wish Station Officer Steele would just accept that I am never, *ever* going to be capable of passing my driving test.'

'It's all right, Bella, it's over for today,' Winnie reassured her. 'Let me introduce you to Mac; he's the new driver you're going to be working with.'

Mac held out his hand. 'Pleased to meet you, Bella, and don't worry, I won't ask you to drive.'

'I'm a much better attendant than I am a driver,' Bella said, shaking his hand. 'Much better.'

Bella sat cross-legged on the flat roof of the ambulance station, finishing off her sandwiches. She'd come up here to calm down after her traumatic driving lesson and was glad to be distracted by the dog fights going on in the blue sky above east London and out towards Kent. Crew members often came up here to watch what had become a common sight over the past few weeks.

'There you are.' Winnie's voice made her jump. 'I thought you might be up here.' She sat down beside Bella, leaning her elbows on her bent knees. 'Was this morning's lesson truly awful? I thought you were getting better.'

Bella sighed. 'It isn't *how* to drive. I know how to change gear and which pedal to press and when; I can do all that perfectly well. It's just being out in the traffic with Sparky snapping and grumping at me. He makes me so nervous it all starts to go wrong and I just want to get out of there...' Her voice cracked.

Winnie put her arm around Bella's shoulders and squeezed her. 'Perhaps someone else should take you out, someone who'll be more patient with you. We could speak to Station Officer Steele about it.'

'Who else is there? Sparky does all the practice drives and the boss might not want anyone else to do it.'

'We don't know that for sure, not until we ask. Perhaps if we suggested someone else who might be willing to take you out instead, it might persuade her.' Winnie smiled. 'In fact I know just the person.'

'Who?'

'Mac.'

'But he's only just arrived,' Bella said.

'Yes, but he's an experienced driver and seems to be a kind and caring man.'

'How do you know?'

'I've talked to him, and he's a conscientious objector.'

61

'A conchie!' Bella whistled.

'Yes, if you must put it like that, but he seems an honest, thoughtful man and he might be willing to help. Of course if you'd prefer to keep on with Sparky...'

'All right, but only if Station Officer Steele agrees. So why has Mac come to work here?'

'Because unfortunately some biased and short-sighted people at his last station didn't like working with a conscientious objector. They made things extremely difficult for him,' Winnie explained.

'Do you think it's the right thing to do, refusing to fight?' Bella asked. 'If everyone did that, then where would the country be now? Probably invaded and with Hitler living in Buckingham Palace.'

'Everyone's entitled to their own opinion; it's a free country.' Winnie looked thoughtful for a moment, then went on. 'If you think about it, isn't that what this war's about? Hitler's out there taking over people's countries, telling them what they can and can't do. If we stopped people saying no when they felt strongly that they couldn't fight, we'd be following in his footsteps. That must never happen.'

Bella clapped. 'Hark at you, Winnie. You sound like a politician. Thinking about it, if my brother had become a conscientious objector, I'd have a lot less to worry about. I wish he had been driving an ambulance around London instead of nearly dying at Dunkirk.'

'Is he out of hospital yet?'

'He will be soon. He said in his last letter that

he'll be getting some home leave, but then what will happen to him? They'll probably send him off somewhere else to fight.' Bella sighed. 'What about your brother, Harry; wouldn't you rather he was doing some safe job than flying up there?' She shielded her eyes against the sun and looked up to where aircraft were circling around, following each other, ducking and swooping.

Winnie shrugged. 'It's not for me to tell him what to do. I know how much he adores flying and doing his bit. Everyone has to make their own decision and we should respect whatever they choose, even if we don't agree with them.'

'Look!' Bella grabbed hold of Winnie's arm as a plane started to tumble from the sky, a trail of black smoke streaming out behind it. 'Is it one of theirs, or ours?'

Before Winnie could answer, a tiny white parachute opened up and floated downwards, carrying the escaped pilot slowly back to earth while his plane hurtled towards the ground ahead of him. They couldn't see where it hit; only the pall of smoke that rose on the horizon.

Winnie blinked back tears. 'Whoever it is has a chance now. Good luck to them. If it's one of theirs, at least the war is over for him now; and if it's one of ours, he's survived to fight another day.'

Frankie felt sick. Her stomach was in knots and the palms of her hands were damp. She'd happily spent the morning poring over maps, learning the quickest routes to the nearest hospitals, but now she and Winnie were on their way to an incident, and a great black cloud of doubt had draped itself heavily around her shoulders. Would she be able to do her job properly this time? And what if she couldn't...

'What do you think it might be?' she asked.

Winnie glanced at her and smiled. 'I still have no more idea now than I had when you asked me that very same question a few minutes ago. Will you please stop fretting, Frankie. Whatever it is, we'll manage it together. I promise you.'

Frankie looked down at the chit Station Officer Steele had given her, reading again the words *to proceed to Carron Wharf St Katharine Dock*, desperately searching for any other clue to the injuries of the patient, but there had been none there the first time she looked, and there were still none now. No miracle had occurred to ease her worrying.

If she couldn't deal with today's incident, then she must leave. Winnie, kind and caring as she was, couldn't manage with an attendant who was useless, and it wouldn't be fair on her to stay. Frankie knew that Winnie would never tell Station Officer Steele about her inability to do the job, so she'd have to confess herself. Her conscience won't let her do anything else. If it came to that, she'd be back at her old sewing machine in Cohen's factory, and her dream of being an ambulance driver would have blown away like the mist that swirled off the Thames.

'Here we are.' Winnie drove in between the two wide gateposts that marked the entrance to St Katharine Docks and brought the ambulance to a stop. A Port of London constable stepped out of one of the police boxes that stood either side of the gateway and Winnie leaned out through the open window. 'Good afternoon, Constable. We've been called to an incident at Carron Wharf, could you please give us directions on how to find it?'

'I'll do better than that,' he said, smiling. 'If you'd like to follow me, I'll walk you through to the wharf. Don't want you gettin' lost.'

'Ask him if he knows what it is,' Frankie hissed.

'Constable, do you happen to know what injuries we can expect?' Winnie asked.

'A broken leg. A bale of cargo fell on 'im; could have been a lot worse. Follow me...' The constable set off briskly.

'How does a broken leg sound?' Winnie asked, putting the ambulance into gear and slowly following the policeman.

Frankie let out the breath she didn't realise she'd been holding, and smiled. 'I think I can manage that.'

With the heavy dread of what she might be facing finally lifted, Frankie took the chance to have a good look around as they drove towards the wharf, weaving their way between tall warehouses where horses stood patiently waiting as the carts they were harnessed to were piled up with sacks and crates. As they neared the wharves, the tall cranes used to unload cargo from the moored ships towered over them.

'Looks like this is it,' Winnie said as the policeman waved to them and pointed to where she should park the ambulance, not far from where they could see a man lying on the ground surrounded by a small crowd. 'This incident is a huge improvement on yesterday's. Remember I told you that they're not all as bad as that one.' She turned off the engine. 'Let's get to work.'

''Ere come the angels to the rescue,' a man called out as Frankie and Winnie carried the stretcher over to where the injured stevedore lay on the ground, his face pale and pinched-looking with pain.

'You telephoned and we came.' Winnie smiled at the men. 'Frankie, would you like to do the honours?'

'Of course.' After they'd laid the stretcher down, Frankie quickly examined the man's leg, gently feeling along his thigh.

'Ow, that 'urts.'

'Sorry.' Frankie smiled at him. 'I needed to check where the break is. Now I'm going to splint your legs together so they won't move around too much on the way to hospital.'

''Ave you done this before?' the man asked as Frankie unpacked some splints and bandages from her bag.

'Oh, don't worry, Frankie's an expert; she's splinted up hundreds of broken bones.' Winnie knelt down near the man's head and patted his shoulder. 'I can assure you that you're in quite safe hands.'

Frankie felt the crowd's eyes on her as she set to work carefully splinting and bandaging the man's legs, taking care to keep them from moving any more than necessary. She focused hard, vaguely aware of Winnie's plummy voice chatting away in the background, making the watching men laugh and doing her best to distract the patient from what Frankie was doing.

'There, all finished. I told you that you were in safe hands; she's done a splendid job.' Winnie smiled warmly at Frankie. 'It's much better than I could have done. Right.' She squeezed the man's shoulder. 'Are you ready to go?'

Five minutes later, their patient was safety stowed in the ambulance, lying on a stretcher with some of the sandbags they always carried for fractures firmly positioned alongside his legs to stop them from being jolted around as they drove. Winnie closed the back doors and went round to the driver's seat, leaving Frankie in the back to keep an eye on the man.

''Ow are you feeling?' Frankie asked, spreading a blanket over him to keep him warm.

'I've been better, I've got to be honest.'

Frankie smiled. 'Don't worry, the hospital will soon have your leg sorted out.'

'Everyone all right in the back?' Winnie shouted through the little grille behind the driver's seat.

'Yes, we're fine. Remember to take it slow, no jolting around,' Frankie said.

'Right you are. One smooth journey to St George's Hospital coming up.'

Winnie started the engine, and as the ambulance began to move slowly forward, Frankie remembered the pail of water she'd driven around on her driving test. It was there to represent an injured patient being taken to hospital, and here she was doing that for real. She wasn't doing the driving yet, but one day soon she would be.

After the shock and horror of yesterday's incident, she'd proven to herself that she *could* take care of patients, give them the necessary first aid and get them to hospital. But would all her call-outs be as easy as this? a traitorous voice whispered in her mind. What would happen if she was called to another incident like yesterday's? What would she do then?

'Come out for a walk with me. Please.'

Winnie looked at her older brother's exhausted face. 'Don't you think you'd be better off getting some kip, Harry?'

'If I'd wanted to do that, I would have stayed where I was,' he snapped. He sighed heavily, running his hand through his light-brown hair cut to RAF regulation shortness. 'I'm sorry, forgive me. I shouldn't have spoken to you like that. I don't *want* to sleep. I was damn lucky to get a twelve-hour pass and I don't want to waste it.' He stood up and started pacing up and down the kitchen. 'I want to live a bit ... do something normal. We could have a walk in Regent's Park and then have tea and cakes somewhere; what do you think? It would set you up for your shift later on. I promise I'll get a couple of hours' kip here before heading back.'

Winnie had an urge to throw her arms around him and squeeze him tight to make him feel better, but they didn't go in for such behaviour in their family. Something she always thought was a great pity, because back in India when they were growing up, dear Sita, their ayah, had often hugged them to her like they were her own children, and Winnie had loved that. But her parents had never displayed their emotions so freely, and sadly it had leached downwards so that Winnie and her brothers didn't show each other physical displays of affection either.

Despite this, the three siblings had a good relationship, something Connie had helped to foster over the many school holidays they'd spent with her. They were far closer to each other than to their parents and knew that they could always rely on one another.

'Of course I'll come out with you. It won't take me long to get ready; why don't you finish off the toast while you're waiting.' Winnie pushed the half-full toast rack across the table to where Harry was sitting. 'Waste not want not and all that.'

Running up the stairs to her room, Winnie couldn't help wondering at the wisdom of Harry going out when he clearly needed rest. When he'd turned up unexpectedly a short while ago while she was eating a late breakfast, letting himself in with the key Connie had given him, she'd been shocked by his appearance. His normally handsome face looked pale and haggard; his grey eyes had an odd feverish look about them, as if he was drinking everything in because he didn't want to miss out on anything.

Connie had already left to go to her voluntary job at the Red Cross and wasn't here to make him see sense and rest, but then perhaps going out and doing normal things would be as good as a rest for Harry. His life now revolved around waiting for the command to scramble, running for his Spitfire and taking off into the blue, not knowing when he'd come back. Or even *if* he'd come back. He was living on a knife edge, wondering if he'd survive to see another day.

Regent's Park was bathed in sunshine, and Winnie was glad to see the fresh air bringing some colour back to Harry's face.

'You're lucky that my shifts have just swapped around, or there'd have been no one at home when you turned up,' Winnie said as they walked along. 'I'm not terribly fond of this shift; it's a devil coming home in the blackout in the middle of the night. When there's no moon it's terribly hard to see where I'm going, and I've had a few scrapes bumping into things, though I suppose it's only fair we rotate the shifts every few weeks so we all get a share of the good and the bad bits.'

'I thought it was worth the chance. If you or Connie hadn't been at home, I'd have just slept on the sofa and gone back.'

'Well I'm glad you came.' Winnie smiled at him. 'It's lovely to see you.' She paused. 'What's it like?'

Harry shrugged. 'It's a lot of waiting around and then some flying.'

'I've often watched the dog fights from the roof of the ambulance station. It looks terribly scary. Is it awful up there?'

'We just get on with it. You know, there isn't time to worry while it's happening; we're too busy doing the job. It's them or us.' He stared across to where some people were busy working on their allotments.

'How's Peter?' Winnie asked. 'Perhaps you could bring him with you next time you get some leave.'

Harry took a cigarette out of his silver holder and lit it, blowing the smoke out in a long stream.

'He bought it a few days ago.' His voice sounded

strangely matter-of-fact. 'I saw him go down … didn't stand a chance.'

Winnie felt like she'd been punched in the stomach. She stopped walking and turned to face him. 'I had no idea. I'm so very sorry to hear that.' Her eyes filled with tears at the thought of dear, funny, happy Peter dead. He'd been Harry's best friend from university, whom Winnie had got to know when he'd come to stay in the holidays. The two young men had joined up together and been delighted when they'd found themselves both posted to North Weald airfield. And now Peter was gone forever.

Harry cleared his throat. 'He wasn't the first in my squadron who's bought it, and he won't be the last. It's what happens.' A flash of pain crossed his face, then he smiled at her, a smile that didn't quite reach his eyes. 'How about that tea and cake? I'm suddenly ravenous.'

'Yes, of course.' Winnie did her best to smile as they started to walk towards the park gates, but a horrible chill feeling had settled around her heart, like a freezing fog in winter. This dreadful war was exacting a terrible price, with young vibrant lives being snuffed out so readily. She closed her eyes and sent up a silent prayer that Harry didn't meet the same fate.

Chapter Three

'You're on picket duty tonight, Frankie, your first one.' Station Officer Steele pointed to her name on the list. 'Half past ten to half past eleven, just an hour to keep guard so that no one comes in and pilfers our precious petrol.'

'Right, I'll be there.' Frankie had been warned that the shifts that covered the night hours brought another duty with them, with all crew members having to take their turn to patrol the area outside the garages.

'I'll do it with her,' Bella said. 'It helps pass the time if you've got someone to talk to.'

'If you wish,' Station Officer Steele said. 'But it won't excuse you from doing your own picket duty later in the week.'

'I'll come out and keep you company then,' Frankie said.

'I'm pleased to see you helping each other out; that's what makes a good ambulance station crew.' Station Officer Steele smiled, her brown eyes warm behind her glasses. 'Keep an eye on the time so you don't forget. Ah, Sparky, can I have a word...' She wandered off to speak to him, leaving Frankie and Bella to finish the preparations on their ambulance. They were now working as a pair, Frankie as driver and Bella as attendant.

'Thanks for offering to do the picket duty with me,' Frankie said, polishing the wing mirror on the front of the cab while Bella swept out the inside.

'I'm glad to help. It can get a bit lonely down here in the dark when everyone else is up in the staffroom. Like I said, it makes the time pass quicker if you've got someone to talk to.'

Just before half past ten, Frankie and Bella left the blacked-out common room, where the other crew members were passing the time until the end of the shift, reading, playing cards, knitting or simply dozing in the armchairs. As they stepped out into the darkness of the courtyard, their eyes needed time to adjust to the dark, but their ears had no problem picking up the sound of the Jones sisters sweetly singing 'Three little maids from school are we', filling the night with a feeling of fun and cheerfulness so typical of the two women.

Frankie and Bella waited for them to finish the song before they clapped.

'Thank you. Is it time to change over already?' Jones the elder asked.

'Yes, it's half past ten,' Bella said. 'You can go and have a cup of tea, and then it'll soon be the end of the shift.'

'Tea sounds wonderful. My throat's a bit dry after all that singing,' Jones the younger said. 'We'll leave you to it. It's been as quiet as a mouse out here, nothing stirring.'

'I dare say our singing's enough to scare off any prospective burglar.' Jones the elder laughed. 'We're like a couple of howling guard dogs out here.' She linked her arm in her sister's. 'Come on, tea's needed.'

The two women headed off to the staffroom, humming another song together like a pair of bumblebees.

'Do they always sing out here?' Frankie asked when they'd gone in.

'Yes, and other times as you've heard. They're wasted here; they ought to join ENSA and tour round entertaining the troops,' Bella said. 'They were involved with the theatre before the war and must miss doing shows.'

'This war has changed so many people's lives. I sometimes still can't believe I'm an ambulance driver. I think I'm goin' to wake up and it's all been a dream.'

'You really are here, I promise you.' Bella nudged Frankie's arm. 'See, that's real enough. Do you like being here?'

'Yes, it's much better than sewing uniform after uniform. What did you do before you joined the ambulance service, Bella?'

'I was in service here in London. I was a house-maid.'

'Did you enjoy it?'

'No. But it was a job and it gave me a home of sorts. I much prefer being in the ambulance service, though.' Bella laughed. 'That's one good thing about the war: it's given us better jobs. You seem to have settled in well after that horrible first incident.'

Frankie shivered. 'Don't remind me of that. I've been lucky that all my other call-outs have been nicer: broken bones, a woman in labour, nothing too gory, but...'

'But what?'

74

'I still worry what I'll do if there's another incident like that one – you know, with lots of blood, or–'

Bella put a hand on her arm. 'Then you'll do what's necessary, I know you will. You get more experience every incident you go to. Don't worry, your training will kick in and you'll do the job.'

'Do you think so?'

'Yes, I do. We work together as a team; I'll be there with you.'

Frankie looked up at the star-pricked sky and hoped that Bella was right, because at the back of her mind, a little voice still questioned her ability to cope when things got difficult and she was tested to her limit.

Frankie sat cross-legged on the flat roof of the ambulance station in the warm early-evening sunshine. She was wearing a pair of dungarees like the ones Bella had loaned her on her first day at Station 75. She'd made them herself, buying enough navy fabric for two pairs so that she wouldn't have to wear her normal clothes and risk spoiling them.

With her small sketchbook resting on her knees, she was drawing the view across the rooftops towards the Tower of London and Tower Bridge. She loved these moments when all the preparation work was done, ambulances checked and ready go, and the crews had some time to relax. Winnie and Bella were sitting nearby, both busy. Winnie was concentrating on turning the heel of the sock she was still knitting, and Bella was engrossed in a book.

Looking back and forth from the view as she worked, Frankie lost herself in the joy of drawing, focusing on the shapes that made up the familiar buildings. Line by line, the sketch grew across the page. The sudden wail of the air-raid siren, the 'Moaning Minnie' as her grandfather called it, startled her, its mournful sound rising and falling across the rooftops.

'Not again!' Winnie sighed loudly, stuffing her knitting into her bag.

Bella stood up. 'Come on, down to the shelter, everyone.'

'Hold on, I just want to finish this bit,' Frankie said, adding some more lines to her drawing.

'Oh no you don't. You know how Station Officer Steele is if we take too long getting to the shelter.' Bella held out her hand. 'Up you get.'

Frankie took hold of Bella's hand and stood up. 'Thank you.'

The thought of going to sit in the stuffy shelter wasn't very appealing after being up here in the sunlight and fresh air, but Station Officer Steele was insistent, even if it turned out to be just another small nuisance raid – and there'd been plenty of those during the last week, mostly doing damage to people's nerves, scaring them and sending them fleeing to the nearest shelter as yet again their lives were interrupted by the wail of the siren and the threat of bombs falling. Frankie had lost count of the number of times Moaning Minnie had gone off during the past week. She glanced at her watch. It was almost quarter to five; how long would it be before the all-clear went this time and everyone could get back to what they should be doing?

As she followed Winnie and Bella across the roof to the doorway leading downstairs, Frankie suddenly realised that the light would have changed by the time they came out of the shelter; the shadows on the buildings wouldn't be the same as they were now. She glanced back to take a last look towards Tower Bridge, hoping to commit some of the view to memory so at least she could carry on with her drawing in the shelter. Gazing eastwards across the rooftops, she saw a sight that chilled her blood. High up in the clear, brilliant-blue sky were countless black specks flying in V formations, like a huge swarm of flies. Smaller planes darted around them, sunlight glinting off their silvery bodies. Planes. German planes.

'Look!' she shouted, pointing towards them.

Bella and Winnie turned back and stared.

'Bloody hell!' Winnie gasped. 'There are hundreds of them.'

The deep, rumbling sound of the German planes' engines was growing louder and louder.

'Quick! Get to the shelter,' Bella said, but they all stood rooted to the spot as the sound of distant crumps reached them from further downriver, where the banks of the Thames were crowded with docks and warehouses. Smoke, black and ominous, began to curl up into the air.

'They're bombing the docks.' Frankie's stomach lurched at the sickening sight. She'd lived all her life within sight of the docks, with their tall cranes peppering the skyline like trees, alongside the funnels of the ships that brought cargo from distant lands. She remembered when she was little how Grandad had taught her to recognise a ship from the West Indies, its red-painted funnel with yellow and black bands and the letter W on it. They were the ones that brought the bananas in, he used to say.

'Frankie! Come on!' Bella grabbed her arm and pulled her towards the door. 'We need to get the helmets on the way down.'

'Here they come,' Sparky called out as the three of them burst into the shelter a few minutes later.

Frankie was blinded for a few seconds, after rushing in from the bright light outside into the dimmer shelter that had been built for the crews in the courtyard. Once her eyes had adjusted, she could see all the other crew members sitting on the benches that ran around the brick walls.

'Bombers!' Winnie panted. 'They're bombing the docks.'

'There are hundreds of them,' Bella added.

'What exactly did you see?' Station Officer Steele asked.

As Winnie explained what they'd seen from the rooftop, Frankie could hear the droning noise of hundreds of planes growing louder, punctuated by thumps as more and more bombs rained down and the hollow boom of the ack-ack guns firing back at the bombers.

'Right, this is what we've all trained for.' Station Officer Steele's voice was calm and firm. 'We'll–'

The telephone suddenly rang, making Frankie jump. Bella clutched Frankie's elbow as Station Officer Steele grabbed the receiver and listened. 'Yes, yes. I see. Thank you.' She replaced the receiver and turned to face the crews. 'That was the red alert.'

'Bleedin' obvious it's a red one,' Sparky muttered. 'Listen to the buggers.' He looked up at the roof as if he expected to be able to see the bombers through the brick.

Station Officer Steele ignored him. 'Let's just keep calm; we're trained and ready for this. Expect a busy shift, everyone.'

'Are you all right, Frankie?' Bella whispered as they squashed into a space on a bench.

Frankie nodded. 'Just a bit shocked. Seeing all those bombers up there, and the smoke going up...'

Bella squeezed her arm again. 'We'll be fine. I–'

The telephone rang again and Station Officer Steele pounced on the receiver. 'Yes, I see.' She started to write rapidly on a slip of paper. 'Right away. Goodbye.'

Putting down the receiver, she cleared her throat. 'It's started. First incident's for you, Sparky, with Paterson. Good luck.'

Sparky jumped up from where he'd been sitting next to Mac and rushed out of the door. Frankie watched as his attendant, Paterson, an older man who'd fought in the Great War and who was one of the unpaid volunteers, collected the chit to find out where they were going and dashed after him. Neither of them had hesitated about going out in the middle of a raid to do their job. It didn't matter that bombs were raining down; the call for help had come and they'd gone to do what was needed. Frankie would do the same when her turn came. She was glad that she'd have

Bella with her. Since they'd been paired up together a week ago they'd made a good team, and Bella was always calm and reliable.

Sitting waiting for their turn to go out was hard. Some crew members were knitting or reading to pass the time, and the Jones sisters had a game of cards in full swing down the other end of the shelter, but Frankie knew she wouldn't be able to concentrate on anything. Her drawing of the Tower of London would go unfinished for now, because her mind was taken up with what was going on outside. The sounds penetrating the walls spiralled her mind into a mass of questions. How widespread was the bombing? Had Stepney been hit? Were her family safe? She had no answers to any of them, and her imagination started to weave various scenarios, many of them not to her liking. There was nothing she could do to help her family from here, apart from hoping and praying that they were safe and that they'd all live to see another day.

Winnie drove carefully, her knuckles standing out white as she gripped tightly on to the steering wheel. She had to stay focused on the road ahead and try her hardest to block out the cacophony that was filling the London streets – the clanging of fire engine bells as they raced to tackle blazes, the screaming of falling bombs accompanied by the bangs and thuds as they landed, and blanketed over all this, the constant roaring of engines as squadrons of bombers passed overhead.

'Oh God, I never thought it would be like this,' Hooky whimpered from the passenger seat. 'Will

80

we be all right, Winnie?'

Winnie bit down on her bottom lip to stop herself from snapping out the unkind reply that had popped into her mind. She hadn't been happy when Station Officer Steele had paired her up with Hooky. Hooky was far more interested in herself than taking care of any patient who needed help; it was a mystery to Winnie why she'd joined the ambulance service in the first place. She'd been whining and complaining since they'd left the ambulance station, but Winnie couldn't take out her dislike on her now; it wouldn't have been kind, because the simple fact was that Hooky was scared. And so was Winnie.

'Of course we will.' Winnie glanced at Hooky and did her best to smile, but it probably came out as more of a grimace, because her face felt strangely frozen, with her jaws clamped firmly together.

'What will happen if one of those bombs hits us?'

Hooky peered up at the sky through the windscreen.

Then hopefully we wouldn't know a thing about it, Winnie thought. 'We'll be fine, try not to worry.'

Bearing left out of Minories and past Tower Gardens, they had a much clearer view to the east, and the sight before them made Winnie gasp. A huge roiling pall of grey smoke was rising up from the docks, blotting out the blue sky.

'Oh my God! Look at that!' Hooky shrieked.

Winnie swallowed hard. 'The warehouses are on fire. What a waste.' The bombers were clearly targeting the docks to cause as much damage as possible. They knew where the precious goods came into London from overseas, and where to hit hard to destroy them.

Turning the ambulance towards East Smithfield, Winnie changed into a higher gear as she picked up speed, but her haste made the gears crunch horribly, something that would normally have made her swear.

'We can't go into that,' Hooky said.

'Well we are,' Winnie snapped. 'There are people who need help, and it's our job to give it to them – it's what we both signed up for.' And it would be a whole lot easier if she didn't have someone with her who was turning into a drain rather than a support, she thought.

The acrid smell of burning irritated Winnie's nose, and her eyes were streaming in the smoke-filled air. Wiping away her tears with the back of her hand, she squinted so that she could focus on filling in the label for their last patient – an unconscious woman around whom Hooky was tucking a blanket. They'd already loaded up three other casualties into their ambulance, all of them victims of a collapsed wall that they'd been sheltering beside when a bomb had gone off nearby.

Winnie pencilled in a question mark for the woman's name and quickly filled in the rest of the details: time, date and place of incident and a bold 'X' to indicate a crush injury so that she'd get priority treatment when they reached the hospital. She tied the label securely onto the patient and took hold of the handles at one end of the stretcher.

'Ready?'

Hooky nodded, grabbing hold of the other handles.

'On the count of three. Onc, two, three.' The two girls stood up together, bearing the weight of the woman between them as little cinders of ash continued to drift down like grey snow. 'Watch your step,' Winnie reminded Hooky as she led the way, picking her path carefully back to the ambulance across the remains of the wall and then over the fire service's thick canvas hosepipes, which lay like giant snakes across the road, feeding the jets of water that the firemen were aiming at the fire raging further down the street.

It all seemed surreal, Winnie thought, as if she were living in a terrible dream. But it wasn't a dream. The injured people, the spilt blood, the fires burning all around them made it all too real. Reaching the ambulance, she glanced up at the planes still roaring overhead. Did they know what chaos and hurt they were inflicting on innocent people? Did they even care?

'It's as if the sun has set in the east tonight.' Bella stared out of the front of the ambulance at the ominous red and orange sky that should have been falling into darkness by now. It was as if the fierce flames devouring the docks were holding back the night, painting the heavens with a strangely beautiful glow, against which the black silhouettes of buildings stood out in sharp contrast.

'The blackout's completely useless when they've got that inferno to guide them in.' Frankie swerved the ambulance over to the right to avoid a crater in the road. When the all-clear had gone at about half past six, she'd hoped that the worst was over, but it had only been a lull in the horror – the planes had come back for a second attack. She and Bella had just made it back to the ambulance station at about half past eight when the siren had gone off once more and the bombing had started all over again.

Now, driving down the Highway to yet another incident, she could hear the drone of more bombers going over and the sound of high-explosive bombs hitting their targets. Shrapnel rained down on the cobbles, hitting the outside of the ambulance with a patter.

'Watch out!' Bella shouted, pointing to something ahead.

Frankie braked hard and stopped a few yards from where two figures lay sprawled in the road. Beyond them, further down the street, there was a large crater, and debris spilling out from nearby damaged buildings.

Checking that the chin strap of her steel helmet was securely in place, Frankie climbed out of the ambulance and hurried over to help, with Bella close behind. The two bodies lay at strange angles, like rag dolls tossed aside, and as Frankie approached, she could see that the nearer one – a woman – was dead, her eyes open and staring sightlessly up at the sky. It was only as she bent down to gently close the woman's eyes that Frankie realised one of her legs was missing. An icy-cold hand gripped at her heart and she could hear the blood starting to rush in her head. The memory of the man speared on the railings flashed into her mind and a sense of panic started to creep through her. It was as she'd feared: she was crumbling...

A sudden loud bang from a few streets away made her jump and brought her back to the present, where the constant drone of the bombers passing overhead, dropping their deadly weapons as blithely as confetti, ignited a surge of anger in her. It coursed through her like molten metal. What had these people done to deserve this? Nothing! Nothing at all! And look what had happened to them... She stared at the woman, who was dressed up nicely in a pretty floral-patterned dress. It was now torn and dirty, and her lips, so carefully painted with red lipstick, stood out against her deathly white face.

Frankie?' She looked over to where Bella was crouching by the other body and noticed that it was missing limbs too. 'What shall we do?' Bella asked. 'We're only supposed to deal with the incident we're sent to.'

'I know.' Frankie sighed. 'But we can't just leave them here like this; they might get run over. Let's move them so at least they're out of the way and can be picked up later.'

Between them they carefully lifted the bodies and carried them to the side of the road, laying them gently side by side.

'And the rest of them?' Frankie said.

Bella nodded, her face pale.

Frankie bit hard on her bottom lip as she stooped down to pick up the woman's missing leg. It still had her shoe on, a high-heeled, peep-toed white sandal, probably her best pair, saved to wear on a night out with her young man. The leg was surprisingly heavy. Frankie had never appreciated how much a leg weighed before; her own legs just walked, but carrying someone else's... Hot tears slid down her cheeks. This wasn't a normal thing to do, it wasn't natural, but she had to give the poor woman some dignity in death. She gently laid the leg in place so that at least for the time being the body looked whole again.

Bella replaced the man's missing limbs and they both stood back and bowed their heads in silence for a few moments.

'We've done what we can for them.' Bella squeezed Frankie's arm. 'We'd better get going; they'll be waiting for us at the incident.'

Frankie nodded and they walked back to the ambulance arm in arm.

Frankie parked the ambulance where the ARP warden indicated and climbed out. They'd been sent to a house that had taken a direct hit, pulverising it into piles of bricks, powdery dust and slivers of glass. Rescue service workers were busy digging down into the rubble.

'Who's in there?' Frankie asked the warden.

'An old couple, wouldn't go to the street shelter... I kept tellin' 'em, but they wouldn't listen. They're nearly through to 'em now.'

'What's that?' Bella asked, as a weird whistling scream filled the air, growing louder by the second.

'Get down!' the ARP warden roared, pushing the two girls to the ground and throwing himself down beside them.

Frankie fell half on top of Bella and covered her ears. She was aware of a bright flash of light, earth and debris flying into the air and the ground heaving beneath her as a strong wave of turbulence sucked and pressed at her, flinging her hard against the side of the ambulance.

She lay stunned for a few moments, her ears ringing from the bang while a strong, acrid smell of cordite irritated her nose. She could feel Bella moving beside her.

'Are you all right?' she managed to say, her voice coming out in a hoarse whisper.

'I think so.' Bella sat up and leaned against the side of the ambulance, blinking the dirt out of her eyes. 'What was that?'

'High-explosive bomb.' The ARP warden's voice was thick with dust. He struggled to his feet, looking down at them. 'Are you both all right?'

Frankie nodded, pulling herself into a sitting position and leaning against the ambulance beside Bella. 'Bit shocked and bruised, but I think everything's in working order.' She wriggled her toes and fingers to make sure.

'Bloody bombers.' The warden shook his fist at the sky, where the searchlights were trying in vain to pick out the planes through the canopy of thick grey smoke that stretched above them. ''Scuse my language, ladies, but they deserve it. It's bad enough trying to rescue people without them buggers throwing more bloody bombs at us while we do it.'

Bella smiled, her face and clothes covered with plaster dust and dirt. 'If this doesn't deserve some choice language, then I don't know what does.'

'We need some help over here!' one of the rescue service workers shouted from further down the street, closer to where the bomb had fallen. He was kneeling beside one of his colleagues, who only moments earlier had been digging to try and free the old couple in the house. 'We need a stretcher.'

'Come on.' Frankie struggled to her feet and put out her hand to pull Bella up. Grabbing their kitbags out of the back of the ambulance and sliding a stretcher out, they picked their way across the jagged, dusty debris covering the road.

'He's hit bad,' the rescue service man said. His colleague's uniform jacket had been ripped open, revealing a deep bleeding gash on the man's chest.

Frankie's first-aid training took over and she quickly assessed what needed to be done. While she got to work applying a field dressing, Bella was called over to help another man.

Ten minutes later, they'd loaded up three injured rescue workers into the back of their ambulance, all carefully labelled and covered in blankets, with hot-water bottles tucked in beside them to help with the shock.

'What about the old couple in the house?' Bella said. 'We won't have room for them now.'

'We'll take these to hospital and come back for them later; they've still got to dig them out yet.' But whether the couple would still be alive by then, Frankie didn't know.

It was a beautiful Sunday morning, sunny and warm, but it seemed to Frankie that what she was seeing was unreal. Walking home along Commercial Road, exhausted from a seventeen-hour shift, it was as if she were in a living nightmare. It was heartbreaking to see the devastation around her; orange flames were still shooting upwards from the docks, reaching higher than the cranes, the fire like a monster engulfing everything in its path. Black smoke billowed into the sky and the air was filled with a horrible smell of burning as the precious contents of the warehouses – wood, rubber, sugar, tea and spices – were consumed in the inferno.

It wasn't just the docks that had been hit; the bombs had shown no mercy, landing indiscriminately on houses, shops and churches. Slivers of glass were strewn across the pavement where windows had been blown out, and Frankie's boots made a crunching sound as she carefully picked her way homewards over smashed roof slates, rubble and the many pieces of shrapnel pitted into the ground. The gutters ran with water from smashed pipes. It was chaos. A world far removed from a normal East End Sunday morning.

Frankie hurried on as fast as she could. Please be all right, please be all right, she thought, desperately hoping that her house hadn't suffered the same fate as many of those she passed, some with their facades blown apart to reveal their contents to the world like doll's houses, others collapsed into piles of rubble and dust. She saw people scrabbling about in the ruins, looking for anything that might have survived the blast, scavenging whatever they could of their former lives.

Turning into Matlock Street, she sighed with relief to see that the whole street was still standing. A few slates had come off here and there, smashing across the cobbles, but thankfully no bomb had found its way here.

Bursting in through the front door of number 25, she was relieved to hear the sound of the wireless playing in the kitchen. Ivy appeared in the doorway, one hand on her hip and a cigarette in the other.

'Oh, it's you. I thought it was Reg.' She looked Frankie up and down, a sneer on her face. 'Look at the state of yer!' She tossed her head and went back into the kitchen.

Clearly the raid hadn't had any effect on Ivy then, Frankie thought, following her into the kitchen.

'Where's Stanley, is he all right?'

'He's gone out somewhere, wanted to see what's 'appened.' Ivy poured herself a cup of tea. 'Oh, sorry, that was the last of it.' She sat down in the armchair and put her feet up on the little stool. 'You're late 'ome.'

Frankie filled the kettle at the sink, lit the gas and put it on to boil. 'We were very busy and not everyone from the next shift made it in, so we 'ad to keep going.'

Even when the all-clear had gone at five o'clock that morning, after eight solid hours of bombing, their work hadn't stopped. There'd still been plenty of incidents to attend, but at least they hadn't been in danger of being hit by a bomb any more. Frankie had found the silence after the long night of screaming bombs and droning engines strangely eerie.

A weary-looking Station Officer Steele had

finally sent everyone from Frankie's shift home at eight o'clock, and with so many buses and trams not running it had taken Frankie nearly an hour to make her way home through the devastation.

'Where's Grandad?'

Ivy shrugged. 'Still on duty. 'E's been out all bloomin' night.'

'Shouldn't he 'ave been back by now?' A prickle of fear ran through Frankie. Her grandfather had been out in the thick of the bombing and could have been hurt. Or worse.

'Course he should, but knowin' 'im, 'e's still 'elping out.' Ivy took a deep puff on her cigarette. 'Leaving me and Stanley 'ere on our own.'

'He was out doing his job, Ivy. It was hell out there last night.' Frankie took a deep breath. She didn't have the energy to put up with Ivy's selfish moaning. 'You were quite safe in the shelter.'

Ivy rolled her eyes. 'I 'ate it in there. If you were still workin' at Cohen's you'd have been 'ere with us, not gaddin' about drivin' ambulances.'

Gadding about driving ambulances was hardly how Frankie would describe what she'd been doing last night, but she wasn't going to give Ivy the satisfaction of rising to the bait.

'You're much safer in the Anderson than in 'ere. You should see what's happened to 'ouses that got a direct hit.'

Ivy ignored her. 'Are you going to clean yourself up? I don't want dirt all over my nice clean kitchen. You're filthy.'

Frankie glanced at herself in the mirror hanging over the fireplace. She looked like all the others had when they'd come back to the ambulance station, their faces smudged and grimy with dirt and smoke, their clothes and hair powdered with plaster and brick dust.

'I'll go and get the worst of it off outside.' Leaving the kettle to boil, she went out to the back garden and brushed off her clothes as best she could, then she undid her hair and hung her head upside down, running her hands through the heavy waves, dislodging dirt and dust. She'd give it a proper wash after she'd had a cup of tea. Then she needed some sleep or she'd be no good for tonight's shift. Hopefully by the time she woke up, Grandad would be home; if not, she'd go looking for him.

Bella stared at what was left of her home. Number 15 Garden Street was now just a pile of rubble, with broken wooden beams sticking out of the crumbled bricks like matchsticks that had been tossed aside.

'You all right, love?'

Bella turned to the ARP warden, whose face was smudged and dirty under his steel helmet. She recognised him; he was their local warden, who had a list of all the residents in his area and where they'd be sheltering during a raid. He knew that Mrs Taylor always stayed in her house. She opened her mouth to speak, but no words came out.

'Did you live 'ere?' he asked. 'You one of Mrs Taylor's lodgers?'

She nodded. 'Where's...' Her voice emerged as little more than a whisper. She swallowed and took a deep breath. 'Where's Mrs Taylor? She

92

always sheltered under the stairs when the siren went.'

'I know.' The ARP warden sighed. 'That's where we found her.'

'Is she in hospital?'

'I'm sorry, love, she didn't survive. We pulled her out but she was already gone.'

Bella shivered, suddenly feeling chilled to the bone. 'But...'

'Listen, get yourself along to the rest centre at the school and get a nice 'ot cup of tea inside you. They'll 'elp you out with somewhere to stay and tell you where to get new ration books.' The warden smiled kindly at her. 'It was one hell of a raid last night. She wouldn't 'ave known a thing about it.'

'Thank you,' Bella said. 'I'll go along there in a moment.'

'You make sure you do.' The ARP warden touched the front of his steel helmet and Bella watched him walk further down the street to where a family were searching through the rubble of their house, pulling out any possessions that could be recovered. They'd lost their home as well, but at least they were still alive – they must have gone to shelter somewhere else and weren't at home when the bomb dropped. But Mrs Taylor had refused to go anywhere else. Bella had tried her hardest to persuade her to use one of the street shelters, but Mrs Taylor wouldn't be shifted. Her home, she said, was the safest place for her, but it hadn't turned out to be safe at all. It had killed her.

Bella turned her back on the family that had survived and stared at what was left of her home.

Sticking out of the rubble were a few recognisable bits and pieces: shreds of curtain material from the front room, a shard of dark green pottery from the pot in which the aspidistra stood. A splash of red stood out against the grey dust. She knelt down and pulled it out. It was one of her books. She blew the dust off the cloth cover and ran her fingers over the golden print on the front, reading the words she'd read so many times before: '*A Christmas Carol* by Charles Dickens'. Opening the book, she saw her own name written on the flyleaf; her father had inscribed it there when he'd given her this book for Christmas. The words swam and distorted in front of her eyes and she didn't try to stop the tears from sliding down her cheeks. Sniffing hard, she closed the book and hugged it to her. It was all she had left now.

The rest centre was full of people, young, old, in families and on their own. To Bella's surprise, most of them seemed astonishingly cheery and were tucking in to the tea and sandwiches provided by women from the WVS. Not knowing quite what else to do, she joined the queue.

'There you go, dear. You look like you could do with that,' a woman said, handing her a mug of tea. 'Take a plate of sandwiches too.'

'Thank you.' Bella smiled and took a plate, then looked around her for a space to sit down to eat.

'Come and sit 'ere,' a woman with two small children called, picking up a little boy from the chair beside her and plonking him on her lap.

Bella did as she was told and sat down next to the woman, who smiled at her warmly.

'Didn't think we'd end up in 'ere,' she said, jiggling the little boy up and down to stop his grizzling. He put his dirty thumb in his mouth and sucked hard, his tears quickly subsiding as he leaned against his mother's chest, eyes fluttering closed. 'Least we're all alive and not 'urt, that's the main thing, ain't it?'

Bella nodded.

'You on your own?'

'Yes, my lodgings got hit,' Bella explained.

'You bin dug out?'

'No, I was at work. I've just come home.'

The woman nodded. 'They're trying to sort out somewhere for us all to stay, only it's goin' to take a while.' She looked around her. 'Some people 'ave got family they can go to, but I ain't. My old man's in the army and there ain't no one else.' She took a deep breath, her chest under her faded crossover apron puffing out. 'We just 'ave to sit and be patient.'

Bella took a bite of corned-beef sandwich and nodded as the woman continued to talk, explaining how she'd arrived home after the all-clear had gone to find the side of her house blown clean off.

'That's perked you up a bit,' the woman said when Bella had finished her tea and sandwiches. 'Nothing beats a cup o' tea. Now all you got to do is wait for somewhere to go.'

Bella looked around at the other people in the rest centre. Many were caked in dirt and dust from the bombing; every one of them needed a new home. It was going to take a long time to find them all somewhere to go. A heavy wave of exhaustion pressed down on her. She needed some sleep, and soon, because she was expected back on duty at half past three this afternoon, but the chances of getting any in here were low, even if she could find a space to lie down.

She stood up.

'Should I save your seat?' the woman asked.

'No thank you. I'll come back later. Hope they sort you out soon.'

She returned her plate and mug to one of the WVS women and left the rest centre, heading back to the one place where she knew she could get some sleep – Ambulance Station 75.

Bella wrung out her dungarees, blouse and underwear, squeezing them tight to get as much water out of them as she could. She'd had a much-needed wash and changed into the spare set of clothes that she always kept at the station. It had been a relief to be clean again. Then she'd scrubbed the dust, dirt and dried blood out of her clothes from last night. She'd be needing them again soon, as she hadn't been able to salvage anything else from the bombed-out house.

Luckily no one had questioned why she was here; they were all too busy working on the ambulances, which were in a mess after last night, pitted and scratched by shrapnel and dusty with soot and brick dust, the insides stained with dried blood and vomit. It was usually a crew's responsibility to clean their own ambulance when they got back to the station, but after their seventeen-hour stint, Station Officer Steele had sent Bella's exhausted shift home, leaving the next shift to do the cleaning-up.

Satisfied that she'd got every drop of water out that she could, Bella took her washing up to the flat roof and spread it out to dry in the sun. It was a beautiful day, a warm late-summer Sunday, but as she looked out across the rooftops towards the docks, where the black smoke was still writhing upwards, she knew that for many people, like those she'd seen in the rest centre, life had suddenly changed for the worse.

She yawned. She needed to sleep. Leaving her washing to dry, she went downstairs and into the women's rest room, where mattresses were laid out on the floor for people to grab some sleep during the night shifts. Taking a blanket from the neatly folded pile on a table, she settled herself down, closed her eyes and quickly fell into a deep sleep.

It was the telephone that woke Winnie. Its insistent ringing had penetrated her dream, catapulting her back into consciousness. She turned over and looked at the clock on her bedside table: half past twelve. She groaned. She could have done with another couple of hours' sleep, as she wasn't due back on duty until later in the afternoon.

Her bedroom door opened quietly and she could see Connie peering inside. 'You can come in, I'm awake.'

'I didn't wake you, did I?' Connie asked, sitting down on the side of the bed.

'No, it was the telephone.' Winnie pulled herself up into a sitting position, rearranged her pillows against the dark wooden headboard and leaned back against them.

'I'm sorry, I got to it as quickly as I could.' Connie paused. 'It was your mother; she wants you to telephone her back.'

Winnie sighed, rubbing the back of her neck. 'Does she know what happened last night?'

'Oh yes, she saw the red glow over London. She's heard from your father; that's why she's rung. She wants to talk to you about something.'

Winnie sat upright, instantly suspicious. 'What does she want to talk about?'

'She didn't tell me; all she said was that she needed to speak to you.' Connie stood up. 'Go and get yourself washed and dressed and I'll make you some breakfast; you'll need some food inside you if you've got to speak to your mother. It'll be ready for you downstairs in fifteen minutes.'

After Connie had gone, Winnie lay back against the pillows, pleating the sheet between her fingers. After last night's horrors, the last person she felt like speaking to was her mother; the very thought of it made her body tense up and her heart beat harder.

The welcome smell of freshly made toast and tea that met Winnie as she walked into Connie's basement kitchen made her realise how hungry she was. There'd been little chance to eat much last night; she'd grabbed a bun and a mug of tea from one of the WVS mobile canteen vans at one point during her long shift, but that had been hours ago, and when she'd come home that morning, all she'd wanted to do was sleep, so after a quick bath to remove the dirt, she'd gone straight to bed.

'Sit yourself down and eat.' Connie poured a cup of tea from the china teapot and put it by Winnie's place. 'And as a special treat, there's some honey from my friend Beattie's bees to go on your toast.'

'Thank you, Connie.' Winnie sat down and took a sip of tea, enjoying the way it soothed her parched throat, which felt sore this morning after breathing in acrid, smoky air.

'How was it last night?' Connie asked as she sat down opposite Winnie and poured a cup of tea for herself.

'Bad.' Winnie spread a thin layer of margarine on her toast, then spooned some honey on top. 'There's been an awful lot of people hurt and killed, and the docks have been terribly damaged.' She bit into the toast, savouring the flowery taste of the sweet honey against the rougher texture of the National Loaf, which she actually rather liked.

'I–' Connie began, but stopped at the sound of the telephone, its insistent ringing echoing loudly around the hall. 'Keep eating, Winnie.'

Winnie could faintly hear her godmother talking on the phone upstairs but couldn't make out the words. A moment or two later, Connie came back down to the kitchen. 'It's your mother, she wants to talk to you. I told her you were having your breakfast...'

'I'll telephone her back later when I've finished.'

'I'm afraid she's waiting and insists on speaking to you now.' Connie squeezed Winnie's shoulder.

'It might be better to get it over with; she's clearly not going to leave you in peace until she's had her say.'

'Very well.' Winnie stood up. 'If it's about having another dinner with the awful Charles Hulme, I'm not sure I can promise to stay polite.'

Upstairs in the hall, Winnie took a deep breath and picked up the telephone receiver. 'Hello.'

'Margot. There you are at last. Your father and I have decided that it's no longer safe for you to stay in London. You've been playing at this ambulance driving for long enough now. Father's going to sort a nice driving job for you in the Wrens.'

Winnie did her best to stay calm as she listened, squeezing her free hand into a tight fist. 'Why?'

'Why?' The tone of her mother's voice altered slightly, a steely undertone creeping in as it always did if someone dared to question her. 'I would have thought it was patently obvious, Margot. Hitler has finally turned his attention on our capital and it's not a safe place to be any more, especially if one is out driving around during an air raid. I could see the red glow from home. Your father and I simply don't want you to get hurt.'

'So it's all right for other people to be out in a raid, but not me?'

'Well, of course, neither your father nor I wants *anyone* to get hurt; we're just moving you into a situation where you can still use your driving skills but won't be in so much danger. You'd still very much be doing your bit for the war effort.'

'Are you going to ask Harry to stop flying his Spitfire?'

'Of course not!' her mother snapped. 'But that's a different matter. Father's going to telephone the right people and you won't have to go back to the ambulance station. In fact it would be best if you came home to Oxford today, so that you're out of London altogether until you can take up a post in the Wrens.'

A tingling, fizzing pressure was building up inside Winnie. How dare her parents try to force their demands on her? How could they think of snatching her away from the work she loved doing? She couldn't go off and leave Frankie, Bella, Sparky and all the others who'd been out risking their lives to help the injured last night. Why should she do some safe, cushy job while they faced who knows what in the days and weeks to come?

'No, absolutely and completely no,' she said, her voice coming out in a strange, clipped manner as she held on tightly to her emotions, which were threatening to explode.

'What do you mean, no?' Her mother's voice was incredulous. 'You don't have any say in the matter. We're your parents.'

'And I'm over twenty-one and perfectly capable of deciding for myself, thank you. Please listen to me, Mother. I will *not* be leaving my job at the London Auxiliary Ambulance Service. I enjoy it, I like the people I work with, and after last night, we're needed more than ever.'

'But Margot—'

'Thank you for calling. Goodbye, Mother.'

Winnie put the receiver back in its cradle very carefully. She doubted this would be the end of the matter; she knew that her mother was used to getting her own way, but Winnie was not going to give in. Not now, not ever.

Chapter Four

'Look, 'ere's another bit.' Stanley bent down and picked up a piece of twisted shrapnel that had speared itself in between some cobbles. He held it out on the palm of his hand for Frankie to admire.

'Lovely. So 'ow many bits is that now?'

Stanley grinned. 'That makes nineteen just this morning.'

Frankie smiled at him, glad that he, like many of his friends, had a more rosy view of the war. They knew the names of all the planes, both British and German, and could identify them from their shapes. She hoped he wouldn't ever be forced to face the true reality and horror of what war could bring – she'd seen plenty of that for herself last night.

'Whatcha want to talk to me about?' Stanley asked as they walked along.

Frankie had asked him to walk part of the way to work with her as she wanted to speak to him out of earshot of Ivy.

'I wanted to ask you about last night. Were you all right in the shelter?'

'Course I was. I like it in there. Bit loud, though.' He grinned. 'Ivy kept shrieking every time a bomb went off. The closest ones made the ground rock.'

'Did you get any sleep?'

'A bit, but I kept waking up.'

'What about Ivy, did she go to sleep?'

Stanley shrugged. 'I don't know. She wasn't in there all the time.'

'What?' Frankie made herself sound calm even though a dart of anger sliced through her. 'She left you in there all on your own?'

'Well I woke up a couple a times and she wasn't there then. I thought I should go out and look for 'er, but Grandad made me promise to stay in there until the all-clear goes, so I didn't dare.'

Frankie put her arm around his shoulder and squeezed him to her. 'You did the right thing. Grandad's right; he knows all about what to do in an air raid, so never, ever go out until you hear the all-clear. It's not safe.'

'What about Ivy? It's not safe for 'er either.'

Frankie didn't really care whether it was safe for Ivy or not; if the woman was fool enough to leave the shelter in the middle of a raid, that was up to her, but the danger was that Stanley, dear, kind-hearted Stanley, might go out looking for her and end up getting hurt or worse.

'No, it ain't. Ivy shouldn't go out in a raid either, but if she does, you must never go out with her or go looking for her, you 'ear me? Never.'

'I won't, I promise. Cross my 'eart.' He made a cross shape over his chest.

Frankie smiled at him, trusting that he would keep his word. It was hard enough worrying about him getting into a shelter before the bombers started dropping their deadly loads without the

103

thought of Ivy leaving him there on his own. Or perhaps not even bothering to take him into the shelter in the first place but just staying in the house.

'When the siren goes, make sure you get to the shelter quickly. No dawdling to look for planes or pick up shrapnel; it's not safe.' Frankie stopped walking and turned Stanley to face her so that she looked directly into his eyes. 'Promise me?'

He nodded. 'I promise, cross my 'eart again.' He made another cross over his chest. 'What about you, will you go to the shelter?'

'Of course. Station Officer Steele gets cross with us if we're not there sharpish, and we all have to have our helmets on as well. Right, you'd better start heading 'ome now, and I'll see you in the morning. Remember, if the siren goes...'

'Get to the shelter fast and stay there.' Stanley smiled. 'See you tomorrow.'

Frankie stood watching him wander off down the road, inwardly seething that Ivy should be so reckless, leaving Stanley on his own. He hadn't said so, but he'd probably been scared. She'd known the woman was selfish and uncaring, but to leave a ten-year-old boy alone in the middle of a huge bombing raid was unthinkable. Frankie would be telling her exactly what she thought about that tomorrow – she was not going to simply ignore it, not when a boy's life was at stake.

'There's someone else in 'ere. Quiet!' one of the rescue service workers shouted out.

In an instant everyone fell silent. Other rescue workers, who'd already dug three casualties out of the bombed house, stopped digging and waited.

Thankfully the all-clear had gone a short while ago after a second night of fierce bombing, when smouldering fires had been reignited and new ones started, so that once again the night sky over the East End was lit up with a hellish orange glow. Now the sky was lightening as dawn approached, but the sunrise to the east was blotted out by the dirty grey smoke rising from the docks.

Winnie watched as the rescue service man lay down on the pile of rubble, placed his ear to the ground and listened carefully. Could there be someone still alive down there? Strangely, she found herself straining to hear too, even though from where she stood by the ambulance, she was unlikely to hear anything.

'There's definitely something there,' the man shouted as he started to pull bricks out with his gloved hands. The other workers joined in, removing bits of broken timber and lumps of masonry.

'It looks like there's someone else buried in the rubble,' Winnie said to Hooky, who was in the back of the ambulance, making their patients comfortable. 'We should wait a few minutes to see what they find.' She had been about to close the doors and drive the casualties to hospital. They could afford to wait, though, since none of the three people who had been pulled out of the collapsed building appeared to be suffering from anything more than broken bones and gashes. They'd been lucky.

'Must be Mr Crow,' one of the casualties said in a croaky voice. ''E lived in the bottom two rooms.'

Like many of the houses in the East End, this one had been occupied by more than one family.

'Thank you, I'll go and tell the rescuers,' Winnie said. But before she got to where they were digging, they'd found something.

'It's a dog!' someone shouted. Moments later, they lifted a small grey creature out from the ruins, the lead attached to its collar still trailing back into the rubble.

'Can you come and 'old it while we dig down a bit further?' the rescue service man called over to Winnie, unclipping the lead.

'One of the casualties just told me that a Mr Crow lived downstairs,' Winnie said as she carefully climbed across the rubble and took the grey bundle gently in her arms. It was quivering and shaking so much that its bones seemed to be rattling around inside it. 'It's all right, you're safe now,' she whispered, holding it against her chest and gently stroking it. Her hand brushed off some of the brick and plaster dust to reveal golden fur underneath, and the dog looked up at her, its chocolate-brown eyes wide with terror.

At the sound of a shout from the rescue workers, Winnie turned to see a hand sticking out of the rubble, the other end of the lead still around its wrist. She smiled, glad that they'd found the dog's owner and that the two would soon be reunited. Gently the rescue service man slipped the lead off the wrist and passed it to Winnie, then leaned back into the hole and felt for a pulse.

He waited, checking again, and then again. Finally he looked up and shook his head. 'He's gone. Nothing we can do for him now but dig him out.'

The animal whimpered and Winnie hugged it to her. 'What about the dog?'

'They've been rounding up all the stray dogs and cats and putting them out of their misery. Here's another one for them.'

Winnie's throat tightened. She couldn't let this innocent creature be destroyed just because its owner had been killed. 'I'll take him.'

The rescue service man shrugged. 'If you want to, miss. I ain't goin' to stop you.'

Winnie turned away before he could change his mind. 'Thank you.'

Carrying the dog back to the ambulance, she recalled the little dog she'd had in India and been forced to leave behind when she'd been sent to school in England. She'd never forgotten the gut-wrenching sorrow of saying goodbye to her precious pet, and that last view of July in Sita's arms as they'd driven away to catch the train. Poor July had watched her so loyally, with no idea that she'd never be coming back.

'What have you got there?' Hooky asked, staring at the trembling animal clutched to Winnie's chest.

'Mr Crow's dog. I'm afraid he was killed, but this poor little mite survived.'

'That's Trixie, that is.' The woman who'd told them about Mr Crow earlier strained to sit up and look.

'You must stay still.' Hooky pushed her gently down. 'You've got broken bones and they don't take kindly to being jostled around.'

'Mr Crow loved that little dog,' the woman said.

'Don't worry, I'll take care of her for him,' Winnie said.

Hooky folded her arms and glared at her through narrowed eyes. 'But you can't.'

'Why not? If we leave her here, she'll have nowhere to go and end up being rounded up like all the other strays and killed.' Winnie stroked the dog's ears gently. 'We can't let that happen to you, can we, Trixie? Would you pass me a blanket to wrap her up in, please; she's probably suffering from shock and needs to be kept warm.'

Hooky sniffed and grudgingly passed her a blanket. 'That dog's filthy, and so will that blanket be after you've finished with it.'

Winnie gently swaddled the dog. 'You'd be filthy too if you'd just been buried alive.'

'Well I'm not having a dog in here with the patients,' Hooky declared, hands on her hips. 'It's my job to look after people, not dogs.'

'I wasn't going to ask you to.' Winnie smiled at her. 'She can sit in the front with me.' Before Hooky could answer, Winnie closed the back doors and carried Trixie round to the front of the ambulance, where she settled her on the passenger seat. Smiling at the dog, who looked back at her with sad eyes, she couldn't help thinking that she much preferred sitting next to Trixie than Hooky.

'Come on, try and eat something, just a little bit.' Station Officer Steele spoke softly as she offered Trixie a morsel of corned beef from her sandwich, trying to tempt her to eat, but the little dog turned her nose away, trembling and whimpering softly. 'Very well, we'll leave it for now, but I'll try

108

again in a while. You need to eat.'

'Has she had anything yet?' Sparky kneeled down on the floor beside the armchair where Winnie had put Trixie, still wrapped in a blanket.

'Nothing.' Station Officer Steele sighed. 'Poor little thing, she must be terrified and have no idea what's going on. Animals don't have any notion of war; they're just innocent victims. Have they finished cleaning up the ambulances?'

Sparky nodded. 'Nearly done, but they were in a right mess again this morning. Dirt, dust, blood...' He shook his head. 'It was just as bad last night. I 'eard the railway lines going south 'ave all been smashed up.'

'They're giving us a real battering.' Station Officer Steele gently stroked Trixie's ears. 'Do you know what Winnie is going to do with her?'

'Take her 'ome, so she says. She's a lovely little dog, ain't she?'

'She is indeed. If Winnie can't give her a home, I'd be rather tempted myself.'

'You?'

Station Officer Steele nodded. 'I'm very fond of animals, as a matter of fact.'

'Who'd've thought?' Sparky smiled. 'You want to watch out; people might start to think you've got a soft side to you.'

Station Officer Steele smiled. 'There's a time and place for everything, you know, I can be as soft as butter or as hard as–'

'Steel,' Sparky interrupted, grinning at her.

'Come on, Bella, are you comin'?' Frankie asked. 'I don't know about you, but I need to get 'ome

109

and get some kip.'

'I'm not quite ready yet,' Bella said, drying her hands slowly. They were in the ladies' changing room, where they'd both had a quick wash to get the worst of the dirt off their faces and hands before heading home. 'You go on and I'll see you tomorrow.'

Frankie yawned. 'If you're sure? It was a long, long night.'

Bella smiled at her. 'Go home, Frankie, before you fall asleep on your feet.'

'See you tomorrow then.' Frankie went out and Bella sighed with relief. Winnie had left earlier, taking the little dog with her, and all the others from her shift had gone home too, leaving the new crews busy doing the checks and preparations on the ambulances. Bella hadn't told anyone about what had happened to her house.

She quickly changed out of her dirty dungarees and blouse and put on the ones she'd washed the previous day. Then she did the same as before, washing out the dirty clothes and taking them up to the roof to dry while she slept. All she needed to do was make sure she brought them down again before the start of her next shift so no one asked questions. No one need know what she was doing.

Walking into the ladies' rest room a short while later, she was startled to see Station Officer Steele lying stretched out on one of the mattresses.

'Ah Bella, there you are.' She swung her legs around to the side and pushed herself upright. 'These mattresses aren't very comfortable, are they? They're fine for a quick snooze on shift, but not wonderful for a proper night's sleep.'

'I ... I'm not sure.'

'Aren't you?'

Bella's face grew warm. Did she know? How could she, when she hadn't been there to see?

'Bella, are you feeling all right?'

She nodded. 'Yes thank you.'

Station Officer Steele looked at her for a moment, her shrewd brown eyes appearing to see right into Bella's mind. 'So can you tell me why you slept here yesterday after your shift?'

'I...' Bella began, but was hushed by Station Officer Steele raising her hand.

'As I've said before, very little goes on at this ambulance station that I don't know about. So what's happened?'

Bella sighed and sank down on to the nearest mattress, hugging her knees to her chest and wrapping her arms around them. 'I've been bombed out. I went home yesterday after my shift and there was just rubble left, and Mrs Taylor, my landlady, had been killed...' Her voice cracked.

Station Officer Steele nodded, her eyes gentle. 'Go on.'

'I went to a rest centre like the warden told me to, but it was so full of people, all of them with no home, people with little children to take care of. They all needed somewhere else to live too. And I was so tired, I just needed to sleep ... so I came back here.'

Station Officer Steele stood up. 'Well you can't live here, Bella. It's an ambulance station, not a refuge for homeless people.'

Bella's stomach knotted. She was going to be

thrown out. Where would she go?

'You'd better come home with me. I've got a spare room and you need a place to stay for a while.'

'But...'

Station Officer Steele held out a hand. 'Come on, up you get. I'm not going to argue with you. You need a proper place to stay where you can get some decent sleep, and I need my crew members to be fully fit for work.'

Bella took the offered hand and stood up. 'I don't know what to say.'

'Yes will do. Now come on, I'm exhausted. Let's go home.'

'There you are, there's nothing like a cup of cocoa before bed.' Station Officer Steele handed Bella a steaming cup and then sat down in the armchair opposite.

'Thank you.' The warmth from the cup seeped into Bella's fingers as she cradled it in her lap. She was sitting perched on the edge of the sofa, not quite believing that she was going to be staying at Station Officer Steele's flat in Holborn.

'You can sleep in my brother's room. He's away at the moment and won't mind.' Station Officer Steele sipped her cocoa.

'I don't want to intrude. I'll be fine sleeping on here.' Bella patted the sofa.

'Nonsense. If you do that, you'll end up with a crick in your neck and a bad back in no time. As I said, I need my crews to be well rested and fit for duty. I won't hear of you sleeping anywhere else except my brother's room.' She raised her eyebrows. 'If you're worried that he'll mind or might suddenly come back in the middle of the night, then don't be. Gerald is working up in Scotland for the navy and won't be back for some time. He'd be glad that his room is being put to good use.'

'Thank you.'

'That's settled then.' Station Officer Steele sighed and suddenly looked very tired. 'It's been one hell of a shift again. The telephone never seemed to stop ringing; we could have done with more ambulances. They've been drafting them in from other areas to cope with the number of casualties. We never had enough last time either.'

'Last time?' Bella asked.

'In the Great War. I was an ambulance driver in France. It was hard work, but I enjoyed it – I was with a great bunch of women. You young women remind me so much of how we were then.' Station Officer Steele stood up and went over to a small bureau, picking up a photograph in a frame and bringing it over to Bella. 'There we are; that's me,' she pointed to the figure on the left, dressed in a smart uniform, 'and that's Elsie, my co-driver and best friend.' She smiled, her face softening. 'We were a right pair.'

'I never knew you were in France,' Bella said.

Station Officer Steele shrugged. 'It's not something I talk about much, I suppose. I do understand what it's like for you young women, I really do. This time's harder in a way because the war has come to us, right to our doorsteps, and innocent people are being killed or injured, their homes destroyed.' She reached out and patted Bella's

113

arm. 'Last time was bad enough, but at least most people were spared being in direct danger.'

'Do you think they'll keep bombing us?'

'Probably. Hitler won't stop until he gets what he wants, and that's Britain, but we can't let him get it.' She paused. 'Drink up. It's time to get some sleep, or we'll be in no fit state for the next shift.'

'I'll do what I bloody well like.' Ivy spat the words out. 'You ain't going to give me orders. If you're that bothered, you should be 'ere yourself instead of prancing off to drive an ambulance.' Her last few words dripped scorn.

Frankie waited a moment before answering. She felt like slapping Ivy's heavily made-up face, giving the self-centred woman what she deserved, but that would only add fuel to the woman's fiery temper.

'You shouldn't leave a ten-year-old boy on his own in the middle of an air raid, Ivy. What were you thinking? You know Grandad doesn't want you out of the shelter either.' Frankie spoke calmly, holding tightly onto the back of the chair. 'It's for your own safety.'

'Well he ain't been 'ere either when the bombs are droppin'. I 'ate it in that shelter; makes me feel all closed in. Bloomin' metal coffin it is.'

'If you keep coming out in the middle of a raid, you might well end up in a real coffin – that's if there's enough of you left to put in one.'

'What do you mean by that?'

'I've seen enough victims of bomb blasts to know exactly what can happen to a person that's caught in one.' Frankie paused, letting her words sink in. 'So if I'm at 'ome when that siren goes, you won't see me taking any chances by staying in the 'ouse or leaving the Anderson in the middle of a raid. Look, if you don't want to do it for yourself, do it for Stanley. Think how scared 'e must be on 'is own.'

Ivy squared up to her, her face no more than a few inches away, her hands on her ample hips. 'He ain't my son, or even my responsibility.' She prodded a finger towards Frankie. 'If you're so concerned, then give up that fancy job and be 'ere with him.'

The woman's sheer cold-heartedness was incredible. Stanley might not have been a blood relation, but it didn't matter – Frankie's grandparents had taken him in from next door to save him from being put in an orphanage after his widowed mother died. Ivy clearly didn't care anything for the boy; her only interest in him was when she wanted him to do something for her.

'You know I can't do that,' Frankie retorted. 'They need drivers more than ever now. Stanley's part of this family – the family you married into – and as you're not working, your duty is to make sure he's safe in the shelter, and to stay there with 'im.' Her blood was fizzing inside her at the nerve of the woman. 'Very well then, I'll make other arrangements for 'im so I know he's safe. I'll speak to Josie at number five, see if she can squeeze him into her shelter with the rest of her brood. I know she wouldn't ever see a child left on its own in the middle of a raid. I'll call in on my way to work.'

As she turned to go, Ivy grabbed her arm.

'Wait. I've reconsidered. I'll stay with 'im. 'E don't need to go to no neighbour's shelter, not when we've got a perfectly good one of our own. Your grandfather wouldn't like that.'

No, he wouldn't, thought Frankie. He'd be furious that Ivy was leaving Stanley on his own, and no wheedling would get her out of that one. Frankie hadn't had a chance to speak to him yet, as she hadn't seen him for the past few days, and she hadn't wanted to wake him up from much-needed sleep. 'If that's what you want but rest assured, Ivy, I will check with Stanley, and if I'm passing by during a raid, I'll drop in and check for myself.'

Ivy's face blanched. 'But you don't come out this far east.'

'Oh we do, especially if bombs are dropping around 'ere.' Frankie smiled at her. 'I must go. Remember to get Stanley to the shelter as soon as the siren goes and stay there with 'im till the all-clear, yes?'

Ivy nodded, her mouth pressed in a thin line.

'See you in the mornin', if not before when I'm out this way.' Frankie got out of the house as quickly as she could, her legs shaking as she went. She hadn't been called to an incident round here yet, as there were other ambulance stations closer, but Ivy didn't need to know that. If she thought Frankie might drop in at any time, so much the better.

Walking down Matlock Street, Frankie smiled with relief. That was the first time she'd got Ivy to back down, and it hadn't been fear of what might happen if a bomb dropped on her that had made her step-grandmother change her mind; rather the worry about what the neighbours would say. She didn't want them to know what she was really like. Putting on a show was all important for Ivy. It was her weak spot.

Trixie fitted nicely into the basket on the front of Winnie's bicycle. Instead of facing the direction they were travelling, she sat looking at Winnie, her brown eyes fixed on her as if to make sure she didn't suddenly disappear.

'Nearly there,' Winnie said, 'though I don't know what they're going to say about you coming to work with me. I don't mind, of course, but the others...'

She had left Trixie at home with Connie the day before, thinking that the peace and quiet would be best for the little dog; give her a chance to rest and recuperate after her traumatic burial, but it had turned out quite the opposite. Trixie had been inconsolable and had whined non-stop until Winnie had returned after her shift. She had refused to leave Winnie's side ever since, even sitting beside the bath while she washed off the dirt from another night of ferrying casualties to hospital.

Turning into Ambulance Station 75, Winnie rode in under the arched passageway and bumped her way over the cobbles to the garages, where she dismounted and wheeled her bicycle inside to stow it out of the way at the back.

'Who've you got there?' Sparky's voice made her jump as he stepped out from behind one of the ambulances with a screwdriver in his hand.

'None of your business,' Winnie said, moving in

front of her bicycle basket to shield Trixie from his view. 'And what have you been doing with that screwdriver?'

'None of your business either,' Sparky retorted with a grin on his face. 'If you must know, I was fixing one of the stretcher runners – last shift said it was sticking.'

Winnie smiled at him and stepped aside. 'I've brought Trixie to work with me; she won't leave my side now. Poor little mite was terribly upset all day yesterday while I was away.' She lifted the dog out of the basket and held her in her arms, stroking her soft golden head. 'I didn't have the heart to leave her at home. She's suffered enough and I don't want to upset her any more.'

Sparky whistled. 'I don't think that'll go down well with the boss.'

'I don't see why not. She was very kind to Trixie when I brought her in; you told me so yourself.'

'Indeed I did, but just because she tried to feed a scared dog her corned-beef sandwich, it don't mean she'd want it here all the time. We're busy enough as it is, Winnie; you ain't going to 'ave time to be looking after Trixie. She'd only get in the way.'

'Well I'm not taking her home,' Winnie snapped. 'She's staying with me. And she won't be any trouble, I can assure you.'

'If you say so, but don't say I didn't warn you.' Sparky stroked Trixie, ruffling the soft fur on her ears. 'She's a sweet little thing, but this ain't the place for her.'

'We'll see.' Winnie smiled at him and put Trixie down on the ground. 'Come on, Trix, this way.'

She headed towards the stairs leading up to the staffroom with the little dog trotting at her heels.

'You can't have a dog at an ambulance station, Winnie. This is a place of work and people's lives depend on us. She might get in the way and delay us getting to an incident; she could end up costing someone their life.' Station Officer Steele reached out and gently stroked Trixie's ears, and the dog responded by wagging her tail. 'Look, I've nothing against her, she's a dear little creature, but this really is no place for a dog.'

'But she won't be in the way, I promise you. She stays right by my side; where I go, she goes.' Winnie held Trixie protectively in her arms.

'You are not seriously thinking of taking her out to an incident, are you?' Station Officer Steele's voice had an icy edge to it. 'In one of my ambulances?'

'Why not? She can sit in the cab and she won't be any trouble.'

Station Officer Steele took in a sharp breath. 'If I didn't need you here on duty today, I'd send you straight home.' Her voice was clipped and crisp. 'As it is, you'll have to stay for the duration of your shift, but I want that dog kept out of everyone's way. You leave her at home tomorrow or you'll be dismissed. Do you understand?'

'But–' Winnie began.

Station Officer Steele held up her hand to stop her. 'That's my last word on the matter.' She gave Trixie a final pat, then turned on her heel and went into her office, closing the door quietly behind her.

'That's told you,' Mac said, getting up from the chair where he'd been sitting drinking tea and going over to the sink to rinse out his cup. 'Bring Trixie down and she can sit in the cab while we get the ambulance ready. I've been teamed up with you today as Hooky's off with a bad back.'

'That's one small mercy then,' Winnie said. 'I was dreading her kicking up a fuss if we had Trixie with us in the ambulance. I honestly don't think she'll get in the way... I wouldn't put anyone in danger.'

'I know you wouldn't, but rules are rules, I suppose.'

'Yes, but aren't they made to be broken if there's a good enough reason?'

Mac shook his head and smiled. 'You are quite irrepressible, Winnie, did you know that?'

Winnie laughed. 'I have been told that before. I can't help myself; as soon as someone says I can't do something, I get a terrible urge to do it.'

'So if I want you to do something, I should try telling you to do the opposite?'

Winnie shrugged and grinned. 'I'd only do it if I thought it was the right thing. And that's for me to know and you to wonder at.'

Trixie sat quietly in the ambulance cab, watching intently through the windscreen as Winnie worked her way through the necessary daily checks – oil, water, petrol, tyres and lights – before cleaning the engine and polishing the bonnet, wings and cab.

'See, she's quite happy,' Winnie called to Mac, who was up a ladder cleaning the sides of the ambulance.

'Course she is.' He smiled down at her.

'And she's a lot cleaner than when you found her,' Bella called over from where she was kneeling on the roof of her ambulance scrubbing off bomb debris. 'How'd you manage that?'

'Two baths,' Winnie said. 'You should have seen the colour of the water when I'd finished.'

'Aye, aye,' Mac whispered. 'Have you seen who's watching?' He indicated upwards with his eyes while he carried on working.

Winnie glanced up and saw Station Officer Steele at her lookout post at the staffroom window, watching what was going on. That was nothing new, of course – the whole crew knew that she liked to keep an eye on them – but Winnie felt her hackles rise, and she had to clamp her lips together hard to stop herself from calling out to her that Trixie wasn't causing any problems or getting in the way.

'You feeling all right?' Mac asked. 'Only you've gone a bit pale, except for those pink spots on your cheeks.'

'If you must know,' Winnie said stiffly, struggling to quell her emotions, 'I'm trying hard to control myself and not say what I think for once, because if I did, I might just dig myself into such a deep hole that I couldn't crawl out of it. I don't want to lose this job – I love it.'

Mac nodded. 'Good for you, Winnie. I admire your spirit and your self-control.' He lowered his voice. 'If it's any help, I'm on your side. I can't see that having Trixie around would be a problem. She's more likely to be good for us, to be honest; we're seeing enough horrible things, and having a

121

dog here to make a fuss of might help to take our minds off it.'

'Thank you, Mac, I appreciate that, but I don't have any choice if the boss says otherwise, do I?'

'This looks like it,' Winnie said, parking the ambulance where the ARP warden was indicating. Mac had insisted that she drive to keep everything as normal as possible and not give Station Officer Steele the slightest reason to question Winnie's dedication just because she had Trixie with her. The dog was quite happy going out in the ambulance with them and had sat on Mac's lap the entire journey looking out of the window, as if she'd been doing it forever.

Winnie wound down the window and spoke to the warden. 'What have you got for us?'

'Buried casualties; they've nearly finished digging 'em out. Both unconscious, man and a woman.'

'We'll get the stretchers ready.' Winnie turned to Trixie and took the dog's head between her hands, looking her straight in the eyes. 'You stay here while Mac and I go and do our job. We won't be long.'

'Anyone would think that dog can understand what you say, the way you're talking to her,' Mac said.

'She's a bright little button, aren't you, Trixie? Who knows what they understand? Come on, there's work to be done.'

'Make sure your window's shut,' Mac reminded her. 'You don't want Trixie jumping out.'

Winnie smiled at him gratefully. 'Thanks.'

Barely ten minutes later, both casualties were safely stowed in the back of the ambulance, with labels written out and tied on, blankets tucked around them and hot-water bottles keeping them warm.

'All set?' Winnie asked Mac, who was staying in the back with the patients while she drove them to hospital.

Mac nodded. 'I'll keep a close eye on them, don't worry.'

'I won't then.' Winnie grinned and shut the doors.

The moment she opened the door of the cab, a streak of golden fur jumped out and rushed over to the remains of the house where the two casualties had been dug out.

'Trixie!' Winnie yelled, but the dog took no notice of her and started to scrabble and dig in the debris, sending brick dust and plaster shooting out behind her.

Winnie rushed over and grabbed hold of her collar, trying to drag her away, but Trixie dug her claws in and barked loudly.

'What's going on?' the ARP warden said.

'She got out of the cab. I'm sorry, I'll take her back.' Winnie bent down and tried to pick Trixie up, but to her surprise, the dog growled at her and then started madly digging again.

'Looks like she's searching for something,' the ARP warden said.

'She was buried in a bombed-out house herself, maybe she thinks this is it and is looking for her owner,' Winnie suggested.

'What's goin' on?' One of the rescue service

workers who'd dug the casualties out came over carrying a mug of tea from the nearby WVS mobile canteen van.

'Her dog keeps digging, won't leave it,' the ARP warden said.

'Could mean there's someone else in there, though according to your list there were only two people living here.' The rescue worker looked at the warden.

'That's right, Mr and Mrs Shaw. That's them we pulled out; I know them both. There ain't no one else on the list for this address, otherwise we'd have got one of the rescue dogs in.'

Winnie had seen the rescue service using dogs to sniff out buried casualties at some of the other incidents she'd been to.

'I'm inclined to believe this dog; they don't behave like that for nothing. If we don't dig and someone's down there ... even if they ain't on your list...' The rescue service man gulped back the remains of his tea and handed the mug to Winnie, then bellowed to his colleagues gathered around the WVS van. 'Over 'ere, you lot! Looks like there could be someone else down 'ere.' He knelt down and started to remove bits of brick with his hands as the others hurried to help.

'Come on, Trixie, you mustn't get in the way.' Winnie bent down again to the dog, who'd been digging all the while and was now more a dirty grey colour than gold. To her relief, Trixie let her pick her up, and rested quietly in her arms, watching as the rescue service workers dug downwards.

'What's happened?' Mac appeared at Winnie's shoulder. 'I wondered what was going on when we didn't leave, and then I heard the shouting.'

'There could be another casualty,' Winnie said. 'I'll go and get a stretcher.'

It seemed like an age but could only have been a minute or two before one of the rescuers removed some debris to reveal a woman's face looking up at them. She blinked in the light, her eyes standing out starkly against her dusty grey face.

'It's all right, love. We'll 'ave you outta there in no time,' one of the rescuers said. He quickly issued instructions to the other workers, then turned and smiled at Winnie. 'You've got a good dog there, saved this woman's life.'

Winnie, lost for words for once, hugged Trixie to her. Station Officer Steele had been wrong. Trixie hadn't got in the way, or stopped them from saving someone; in fact she had done quite the opposite. Without the little dog, that poor woman would have lain there undiscovered and died alone in a tomb of rubble.

'Well, I'm surprised, happily surprised, and I'll admit I was wrong,' Station Officer Steele said after she'd listened to Winnie and Mac telling her what had happened at the incident.

Winnie held Trixie to her chest, wary of what was coming next.

'It's highly irregular and goes against my own rule, but as I'm the boss, I don't see why I shouldn't amend that rule.' Station Officer Steele smiled, her brown eyes warm behind her glasses. 'I need to take into account how Trixie saved a woman's life today. Despite what I said earlier, she's proven herself to be an asset to this station.' She stroked the dog's head which was still covered in grey dust. 'I apologise to you, Winnie, and would be delighted if you brought Trixie to work with you from now on. You can take her out with you to incidents if you wish, or she can stay behind with me and I'll look after her.'

'She can come to the station?' Winnie asked.

Station Officer Steele nodded. 'She certainly can, and I've even saved her a bit of corned beef from my sandwich. I expect she'll be hungry after all that digging.' She smiled warmly. 'Welcome to Station 75, Trixie. I've got a feeling you're going to be a help to all of us.' She nodded at Winnie and Mac. 'Right, I'll go and find that piece of corned beef.'

Mac nudged Winnie's arm as they watched the station officer hurry across the courtyard towards the stairs. 'How about that, then? She wasn't ashamed to admit when she was wrong; there aren't many bosses that'll do that.'

'I'm delighted she's changed her mind. I thought I was going to have to leave Trixie at home and dreaded how the poor thing would react, but now...' Winnie beamed at Mac, 'she can come here with me.'

'You've broken a rule today and had a new one made; that's pretty good going,' Mac said, stroking Trixie's dusty head. 'Even for you.'

Winnie laughed. 'What did I tell you? Rules are made to be broken...'

Frankie stared at what remained of the back garden. The house had caved in on itself like a pack of cards, with any remaining walls leaning drunkenly inwards. Debris was strewn across the garden: brick and plaster dust, splinters of broken glass, wooden beams sticking out of the rubble at awkward angles – all the work of today's daylight raid.

'What's going on?' Bella asked the ARP warden.

'Family of three trapped inside their Anderson shelter.' He took his steel helmet off and wiped his dirty forehead with his sleeve before replacing it again. 'Mother and two children; we've spoken to the boy, but there's no response from the mother or daughter.'

An icy hand gripped Frankie's heart. Shelters were supposed to do just that – shelter people and protect them from harm. That was what this family had thought, only ... it hadn't been safe, had it? If a bomb hit Frankie's home, Stanley could be killed even if he was in their shelter. The thought made her feel sick. Were they living in false hope, scurrying to the Anderson the moment the siren went, thinking they would be perfectly safe in there? It seemed that nowhere was entirely safe any more. Whether you survived an air raid depended on pure chance and where you were when the bombs fell.

Frankie watched as the rescue workers carefully dug their way through the debris heaped around what remained of the Anderson shelter. They'd exposed part of the corrugated iron at the front, which had twisted inwards, and she could see that the door was gone and the dark interior was only visible through a small gap.

'How long before they dig them out?' Bella asked.

The ARP warden shrugged. 'They're working on it, but they've got to be careful; there's so much debris that it could collapse and pour into the shelter and suffocate them. They're going as quickly as they can.'

The chief of the rescue service workers came over and nodded a greeting to Frankie and Bella. 'We're opening up a big enough 'ole to get someone in to the boy and see what can be done for the mother and daughter. We need someone small and slim to crawl through. Would–'

'I'll do it,' Frankie blurted out, before her brain had a chance to catch up with her tongue.

'I'm happy to go in as well,' Bella said.

'Thank you both, but there's only room for one of you.'

'I'm used to small boys and know what they like to talk about, because of Stanley... I know I could keep 'im talking, take his mind off it.'

Bella put her hand on Frankie's arm. 'Are you sure?'

Frankie nodded. She wasn't really sure at all, but it was better than standing around waiting until they finished digging the family out. She'd be doing something to help, and that poor boy needed someone in there with him, because he must be terrified.

'You'll need to take it slowly and try not to dislodge anything,' the rescue service chief said a short while later as he shone his torch through the gap that they'd excavated for her to crawl through. Frankie could see the mother slumped

128

on the floor, partly buried by the remains of a bunk bed, which had toppled over.

'Where's the boy?' she asked quietly.

'Right at the back. You can just make out his head, see?' He waggled his torch so that its beam pinpointed where he meant. 'He keeps drifting in and out of consciousness; he responds for a bit and then is gone again. If you can get 'im talking it'll 'elp. Tell 'im we'll get 'im out soon.'

Frankie nodded, taking a deep breath to steady the nerves that were swarming around her stomach. Could she do this? There was no question to answer. She *had* to do it. Imagine if that boy was Stanley; she'd hope someone would go in to be with him, wouldn't she? This boy wasn't Stanley, but he needed someone, and that someone was her. 'All set.'

She checked that her torch was working and then slowly began to slither her way in head first through the hole, which was barely wider than her shoulders, crawling along inch by slow inch on her belly, making every movement as gentle as she could, taking care not to dislodge debris and keeping her head down to stop her steel helmet scraping along the roof.

As her body plugged the hole, blocking out the light from outside, the inside of the shelter was plunged into darkness except for the thin beam of light from her torch. It was as if she were descending into the depths of the earth, and her blood started to whoosh noisily around her head. She had to fight hard against a surge of panic that was threatening to rise up and engulf her. She breathed slowly and deeply, reminding herself that it was only an Anderson shelter she was going into, just like the one in the back garden at home.

There was a drop down into the shelter, and once her head, shoulders and chest were free of the hole, she had to use her arms to brace herself so that she didn't fall, walking her hands carefully forward until she could curl her knees up and pull her whole body through.

'That's it, you're in. Well done,' the chief rescue worker called. 'Get your bearings first and then check the mother, as she's closest.'

Frankie shone her torch around, visions of the neat Anderson shelter at home flashing into her mind. The inside of this shelter looked as if it had been shaken up and thrown down like dice out of a cup, making the small space a chaotic maze of broken furniture and people that she'd have to negotiate her way around.

With adrenalin now firing the blood in her veins, she began to pick her way slowly towards the mother, checking before each movement to make sure it wouldn't dislodge anything and cause more damage.

Reaching the woman, she crouched down next to her. 'Hello, my name's Frankie. I'm here to help you.' She shone her torch over the woman's face. It looked pale, and her eyes were shut. Gently putting her fingers on the woman's neck, she felt for a pulse. She waited, and waited. But there was nothing. Not a beat, not a twitch. She was gone.

'Anything?' the chief rescuer's voice called from the entrance, where she could see his form blackly silhouetted against the daylight.

She lit up her own face with the torch so that

he'd be able to see it, and shook her head. She didn't want to say it out loud in case the boy was conscious again, because news like that wasn't going to be good for him.

'Can you see the girl?' the rescuer called through.

She shone her torch around, and spotted a leg sticking out from under some blankets towards the back of the shelter. Carefully she made her way across, stepping over bits of broken wood and a battered kettle. She took hold of the blanket and gently pulled it to the side, biting back the gasp that heaved in her chest at the sight of the girl's sightless blue eyes staring up at her. She didn't have to check for a pulse to know that she was gone too.

'I've found her,' she said, and once again shook her head in the torchlight so that they got the message outside.

Turning her attention to reaching the boy, she bent down and squeezed her way between some wooden poles that had fallen diagonally across the shelter. Reaching the back, she could see a small bed, just wide enough to fit across the end wall; it was tipped up against the corrugated iron, and the boy's head could be seen sticking out from underneath it.

Taking care not to knock against anything, Frankie gently pulled the bed back a few inches, enough to reveal the side of the boy's face, which she was relieved to see had a pink tinge to it, unlike the ghostly pallor of his mother and sister. His eyes were shut, but they flickered open, then quickly closed again, screwing up against the beam from

131

her torch.

Frankie touched his head lightly with her fingers. 'Hello, I've come to help you.'

The boy turned his head to look at her, blinking his eyes and gradually opening them wider as he grew used to the light. He stared at her steel helmet. 'Who are you?'

'I'm Frankie and I'm an ambulance driver come to take you to the hospital. What's your name?'

'Johnny Watson,' he said, then winced.

'Are you in pain?' Frankie asked.

He nodded. 'My leg's 'urt.' Tears filled his eyes and trickled sideways down his dirt-smudged face.

'We're going to get you out of here soon, I promise you,' Frankie said. 'The rescue service are busy digging you out as fast as they can.'

'But it 'urts,' Johnny whimpered.

'I'm going to see if we can get you something to help with that. I'll be back in a moment.'

She made her way carefully back to the opening, which was noticeably bigger than when she'd come in, and spoke to the chief rescue worker. 'He's in pain, says his leg hurts. I can't tell what the problem is without moving the bed more, but there's no sign of bleeding that I can see. We need the doctor to come and give him some pain relief.'

'Don't move him yet. The doctor's on his way; shouldn't be long now. Go back and keep talkin' to the lad, try and take 'is mind off it.'

'I'll do my best,' Frankie said.

Back beside the boy, she crouched down so that he could see her as they talked. 'How old are you, Johnny?'

132

'Seven. Where's my mum?'

'It's all right, she's over there.' Frankie chose her words carefully, treading a fine line between not lying to him but not telling him the terrible news that she was dead either. He would have to know, but not yet when he was in such a difficult situation. 'We'll get her and your sister out too, don't worry.'

'When? It still 'urts.'

Frankie wriggled her hand under the bed frame and managed to find his. ''Ere, you grab hold of my hand, Johnny, and squeeze when it hurts, and that'll help.'

Johnny's hand immediately latched onto hers and held it tightly, his small fingers pressing hard into her flesh.

'That's it, good boy, you're doing really well. I live with a lad who's ten years old, Stanley's his name. Him and his mates keep collecting shrapnel, do you?'

Johnny nodded. 'We swap bits at school.'

Frankie couldn't be sure how long she sat there talking to Johnny; it could have been a matter of minutes, or much longer, it was hard to say, but it seemed like an age as she watched him wincing with pain and felt his hand clamped as tightly around hers as the little boy could manage.

'The doctor's 'ere and coming through,' the chief rescuer called at last.

'Hear that, Johnny? 'Elp's on its way now. It won't be much longer; you've been such a brave boy.'

She watched as the black silhouette of a figure climbed through the hole and then a bag was handed through to him.

'I'm going to flash my torch around to get my bearings, so mind your eyes,' a warm, Scottish voice said. Frankie dropped her gaze to the floor as the beam of torchlight swept around the confined space of the shelter. 'I see where you are and I'm on my way.'

'This is Johnny. He's seven years old and his leg's hurt,' Frankie explained when the doctor reached them.

He nodded and smiled at her, his eyes kind under his steel helmet. 'Hello, Johnny, I'm Dr Munro. We'll have a look at you and then give you some medicine to help you feel better.' He quickly assessed the situation. 'Can you help me move the bed back?' he said to Frankie. 'We need to take it steady and be prepared...' His eyes held hers and she knew what he meant. Moving the bed away from the wall could relieve the pressure on Johnny's legs, and, depending on how he was hurt, could cause blood loss. 'You take hold of this end near Johnny's head and I'll go to the other end. Ready on the count of three. One, two, three.'

Slowly and smoothly they eased the bed back, and Frankie was relieved to see no sign of blood spurting out. She took hold of the little boy's hand again.

'Are you all right, Johnny?' she asked. 'Remember to squeeze my 'and when it hurts.'

He immediately clamped his fingers around hers, and increased the pressure further as the doctor gently examined his legs. 'Ow, ow.'

'I'm sorry, I don't mean to hurt you. I'm going to give you a wee injection to help with the pain and you'll soon feel better.'

'I don't like injections,' Johnny whimpered.

'Oh, you've no need to worry with mine.' Dr Munro smiled. 'They make us doctors practise on ourselves so we get very, very good at it. You won't feel a thing.'

He was as good as his word, because Johnny didn't make a fuss as Dr Munro injected him; in fact he didn't even know when he was doing it because Frankie stood in the way so that he couldn't see what was going on.

'There you go, young man, all done,' the doctor said. 'How does that feel?'

'Better.' Johnny's face relaxed as the painkiller started to work, and his grip on Frankie's hand loosened, although he still kept hold of it.

'You're doing brilliantly,' Frankie said, squeezing his hand. 'It won't be long before we have you out of 'ere, then I'll take you to hospital in my ambulance.'

'And I'll see you there later,' Dr Munro said, closing his bag. 'I'm going to have to go and see my next patient now, Johnny.' He squeezed Johnny's shoulder. 'You've been a very brave boy.'

Johnny nodded sleepily, his eyes drooping, and moments later he was asleep.

'Will you stay with him till they get him out?' Dr Munro asked.

'Of course,' Frankie said. 'I couldn't leave him in here on his own.'

Dr Munro smiled, his blue eyes warm. 'It's hard to see little children caught up in it...' He sighed, shaking his head. 'Thank you for your help. Having someone to keep patients calm is a godsend.'

Frankie nodded. 'I'm glad I could help him. Poor lad, it's not going to be easy for him...'

'Aye, there've been far too many families destroyed since the bombing started.' He picked up his bag. 'I must go, there are more patients waiting. Cheerio then.'

'Goodbye.' Frankie watched as he clambered over the broken furniture and climbed out of the hole, off to tend to other people hurt in today's raid. He seemed like a very kind man; perhaps she'd see him again sometime when he was out with the mobile medical teams that went to incidents where casualties needed help before they got to hospital.

Left on her own in the shelter, Frankie crouched down beside the bed and gently stroked Johnny's hand as she waited for the rescue workers to finish digging out a big enough hole to carry the casualties through. She was glad that the boy had fallen asleep so that he couldn't see his mother and sister being taken out of the shelter before him.

He was still asleep when it was his turn to be removed. She helped to gently lay him on a stretcher, taking care to secure his broken leg before tucking a blanket snugly around him. Just as she and the rescue worker who'd come into the shelter to help carry Johnny out were about to lift the stretcher, Frankie noticed a small toy dog made from cloth that had fallen to the floor beside the bed. Was it Johnny's? If she tucked it in beside him, it would more than likely get lost when he got to the hospital; they were far too busy tending the injured to worry about toys. If it was left here, he might never get it back, and he'd lost more than enough already today. Frankie picked it up and put it in her pocket, promising herself that she'd take it to Johnny in hospital and make sure that he and his precious toy were reunited.

Chapter Five

'Visiting day for families is Sundays, two till four,' the nurse informed her as she stood in the doorway of the ward, blocking the way in.

'I'm not family,' Frankie said. 'I'm an ambulance driver; I brought Johnny into the hospital yesterday. I was with 'im in the shelter until they dug him out. I just wanted to know how he is.'

'As good as expected after losing his mother and sister like that. We've fixed his leg, but his heart is going to take longer to mend.' The nurse considered for a moment. 'Look, I shouldn't really as it's against the rules, but Sister's on her dinner break, so if you're quick, you can have five minutes with him. It might do him good to see someone else, and since you helped him...'

'I brought him this; it was with 'im in the shelter.' Frankie pulled the toy dog out of her dungarees pocket. 'It was a bit dirty after being bombed, so I've cleaned it up for him.'

'They won't let him keep it in here, I'm afraid, because of infection. There's an aunt, his mother's sister, who he'll be going to live with while his father's away in the army; she's coming to see him, so I'll see it's given to her to keep for him.' Frankie handed the dog over. 'Five minutes now, no more, or Sister will have us both hauled over the coals. He's in the third bed along on the left.'

'Thank you,' Frankie said and went into the ward before the nurse could change her mind. The sight of injured children was heartbreaking and she had to swallow back tears as she walked past the beds, where large eyes in pale faces followed her movements, or, even worse, just stared blankly at the ceiling.

'Johnny?' Frankie spoke gently as she came to the bed where he lay with a frame over his legs holding the bedclothes off his injuries. He looked at her, frowning. 'It's me, Frankie, do you remember me?'

He nodded, and Frankie knelt down on the floor beside the bed and took hold of his hand. 'They've fixed your leg, I see.'

Tears welled up in Johnny's eyes and spilled over, running down his cheeks.

'I've come to see how you are.' Frankie took out her clean handkerchief and dabbed at his cheeks.

'My mum and my sister are dead...' He broke down into sobs and Frankie leaned over and gathered him into her arms, careful not to move him too much because of his leg.

'I'm sorry, Johnny. There was nothing we could do to save them. The bomb killed 'em outright. They wouldn't have suffered.'

'No, they wouldn't have, Johnny,' a Scottish voice said. 'I promise you.'

Frankie turned around and recognised Dr Munro from the shelter, this time looking a lot cleaner and dressed in a white coat rather than a steel helmet.

He smiled at her. 'I see I'm not the only one to come and visit you, Johnny. You're a popular young man to have ambulance drivers drop in on you.'

Johnny managed a smile.

'The nurse only let me in for five minutes.' Frankie gave Johnny a final hug and then stood up. 'I'd better go. I'll come and see you again soon. You do what the doctors and nurses tell you and you'll be out of 'ere in no time. All right?'

Johnny nodded. 'Goodbye, Frankie.'

Frankie squeezed Johnny's shoulder and quickly left. When she stopped at the ward door to give a final wave, she saw that Dr Munro was talking to Johnny, holding the boy's hand.

'How was he?' The nurse who'd let her in stepped out of a side room as she went past.

'He's upset about his mother and sister of course, poor boy. We didn't tell 'im while he was in the shelter.'

'It's a sad tale but not such an unusual one these days, unfortunately. At least he's got an aunt who will take him in.'

'Can I come back and see 'im again?' Frankie asked. 'On Sunday between two and four?'

The nurse grinned. 'Of course. I'm sure he will be pleased to see you.'

Frankie had almost reached the top of the stairs down to the ground floor when she heard footsteps behind her and her name being called.

'I thought I'd missed you.' It was Dr Munro. 'Thank you for coming to see Johnny; it was very kind of you. I've not seen an ambulance driver come back to check on a patient before.' He smiled, and Frankie noticed that his eyes were almost aquamarine.

'I've got to admit, Johnny's the first casualty I've ever come to visit,' she said. 'I was worried about 'im and wanted to see for myself that he was all right – well, as all right as he can be after what happened.'

'So was I,' Dr Munro said. 'Worried, I mean. We haven't been properly introduced; a bomb-damaged shelter wasn't really the time or place.' He held out his hand. 'Alistair Munro.'

'Stella Franklin, otherwise known as Frankie.' She shook his hand.

'Pleased to meet you, Frankie. I'm due a break now; would you like to join me for a cup of tea, or are you due on duty soon?'

'Not till half past three, so yes, thank you, I'd love a cup of tea.'

'So how long have you been an ambulance driver?' Alistair asked as they sat in the hospital canteen with mugs of tea in front of them.

'Only a few weeks. I used to sew uniforms before that.' Frankie took a sip of tea.

'That's quite a change. You'd have saved yourself from having to see some terrible sights if you'd stayed sewing uniforms.'

'I know, but I wanted to do somethin' more useful, and it had to be somethin' I could do while still living with my family. Joining the WAAF or the ATS wouldn't have been any good as I'd have had to leave home, so the Auxiliary Ambulance Service

140

was perfect, interesting and challenging, though...' She paused, turning her mug round and round in her hands. 'I failed on my very first day; I couldn't do my job.' She told him about her first incident, with the man skewered on the railings. 'I've seen things as bad as that since then, only I've learned to cope with it by getting angry.'

'Who with?'

'The bombers. First night of the Blitz, when I heard them flying over, droning on and on and the bombs screaming through the air, and I saw what they'd done to innocent people...' She sighed. 'It made me so angry ... made me keep going and got me through it. I don't like some of what I do – it makes me feel scared and sick – but I 'ave to do my bit and help these people. You must see awful things as well.'

Alistair shrugged. 'Yes, but being a doctor I'm used to it.'

'Do you go out much with the medical team?'

'I'm on call once a week – people often need help out there where they've been hurt – but most of the time I'm in the casualty department, and I see the injured when they get to hospital.'

'You don't sound like you're from round 'ere,' Frankie said.

'Now how'd you guess that?' He made his accent stronger and grinned at her. 'I come from near Edinburgh. I trained there and then thought I'd see a bit of the country. I came to London a year ago.'

'Do you like it?'

'Yes, but I prefer it when it's not being bombed to smithereens.'

'I'm with you on that one.' Frankie drank the last of her tea. 'I'm going to 'ave to go or I'll be late for my shift. Thanks for the tea.'

Alistair stood up as she got to her feet. 'You're welcome, any time. Don't worry, I'll keep an eye on Johnny; he'll be fine in time. Have a good shift.'

'I will, though it will be a better one if the bombers don't come back again tonight. What do you think the chances of that are?'

He ran his hand through his dark brown hair. 'Going by the fact that they've been back every night for over a week, I'd say it's pretty unlikely.'

'Yeah, that's what I think. I suppose with all this practice we're getting pretty good at it.'

'Stay safe, Frankie. I'll look out for you when I'm next out with the medical team.' He smiled warmly.

'You too.' Frankie walked away smiling.

'I'm nearly falling asleep.' Bella sat up straighter and stretched as much as she could within the confines of the ambulance cab in an effort to wake herself up.

She and Frankie were heading back to Station 75 after another long night. Their shift was still being stretched well beyond its normal finishing time as it was impossible to go home in the middle of an incident, and it was often difficult for crews from the next shift to get to work in the middle of a raid. Last night had been no different. The bombers had come back and the telephone had kept ringing with incidents to go to. Now the all-clear had gone and people were stirring from the shelters, emerging onto the streets and heading home to see if they still had a home to go to.

'We're nearly back.' Frankie yawned as they drove past the Tower of London. 'I'm looking forward to crawlin' into my bed.'

'Me too,' Bella said. Though it wasn't strictly her bed, she thought, but Station Officer Steele's brother's. She still hadn't told anyone that she was staying there; she didn't want a fuss, and it would only be for a day or two, until she could find somewhere else to live, though that was proving harder than she'd thought because so many people had been made homeless by the bombing, with more being added every night.

A lone figure in army uniform striding along the pavement caught Bella's eye as they drove past him. There was something familiar about the man; it was the way he walked. She quickly turned around for another look but couldn't see him beyond the bulk of the back of the ambulance.

'Can you stop, Frankie?' she asked.

'What's wrong?' Frankie pulled over to the side of the road. 'Are you feeling all right?'

'I thought... Wait here a moment.' Bella opened her door and jumped out, looking back at the figure walking towards her along the pavement. It *was* him! There was no mistaking her brother. 'Walter!' Bella's tiredness evaporated and she ran towards him full pelt, calling out, 'What are you doing here?'

'Came to see you.' He grinned as he caught her up in his arms and lifted her small frame off the floor in a great bear hug.

'How are you?' Bella asked when he'd released

her and put her down again. She looked him up and down. 'You look well.'

He shrugged. 'They say I'm fit for service again.' He smiled, but Bella noticed that it didn't quite reach his serious brown eyes.

'What do you think?'

Walter shrugged. 'The army never asks a soldier for his opinion – they just tell you what to do.'

'Well I'm very pleased to see you here. Come on, we're on our way back to the station and then I'll be finished.' She linked her arm in his and marched him towards the waiting ambulance. 'Frankie, this is my brother, Walter. Can we give him a lift back?'

'Course we can. Pleased to meet you, Walter.' Frankie stretched her arm across and shook his hand.

'And you, Frankie. Peggy's told me in her letters about working with you.'

'Climb in and we'll get this ambulance back, then we can all go 'ome, and you two can have a good catch-up.'

'I won't be going straight back to the flat today, but I'll be really quiet when I do come in,' Bella said. She'd come to Station Officer Steele's office before she left the station, knowing that her boss would be the very last to leave as she always was, checking that all her crews had gone home before her.

'But you need some sleep,' Station Officer Steele said. 'You've done more hours than you should have again.' She raised her eyebrows, her keen brown eyes searching Bella's face. 'Is there any-

144

thing wrong?'

Bella smiled. 'No, quite the opposite. My brother's here, he's waiting for me outside, and I want to spend some time with him.'

'He's been released from hospital then?'

'Yes, he got a train to London yesterday evening and spent the night in the Underground during the air raid, and now he's here to see me.'

Station Officer Steele smiled. 'Then bring him back to the flat. Remember, I've told you to treat it as your home while you're staying. You need to make the most of every precious moment you can with him, as no doubt they'll be sending him off somewhere else again soon and you might not get the chance again for who knows how long. Bring him home, Bella, and I look forward to meeting him.'

'If you're sure, thank you.'

Back downstairs, Walter was waiting for her, watching as the crews from the next shift cleaned the ambulances.

'Do you do that?' he asked as she linked her arm in his and steered him in the direction of the arched passageway leading out to the road.

'Yes, usually we do it at the end of our shift, but with our normal shift overrunning they often send us home and get the next shift to clean them out. They'll have more time to do it now things have calmed down after last night's bombing.' She steered him to the left, in the direction of Station Officer Steele's flat.

Walter grinned. 'Makes a change from cleaning houses, I suppose.'

'Rather this than cleaning up after people too

145

rich and idle to do it for themselves. I'm not going back to that after this is over,' Bella said. 'I've promised myself I won't.'

'What'll you do then?'

'I've got a dream of continuing my education. I still want to be a teacher; remember that's what I always wanted to do, before...'

Walter squeezed the hand that was linked through his arm. 'I know. Your dream was shattered when Father died and that bastard threw us out.'

'Walter! You shouldn't use language like that.'

'Well he deserves it; he behaved like one. He didn't care that Father had put his life and soul into that garden. And for what? He was barely in his grave before they evicted us.' Walter's voice cracked and he paused to clear his throat. 'And what was left of our family was broken up and scattered to the four winds just to survive.'

Bella closed her eyes, remembering how her family had been blown apart. As if her father's death wasn't enough to cope with, his employer had sent his estate manager around the day after the funeral to inform her mother that they had one month to vacate their home – the cottage that went with the head gardener job at the Hall. There'd been no loyalty or compassion shown to the family despite the many years of service her father had given. With no place to go, they'd all had to find somewhere new to live and work. Walter had joined the army; Bella had had to abandon her education and go into service, and her mother had returned to working as a cook at another grand house.

Bella understood her brother's bitterness; she'd felt the same way for a time, but had put it behind her now. There was no point in dwelling on it; it didn't help. The best thing to do was move forward and prepare for the future so it could never happen again.

She stopped walking and turned to face her brother. 'It's past and done with now, Walter, you mustn't let it keep bothering you.' She took his hand in hers. 'It wasn't right and it wasn't fair, but it's the way things were for people like us – servants. It's what we do next with our lives that matters. We can't change the past, but we can learn from it, and that's why I'm never going back to being a housemaid again.'

Walter nodded. 'I know. I'm trying, I really am.' He nudged her with his elbow. 'I bet you hated being told what to do: clean this, dust that.'

'Of course I did. Mind you, I made good use of their library. I bet I read more of the books in there than the family ever did.'

They were walking past St Paul's Cathedral en route to Station Officer Steele's flat in Holborn when Walter said, 'Can we sit down for a minute? I need to tell you something.' His face looked serious.

'Of course.' Bella led the way over to the steps at the front of the magnificent building and sat down on them, patting the cold stone beside her for Walter to do the same. 'Go on then, spill the beans.'

'I'm not going back.'

'What, to where we used to live?'

He shook his head. 'No. The army.' He cleared

147

his throat. 'I'm supposed to report back fit for duty next week, but I'm not going... I'm going AWOL.'

Bella stared at him. 'What? But why? I thought you loved it in the army.'

'I did. But not any more, not after Dunkirk. What I...' His voice caught in his throat and he leaned forward, resting his elbows on his knees and his head in his hands. Bella put her arm around his shoulders. Walter sat motionless for a few seconds, then sat up and looked at her, his eyes bright with unshed tears. 'It was hell there, stuck on that beach with those bastard Jerries firing at us and bombing us. I saw my best mate blown to bits. I don't know what it's all for any more.'

'I'm so sorry, Walter, you should never have had to go through that.' She leaned against him, her head on his shoulder. 'None of our men should. But you came through it, thank God.'

'Sometimes I wish I hadn't... It would have been easier if I'd been killed.'

'No it wouldn't!' Bella snapped. 'We had no idea what had happened to you for days, whether you were dead or alive.' She stopped. Her throat felt too thick to speak. 'When we did find out you were safe, I was so grateful ... so relieved.'

'I'm sorry. It just feels sometimes... I feel guilty that I'm still here and some of my friends aren't. It was down to luck where you were on that beach and whether a bullet or a bomb got you.'

'You were lucky, thank God. But you don't have to decide yet, you know; you've got a few days before you have to report for duty. Promise me you'll think about it before going AWOL, and don't go off and do anything stupid without telling me first.'

Walter shrugged. 'I've made up my mind. I don't care if they throw me in the slammer for it; at least I'd be out of it and wouldn't have to go through all that again.'

'Promise me,' Bella insisted.

'You always were bossy,' Walter replied. 'Very well then, I promise, but only for a few days, mind.' He stood up and held out his hand. 'Come on, I'm hungry. Let me treat you to some breakfast.'

Bella took his hand and let him pull her to her feet. 'That's an offer I don't get every day. You're on; there's a British Restaurant not far from here.'

Station Officer Violet Steele couldn't sleep. The words that Bella had whispered to her kept going round and round in her mind. Walter wanted to go AWOL. She'd known something was bothering Bella the moment she and Walter had arrived at the flat, and she'd asked her quietly what the matter was while they were in the kitchen preparing mugs of cocoa.

It was no good, sleep wasn't going to come, and the harder she tried, the further away it crept. She needed something stronger than cocoa today. Putting on her slippers and woollen dressing gown, Violet went through to the sitting room, where Walter was sprawled in an armchair, his chin resting on his chest. Trying not to wake him, she tiptoed over to the cabinet where she kept the bottle of single-malt whisky that her brother had brought back from Scotland on his last trip home, and poured herself a generous measure. A movement made her look around and she saw that Walter was awake.

'I'm sorry if I woke you.'

He shook his head. 'I was just dozing. I didn't get a lot of sleep down the Underground last night.'

'Can I pour you some?' She held up the bottle. 'A wee dram?'

'If you're sure, then thank you, I'd like that.'

'Cheers.' Violet clinked her glass softly against Walter's, then sat down in the armchair opposite him. 'I apologise for not being properly dressed. I couldn't sleep, too much going on in my mind.'

'I get that a lot, especially since I was injured.' Walter took a small sip of whisky. 'I keep reliving it in my mind, seeing it all over again, hearing it ... the screams ... the planes...'

Violet nodded. 'It'll take some time to learn to live with that. It was the same in France during the Great War. I knew men who couldn't escape from the noise and hell of it, even when they weren't at the Front. It got into their minds and wouldn't let them go.'

'Were you in France?'

'Yes, I drove ambulances. I had a fiancé at the front line and wanted to be near him.'

'What happened to him? Did he survive?'

'No.' Violet took a mouthful of whisky and let the fiery liquid trickle down her throat, leaving a trail of warmth in its wake. 'No, he didn't, because our own side shot him when he couldn't cope any more.' Her throat tightened and she waited for the

150

tears that threatened to spill over to subside; she only ever cried for him in private. 'William tried so hard, but in the end he had to leave. Desertion, they called it. He'd volunteered to join up, done over two years at the Front and had earned some time away to recover from his shell shock, but they wouldn't listen to him, wouldn't give him a chance. Court-martialled him as a coward and shot him at dawn on the fifteenth of October 1916.'

'I'm sorry.' Walter shook his head. 'My father told me what it was like out there; he was lucky to come back.'

'Thank you.' Violet nodded and glanced down at her whisky, swishing the golden liquid around the glass for a few moments before looking up again at Walter. 'The reason I'm telling you this, Walter, is because I want you to think very carefully about what you do next.'

Walter sat up straight and stared back at her. 'What do you mean?'

'I know what you're thinking of doing,' Violet said softly. 'Going AWOL.'

Walter took a sharp breath, frowning. 'She shouldn't have told you.'

'She didn't tell me. I asked her what was wrong. I know my crews well, Walter, and see it as part of my job to take care of them. What bothers them bothers me. So don't go blaming your sister; this is too big for her to shoulder on her own.' Violet sighed. 'Look, you can tell me to mind my own business, but I'd like to help you if I can, because I do understand how you're feeling. I went through every painful step with William.'

151

'I'm not a coward!' Walter snapped.

'I know. It takes a brave a man to consider stepping out of line. What is it that makes you not want to go back?'

Walter considered for a moment before giving his reply. 'I don't think we can beat them. It's pointless, and then all my friends would have died for nothing.' His eyes took on a faraway look. 'You should have seen what happened on that beach. We had nothing to match them; we'd had to abandon most of our equipment, and we were sitting ducks being picked off.' He shrugged. 'Look what they're doing to London now, pounding it with bombs night after night. They overran Holland and France; it's only a matter of time before they do the same to us.'

'So you think we should surrender?' Violet asked.

'God, no!' Walter ran a hand through his dark hair. 'I don't know. I feel so confused. I just want to run away from it all and never go back to having to follow orders I don't agree with.'

'William felt the same way about being told what to do by idiots far behind the line who had no idea what the actual fighting was like.' Violet gripped tightly onto the arm of her chair. 'They seemed to be running the whole damn war like a game on a board, never considering the real flesh-and-blood people who were paying the price for their mistakes. You know, they ordered men to walk across no-man's-land when any fool could tell you it makes more sense to run; you're less likely to be hit and will reach the enemy quicker. William lost most of his company at the Somme as they walked across.' She shook her head and swirled the whisky around in her glass again.

Walter shook his head sadly. 'They were lions being led by donkeys.'

'Indeed, they were.' Violet looked him directly in the eye. 'I fear the country is hanging on by its fingernails. It's very vulnerable right now and invasion may well be just around the corner.'

'If they come here, I'd fight to the death to defend my family from those bastards.' Walter blushed. 'I'm sorry, I shouldn't have said that.'

Violet smiled. 'I can assure you, Walter, I have heard far worse in my time.' She sipped her whisky, considering for a moment. 'It seems to me that you need time to think about what you want to do. Remember, you've only just come out of hospital after a horrendous experience. When do you have to report for duty?'

'Not until next week. I'm going to see my mother this afternoon, get back to the countryside for some peace and quiet.'

'Then you have time on your side. Consider all your options carefully and I'm sure you'll find the right answer. Whatever you decide, you have my support.'

Walter looked surprised. 'You've only just met me today.'

'Perhaps, but I understand how you feel, and I have seen what can happen when people aren't listened to and helped.' She stood up. 'I must get some sleep. Please make yourself tea if you'd like some.' She glanced at the clock. 'I'll be up again about one o'clock.'

'Thank you.' Walter held out his hand to her.

'It's helped to talk about it.'

Violet smiled as she shook his hand. 'I'm glad. It's a terrible thing that your generation is having to go through another war. They called the Great War "the war to end all wars", but it seems that those in charge never learn, and it's the ordinary people who pay the price.'

'Well hello to you too, Trixie.' Winnie laughed as the little dog launched herself at her, skipping and wriggling around, her feathery tail wagging in a blur of golden fur, making it quite clear that she was delighted that Winnie had finally woken up. Trixie still stuck close by Winnie and slept in her bedroom, snuggled up in a blanket on the floor beside her bed.

Winnie gave her a cuddle and then checked the time. It was nearly twelve o'clock. She'd slept later than normal, but she'd been so tired after the previous night. The bombers had come back and people were still being killed and injured, and it had been another busy shift, draining physically and emotionally.

'Time for some breakfast for both of us.' Winnie put on her slippers and dressing gown and with Trixie following at her heels made her way downstairs. As she reached the bottom of the flight of stairs leading into the hallway, a figure stepped out of the sitting room, making her start. It was her mother.

'There you are, Margot.' Her tone of voice suggested that Winnie was late for an appointment.

'Mother, what are you doing here?'

'I've been waiting for you. Constance made me

some tea before she went out...' she glanced at her watch, 'some two hours ago now.' She sighed. 'She made me promise not to come and wake you. Apparently you had ... a difficult night.'

Trixie started growling and Winnie picked her up and tucked her under her arm, stroking the dog's head. 'It's all right, Trix.'

'So this must be the dog you found. Constance told me you'd adopted her.'

'Yes, this is Trixie. You wanted to see me then, Mother?' Winnie mentally braced herself for what would come next. Her instinct told her this was no mere social call; her mother didn't make those types of visit to her. There was always an ulterior motive, something she wanted.

'Yes, I've come to tell you about your new job.' Her mother smiled as if she was delivering news of something that Winnie had longed for.

Winnie opened her mouth to speak, but no sound came out. She gave herself a mental shake and managed to croak, 'What new job?'

'It's a perfectly splendid one; your father and I are delighted. You'll be working for a friend of your father's at the Ministry; he travels around the country on government business and needs a new driver.'

She knew it. Her mother had taken no notice of what she'd said on the telephone a few days ago. Winnie's heart was beating hard and the blood was surging through her body. 'Please listen to me, Mother. I. Do. Not. Want. A. New. Job.'

'You're being very brave, and that's highly commendable, but you've done your bit now and it's time for something different, something safer.' Her mother moved towards her, then quickly stepped back as Trixie growled again. 'You can leave with me today; you won't ever have to drive an ambulance again.'

'No!' Winnie didn't trust herself to say more in case everything she'd held back over the years came pouring out. 'If you'll excuse me, I'm going to have my breakfast. I'm due back on duty this afternoon. Please let yourself out.'

Not waiting for a response, she fled down the stairs to the kitchen, closing the door behind her and leaning against it, her whole body shaking. Would her parents never stop interfering? Why could they not understand that she knew what she wanted in life?

Trixie whimpered in her arms and Winnie put her down and let her out of the back door into the small garden. Leaving the door ajar so the little dog could find her way back in, she made herself some tea and toast. She didn't feel like eating any more, her appetite snuffed out by her mother's visit, but she knew she must; her job needed her to be fit and ready.

She was sitting at the table, Trixie back inside and leaning against her legs, when the kitchen door opened a crack and her mother's voice called, 'Can I come in?'

Trixie growled softly and Winnie felt herself tense. What did she want now? She'd hoped she'd gone. 'Yes, if you must.'

Her mother came in and sat down. 'Margot, if you don't want to do it for yourself, then at least do it for Trixie. She could get hurt if she goes out with you in the ambulance as Constance tells me

156

she does. You wouldn't want that. She could come and live at home; I'm sure our gardener would look after her.'

Winnie stared at her. 'I beg your pardon?'

'He's very good with animals. She'd be well looked after and you'd be free to do your new driving job.'

Winnie stood up so fast her chair fell over backwards. 'Please accept this as my final word on the matter. I am not leaving the ambulance service and Trixie is staying here with me.' She strode across to the door that led to the steps up onto the street, and held it open. 'I need to get ready for work, so thank you for your visit.'

Her mother stared at the door, her lips tightly pursed. 'I'm not going out that way; that's the servants' entrance.'

Winnie shook her head. 'Connie doesn't have any servants. I often come and go this way, and so does Connie. It's your quickest way out.'

'You'd never have spoken to me like this before you started working at that ambulance station.' Her mother stood up, her body rigid. 'I'm very disappointed in you, Margot.' She tossed her head. 'I shall go out the way I came in. You haven't heard the last of this.' She nodded curtly and left the kitchen, her heels tip-tapping on the wooden stairs as she made her way up to the next floor.

'Goodbye, Mother,' Winnie called after her as the front door slammed loudly. 'Well, Trixie,' she said, bending down and scooping the dog up in her arms, 'I'm sure I haven't heard the last of it. I might not have won the war, but I think I just won that battle.'

157

The alarm clock shattered Bella's dream and she woke with a start, rolling over and switching it off. She sighed and started to close her eyes again, and then remembered – Walter was here and he was going AWOL. Fuelled by a mix of fear and worry, she launched herself out of bed and hurriedly dressed, wondering whether he had already made a run for it. To her relief, she found him sitting in the kitchen drinking tea.

'Morning, sis, want a cuppa?' he said cheerfully.

'You're still here! I thought you might have gone.'

'I wouldn't go without saying goodbye.' He poured her a cup. 'Sit yourself down. Your boss has already gone, said she wanted to do some shopping before her shift started.'

Bella sat down opposite him.

'What are you having for breakfast, then, if you can call it that at this time of day?'

Bella shrugged. 'That's the joy of working shifts. It's all right, I'll get myself something in a minute. I want to talk to you first. You know what you said yesterday ... about going AWOL?'

'Yes.' Walter looked at her, his face deadly serious.

'Did you really mean it?'

'Of course.' He sighed. 'I did when I told you, but now I'm not so sure.'

Bella's heart leapt with hope. 'You've changed your mind?'

'Not necessarily. Your Station Officer Steele and I had a good talk about it while you were asleep.

She understands how I feel and made me think. Did you know her fiancé was shot for desertion in the Great War?'

'No! She's never talked about him. Poor woman, that must have been terrible for her.' It showed how very little the crews at Station 75 knew about their boss. Station Officer Steele always seemed such a strong and capable person, and yet she'd suffered awful loss and kept it well hidden.

'Don't go spreading it around, will you? She's a private person and wouldn't want her business aired in public,' Walter warned her.

'Don't worry, I won't. She's been very good to me.' Bella drank some tea. 'So what are you going to do, Walter?'

'I'm going home to see Mother for a few days. It'll be good to spend some time with her in the countryside. I can think properly there, make up my mind.'

Bella reached out and took hold of his hand. 'I'll stand by you whatever you do.'

'Thank you.' He squeezed her hand. 'It means a lot to me to hear you say that. I'll write to you and tell you what I decide.'

'You could register as a conscientious objector and come and work for the ambulance service like Mac,' she suggested. 'You'd make a good driver.'

'I think it's a bit late for that. If I was a genuine conchie I'd never have joined the army in the first place, would I?'

'I'm scared for you.' Bella held on tightly to his hand.

'Don't be. I'll be all right whatever I do. You

159

and I are survivors, keep remembering that.'

Bella did her best to smile at him. She hoped he was right. Going AWOL would land him in big trouble with the army, but going back would put him in even more danger, as he'd probably be sent off to fight the enemy again. Whatever he decided to do, there was no guarantee he would be safe.

'I'm sorry, but he's been sent out to our sector hospital in the countryside until he's better. It's safer there for him,' the nurse explained.

Frankie had waited until the proper visiting time on Sunday afternoon to come back and see Johnny, calling in on her way to work, and now he wasn't there. She bit back her disappointment. 'I brought him this.' She held up a comic that she'd managed to find in a shop.

'You could always leave it here for other children to read,' the nurse suggested. 'They'd appreciate something to look at.'

'Of course.' Frankie handed it over to her. 'Thank you anyway.'

As she walked back towards the main staircase, she knew she should feel glad that Johnny was now safely out of London. There'd still been no let-up in the bombing raids; they came each night and sometimes during the day as well. At least out in the countryside he was away from all that, and the fresh air would do him good, bring some roses to his cheeks, as her grandmother used to say, but it was disappointing not to see him again and be able to reassure herself that he was doing well.

Walking out through the hospital's main front

doors, Frankie passed a parked ambulance. She recognised the driver and attendant from another ambulance station and smiled at them. She was halfway to the gates when she heard her voice being called in a familiar warm Scottish accent, and looking round, she saw Alistair hurrying towards her dressed in his normal clothes.

'What are you doing here?' he asked.

'I came to visit Johnny, only he's been sent to the countryside; went this morning, so they said.'

'That's good. I mean him being sent to a safer place, that is, not that you didn't see him.' Alistair cleared his throat. 'Could I speak to you a minute, Frankie?'

'Yes, of course.'

He took hold of her elbow and guided her to the side of the path, which was busy with people coming and going. Usually confident, he suddenly seemed very uncertain of himself, and a feeling of dread crept through her. Was he going to break some bad news to her about Johnny?

He ran a hand through his dark brown hair, making it stand up. 'I was wondering if you'd like to come out with me ... to the pictures or for a meal sometime...'

Frankie pressed her hand to her chest. 'Phew! I thought you were going to tell me something bad about Johnny.' She looked at him and smiled. 'Yes, I would love to go out with you sometime. Thank you.'

'Really?'

'Yes, really.'

Alistair smiled in delight, his blue eyes crinkling at the corners. 'Excellent.'

'I've got the whole day off next Saturday; we've worked so much extra time lately that Station Officer Steele is letting some of us have time off.'

'Would you like to go to one of the concerts at the National Gallery to start with?'

'I've never been to a concert before.'

'There's a first time for everything. I've been to a few there and they're very good.'

'All right then, why not? I'd be delighted to go. Thank you.'

Alastair beamed at her. 'Excellent. I'll swap my shifts around and we'll do just that. I'll look forward to it.'

Frankie smiled at him. 'Me too.'

'I'm sorry, dear, but if you already have somewhere to stay then you're not homeless, are you?' the woman in the town hall office said. 'Our priority is rehousing people who have no home because they've been bombed out.'

'I *was* bombed out!' Bella said, barely keeping control of her temper. This was the third time she'd been to the office this week. She had spent hours queuing up only to be told she was not a priority case and to come back again another day when they might have more to offer her. But they never did, because the bombers kept coming and more and more people were being made homeless and needed somewhere else to go, and Bella's request slid further and further down the list.

The woman smiled at her over her horn-rimmed glasses. 'You're lucky you've got somewhere for now. I know it might not be ideal, but there's a war on and we've all got to make sacrifices.'

162

Bella nodded. 'Thank you.'

As she turned and walked away, the next person in the queue, a woman with two small children clinging to her skirts, stepped forward. Bella wished her luck.

She'd been staying at Station Officer Steele's for more than a week now and she didn't want to overstay her welcome, though her boss hadn't shown any indication that she wanted her to leave. Bella liked to be independent and make her own way, but the shortage of housing was making it difficult. She'd spent every moment she could looking for somewhere else to stay and had only come to the housing office in desperation in case they could help her, but there were plenty of people more in need of rehousing than her.

She'd had enough of searching for one day, and it was too early to report for her shift, so she headed to the one place where she could do something useful to take her mind off her problem – Station 75's allotment. She knew from many hours spent helping her father when she was a child how calming repetitive jobs like weeding could be, and she needed some of that right now.

The allotment was in the moat surrounding the Tower of London. Where once water had surrounded the high walls, Londoners now grew food to eke out their meagre rations. Bella enjoyed coming to work here, but since the bombing had started she hadn't had any time to spare, sleep and finding a new home being her priorities. It was good to be back. The once neat rows of vegetables were looking a bit scruffy around the edges where weeds were poking their way through; the allotment had been neglected lately while the crews coped with the huge increase in incidents that the bombing had brought.

Kneeling down on the ground, Bella set to work pulling out unwanted plants from between the vegetables, the methodical task helping to soothe her. It also took her back to happier times working side by side with her father in the large walled garden at the Hall. He'd loved his job and had taught her a lot about plants and the natural world. Living in London she missed that strong connection with nature and the passing seasons. When Station 75 had been given the allotment, she had jumped at the chance to get involved and had spent many happy hours working there.

A cold, wet nose suddenly nudged her arm. 'Trixie! What are you doing here?' As she scooped the tail-wagging dog into her arms, she looked around to see where she'd come from, and saw Winnie propping her bicycle against the moat wall.

'Are there any weeds left for me?' Winnie asked as she came over to join Bella. 'I need to be busy.'

'Help yourself, there's plenty to go around.' Bella let go of the wriggling Trixie, who launched herself at her mistress as Winnie stood, hands on hips, surveying the allotment.

'You can tell we haven't had much time to look after it lately; it's looking a bit tattered and not up to its usual standard, but nothing a bit of hard work won't sort out.' Winnie knelt down and set to work. 'So what brings you here? Couldn't you sleep?'

'No, I slept fine, thank you. I've missed coming

here so thought I'd put in an hour or two before shift started.' Bella pulled out a deep-rooted weed, sending soil pinging up into her face.

'I'm here to vent my frustration and thought that at least this would be productive.'

'What's wrong?' Bella asked. Winnie didn't look her usual cheerful self; she'd even forgotten to put her usual pillar-box-red lipstick on.

'My mother. She ambushed me as I was coming down for breakfast. She'd come specially to tell me about my new job,' Winnie explained. 'My father has arranged for me to go and work as a driver for a friend of his in the Ministry so that I'll be out of danger.'

Bella reached out and grabbed Winnie's arm. 'We'll miss you.'

'No you won't, because I'm not going anywhere. And I told my mother precisely that. I love my job, and what we're doing is essential war work.'

'But it is dangerous, though. We go out in the middle of raids when most sensible people are tucked up safely in shelters.'

Winnie shrugged. 'My brother's job flying Spitfires is even more dangerous, but they don't turn up at his fighter station and tell him they've got him a nice cosy position driving some bigwig around.' Her voice was gradually getting louder and angrier. 'It's not fair, they treat me as if I'm some sort of idiot who doesn't know what she wants.' She suddenly stopped and looked at Bella, then started to laugh. 'Goodness, listen to me. Weeding is supposed to be calming me down. I'll stop talking about it now and try to forget about it.'

'It's all right, Winnie, you're entitled to be angry. We all get upset from time to time; it's allowed, you know.'

Winnie smiled at her. 'Thank you, Bella, you're a dose of common sense.' She paused, dirt-smudged hands on her hips. 'I wish I could take things as calmly as you do. I've never seen you get upset about anything, even when Station Officer Steele is in a mood with us for some misdemeanour or other.'

'She's a good boss really. If you knew what she'd been through...' Bella stopped talking; she'd said too much. It had slipped out in defence of the woman who had helped her, given her a roof over her head and her brother some good advice.

Winnie narrowed her eyes and stared at her. 'What do you know that you're not saying? I wonder...'

'Nothing.' Bella's cheeks grew warm and she looked down at the weeds, taking more care than necessary as she selected the next one to pull out.

'Come on, I can tell you know something. Has the boss got a secret admirer that she's been hiding from us?'

'No, she hasn't, not after what happened to her fiancé,' Bella snapped.

'Fiancé? What fiancé?'

Bella sighed. 'Look, I can't tell you. She's a private person and wouldn't want it spread around the station.'

Winnie's grey eyes widened. 'I'm sorry, Bella. I didn't mean to be intrusive. I honestly wouldn't spread anything about her... I do actually respect her immensely, you know. I know it doesn't always

166

seem like that, I suppose because she doesn't approve of everything I've done, but she's always fair and if she does reprimand me then I jolly well deserve it. I might not like it, but I do know it's my own fault.' She held up her hands. 'I won't bother you about it any more, I promise.'

Bella nodded and smiled at her. 'Thank you.'

The two of them fell into silence, working their way through the weeds while Trixie snoozed in the sunshine close by.

'Her fiancé was killed in France during the Great War,' Bella said, sitting back on her heels and looking at her soil-stained hands. Winnie didn't need to know the terrible detail that he'd been shot by his own side.

Winnie sighed. 'That's so sad. Like Connie's fiancé too. So many young women lost the men they loved and have never married. Connie always says that no one could ever match up to her fiancé.' She leaned over and touched Bella's hand. 'Don't worry, I won't breathe a word of that to anyone.'

'I know you won't, otherwise I wouldn't have told you.' Bella grinned and threw a weed at Winnie from the pile she'd pulled out.

'A weed fight!' Winnie retaliated and the two of them bombarded each other furiously, ending up sprawled on the ground helpless with laughter while Trixie skipped around them, barking and wagging her tail furiously.

'Goodness, that feels better,' Winnie said, lying on her back and looking up at the blue sky, where she could see silver barrage balloons bobbing around in case any daylight raiders came in on a surprise attack. 'I haven't laughed so much in ages.' She rolled onto her side, her head supported in her hand. 'How did you find out about her fiancé?'

Bella stared up at the sky for a few moments and then sat up. She chewed on her bottom lip, wondering what to say; in the end, she couldn't make herself say anything other than the truth, because that had been drummed into her by her parents.

'I'm staying with her.'

Winnie quickly sat up and stared at her, her mouth open wide. 'Did I hear that correctly? You're staying with Station Officer Steele? But why? I thought you lived in lodgings.'

'I did, but I was bombed out...' Bella poured out the whole story, finishing with being turned away again this afternoon at the housing office.

Winnie grabbed hold of her hand. 'Oh you poor darling, I had no idea. Why didn't you say?'

Bella shrugged. 'I didn't want to make a fuss; I'm not the only one who's been bombed out. I thought I could sort it out quickly, and I've been trying to, I really have. I will find somewhere in time, I've just got to keep on looking.'

'You don't need to do that, Bella. You can come and live with Connie and me. We've got plenty of space and I'm absolutely sure she'll be more than happy to have you there. Trixie and I certainly would. It would be such great fun having you living in the same house.'

'I couldn't, but thank you.'

Winnie stared at her, her head on one side. 'Why not? I don't understand. If you're worried

168

about Connie, don't be; she's the most generous person you'll ever find, and she's always having people to stay. Would it help if I asked her first and got her to write you a letter to say that it's absolutely fine with her? Would you think about it then?'

Bella nodded. 'All right then, thank you, but I really don't want to intrude.'

Winnie laughed. 'You wouldn't be. We've all got to help each other out these days – remember, there's a war on.'

They were the same words the woman at the town hall had used, and Bella remembered how dire the housing situation was. 'Thank you, Winnie, I appreciate your offer, and if your godmother says it's fine with her, then I'll be happy to come and stay with you for a while.'

'Excellent,' Winnie beamed. 'You won't regret it, I'm sure.'

Chapter Six

Bella stood outside Winnie's home in Bedford Place, a smart road leading off Russell Square, and stared up at the imposing building, wondering if she'd made a big mistake. The grand Georgian house was five storeys high, and she wasn't sure which door to knock on, the main entrance or the one she was more familiar with – the servants' entrance down in the basement. Before she could make up her mind, the main door was thrown open and Winnie stood in the doorway beaming at her.

'Bella! You're here. I've been watching out for you.' She ran down the short flight of steps onto the pavement, closely followed by Trixie, her tail wagging happily. 'Let me help you with your luggage.' She paused and looked down at the one small suitcase that Bella was holding. 'Is that all you've got?'

Bella nodded. 'I lost most of my belongings in the bombing, not that I had much anyway. Station Officer Steele gave me this suitcase and some clothes.'

'Never mind, it doesn't matter.' Winnie took hold of the case and linked her arm through Bella's, leading her up the steps and into the house. 'We'll go through my wardrobe and find you some more things. We'll have to alter them a bit with me being taller than you, but that shouldn't be a problem.'

Stepping into the hallway with its black and white tiled floor and elegant staircase sweeping upwards, Bella had a sudden urge to turn around and run straight back to Station Officer Steele's more modest flat. She must have been mad to accept Winnie's offer. This sort of house only meant one thing to her: the drudgery of being in service.

'This is it, welcome to Connie's house, I hope you'll be very happy here. Connie says to make yourself at home. She's had to go to a Red Cross meeting, and she apologises that she can't be here to welcome you herself. She–' Winnie stopped and stared at Bella. 'Are you feeling quite well? Only you've gone rather pale. Come and sit down.' She bustled Bella through a pair of double doors into a sitting room and sat her down on a sofa.

'I'm fine, honestly.' Bella looked around her at the beautifully furnished room. Long plum-coloured silk curtains were draped in liquid folds at the windows, and a tasteful painting hung above the large marble fireplace. Memories of many mindless hours spent dusting similar fireplaces flooded back.

'Let me get you some tea, and after that I'll show you your room,' Winnie said. 'I won't be long. Trixie, you stay here and keep Bella company.'

'Don't you get your maid to do that?' Bella asked.

'I'd have a long wait if I did, Connie doesn't have servants; she doesn't believe in them and nor do I. We get along just fine without any help, apart from Mrs Brown, who comes in to clean a few times a week and keeps us in order.'

Bella stood up. 'Let me come and help with the tea.'

'If you'd like to. This way, then.'

Winnie led her down to the kitchen, where Bella instantly felt more at home, although it seemed odd to see a kitchen like this without a cook bustling about preparing meals or other servants doing their jobs.

'Do you mind if we drink our tea here?' she asked as Winnie poured hot water into a china teapot.

'Not at all. I eat most of my meals down here now; too much fuss to take it all up to the dining room. It makes one realise how much work eating in there created for servants in the past.' Winnie sat down at the table opposite Bella and smiled. 'It's going to be lovely having you here; we've given you the bedroom next to mine.'

'I thought I'd be up in the attic.' The words were out of Bella's mouth before she had time to think.

'Why on earth would you think that?'

Bella chewed on her lip for a moment. 'Before I joined the ambulance service I used to live in a house similar to this one ... and I slept up in the attic along with the rest of the servants. I was a housemaid.'

Winnie's grey eyes widened. 'I had no idea; you never said. I always thought you worked in a school or something because you're so clever and always reading.'

Bella shrugged. 'I had dreams of being a school teacher but I had to forget that when my father died and we lost our house. Going into service gave me a job and a home, of sorts.'

'Did you like it?'

'I hated it, but needs must, as my mother kept reminding me.'

'Joining the ambulance service must have been a happy release for you.'

'Though even that came about through following orders.' Bella took the cup of tea Winnie had just poured for her. 'Soon after war was declared my employer insisted that all his staff leave to do war work of some kind. We all had to go, so I chose the ambulance service,' she smiled, 'which I love. I'm free of domestic service now and I'm never going back to it again.'

'Well I hope this place doesn't make you feel uncomfortable remembering your past,' Winnie said gently. 'You must treat it as your home; you're our guest and not working in service any more.'

'It felt strange coming in the front door and seeing such a grand place again,' Bella admitted. 'I didn't even know which entrance to go to; I was trying to work it out when you opened the door.'

'Connie's had lots of people to stay: refugees fleeing Hitler, people involved with her Red Cross work... They all just fit in and we get on with it. Everyone takes a turn at washing up in this house.'

Bella smiled. 'It's very different to what I knew before.'

'Of course, but when you meet Connie you'll understand why. She might have been born with a proverbial silver spoon in her mouth, but she's as different from the rest of her family as can be. They nearly disowned her when she joined the suffragettes but forgave her when she spent the Great War working as a VAD in France.' Winnie leaned across the table and squeezed Bella's arm. 'The past is the past, Bella; don't let it spoil the present. Honestly, we're absolutely delighted to have you stay here.'

'Thank you.' Bella could feel herself starting to relax. It would take some getting used to being in a house like this, but she liked the sound of Winnie's godmother very much. Connie sounded like a woman who knew her own mind and followed it.

'Good, drink up and I'll show you to your room, and you can settle in and get to know the place,' Winnie said.

Frankie closed her eyes and let the music wash over her. Its rising and falling notes and varied rhythms seemed to massage the tension out of her body until she felt as if she was floating away on a beautiful sea of sound.

'You all right?' Alistair whispered to her.

Frankie opened her eyes and smiled at him. 'It's wonderful.'

'I'm glad you like it.'

Coming here, Frankie hadn't been sure what to expect. She'd never been to a concert before; the only music she'd heard was on the wireless, or a dance band playing live, but this was different, more focused, and despite there being many others in the audience, it felt as if Myra Hess was playing for her alone as she ran her hands over the ivory keys of the grand piano, coaxing Mozart's elegant music out of the instrument and filling the dreary basement with a magical sound.

When the last notes died away and Myra stood up to take her bow, Frankie leapt to her feet clapping loudly along with the rest of the audience. She hadn't wanted it to stop. It had transported her away from the everyday, the bombing, the streets in tatters, the threat of invasion, the worry about her family. All of that had been forgotten for a short while and it felt wonderfully refreshing, like rain after hot weather.

'Thank you for bringing me 'ere.' Frankie linked her arm through Alistair's as they joined the queue of people filing out. 'I loved it.'

'In that case, we should come again.' He smiled, his blue eyes meeting hers. 'There's a concert every day at one o'clock, so we could try and fit it around our shifts.'

'I'd like that.'

'Are you feeling hungry? I know I am.'

Frankie nodded.

'Let's get something at the sandwich bar here; they're very good.'

'I ain't sure which one to choose,' Frankie said, looking at the choice of sandwiches a short while later. She was used to the Spam or fish paste sandwiches she took to work with her; she'd never tried anything like these before. Should she have a honey and raisin or a cream cheese and date?

'Let's get one of each and share them, then you can try both,' Alistair suggested. 'And do you want some damp station cake and tea too?'

'Yes please.' Today was turning into a day for trying new things. She hadn't been sure that she'd like a classical concert, and when they'd arrived in Trafalgar Square and seen the long queue of people waiting to get in snaking around the outside of the National Gallery, she hadn't been sure if it was worth the bother joining it, especially as there was a strict limit to the numbers that could be squeezed into the gallery's basement. But they'd been lucky and it had opened a door to a new world for her, one that she'd like to go to again.

'This is lovely. Much better than fish paste.' She took another bite of her share of the honey and raisin sandwich.

'They're supposed to complement the music,' Alistair said. 'What's this one then, do you think?

Sweet and fruity?'

'What about the cream cheese and date?' Frankie grinned. 'Cool and exotic? They make my Spam sandwiches seem very tame.'

'I've got some news for you. I had to telephone the sector hospital where Johnny was sent, and I asked how he is. They said he's doing very well and should be able to go and live with his aunt in a few weeks' time.'

'That's good. Thank you for finding out, I often think about 'im and wonder how he is. It was such a terrible thing for 'im to lose his mother and sister when they were supposed to be safe in the shelter.'

Alistair reached his hand across the table and took hold of hers. 'I know, but something good did come from it.'

'What's that?'

'It's where we met.'

Frankie smiled at him, her cheeks growing warm. 'A place I won't forget in a hurry. Poor Johnny, his family gone in an instant. I kept think-ing the same could happen to Stanley when he's sheltering in our Anderson.'

'Who's Stanley?'

'He's sort of like my brother.' Frankie explained how the little boy had come to live with them. 'I worry he'll get 'urt, or worse, in a raid.'

'Why don't you evacuate him?' Alistair asked, picking up his cup of tea. 'At least he'd be safer out in the countryside.'

'He was evacuated at the start of the war but we brought him 'ome because he was badly treated. He's scared it might 'appen again. We're stuck between a rock and a hard place. Is it better to stay

176

and risk being bombed or be sent away and end up being unwanted and ill treated again?' She shrugged.

'It's a hard choice.'

'Let's not spoil today talking about something I can't fix. What shall we do next? We've got the rest of the afternoon to enjoy before we go to the Lyceum dance hall tonight.'

'How about a walk in St James's Park? It's a beautiful day and it would be lovely to be amongst the trees and greenery,' Alistair suggested.

'As long as we save some energy for tonight. It's been a long time since I went dancing, and I'm looking forward to it.'

Bella scanned the room, thrilled at what she saw.

'Please borrow anything you like,' Winnie said. 'Connie's parents were great readers and she's just the same, so they have a huge collection.'

'Thank you.' Bella beamed at Winnie and then returned her gaze to the hundreds and hundreds of books that filled the dark-wood shelves lining the walls of the library.

'There's enough in here to keep you going for quite some time.' Winnie smiled at her. 'I can see how taken you are with it, so I'll leave you to explore while I take Trixie out for a walk. Please do make yourself completely at home, and I'll see you in a while.'

Left on her own, Bella wandered around the library in a daze. Fancy having so many books in your home available to read at any time! She was going to love this room. Trailing a finger along a shelf, reading the titles, she spotted one that took her fancy and took it over to the leather wingback armchair by the window, settling down to lose herself in the story.

She had no idea how long she'd been there, but she'd read a good chunk of the book when she heard the door open and someone come in.

'Did you have a nice walk?' she said.

'Yes thank you,' a man's voice replied.

Bella peered around the chair and saw a man standing looking at her with a smile on his face. Her cheeks grew warm and she quickly stood up. 'I'm sorry. I thought you were Winnie come back after her walk.'

'She's making some tea and sent me to ask you if you'd like some.' He came towards her and held out his hand. 'I'm James, Winnie's brother.'

Bella shook his hand and noticed that he had the same grey eyes as Winnie, only his were fringed with dark eyelashes that matched his hair. 'Pleased to meet you. I didn't know you were coming.'

'Nor did anyone else till I turned up. I had to come to London for work and decided to drop in on Winnie and Connie for a few days while I'm here. So how about that tea?'

'Yes please.' Bella glanced at her watch, surprised to see that over an hour had passed since she came into the library. 'I lost track of time.'

'I do that all the time,' James said. 'What are you reading?'

Bella showed him the book. 'I'm enjoying it.'

'If you like that, you should try this one.' He went to a shelf, pulled out another book and handed it to Bella, before crossing the room and selecting two more. 'And these.'

'Thank you. You look like you know this library very well.'

James smiled. 'I think I've probably read most of the books in here over the years. We always spent our school holidays here with Connie and I used to raid her library.'

'Ah, I should have known you two would be talking books,' Winnie said, walking into the room with a tray of tea things, Trixie trotting along at her heels.

James shrugged and smiled at his sister warmly. 'You should try it sometime, you might enjoy it.'

Winnie laughed. 'You know I don't have the patience to sit reading for hours on end like you.' She put the tea tray down on the table. 'So have you thought about my suggestion, James? It would be fun.'

'You know I've got two left feet,' he said, bending down and stroking Trixie's ears. 'Who'd want to dance with me? I can't inflict my clumsiness on anyone else.'

'How about you, Bella? You're coming tonight, aren't you?' Winnie asked as she poured out three cups of tea from the china teapot.

Bella nodded. 'But I won't be doing much dancing. I've got two left feet as well. I was never any good at it, always tripping up and going the wrong way.'

'Well then you two should dance together; you'll be perfectly matched and neither of you will mind if the other goes wrong. Please, James. This is our first day off in ages and we want to go out and have some fun. Do come with us.'

James shook his head and looked at his sister. 'I

know I won't have a moment's peace until I say yes, will I?'

Winnie laughed. 'So just say yes and get it over with.'

'Very well then.' James looked at Bella. 'My apologies in advance for my complete lack of co-ordination if you're brave enough to chance a dance with me.'

'Likewise,' Bella replied. 'And when our feet are so bruised that we can't take any more, we can always go and sit down and talk about books.' She threw a glance at Winnie, who sighed and rolled her eyes.

Frankie's fingers were itching to draw. She quietly slipped her sketchbook and pencil out of her bag and set to work, focusing on the shapes and shadows that made up Alistair's face as he lay sleeping under the tree. It was a joy to study him without worrying that she was staring. She was enjoying every moment of the day, from the concert to their leisurely stroll in St James's Park before Alistair had drifted off to sleep in the warmth of the afternoon as they'd relaxed in the shade of a tree.

'Are you drawing me?' His voice made Frankie jump. She'd been so focused on finishing the final part of her sketch that she hadn't realised he'd woken up. 'Let me see.'

'I couldn't resist. I 'ope you don't mind.' She passed him the sketchbook.

Alistair studied it for a few moments, then smiled at her. 'You're very talented.'

Frankie shrugged. 'I just love drawing.'

180

Alistair sat upright. 'Do you draw much?'

'When I can. I often sketch while we're waiting to be called out to an incident. It takes my mind off things for a bit, because sometimes the waiting's worse than going out. You sit there feeling like you're on a knife edge, not knowing when the telephone will ring, when you'll be told to go out, or what you'll find when you do.'

Alistair nodded. 'Being busy stops you thinking about what might happen.' He suddenly laughed. 'Listen to us. This is our day off and we should be enjoying every moment, not thinking about work or the war.'

He looked at her, then reached out and gently touched her hair. 'I love your hair. It's the colour of autumn bracken on the hills.'

'What's bracken?' Frankie asked.

'It's a plant. Have you never seen bracken before?'

Frankie shook her head. 'I'm from Stepney, remember.'

'Bracken's a type of fern that goes a beautiful soft auburn in the autumn. There was plenty around where I grew up.'

'Very different from the streets of Stepney.'

'Aye, and I miss the countryside a great deal. I'll take you out of London and show you some bracken one day if you like.'

Frankie laughed. 'You're opening my eyes to new things: first a concert, then bracken, whatever next?'

'My twinkle-toed dancing tonight, perhaps?' He grinned and stood up, holding his hand out. 'Come on, let's go and find some tea and something to eat. I'm hungry, and we're going to need plenty of energy if we're going dancing tonight.'

The Lyceum dance hall was bursting with people out to enjoy themselves, and the atmosphere felt as if it had been charged with an electric excitement.

Frankie stood on tiptoes and scanned around for her friends, eventually spotting them sitting at a table near the edge of the dance floor, which was already a sea of dancing couples, lots of them in uniform. 'There they are, over there.' Holding on to Alistair's hand, she made her way through the throng.

'Good, you're here.' Winnie smiled. 'I wasn't sure if you'd be able to find us in this crowd. We managed to save you some seats. We've got an extra person tonight, too; this is my brother James, who turned up unexpectedly today.'

James stood up and shook Frankie and Alistair's hands. 'Good to meet you.'

'So, Bella and James, are you going to brave the dance floor now?' Winnie asked. 'You keep putting it off, but you can't sit there all night.'

James shook his head. 'I suppose the only way we'll get you to stop badgering us is to actually go and do it.' He looked at Bella. 'Remember, I did warn you I have two left feet.'

'That makes four left feet between us then.' Bella stood up smiling, her flushed cheeks dimpling prettily. 'Come on, let's get this over with.'

'There's no point coming to a dance if you're not going to actually dance, is there?' Winnie called out to them as she watched them cautiously join in

182

at the edge of the dance floor. To begin with their movements were awkward and halting, but before long they were swept away and swallowed up into the swirling, rotating mass of couples.

'Have you been dancing?' Frankie asked.

'Of course. Mac and I had only just sat down for a rest when you arrived.' Winnie smiled at Mac, who she'd also nagged into coming tonight. 'Mac's a fine dancer; he didn't step on my toes once.'

'I wouldn't have dared.' Mac took a sip of his drink.

'I can't sit still any longer; this music makes me want to dance.' Frankie stood up and held out her hand to Alistair. 'Come on, let's go.'

Leaving Winnie and Mac to rest at the table, they joined the throng of dancers and, like Bella and James, were soon swept away.

'We started the day with music and we're ending it with music,' Alistair whispered into her ear.

'I've enjoyed it very much,' Frankie said, looking up at him. 'I'm still enjoying it. It feels lovely to be out having fun.'

'It's been a good day, Frankie. I've enjoyed myself very much.' Alistair's eyes held hers. 'Thank you.'

Frankie beamed back at him. 'Thank you for asking me.'

They'd been on the dance floor for a good half an hour when the band suddenly stopped playing and the dancers came to a shuddering halt, looking around to see what was going on.

'I'm sorry to interrupt your evening,' said the

bandleader, 'but an air-raid warning is in operation. Those who wish to should proceed to the nearest shelter or Underground station. Those who wish to remain dancing can.'

The band began to play again and many couples started to dance.

'Come on.' Alistair held Frankie's hand tightly and led her as quickly as he could towards the edge of the dance floor.

'I wish we could stay and carry on dancing,' Frankie said.

Alistair stopped and looked at her, his eyes gentle. 'So do I, Frankie, but it's safer in a shelter. We'll go to Aldwych Underground Station; it's the nearest. I know it's spoiled the dance, but we've both seen enough of what can happen in an air raid to know it's the best thing to do.'

Frankie shuddered at the thought of what would happen if a bomb hit the Lyceum when it was packed with so many people. Alistair was right, they had to get to a shelter, but it was annoying when it was her first night off in ages.

Winnie, Mac, Bella and James were waiting for them by the door, and together they headed out into the blackout, where they could already hear the ominous sounds of distant ack-ack guns blasting forth into the sky and the faint drone of bombers heading towards them.

Frankie suddenly felt scared. She'd been out in the middle of air raids plenty of times before, but this felt different. There was no ambulance to drive, no people to take care of, no job to do; she felt exposed and strangely vulnerable as she strode along hand in hand with Alistair.

'Hurry up now,' an ARP warden urged the people streaming towards Aldwych station, 'into the shelter with you.'

It didn't take long to reach the welcoming sight of the station entrance, but every second out in the open felt multiplied a hundredfold, and Frankie was shaking with relief as they funnelled in past the ticket office and down towards the safety of the passageways and platforms. The station was crammed with people, and some had spilled over onto the tracks, where they were settling down for the night in makeshift beds sandwiched between the rails, making themselves as comfortable as they could.

Frankie had to be careful not to tread on anyone as they picked their way along the edge of the platform to find a space to sit. Many people were clearly well prepared for a long stay and had come with blankets and food parcels; no doubt they had fled down here often during the past few weeks. Most of those seeking shelter were civilians, but there were a few people in uniform too.

'So much for our plan to dance the evening away,' Winnie said as they settled down in an empty space near the far end of the platform. 'Our first night off in ages and it's interrupted by another air raid.'

'It might not last long,' Bella said.

Winnie grinned. 'I love your optimism, Bella, but if tonight's raid is anything like all the others, we could be here for a while.'

I hope not, Frankie thought, leaning back against the hard wall of the platform. She didn't like being down here in this stuffy atmosphere

185

that smelled like mouldy bread.

'Are you all right?' Alistair, sitting beside her, put his arm around her shoulders.

Frankie nodded. 'Not used to bein' in the Underground during a raid; it feels a bit odd.'

'Better than being up there.' Alistair nodded to the ceiling.

The wail of the siren suddenly stopped and an eerie silence fell over the platform, as if everyone was holding their breath waiting for what was to come.

Frankie stared at the ceiling, silently praying that it was a false alarm. Seconds passed and nothing happened; people started to talk again, their voices giving her hope that perhaps tonight the bombers wouldn't come, that it had been a mistake and that soon the all-clear would sound and they could walk back out into the fresh air under the star-studded night sky. She was just beginning to relax when the thumps of closer ack-ack guns started up, followed by muffled crumps that shook the platform and made the train tracks rattle as somewhere out in the night bombs hit home. Dust fell in thick clouds from the ceiling, and as the lights flickered off and on, someone screamed from the other end of the platform. Frankie leaned her head against Alistair's shoulder and gripped his hand, her stomach knotted with fear. She would rather be out driving through the raid than down here.

A lone woman's voice suddenly started to sing, quietly at first but growing louder with confidence, and then others joined in until the singing dulled the sounds from above. Frankie could still feel the ground shake when a bomb hit, but somehow it didn't seem quite as bad now that the platform was ringing with a swell of voices and a sense of camaraderie that they were all in it together and they would get through it somehow. She joined in with the singing, smiling at Winnie and Bella, who had quickly added their voices to the mix.

She nudged Alistair to join in too, but his attention had been drawn towards a young woman who stood right at the far end of the platform under an advertisement for Guinness. She had her back to them and was leaning forward, her hands on her knees in an odd hunched position.

'Do you think she's all right?' Frankie asked. 'She looks like she's in pain.'

'I'd better go and check. Come with me.' Alistair stood up and held out a hand to help her up and together they made their way over to the woman.

'Hello,' Frankie said. 'Are you all right?'

The woman straightened up and looked at them. She opened her mouth to speak, but before she could say anything, she grimaced and leaned forward again, resting her hands on her knees and moaning.

'I'm a doctor,' Alistair said. 'Are you in pain?'

After a few moments, the woman nodded and stood up again, and as the front of her open coat swung sideways, Frankie saw that she was heavily pregnant. Alistair grabbed Frankie's arm and nodded at a pool of liquid puddling around the woman's feet.

'It looks like your baby is ready to be born,' he said.

'I'm scared.' The woman's eyes were wide, and tears leaked out and ran down her flushed cheeks.

Frankie put a hand on her arm. 'It's all right, we'll look after you. Alistair here is a good doctor, and I'm an ambulance driver and so are three of my friends over there. We'll all help you.'

Alistair nodded and smiled at Frankie. 'We'll need some water, blankets, soap, alcohol and something to clamp the cord.'

'I'll go and see what I can find.'

'Don't leave me.' The woman grabbed at Frankie's arm. 'Please.'

Frankie took hold of her hand. 'What's your name?'

'Gracie.'

'Listen, Gracie, I'm just going to tell my friends what we need and then I'll be straight back. I'll be one minute, no more. All right?'

Gracie nodded and Frankie darted back to the others, who were sitting watching what was going on.

'What's wrong?' Winnie stood up.

'She's in labour,' Frankie said, and quickly told them what Alistair had asked for.

'We'll all help,' Mac said, standing up along with Bella and James.

'Thank you,' Frankie said. 'Hurry, as quick as you can.'

Gracie was pacing back and forth when Frankie got back to her.

'Should we get her out of 'ere and take her to hospital?' Frankie asked Alistair, who was using his watch to time the contractions.

He shook his head. 'It's too crowded to carry

her through, and with a raid going on up there it would be risky to take her out into it unless we really had to. We'll have to manage here. If the others find some blankets we can use them to screen the area off for some privacy.'

'Ow!' Gracie yelped as another contraction gripped her. Frankie grabbed hold of her hand and held on as Gracie squeezed it tightly.

'You're doing well, Gracie. Keep breathing and try to relax between the pains,' she said, rubbing the young woman's back to help ease her discomfort.

'We've got blankets, and a bottle of gin for you to sterilise your hands with, and the ticket inspector's boiling up water and is going to bring it down with some soap and a towel,' Winnie said when she and Bella returned a short while later. 'Mac and James are trying to find something to cut and clamp the cord with.'

'Great,' Alistair said. 'Spread a blanket out for Gracie, and then can you two hold another up as a screen?'

'Of course.' Bella got to work and prepared a place for Gracie to lie down, then she and Winnie shook out the other blanket and stood holding it up so that the mother-to-be and her helpers were screened off from the rest of the people on the platform, who had been watching with interest what was going on.

Frankie helped Gracie to settle herself on the blanket and knelt down beside her, holding her hand as the pains grew stronger and closer together, while above them the air raid carried on and the ground rumbled and shook with the impact of the bombs.

A little after five o'clock the next morning, just after the all-clear had sounded, the first cry of a newborn baby echoed around the platform of Aldwych Underground Station. The sound brought cheers and applause from the other people who had spent the night sheltering there.

'You have a little girl,' Alistair said, cutting the cord with a gin-sterilised bayonet that Mac had borrowed from a soldier, and then gently wrapping the newborn in a blanket and handing her to Gracie. 'Congratulations.'

'Thank you.' Gracie's eyes sparkled with tears as she hugged her newborn daughter to her.

Frankie's throat felt thick as she sniffed back her own tears and looked up at Winnie and Bella, who were clearly feeling the same way. It had been quite a night. They had gone through every pain with Gracie; Frankie had even found herself panting along with the young woman between the pains. Her hand was sore from being squeezed so tightly, but it was worth it to have been here to help bring the little girl into the world.

'Do you have a name for her?' Alistair asked.

'I thought it was going to be a boy, and I was going to name him after my husband.'

'Where's your 'usband?' Frankie asked.

'He's a prisoner of war; was captured before he could get to Dunkirk,' Gracie said.

'You'll be able to write and let 'im know he has a daughter now.' Frankie smiled at the baby, who was looking at her with wide eyes.

190

'Is Frankie short for Frances?' Gracie asked.

'No, it's short for my surname, Franklin. We get called by nicknames in the ambulance service. My first name's Stella,' Frankie explained.

'Stella. I like that.' Gracie smiled. 'That's what I'll call her, after you. It'll always remind me of how she came into this world and how you helped me and were so kind.'

Frankie's face grew warm. 'Thank you. I'm glad I 'elped, but all I did really was hold your 'and. You did the hard bit and Alistair helped deliver little Stella,' she said.

'You stayed with me and kept me going. I won't forget that,' Gracie said.

'Tea comin' through,' called a voice, and the ticket inspector arrived with a tray of steaming mugs, enough for the new mother and everyone who had helped. Once he had handed them round, he leaned down to look at baby Stella. 'She's a beauty; first baby we've had born on the platforms.' He stood up. 'I've sent for an ambulance, it shouldn't be long.'

Frankie took a sip of tea and enjoyed its warmth spreading through her. She wasn't going to forget her day off in a hurry. It had been a day of new experiences and had twisted and turned in unexpected ways. She looked at Alistair, who smiled back at her, raising his mug in salute, and she felt happy inside, glad that she'd been there with him.

'...and they saved thirty 'orses from a burning building.'

Frankie smiled at Stanley, who was walking along beside her talking about his favourite subject of late – the Dead End Kids.

'*They* don't run and 'ide away in shelters when the bombers come.' Stanley stopped to pick up a piece of shrapnel that was stuck between some cobbles. He examined it carefully and then added it to the collection in his bag before falling into step again beside Frankie. 'I wish I could join 'em.'

'You're far too young to be out during an air raid; you know the safest place for you is in the Anderson shelter.'

Stanley nodded. 'I know, but it's not fair. You and Grandad are out during raids 'elping people. I could 'elp too, I know I could, and I'm not scared.'

'Well you should be,' Frankie snapped. She stopped and put her shopping basket down, then looked down at Stanley. 'It's not a game out there; it's war, Stanley, and it's scary and...' She paused. She didn't want to frighten him, as he'd only end up worrying about her when she was out working during a raid. 'Look, the Dead End Kids are nearly old enough to get called up; they've left school and are much bigger and stronger than you, and they know what to do.'

'I could learn what to do. I'm a quick learner, Grandad says I am.'

Frankie put her hand on his shoulder. 'What they do ain't like a game you play with your friends in the street, Stanley. They're risking their lives every time they go out. Your place is with Ivy in the Anderson, you understand?'

Stanley nodded. 'Wish I was old enough to join 'em. I will when I get to sixteen.'

'I hope the war will be long over by then. Come on, I need to get this shopping 'ome and get the tea started.'

She picked up her basket and they headed for Matlock Street, where she was relieved to see Stanley rush off to join his friends, who were grouped on the pavement comparing their latest hauls of shrapnel. He should be focusing on that, Frankie thought, and not hankering after joining the Dead End Kids, who were the talk not only of Stepney but the whole East End. Their leader, Patsie Duggan, was a Stepney lad who had set up a fire-watching party on Wapping Island and become something of a legend in the area. It was no wonder Stanley was fascinated by them, but what they did was dangerous and not suitable for a ten-year-old boy.

Frankie knew the moment she walked through the front door that Ivy was asleep, as her step-grand-mother's snores could be heard coming from the kitchen. Taking care to close the door quietly behind her, she carried the basket of shopping through, shaking her head at the sight of Ivy slumped in the armchair, mouth open and head lolling to one side. So much for her excuse that she needed to get on with the housework and didn't have time to go out and queue for groceries, Frankie thought, as she started to unpack the meagre shopping, which had taken ages to get. It didn't look as if Ivy had done anything at all; the dirty plates and dishes were still unwashed by the sink where Frankie had put them before she'd gone out.

Frankie sighed. She was tired too, and would like nothing better than to put her feet up and snooze the day away. Everyone in London was suffering from lack of sleep, because October had brought no let-up from the bombing. The German planes kept on coming, dropping their deadly weapons on the city night after night, and sometimes during the day too. The constant worry about when and where the next bomb would land and whether it had your name on it was taking its toll, and people's nerves were starting to fray. Ivy had become nastier and more bad-tempered than ever, so Frankie took the greatest care not to wake her, moving around quietly and then slipping out of the back door to dig up some vegetables from the garden to go with the scrag end of meat she'd managed to get from the butcher. Now that she was on the night shift, from half past eleven until half past seven the following morning, she was at home to cook a meal before she went to work so that Stanley and her grandfather had something warm to come home to.

Coming back inside with carrots, a turnip and some potatoes to go in the stew, Frankie set about washing them ready to chop up. This time she didn't bother to be quiet; Ivy had slept long enough.

'What the bleedin'...' The older woman started awake as Frankie dropped the heavy wooden chopping board onto the table with more force than necessary. She glared at Frankie for a few moments before launching into a vicious tirade. 'What you doing wakin' me up? I only sat down a couple of minutes ago for forty winks.'

Frankie looked at the clock on the mantelpiece. 'I've been 'ome for a good quarter of an hour and you've been asleep all that time.' She started chopping the washed carrots into chunks and throwing them into the saucepan.

'Put the kettle on, will yer, my throat's parched.' Ivy rummaged in her overall pocket, pulled out her ciggies and lit one, blowing the smoke into the air in a steady stream.

'I need to get the veg ready,' Frankie said, moving on to the potatoes.

'I'll do it me bleedin' self then.' Ivy sighed and heaved herself out of the armchair, filling the kettle at the sink and putting it on to boil. 'Whatcha making?'

'Stew.'

'What, again?' She curled her top lip. 'Can't you think of anything else?'

Frankie jabbed her knife hard into a potato and glared at Ivy. 'It's the best way of cookin' the meat; softens it up a bit and it goes with the veg. Course if you'd rather do something else, go ahead.' She stepped back from the chopping board and held her arm out, inviting Ivy to take her place.

Ivy took a deep drag on her cigarette, narrowing her eyes as she blew out a stream of smoke. 'I was only sayin' we often 'ave it, that's all.'

'So you don't want to take over then?'

'Gawd, no, I 'ate cooking.'

And cleaning, and shopping; any work at all, in fact, Frankie thought as she started to chop again. Ivy was as slippery as an eel when it came to avoiding household tasks. She could complain for England, but never wanted to do anything herself. Frankie wasn't making this meal for Ivy, though; she was doing it for her grandfather and Stanley, and she'd carry on cooking for them as long as she needed to.

Babies don't take account of Herr Hitler's air raids, Winnie thought as she negotiated a large crater in the road. From the moans coming from the back of the ambulance, it sounded as if this baby was in a hurry to be born, air raid or not. Poor Trixie, who was sitting beside her on the passenger seat, was whining in sympathy every time the woman groaned in pain. Winnie didn't want a baby being born in her ambulance. She'd been there when Alistair had delivered the baby in Aldwych Underground Station, but then he was a doctor and knew what he was doing. Winnie didn't, and nor did Hooky, so they were both keen to get this expectant mother into the hands of those who could safely help her.

'How long till we're there?' Hooky hissed through the grille between the back and the driver's cab. 'This baby's coming fast.'

'I'm going as quick as I can,' Winnie snapped. 'You know the rules as well as I do, sixteen miles an hour tops or we'll end up cutting the tyres to shreds on broken glass.' Station Officer Steele had warned them about avoiding unnecessary punctures. They had to keep their speed down to protect their tyres, and no rushing, bell-clanging races to hospital were allowed.

It didn't help that the raid was in full swing, with planes droning overhead and offloading their bombs. A loud bang sounded and a flash of light lit up the dark sky as a bomb hit a couple of streets over, making Winnie jump. She'd never get used to this, not if she drove ambulances in raids for the rest of her life.

'We're nearly there,' she shouted through to Hooky as she slowed ready to turn left into the road leading to the nearest hospital. She was glad that they'd soon be on their way back to Station 75, where she hoped they'd have a chance to grab something to eat and drink before being sent out again. This was their third call-out this shift, and her energy was beginning to flag. A Spam sandwich and a hot cup of tea would soon set her right.

Turning left, Winnie's stomach lurched at the sight of the burning building halfway down the street on the right-hand side. Bright orange flames leapt out of the windows while firemen aimed jets of water at the blaze in their battle to control it. She gently braked and brought the ambulance to a halt, quickly calculating what to do. This was the only road leading to the hospital; the other direction had been blocked off by bomb damage the previous night. It had to be this way in or not at all. The other option was to turn around and take the woman to another hospital, but the nearest was a good twenty minutes away, and that was if they didn't get redirected on the way because more roads were blocked. Neither choice was good. What should she do? A load moan from the back decided for her. This baby was coming fast; there probably wasn't time to get the mother to another hospital before it was born, so it had to be this one.

'Hold on,' Winnie called through to the back as she put the ambulance into gear and crawled along towards the burning building.

'Don't come this way!' a policeman shouted at her, waving his arms above his head as she drove towards him. 'The building could come down.'

Winnie ignored him and kept going, steering over some rubble that had spilled out across the road, making the ambulance jolt and lurch from side to side. She gripped the steering wheel hard to keep it steady while her heart thudded inside her.

'What's going on?' Hooky shouted from the back.

'Everything's fine, just some rubble across the road,' Winnie yelled back, concentrating on keeping the ambulance going, all the while aware of the blazing building out of the corner of her eye as she inched past it. Knowing that it could come down at any moment, she sent up a silent prayer that it would wait, at least until she'd got this mother and her unborn baby safely to the hospital.

As the ambulance bumped over the last of the rubble, another load groan came from the back. Ignoring the sixteen-mile-an-hour limit, Winnie pressed on the accelerator and the ambulance sped down the road towards the hospital. She let out a sigh of relief as she turned in through the gates, pulling up as gently as she could so as not to jolt the expectant mother and cause her any more discomfort.

Rushing around to the back, she flung open the doors. Hooky's face was ghostly pale as she jumped out. 'I don't want another one of these sorts of incidents in a hurry,' she whispered as they pulled the stretcher out. 'It's put me right off ever having babies if it's that painful.'

Trust Hooky to think of herself, Winnie thought as she took her end of the stretcher and they carried the groaning woman into the hospital.

'Hooky, there's something I need to tell you,' Winnie said when they were back in the ambulance a few minutes later. 'It could be a bit tricky getting out of here.'

'What do you mean?' Hooky looked at her, her eyes narrowed under the brim of her steel helmet.

'There's a building on fire down there.' Winnie nodded back the way they'd come. 'It's the only way out of here, so we're going to have to go past it again, but don't worry, we'll be fine.' She sounded more confident than she felt, but the last thing she needed was a moaning Hooky when she needed to concentrate.

'We don't have much choice, do we?' Hooky folded her arms firmly across her chest. 'Let's go then.'

Winnie nodded and gave Trixie's head a pat, then started the engine and drove out of the hospital gates. As they headed back down the street, she was relieved to see that the building was still standing, although it was also still very much on fire. Drawing near the rubble that lay directly in front of it, she slowed to a crawl and gripped the wheel hard as the ambulance began to lurch and rock its way over.

'Can't you go any faster?' Hooky snapped, edging away from her window towards Winnie as she tried to distance herself from the burning building.

'I'm going as fast as I dare,' Winnie hissed back through gritted teeth. 'Ambulances aren't built for this.'

'Just keep going.'

When she felt the front wheels grip the road surface again, Winnie let out the breath she didn't realise she'd been holding. Ahead of her the street stretched away; fifty yards of clear paved road and then they'd be out of it and heading back home to Station 75. When the back wheels gripped the road too, and they were clear of the rubble, she pressed harder on the accelerator, watching as the speedometer crept upwards. It was then that she felt a juddering rumble jarring through the steering wheel, and the ambulance skewed slightly to one side.

'Bloody hell!' She bit her bottom lip. 'Not now.' She took her foot off the accelerator and they rolled to a halt.

'Don't stop!' Hooky shrieked. 'What's the matter?'

'Feels like a puncture. Keep hold of Trixie for me while I check.' Winnie opened the door and jumped out, and instantly saw that one of the rear tyres was flat. 'Damn and blast it.'

She opened the passenger door. 'Hooky, I need you to help. Get the spare wheel out of the back while I start jacking it up.'

'But–' Hooky began.

'Now!' Winnie bellowed. 'Leave Trixie in here.'

Winnie had the wheel arch jacked up when she heard shouting.

'You can't stop there!' It was the same policeman as before, running towards her.

'We've got a puncture,' Winnie snapped at him.

'The building could come down at any moment.' There was panic in his voice.

'Stop shouting at me and come and help then!' Winnie ordered.

The policeman did as he was told, working alongside Winnie as they quickly undid the wheel nuts, eased off the flat tyre and replaced the wheel.

'Come on, hurry up,' Hooky said, jiggling from foot to foot, looking from Winnie and the policeman to the burning building and back again.

'We're going as fast as we can.' Winnie strained to tighten the final wheel nut.

'They're running!' Hooky suddenly shrieked. 'The firemen are running!'

'Get out of here!' the policeman yelled. 'It's coming down!'

Winnie glanced at the burning building and saw bricks starting to tumble as the front wall leaned ominously in towards the street.

'Get in and drive!' the policeman bellowed.

Winnie was vaguely aware of him grabbing Hooky by the arm and pushing her into the back of the ambulance, then jumping in himself as she scrambled for the driver's door and leapt in. Mercifully the engine started first time; she pushed the clutch to the floor, slammed the gearstick into position, pressed on the accelerator and the ambulance lurched off down the road.

A rumbling roar filled the confines of the street. Glancing in her wing mirror, Winnie saw a toppling mass of brick and dust, which ballooned and billowed, filling the air and racing towards them, gaining on them every second. She kept driving, focusing ahead, willing the ambulance on and away from the dust, which was getting closer and closer like some avenging beast. It caught them in a blast of hot, choking air, thumping into the ambulance, making it slide out of control and start to spin. Winnie held on tight to the wheel, her heart hammering, knowing that there was nothing she could do, and then everything stopped moving and she was aware of the sound of banging as debris rained down on the roof, while outside the street was filled with dust and dirt, which covered the windscreen like filthy snow.

Slumping back in the driver's seat, Winnie became aware that she was shaking. Trixie crawled across and onto her lap, her wet nose nudging at her hand, and Winnie scooped her up in her arms and hugged her tightly.

'You all right in the front?' the policeman called through the grille.

'Yes, I'm fine. What about you?'

'No harm done 'ere,' the policeman said.

'I'm not all right; look at the state of me.' Winnie smiled as she listened to Hooky complaining. 'I'm covered in dust.'

'Just be glad you're alive, Hooky,' she called back through the grille. It could all have been very different if that building had come down a few minutes earlier, while they'd been driving past it. It would have smashed the ambulance flat, and them with it.

The all-clear had gone by the time they drove back in under the archway in their battered and filthy ambulance. The outside was covered with brick and plaster dust, and thick, gritty powder had blown into the back where the doors hadn't been properly closed in their haste to scramble in. It was going take time and hard work to get the vehicle properly clean again.

Winnie pulled up beside the other ambulances, which were already being cleaned out by their crews. She was tired and rather shaken from their near miss, and desperate for a cup of tea to ease her parched throat.

Switching off the engine, she turned to Hooky, who looked a sight, her clothes and hair grey with dust. 'Would you mind going and making some tea, please? I'll come up and sign off the job, then we can start the cleaning.'

'Why should—' Hooky began.

Winnie held up her hand to stop her. 'Fine, I'll sign off the job and make the tea – I presume you'd like a cup – and leave you to get started on the cleaning, shall I?' She opened her door and started to get out.

'No, no, I'll go and make the tea,' Hooky said quickly, getting out of the cab on the other side.

Winnie watched her go, shaking her head. Hard work and Hooky rarely appeared in the same sentence, she thought.

'Looks like you've been in the wars.'

Winnie turned round and smiled at Sparky, who ran his finger over the outside of the ambulance and examined the dust on his finger. 'Raining brick and plaster dust, was it?'

'Something like that.' Winnie reached into the cab and patted Trixie, who had settled down on the driver's seat for a snooze. 'It's in the back as well.'

Sparky walked around the vehicle and opened the back door. 'What the bloody 'ell 'appened?'

'Building came down and we got caught in the blast,' Winnie said quietly.

'I'd say you were lucky you got out of it in one piece.' Sparky put a hand on her shoulder. 'I'll 'elp you clean it up.'

Winnie smiled at him. 'Thank you, I'd appreciate that.'

'Best to start from the top and work our way down, I think. I'll get a ladder.'

'I need to go and sign off the job first, then I'll get stuck in. I won't be long.' She turned to go, but stopped at the sight of Station Officer Steele striding towards her, her face set and stony, while Hooky followed behind, her hands empty of that much-needed cup of tea.

'What's happened?' Station Officer Steele's voice was clipped and crisp, and Winnie instantly bristled. She knew that tone well and it didn't bode well.

All the other crews stopped work on their own ambulances and watched as Station Officer Steele stalked around Winnie's vehicle, examining the damage, feeling the dents with her fingertips and shaking her head when she saw the state of the inside.

'Upstairs in my office, please, Winnie.' Station Officer Steele didn't wait for her to respond, but stalked back to her office, slamming the outside door behind her.

Winnie sighed. 'What does she know, Hooky?'

Hooky shifted from foot to foot. 'I was making tea and she asked me why I was so dirty. So I told her.'

'Everything?'

Hooky shrugged, looking Winnie defiantly in the eye. 'I couldn't lie, could I?'

'Couldn't you?' Winnie took a dripping-wet cloth from Sparky and thrust it into Hooky's hands. 'You can get on with the cleaning up, then.' She turned to Sparky who smiled at her sympathetically. 'Keep an eye on Trixie for me,' she said.

'Good luck.'

'Thanks, I think I might need it.'

Station Officer Steele's back was poker straight as she sat behind her desk. She hadn't asked Winnie to sit down.

'You need to sign off the incident.' She slid the piece of paper detailing the call-out across the desk, remaining silent while Winnie filled in the details and signed her name, the scratching of the pen nib on paper sounding loud in the ominous quiet.

Adding the paper to a neat pile on her desk, Station Officer Steele turned back to Winnie and looked directly at her. 'Right, tell me what happened. All of it, mind; don't miss anything out.'

So Winnie told her, plainly and clearly, and when she had finished, she couldn't stop herself from asking a question of her own. 'What would you have done?'

Station Officer Steele's lips thinned and she stared at Winnie through her owlish spectacles.

'What I would or would not have done is irrelevant here; it is what *you* did that I am concerned with. You blatantly ignored a policeman's instructions, which could have endangered the lives not only of a mother and her unborn child, but also of another crew member and yourself, not forgetting risking damage to a London Auxiliary Ambulance Service vehicle. It was highly irresponsible.' She paused, drumming her fingers on her desk. 'It is sheer luck that you have come out of this alive, although your ambulance will have to be thoroughly checked to make sure it's still safe to drive.'

'So you think I should have gone to another hospital then, even though the baby might have been born before we got there?' Winnie asked, folding her arms tightly across her chest.

'In this case, yes, I do. If that building had come down when you first drove past it...'

'But it didn't. And we were only caught when it did come down because we had a puncture. If that hadn't happened we'd have been well on our way back here by then and wouldn't have known a thing about it. At least we were there on the spot ready to take the firemen injured by the falling building to hospital, which saved having to call out another ambulance.'

'The fact remains, Winnie, that you wilfully ignored instructions from a policeman and put a patient and crew member at risk, as well as an ambulance, which I don't have to remind you are in very short supply. Quite frankly, I am *extremely* disappointed. I expected better of you. You are an intelligent, educated woman who I thought I could rely on not to do stupid things when people's lives are at risk. Playing around with stir-rup pumps is one thing, but today you truly surpassed yourself.'

Winnie's cheeks grew warm and she swallowed hard, pinching her finger and thumb together to stop herself from showing how she felt. 'Am I to be given the sack?' She was amazed at how steady her voice sounded, because inside she was anything but. It was as if she were a little girl again and being told off by Sita when she'd done something very silly. Sita's look of disappointment had always had a far greater effect on her than any punishment.

'No, but only because I would be down a driver.' Station Officer Steele's gaze was icy. 'But I will be keeping a very close eye on you, and if you endanger patients or crew members ever again, you will no longer be welcome at Station 75. Do you understand?'

Winnie nodded.

'Now go and get your ambulance clean and I will be down to inspect it before you leave.'

'I–' Winnie began.

But Station Officer Steele put up a hand to silence her. 'Just go and sort out the mess, Winnie.'

Winnie nodded and left the office, closing the door behind her quietly. As she headed downstairs to the courtyard, she mentally braced herself to be strong, keep a stiff upper lip and not show how much Station Officer Steele's words had affected her. All she really wanted to do was run to the women's changing room and cry her eyes out, but she couldn't do that; she just had to get on and sort out the mess that she was responsible for.

Back out in the courtyard, there was much less clearing up to do than when she'd gone inside. Many members of other crews had abandoned their own ambulances and were busy cleaning off the debris from her vehicle; the Jones sisters had taken out the stretchers and blankets and were vigorously shaking off the dust; Frankie and Bella were mopping out the back of the ambulance and Mac, Sparky and several others were washing the outside, sending the water running down the sides in reddish-grey streaks until it dripped and puddled on the cobbles.

'You all right?' Mac asked her as she picked up a small brush and started to clean the dust out of the radiator grille.

Winnie looked up and nodded, doing her best to smile. 'Thank you, everyone, for helping; you are all so kind and I appreciate it.' Then she quickly got on with her work, kneeling down in front of the ambulance so that no one would see the ridiculous tears that had forced themselves into her eyes.

'It's what most of the other drivers would have done. We got the patient safely to hospital – surely that's what matters?' Winnie threw her hands in the air as she stomped out of the kitchen and up the stairs to the hall, with Trixie following close on her heels.

Bella hurried after her, grabbing her arm when she caught up with her. 'I agree with you, Winnie. What was important was that you got the mother to hospital so that her baby could be born with doctors and nurses who knew what they were doing, rather than in the back of an ambulance in the middle of an air raid.'

'Exactly! And there would have been nothing said about it if we hadn't got a bloody puncture and been caught in the blast of that building coming down.' Winnie sighed. 'I just wish Station Officer Steele would look at it like that instead of worrying about damaged ambulances. It's not as if they're brand new, without a scratch on them, is it? Every single one of them is battle-scarred with dents and marks or pitted with bits of shrapnel.' She put her hands on her hips, sending a shower of brick and plaster dust floating down onto the black and white tiled floor.

'The boss has really upset you this time, hasn't she?' Bella said gently, noticing the sheen of tears in her friend's eyes.

Winnie blinked hard and sniffed. 'I was just doing my job, Bella; she should know things like that can happen sometimes. It wasn't my fault that building came down. The ambulance is fine, still serviceable. It's as if she doesn't have any understanding of what it's like out there.'

'Remember she drove ambulances in the Great War; she will have been in tricky situations too.'

'Perhaps, but nothing like the raids we're having. It's just so...' Winnie ran a hand through her thick honey-blonde hair, which had come out of its rolls and hung around her face. Like the rest of her, it had a coating of grey dust from the collapsed building.

'Go and get out of those dirty clothes and have a bath, and I'll bring you up some tea and toast.'

Bella put her hands on Winnie's shoulders and turned her around to face the stairs. 'Go on, you'll feel better once you're clean.'

Winnie did her best to smile. 'I'm sorry for being such an utter misery. It makes me so...' Her voice wavered, and she stopped, sniffed and shrugged her shoulders.

'Off you go now.' Bella gave her a gentle push and stood watching as her friend tramped slowly up the stairs, her usually buoyant spirits as flat as a collapsed barrage balloon.

Winnie had seemed fine after she'd returned from Station Officer Steele's office, and had been pleased with everyone's help cleaning up the ambulance. The other crews were genuinely sorry for the flak she'd taken from the boss, because they might all have made the same decision if they'd been in her situation. It seemed unfair that she'd been reprimanded for it when she had just been doing her job.

It had only been on the way home that her spirits had started to wobble and she'd become quiet and withdrawn. Back at the house, her true feelings had come pouring out. Hopefully a hot bath, clean clothes and some tea and toast would make her feel better.

The letter box on the front door clattered and Bella turned around in time to see several letters fall onto the mat. She scooped them up and quickly looked through them, hoping that there might be something for her. And there was. Two, in fact; one from her mother and the other addressed to her in spidery writing that had become familiar to her. She smiled as she tucked them both into her dungarees pocket to read later, and left the rest of the post on the little table in the hall for Connie to find when she got home.

Winnie sat cross-legged on her bed, wrapped in her blue silk dressing gown, her cheeks glowing pinkly from the warm bath but looking uncharacteristically vulnerable without her usual bright-red lipstick.

'There you go; nothing beats tea and toast to perk you up.' Bella handed her friend a cup and plate and plonked herself down beside her on the bed, her own cup in her hand. 'How are you feeling now? You certainly look cleaner.'

'Better, thank you.' Winnie managed a smile. 'I'm sorry to have been such an awful grump. I honestly thought I was doing the right thing, Bella, and I would never put a patient in danger.'

Bella squeezed her arm. 'I know that.'

'Station Officer Steele said I did, and she also said...' Winnie halted and then went on. 'She said she was extremely disappointed, and that she expected better from me.'

'That's really upset you?'

Winnie nodded. 'I felt like a little girl again when I'd done something wrong and Sita, my ayah, told me off. Knowing that I'd disappointed her was worse than any punishment I got. It was the same with the boss.'

'She's like the queen bee of us workers; we all respect her and don't want to let her down. Even you, it seems, though you've had enough tellings-off from her before.'

'They were just about silly things really, but this

211

was different.'

'Did you tell her how upset you were?' Bella asked.

'Of course not! I was going to say sorry, but she clearly didn't want to talk any more and sent me out before I could apologise.'

'Do you think you should have shown her how you felt?'

Winnie coughed on her mouthful of tea. 'Good heavens, no, got to keep a stiff upper lip and all that.'

'Sometimes it would do you good to let that stiff upper lip wobble a bit, you know,' Bella said.

Winnie shrugged. 'It's how we were brought up, how I survived boarding school, I suppose, not showing when you're upset. It's what I know.'

'You never have to hide how you feel from me, you know. It's better to express your feelings than hold it all in. I think if you told Station Officer Steele how upset you were, she'd be kind. She was to me and my brother.'

'You're a good person, Bella, and much wiser than I am.' Winnie leaned her head against Bella's. 'I was scared, you know, driving past that burning building. Perhaps it was a foolish, irresponsible thing to do, but I was more worried about that baby being born in the ambulance.' She suddenly yawned. 'Excuse me, I need to get some sleep.'

'Me too,' Bella stood up. 'Try not to worry about it, Winnie. We all do things on the spur of the moment that we perhaps wouldn't do again if we had more time to think and consider. The important thing is that no one was hurt; the ambulance got a few more dents and scratches and needed a good clean-out, but it could have been a whole lot worse.'

'I know.' Winnie stood up and hugged her. 'Thank you, darling Bella, for listening to me complaining. I did something stupid today and I've had a jolly good telling-off, which has hurt my pride. Station Officer Steele was right: I have let her down. I've let myself down too.'

Bella smiled at her. 'You're a brave woman, Winnie, crazy and foolish sometimes, but we all love you, and Station 75 would be a much poorer place without you there.'

'You're making me blush.' Winnie fanned her cheeks in a dramatic way.

Bella laughed. 'Get some sleep, and I'll see you later.'

Tucked under the covers in the next room to Winnie, Bella opened the letter from James and read it through, enjoying his wonderful descriptions of things he'd seen and done and the latest books he'd read. He had started writing to her after his trip to London, when they'd gone to the dance and spent the rest of the night in Aldwych Underground Station. She'd written back, and they'd exchanged several letters in the past few weeks.

It was the last line of this letter that gave Bella a jolt of joy. She'd told him that she had a week's leave coming up and would be going to stay with her mother in Buckinghamshire, not far from Bletchley where he worked, and he'd written to invite her to meet him for afternoon tea while she was on holiday. He hoped she'd say yes, he added. Bella hugged the letter to her. She was definitely

213

going to say yes; it would be lovely to see him again. When she fell asleep a few minutes later, she had a smile on her face.

Chapter Seven

The sun was creeping above the horizon, lighting up the sky on what promised to be one of those glorious late-autumn days when the world seemed to be clinging on to some warmth before it faced the plunge into the cold and dark of winter, but Frankie wished it would stay down, because at least the darkness would hide the terrible scene before them.

She swallowed hard, trying to wash away the acrid taste of bile that had rushed into her throat at the sight of what looked like a battlefield. The trees had been blasted clean of their leaves, and in those branches that remained, body parts dangled like pieces of meat hanging in a butcher's window.

'Oh God.' Bella grabbed hold of Frankie's arm and leaned against her.

Frankie shook her head but couldn't speak. She'd seen some terrible sights since the start of the Blitz, but this was by far the worst. It was a parachute mine, the ARP warden who'd told her where to park the ambulance had said. It had blown apart a street shelter full of people, the blast toppling surrounding buildings, leaving jagged shells and piles of debris spilling out across the road and far too many people dead.

'Come on, let's get a stretcher out.' Bella's voice sounded odd. She pulled at Frankie's arm and led her around to the back of the ambulance. 'We need to focus on getting the injured to hospital.' She was doing her best to be strong and get on with the job.

'It's a wonder anyone survived.' Frankie opened the back door, and together they pulled out a stretcher and set off towards where some rescue crews were busy digging through what remained of a building.

As always, Frankie watched where she walked, stepping over spilled rubble and skirting around holes, and it was only when she got close that she realised that the body sprawled in front of her on the road was headless. She halted, and the stretcher bumped into her back before Bella realised she'd stopped.

'What's the matter?'

'Trust me, Bella. Don't look down,' Frankie said. 'Look ahead, keep looking ahead.'

'All right, if you say so.'

Frankie braced herself with a deep breath and started to walk again, gazing straight in front of her. She had to concentrate on her job, on helping those who were still alive, or she would crumble and weep at the sheer horror of what had happened here. There was nothing she could do for those poor souls who had died, but those injured in the blast still had a chance, and it was her job to get them to hospital.

The London's casualty department was already crowded with people injured during the night's

215

raid, the seats filled with people huddled in blankets while they waited to be seen, their faces blackened and shocked-looking. Frankie and Bella carried in a stretcher bearing the only person found alive from the street shelter, a young woman who was badly hurt but thankfully unconscious and unaware of what had happened. There was no guarantee that she would survive her injuries.

'What have we here?' asked a nurse, rushing over to meet them.

Frankie quickly explained what had happened.

The nurse flicked back the blanket for a quick look at the woman's injuries. 'Straight to the emergency treatment room; bring her this way.' She set off at a quick march, leading them past the waiting patients through to the quieter treatment area.

Frankie had been in here many times before and knew the routine. The patient would be transferred onto a treatment table, and the crew would collect their used blankets and leave with their stretcher, their job done.

Walking out of the treatment room door, she almost ran into a familiar figure hurrying in. Alistair stopped dead, and his worried-looking face broke into a smile at the sight of her.

'Frankie!'

'Hello, we've brought you another patient, I'm afraid.'

He grabbed hold of her hand. 'Can we meet after work? I'll be there as soon as I can.'

Frankie nodded and smiled. 'I'll be there.'

'Good.' He squeezed her hand and went quickly into the treatment room.

'What was that about?' Bella asked as they walked back through the busy waiting area.

'Just arranging to meet up again after work,' Frankie said. She and Alistair would often manage to squeeze in a walk or a drink in a café between shifts. It was the only way they'd been able to see each other, as neither of them had had any more time off since their visit to the concert. Time spent with him had become precious to her, like a ray of light in these increasingly dark times.

Frankie stared at the raindrops chasing each other down the outside of the café window, willing her mind to think of something else and wipe out the horrific images from the last call-out. She didn't want to keep seeing the body parts hanging in the trees; it had been bad enough the first time. Watch the raindrops, she told herself; which one is going to win the race to the bottom of the window?

'Here's your tea.'

Frankie turned to the waitress. 'Thank you.'

She wrapped her hands around the cup, glad of the warmth seeping into her skin, and returned her gaze to the raindrops, suddenly thinking that they were like tears running down; the sky crying for the people lost today.

'Frankie!' She looked up to see Alistair standing there, his hair and coat wet from the rain. 'I'm sorry to have kept you waiting; we had another emergency so I couldn't get off on time.' He shrugged off his coat and hung it over the back of his chair, then sat down opposite her and reached for her hand. 'You look tired.'

'So do you.'

He grinned. 'Goes with the job. That woman you brought in, she's going to be all right. I thought you'd like to know.'

'She is? I'm glad.' Frankie sighed. 'It was bad, Alistair.' She shook her head and briefly told him what had happened. 'I–'

'What can I get yer?' the waitress asked Alistair.

'Cup of tea and some toast, please. Frankie, do you want anything to eat?'

Frankie shook her head. 'No thank you.'

Alistair waited till the waitress had gone. 'Try not to dwell on it, Frankie. What you saw was shocking and shouldn't have happened, but it did and there was nothing you could have done to change it. You did your job, got her to hospital in time – you helped that woman to live and now she'll recover.'

Frankie squeezed his hand. 'I don't think I'll ever get used to seeing people ... you know ... blown to bits.'

'I hope you never do. You'd have to have a hard heart not to be affected. I would be.'

'Enough talk of work and war.' Frankie smiled. 'Let's talk about something else.'

'So when are we going to another concert?' Alastair asked. 'You would like to go again, wouldn't you?'

'Yes please, I'd love to, and soon. I need that lovely music to transport me away from all my worries for a while.'

'How many worries have you got?'

Frankie shrugged. 'The usual. Family – Stanley, you know ... nothin' the end of the war wouldn't fix.'

'How is young Stanley? Still collecting shrapnel?'

'Tons of the stuff, though he's fascinated by the Dead End Kids now as well. 'Ave you 'eard of them?'

'Who hasn't?' Alistair said. 'They're the talk of the East End. Very brave lads, from all we hear.'

'Stanley wants to join 'em.'

'He's too young, isn't he?'

'Yes, ten's far too young to be doin' what they are. 'E 'as no idea what it's really like out in an air raid; it ain't like somethin' he reads in one of 'is comics. It's real and 'orrible.'

'Frankie.' Alastair took her hand in both of his. 'I thought you didn't want to talk about the war?'

'I'm sorry.' She pulled a face and squeezed his hands.

''Ere's your toast and tea.' The waitress plonked a plate and mug down in front of Alastair.

He thanked her, then picked up his plate and offered it to Frankie. 'Go on, have a piece. You need something to eat – doctor's orders.'

She smiled at him and took a slice. As she bit into it, she suddenly realised that she was hungry after all.

'That's good; eat it all up, mind.' Alastair took a bite of his own. 'Whatever happens, Frankie, you've got to keep going. I know it's not easy, but you must.'

'I know.' She leaned across the table and kissed his cheek. 'Thank you.'

'What for?'

'For listening to me, and for sharing your toast.'

'Did the boss say what we're going to?' Winnie asked, putting the ambulance into gear and pulling out to follow the Jones sisters in front of them. 'Must be something serious if they're sending three crews.'

'No. All I know is we've been told to go via Barker Street because Tyne Street is blocked.' Hooky shifted in her seat, trying to distance herself further from Trixie, who was sitting in between her and Winnie.

Following the Jones sisters' ambulance out onto the road, Winnie glanced in her wing mirror and saw that Mac and his attendant, Hopper, were driving behind them at the rear of the convoy, the thin beam of light from their cowled headlights barely showing through the slats of the covers. 'You sure Station Officer Steele said to go via Barker Street?'

'Yes, quite sure; it's the most direct way now Tyne is blocked. I wouldn't have said so otherwise.' Hooky ignored Trixie, who had nudged her arm with her wet nose, trying once again to make friends. 'Do we have to have that dog with us all the time?'

Winnie bristled. Hooky complained about Trixie every time they went out. Was she engaged in a war of attrition, hoping that if she kept on moaning, then sooner or later Winnie would give in and leave the dog behind? That sort of tactic wouldn't work with Winnie; she was an old hand at dealing with people who kept on and on in a bid to get what they wanted, otherwise she'd be married to the dreadful Charles Hulme by now.

'Tell me, Hooky, what harm has Trixie ever

done to you?'

'Well ... none, but it's not right, is it, taking a dog out in an ambulance? None of the other crews do it.'

'Perhaps not, but I'm the only one who has a rescued dog, and besides, Trixie has already proven her worth.' Taking one hand off the steering wheel, she stroked the dog's golden head. 'And she has Station Officer Steele's approval, of course. If you don't like sitting next to her, you could always ride in the back. Shall I pull over and you can hop in there instead?'

'No thank you.' Hooky folded her arms crossly. 'I'm going to ask the boss about pairing me up with another driver.'

'If you wish.' Winnie wasn't going to argue with her right now. They had a job to do, and being out in the middle of an air raid still put her on edge. Perhaps she should be used to it by now, but the drone of planes flying overhead, the scream of falling bombs, and the flashes and crumps as they hit still made her stomach clench tight. Tonight was no different from all the other nights since the Germans had started pulverising London, but a strange uneasy feeling was growing inside Winnie, prickling at her like a cool breeze after a swim, making goose pimples rise up on her arms.

Trixie started to whine and leaned in against her mistress, nudging her for attention.

'What's the matter?' Winnie stroked her ears.

'Look out, or you'll miss the turning,' Hooky said, pointing ahead to where the Jones sisters' ambulance had slowed down and turned into Barker Street.

Trixie whined and crawled onto Winnie's lap.

'That dog's a menace. We'll end up having an accident because of her.' Hooky made a grab for Trixie to try to pull her off Winnie's lap.

'Leave her!' Winnie snapped. The streak of stubbornness that ran through her like the writing in a stick of rock flared up, and she deliberately drove straight past the turning into Barker Street.

'Hey!' Hooky shouted. 'We should have gone down there.' She craned her neck to look back. 'You've missed the turning messing around with that dog.' Her voice was shrill. 'We'll have to turn around now and go back.'

Winnie shrugged. 'We'll just go another way; it doesn't matter as long as we still get there.' She looked in her wing mirror and smiled when she saw that Mac and Hopper had missed the turning too and were still following them.

'You did that on purpose.' Hooky turned in her seat, and although Winnie couldn't see her very well in the darkness, she knew that she'd be glaring at her, because she'd done it so many times before. 'We're supposed to take the most direct route so we can get there quickly to pick up casualties. Station Officer Steele's going to be furious when she hears you deliberately went a longer way.'

'It's hardly any further, and anyway, who's going to tell her?' Winnie challenged.

'I will.' Hooky's voice dripped poisonous righteousness. 'I simply have to.'

Winnie shrugged. 'Do what you want, Hooky, I really don't care.'

'Humph! You will after the boss has finished with you. Most likely you'll be looking for another job by the end of this shift.'

'If I am, then so be it,' Winnie said. 'At least you won't have to work with me and Trixie any more, will you?'

Hooky ignored her and turned to stare out of the side window into the darkness, where the silhouettes of buildings could be seen against the bright flare of exploding bombs.

Winnie took one hand off the wheel and ruffled the soft fur of Trixie's ears. The little dog had settled herself on her lap, resting her head against Winnie's chest, her body snuggled warmly against her. Whatever happened later, she wouldn't be sorry to never work with Hooky again, Winnie thought. Until then, she had a job to do.

It was several hours later, and Londoners had once more emerged from their shelters after the all-clear, when Winnie drove the ambulance back under the arched passageway into Ambulance Station 75. Their call-out to the incident at a bomb-damaged Underground station had been one of the worst she'd attended, with many casualties, and they'd been kept busy ferrying full loads of injured to hospital. She felt wrung out and exhausted, but there was still the ambulance to clean before the next shift took over.

'Are you planning on telling the boss straight away, or can you manage to help clean up first?' Winnie asked Hooky as she carefully reversed the ambulance into a space between other returned vehicles.

'I'll do my job first,' Hooky said huffily. Since their argument, she'd only spoken to Winnie when absolutely necessary as part of their work.

'Jolly good.' Winnie switched off the engine and jumped out of the cab, closely followed by Trixie.

'Boss wants to see you both,' Sparky said, stepping out of the back of his ambulance with a pail and scrubbing brush in his hand.

Winnie nodded. 'Righto, we'll go up as soon as we've cleaned out the back. It's in a bit of a mess.'

'Leave it.' Sparky touched her arm. 'I'll sort it out for you. She wants to see you straight away, and Mac and Hopper too when they get back.'

Winnie looked at Sparky's face, which was strangely pale, and his usually twinkly eyes seemed to have lost their sparkle. 'What's going on?'

He shook his head, not meeting her eye. 'She's waiting. Go on.'

'Someone must have beaten you to it, Hooky. She's obviously heard already that we didn't follow her advice. That didn't get long to get back to her.' Winnie glanced at her attendant, who was standing listening, arms folded, with a mulish look on her face.

Sparky shrugged his shoulders, looking very uncomfortable. For once he had no cheeky banter to throw at her.

'Are you all right, Sparky? You look a bit peaky.'

'Go on up, Winnie.' Sparky patted her arm and went back to work.

Winnie stared after him for a moment. Station Officer Steele must really be on the warpath.

'Come on, Hooky, we might as well get this over with quickly.' Winnie bent down and scooped up Trixie, then headed upstairs to the boss's office.

Station Officer Steele was sitting ominously still at her desk, her eyes fixed on some paperwork lying in front of her. She didn't appear to have heard them come up the stairs as she usually would.

Winnie knocked on the door frame and let a struggling Trixie down. The little dog rushed over to the desk, her tail wagging rapidly as she put her front paws up on the station officer's lap. The older woman took Trixie's head in her hands and gently stroked her ears, whispering endearments. Then, slowly, she turned to look at Winnie and Hooky. Winnie was shocked by the pallor of her face. Her usually pink complexion was ghostly white, and if she hadn't known better, Winnie would have sworn that she'd been crying.

'Winnie, Hooky. Come in.' She beckoned them forward and stood up to face them, keeping one hand on the back of her chair, holding on so tightly that her knuckles stood out white.

An uneasy feeling crept over Winnie, running like iced water through her veins. Something was seriously wrong. Could the boss be this upset over her ignoring the advice to go via Barker Street? It wouldn't be the first time Winnie hadn't done as she was told, and not the last time either, but did it matter so much? They'd got to the incident quickly and had done a good job ferrying casualties to hospital. Surely the important thing was that they'd done their job. Winnie knew she'd been warned after the incident with the burning building, but this was different, wasn't it?

'I told Winnie to go via Barker Street, I kept telling her and she wouldn't listen,' Hooky blurted out. 'It wasn't my fault she didn't. I told her to turn around and go back, but she wouldn't.'

Winnie suddenly felt like laughing at Hooky's sense of self-preservation in the face of trouble. She was someone who would always put herself first.

Station Officer Steele stared at Hooky, a flash of irritation passing over her face. Then she took a deep breath and began to speak, her usual calm tones sounding as if she'd swallowed some barbed wire, leaving her voice scratchy and strained. 'I'm glad you ignored my instructions, Winnie, because if you hadn't, neither of you would be standing here right now...' Her voice faltered and she cleared her throat. 'I'm sorry to tell you that the Jones sisters have been killed; they never got as far as the incident.'

It was as if she had been drenched in icy water. Winnie struggled to comprehend what she'd heard. 'What happened?'

'A direct hit from a high-explosive bomb while they were driving down Barker Street. They didn't stand a chance. If you'd been behind them, you'd have been caught in it too.'

'Oh my God.' Hooky looked from Station Officer Steele to Winnie and back again. 'But you *told* us to go that way. The Jones sisters were following your orders. And if we'd done the same, we'd have been killed too.'

Station Officer Steele nodded and slumped down into her chair, her head bowed. Trixie whined and jumped up onto her lap, nudging the woman's hand with her wet nose.

Winnie glared at Hooky, anger bubbling up.

Her fellow crew member had surpassed herself this time. 'Go,' she hissed at her.

'But–' Hooky began.

'Now!'

Winnie put her hand on Hooky's arm and propelled her towards the door, closing it behind her. Then, taking a deep breath, she turned back to Station Officer Steele, who had her face buried in Trixie's fur and was quietly sobbing, her thin shoulders shaking in her smart navy jacket.

Kneeling down on the floor beside her, Winnie put her arm around the older woman's shoulders. 'It's not your fault. That bomb could have landed anywhere. It was pure chance that it fell where it did.'

Station Officer Steele looked up, her eyes redrimmed behind her glasses and her usually neat hair tousled. 'But I told them to go that way. If I hadn't, they'd still be alive.'

'They might or they might not. Every time we go out during a raid there's a chance we might be hurt or killed; it goes with the job, and with many others too, like the fire service and the ARP. The Jones sisters could have gone another way; it was their choice to go the way they did. I made a decision to go the way I did, and Mac followed me...' The thought of Mac being caught in the blast if he hadn't followed her made her stomach knot.

Station Officer Steele shook her head. 'For once I am grateful that your observance of orders is as shaky as it is, otherwise I could have lost three crews tonight.' She sniffed and smiled as Trixie licked her hand. 'You remind me of my younger self, Winnie. I never liked doing as I was told

227

either.' She took both Winnie's hands in hers. 'Never stop being yourself; follow what your gut tells you to do, because it's usually right.'

Winnie blinked back tears and nodded. 'Thank you.'

A knock on the door made them both turn. Mac and Hopper were standing outside the door. Winnie's heart did a sudden flip. 'Do you want me to tell them?' she asked.

Station Officer Steele shook her head. 'No. There's no shame in tears, only in not shedding them over worthy things. You go and sort yourself out.' She took a deep breath and stood up. 'Come in.'

Mac caught Winnie's eye as she passed him, and she reached out and squeezed his arm, wishing that he didn't have to hear the news. Other ambulance stations had lost crew members; until now, Station 75 had been lucky, but tonight that luck had run out.

In the quiet of the women's changing room, Winnie splashed cold water on her face, trying to focus her mind on the feeling of it against her skin so that she could stop thinking about what had happened. But it didn't work. Thinking back, she hadn't seen either of the Jones sisters at the incident, but she'd just assumed they'd arrived first and already gone to a hospital with their first load of casualties. It had been so busy with ambulances, theirs and some from other stations, coming and going, it hadn't struck her as unusual that she hadn't seen them.

The horror of losing two colleagues made her

feel sick and shaky. The sisters had been so kind, thoughtful and fun, volunteering in a dangerous job and always cheerful and happy, often singing one of their beloved Gilbert and Sullivan songs. It was wrong that they were gone, snuffed out in an instant. She leaned against the cold porcelain sink and hung her head.

A question suddenly started to gnaw at her. What if she had taken that turn and followed them? Reaching out for her towel, she buried her head it in and closed her eyes, thinking back to those few seconds that, unknown to her at the time, had been like a crossroads. If she'd turned one way, the way she should have gone, she would probably be dead now; the other way, the way she actually had gone, had led her here. What had made her ignore those instructions? Was it just stubbornness brought on by Hooky's insistence, or did it have something to do with that strange feeling moments before, or Trixie's unusual whining? She would never know.

Throwing the towel over her shoulder, she leaned back against the sink again and silently thanked whatever it was that had made her choose. It had saved her life, as well as Trixie's, and Hooky's for all her complaining, not to mention Mac and Hopper's.

The door of the changing room burst open and Frankie and Bella came rushing in.

'Winnie!' Frankie said. 'We just got back and heard about what happened to the Jones sisters. Sparky said you were in the same convoy. Are you all right?'

Winnie nodded. 'Yes, we're unhurt.' She told

them what had happened. 'For once, Station Officer Steele is glad I ignored instructions. She's very upset.'

'She's a kind person,' Bella said, putting her arm around Winnie and squeezing her tight.

Frankie did the same, and Winnie was sandwiched between her two dear friends. 'What a bloody terrible thing this war is,' she said, hugging them back as she finally gave in and let her tears flow.

There was none of the usual jokey banter as the crews on the late-night shift left Station 75 just after half past seven that morning. A sombre mood hung over everyone as the awful reality of what could happen to any of them out on call sank in.

'I think we should raid Connie's medicinal brandy when we get home,' Winnie said, wheeling her bicycle, with Trixie sitting in the basket, out into the street alongside Frankie and Bella. 'And you should have something for the shock as well, Frankie.'

'I doubt there's anything in the 'ouse,' Frankie said, thinking that if there was, Ivy would have polished it off. 'It'll have to be tea for me, I'm afraid.'

'Will Connie mind?' asked Bella, who was pushing the bicycle Winnie's godmother had generously loaned her.

'Course not, that's what it's there for.' Winnie sighed. 'What a shift. We don't want any more like that, thank you very much, Hitler.' She raised her voice, directing it up to the sky, as if trying to send her words directly to the man himself.

'Bloody, bloody war.'

Frankie reached out and squeezed her arm. 'Go 'ome and 'ave that brandy; you need it.'

Winnie nodded and smiled back, although the smile didn't quite reach her grey eyes, which had lost their usual sparkle. 'See you later, half past eleven tonight, and don't be late.' She swung her leg over her bike and set off with a final wave.

'Keep an eye on 'er, Bella; it could have turned out very different for Winnie tonight but for her disregard of orders,' Frankie said.

'Will do.' Bella climbed onto her bicycle and pushed off, pedalling hard to catch up with Winnie.

Frankie watched her two friends until they disappeared from view at the end of the road, then turned and headed in the direction of Stepney. She'd only gone a hundred yards when she heard her name being called and saw a familiar figure coming down the street towards her on a bicycle. It was Alistair. The sight of him gladdened her heart.

'Frankie! Thank God,' he panted, braking hard and leaping off his bicycle. He dropped it to the pavement and folded his arms around her, holding her tight. The warmth and security felt like sunshine after a thunderstorm, and she rested her head against his chest, where she could hear his heart thumping loudly. They stood holding on to each other, not saying a word, just glad to be together.

'What are you doing 'ere?' Frankie asked when he finally loosened his grip and stood back, looking at her with his blue eyes full of concern.

'I came to find you... We heard at the hospital that a crew from Station 75 had been killed... I was so worried it could have been you.'

'It was the Jones sisters, you know the ones I told you about who were always singin' Gilbert and Sullivan songs.' Frankie's voice wavered. She swallowed hard and went on. 'It could have been Winnie and Mac too if she hadn't gone her own way.' She explained what had happened. 'She's pretty shaken up, though she's trying 'ard not to show it. We all know the risks, but until now our station's been lucky.'

She suddenly yawned. 'Beg your pardon, it's been a long night.'

'I'm going to walk you home, Miss Franklin.' Alistair picked up his bicycle.

'But it's well out of your way. Don't you need to go 'ome and get some sleep? You've just come off shift, 'aven't you?'

Alistair shrugged. 'Yes, but being with you is more important than sleep at the moment.' He studied her intently. 'You mean a lot to me, Frankie.'

Frankie stared at him. 'Do I now?' She couldn't stop a huge smile spreading across her face. 'That's good, because you mean a lot to me too.'

Alistair smiled, and then kissed her gently. 'Come on, let's get you home.' Holding on to the bicycle with one hand, he took hold of her hand with his other, and together they started the long walk back to Stepney.

Station Officer Violet Steele hesitated at the entrance to Station 75, her feet unwilling to turn left in the direction of home. She didn't want to go there; she didn't want to be in the flat, where she knew she would sit and brood, her mind going over and over the events of the shift, with its awful outcome, torturing herself with the knowledge that it was all her fault. If she hadn't told them to go via Barker Street to the incident, the Jones sisters would still be alive and would now be on their way home, instead of having been blown to bits with nothing left for their family to bury.

She'd delayed leaving as long as she could, taking her time in handing the station over to her deputy, who was in charge of the next shift, making extra sure that all the checks had been done and that everything had been signed off satisfactorily. Usually after a busy night, tiredness and the accumulated tension that came from hovering over the telephone, organising the crews and keeping on top of the paperwork would descend on her like a heavy weight, and she would be grateful to hand over and head for home. But not today. She still felt strangely alert, as though she could carry on for another eight-hour shift. In fact she would have been glad to do so, as it would have taken her mind off what had happened.

Hearing the sounds of the crews starting to prepare the ambulances behind her, Station Officer Steele straightened her shoulders and made her choice. She turned right and headed for the River Thames. She always loved it by the water, with its sense of sudden open space after the crowd of buildings, and the fresh air carried in with the tide. Striding along, she passed people going in the opposite direction, heading to work after spending yet another night sheltering from the bombs. Londoners were growing accustomed to sleeping in shelters; their lives had become punctuated by the nightly wail of the air-raid sirens and the rush to seek safety. They had became adept at making their nights as comfortable as possible; she'd seen them queuing up to go into the Underground, their arms full of bedding. The war had shifted their everyday lives, disturbing their natural rhythms and forcing them to seek shelter below ground from the nightly terror that rained down from the sky.

Skirting past Tower Gardens and round by the side of the Tower of London, she glanced over at the allotments, where neat rows of vegetables grew like ranks of marching soldiers. Reaching the wall bordering the river, she leaned against it and breathed in deeply, relishing the fresh air filling her lungs with its tang of salt and tar. A cool breeze was whipping off the river, and she huddled inside her pre-war dark-red wool coat, drawing her scarf up around her neck and pushing her hands deep into her pockets.

'I couldn't face going straight home either.'

Station Officer Steele spun around and saw Mac walking towards her from the direction of Tower Bridge. She did her best to smile at him, but her face didn't respond as it normally would.

'Are you all right?' He came and stood beside her, leaning his arms on top of the wall.

'I keep thinking about the Jones sisters...' She looked up at the sky, where silver barrage balloons floated over London like giant fish, glinting in the weak sunshine that was struggling to break

234

through a bank of cloud. 'It's all my fault.' Her eyes smarted with tears. 'I sent them to their deaths.'

Mac stood upright, his eyes wide. 'No you didn't! Why do you think that?'

She sighed. 'It was me that told them to go via Barker Street. It was me that sent them there. So you see...' her voice wavered, 'it's my fault and mine alone.'

Mac shook his head and smiled at her.

'It's nothing to smile about,' she snapped, and immediately regretted her harsh tone. 'I'm sorry.'

'I smiled because what you said is completely ridiculous.' He looked her straight in the eye. 'The Jones sisters' deaths were not your fault. It was pure chance and due to this blasted war, and nothing more than that.'

'But I told them to go that way. If I hadn't, they might not have been hit.'

Mac touched her arm. 'You told us that Tyne Street was blocked and advised us of an alternative route via Barker Street. You gave us information based on the latest reports of bomb damage; you never ordered us to take that exact route. It's up to each driver to get to the incident the way they choose. The Jones sisters chose Barker Street, Winnie and I didn't; simple as that.'

She nodded and stared out across the water at a coal barge making its way upriver, bobbing as light as a feather despite its heavy load, before turning to Mac and asking, 'Why did you go another way?'

He shrugged. 'Spur-of-the-moment decision. I had planned to go down Barker Street, but when

235

I saw Winnie go past the turning, I did too. I don't know why, I just did.'

'Do you know why Winnie chose to do that?'

Mac shook his head. 'You know Winnie, she's a law unto herself. I'm just glad she did, and that I followed her.' He paused. 'You know, if the bomb that killed the Joneses had been released from the plane a second later, it could have hit Winnie or me a couple of streets over instead. It's pure chance where they fall and whether you're there. There's nothing we can do about it but hope our luck holds.'

'I know that what you say makes sense, Mac, I really do, but I deeply regret their loss.' She sighed. 'When we went through it last time, we never thought another generation would have to suffer the horrors of war.' Biting down on her bottom lip, she looked up at the traffic going across Tower Bridge. 'I lost some good friends when the ambulance they were driving was hit by a stray shell just yards from mine. I understand how chance plays a part in whether you live or die in war.' She reached out and touched his arm. 'I want to keep my crews safe from harm, but I can't, I have to send them out in the middle of raids. I worry about you...'

'You don't need to worry. We know how to look after ourselves as much as anyone can in a raid.'

'But I do, and I always will, Mac, because I care. I worry about you all.'

'Even Winnie?'

'Especially Winnie.' Station Officer Steele managed to smile. 'Only please don't tell her I said that, will you?'

Turning into Matlock Street, Frankie felt exhausted. The shift had been busy, as it always was, and the emotional impact of the loss of two well-liked crew members was starting to hit her. She was desperate to drop off into the blissful oblivion of a deep, dreamless sleep.

Josie from number 5 was out scrubbing the dust that had settled on her front step after the night's raid, but she quickly spotted Frankie and sat back on her heels, a smile lighting up her face. 'Mornin', ducks. They were back again last night. 'Ad a busy shift, did you?'

'Mornin', Josie, they kept us busy all right.' She could see Josie giving Alistair the once-over. 'I'm ready for some sleep.'

''Ope you get more than I did last night, sitting in that shelter with the noise of planes and fallin' bombs all around. Good luck to yer, ducks.'

As they continued down the street, Frankie whispered, 'That's it, it'll be all round the neighbours now that I came 'ome with a young man this morning.'

Alistair grinned. 'It'll give them something to talk about instead of the war.'

Nearing number 25, she stopped and looked at him. 'I'd ask you in for a cup of tea, only Ivy will be there...' She'd told him about her step-grandmother and how things were with her.

Alistair squeezed her hand. 'It's fine, Frankie. I need to go home and get some sleep myself.' He bent down and kissed her gently. 'I'll see you soon, look after yourself.'

'You too. I–' Frankie stopped as the front door

was thrown open and Ivy stepped out. Her peroxide hair was tousled and a cigarette drooped from her mouth.

'At last! I've bin waitin'...' she began. Spotting Alistair, she instantly whipped the cigarette from her mouth and stood up straight, one hand on her hip as she pushed out her chest. 'Who's this?' She looked him up and down.

'I'm Alistair Munro.' He stepped forward and held out his hand.

'Ivy Franklin.' She shook his hand politely. 'You're a Scot. Stella hasn't told me anything about you.' She darted a questioning look at Frankie.

'He was just leaving, Ivy,' Frankie said.

'Oh, but he might be able to help...' Ivy's voice had that pathetic tone that she often used with Frankie's grandfather when she wanted something.

Frankie sighed. 'What do you want 'elp with?'

'It's Stanley,' Ivy sniffed, taking a crumpled handkerchief from her pocket. ''E's missing.'

'What do you mean, missing?'

'We were both in the shelter last night, and I thought he was asleep so I nipped inside to get me ciggies, and when I came back, 'e was gone. I called for 'im but I daren't go out after 'im in the middle of a raid.'

'What time was that?' Frankie asked, a wave of fear rushing through her.

'About 'alf past midnight. I don't know where 'e's got to.'

'I told you not to leave 'im alone in there,' Frankie snapped.

'I was only gone for a couple of minutes,' Ivy whined.

'Are you sure he's not in the 'ouse somewhere?' Frankie asked. 'Have you checked everywhere, under the beds, in the cupboards?'

Ivy shrugged.

'Go and look while I ask the neighbours.'

'I'll help you,' Alistair said.

Ten minutes later, there was still no sign of Stanley. Frankie and Alistair had gone from house to house checking with all the neighbours. Stanley's best friend Billy from number 18 hadn't seen him since they'd been playing out in the street together the night before.

'Where can 'e be?' Frankie said, trying hard to remain calm as they walked back to see if Ivy had found him. Her mind was running through various scenarios, and none of them were good. 'Why on earth did 'e go out in the middle of a raid? He promised me 'e wouldn't, 'e knew it weren't safe.'

Alistair put his arm around her shoulders. 'He might be hiding in the house.'

But Frankie knew from the look on Ivy's face as she met them at the door that he wasn't there. 'I don't know what yer grandfather's going to say.' Ivy was wringing her hands.

'We'll look further afield for him,' Alistair said. 'Try not to worry, he might have ended up in a street shelter or the Underground and be on his way home right now.'

Frankie leaned her head against his shoulder. Dear, kind Alistair, she thought, doing his best to allay Ivy's worries. He didn't know her well enough to understand that it wasn't Stanley Ivy was worried about, but what Grandad would say when he found out that she'd left him alone in the shelter again. He'd been angry when she'd done it the first time, and Ivy had promised him it would never happen again. She'd lied. Now she wanted Stanley back to save her own skin.

'You stay 'ere in case he comes 'ome, and we'll go and search,' Frankie told the older woman.

'I'll be 'ere with her, ducks.' Josie came bustling up to them and linked her arm through Ivy's. 'Don't you worry, 'e'll turn up, just you wait and see.'

Frankie desperately hoped she was right, but she'd seen enough of what could happen in an air raid to know that not everyone came home again. Bombs didn't discriminate between children and adults; they were all targets, and if Stanley had left the relative safety of the shelter to go wandering the streets in the middle of a raid... Frankie shivered. If they found him ... no, she had to be positive; *when* they found him, she hoped with all her heart that he would be whole and well and not...

'Which way?' Alistair asked. 'Where should we look?'

Frankie had been so wrapped up in her thoughts that she hadn't realised they'd reached the end of Matlock Street.

'I don't...'

'Let's try the nearest shelters first and keep a good lookout as we go. Someone might have seen him.'

Frankie nodded. 'You should go 'ome and get some sleep, you know. You've got patients to look after on your next shift.'

'I'm not going to leave you to deal with this on your own.' Alistair squeezed her hand.

'Thank you. I'm glad you're 'ere.'

'Wait!' There was the sound of running footsteps over the cobbled street. Frankie turned around and saw Stanley's friend Billy hurrying towards them. 'Wait!' he called again.

'Have you seen 'im?' she asked.

Billy shook his head. 'No, but I think I might know where 'e's gone. 'E's been talkin' a lot about them Dead End Kids and about 'ow he wants to join them.'

'But he's too young,' Frankie said.

'I know, but 'e said 'e wanted to try anyway. He thought if they saw 'ow keen 'e was then they might let 'im.'

Frankie's stomach knotted at the thought of the Dead End Kids out in the thick of it, doing their best to rescue people and put out fires.

'Did 'e tell you 'e was going to go and find them?'

Billy looked shifty. 'Not exactly. He never said 'e was going in the middle of the night. I thought we'd go to Wappin' and have a look in the daytime, not run off in the middle of a raid.'

'All right, thank you, Billy.' Frankie smiled at the boy, who looked relieved that she wasn't going to tell him off. 'You'd best get 'ome or you'll be late for school.'

'I don't mind bein' late, or missin' it altogether.' Billy grinned.

'Don't let your mother hear you say that,' Frankie said. 'Off you go.'

She watched him head slowly home. 'Are you up for going to Wappin', Alistair?'

'If you think that's where he might be. We haven't any other clues, so why not.'

They'd got no further than the Commercial Road when Frankie spotted two familiar figures coming towards them. The hand of the taller, uniformed one was firmly clamped on the shoulder of the smaller one. It was her grandfather and Stanley.

She stood and stared for a moment, then ran towards them.

'Stanley!' she cried, scooping him up in her arms and hugging him tightly. 'Where 'ave you been?'

'He tried to get to Wappin',' her grandfather's deep voice said. 'Another constable who knew me found 'im out on 'is own in the middle of a raid.'

Frankie put Stanley down and placed her hands firmly on his shoulders. 'You promised me you wouldn't leave the shelter during a raid.'

Stanley's face grew red and he looked down at his boots. 'I'm sorry.'

'Wanted to join the Dead End Kids,' her grandfather said. 'We've 'ad a serious talk about it and 'e won't try again, will you, lad?'

Stanley shook his head. 'I only wanted to 'elp. You drive ambulances and Grandad's on duty during the raids. I wanted to do something as well.' Tears started to run down his face, making tracks in the dirt.

'We were worried somethin' had happened to you. It could 'ave, you know,' Frankie said. 'If a bomb goes off near you then you're in trouble.'

'I was frightened,' Stanley admitted. 'I ain't seen any explode before last night. There was one in the next road.'

Frankie put her arm around him and hugged him close. 'I 'ope you've learned your lesson. You're far too young to be out in a raid. Those Dead End Kids are older, sixteen or seventeen. You're only ten years old.'

She glanced at her grandfather, who nodded at her. Frankie's heart squeezed as she noticed how tired and strained he looked. If this war hadn't happened, he'd have been enjoying his retirement now, not still out on the beat because so many younger policemen had been called up.

'So who's this then?' her grandfather asked, holding out his hand to Alistair, who had been quietly waiting while Frankie and Stanley were reunited.

'I'm Alistair Munro,' he said, shaking hands.

'Ah, the doctor.'

'He's been helpin' me look for Stanley,' Frankie said. 'He should have been getting some sleep after his shift at the 'ospital.'

'I'm much obliged to you,' Grandad said. 'I think we all need some sleep. Come on then, Stanley, 'ome we go.'

As the four of them walked back towards Matlock Street, Grandad touched Frankie's arm. 'Did you see Ivy?' he whispered.

Frankie nodded. 'She waited at the 'ouse in case Stanley came 'ome.'

'I've been wondering 'ow he got out without 'er noticing. Did she leave 'im alone again?'

Frankie didn't say anything, just nodded.

A look of bitter disappointment flashed across her grandfather's face and she reached out and squeezed his arm.

'No 'arm done, thank goodness,' she said.

'Not this time,' he said.

There was nothing like a hot cup of tea when you woke up, Frankie thought, even if it wasn't the strongest of brews, as the tea leaves had already had more than one wetting in the pot.

She took a sip, leaned back in her chair and smiled at her grandfather, who was tucking into his breakfast, though it was well past noon. They'd both got up a short while ago after catching up on much-needed sleep, and were enjoying some rare time together. Stanley was playing out in the street with his friends, a game of cricket in full swing, and Ivy had gone shopping after cooking their breakfast of fried bread and precious eggs from the hens they kept in the garden. The events of the night had clearly shaken her up, and she was trying hard to act the perfect wife.

'I needed that,' Grandad said, wiping up the last of the egg yolk with a piece of fried bread. He put his knife and fork down and sat back in his chair. 'Yer young man seems a nice enough fellow.'

'I think so. I wouldn't be steppin' out with 'im if he wasn't. I'm quite picky, you know that.' Frankie grinned.

'You should invite 'im round for tea sometime. I'd like to get to know 'im better.'

'I'd have to tell Ivy about 'im then, won't I?'

'If he means that much to you, she'll 'ave to

244

know sometime.' Her grandad smiled at her. 'I know you and Ivy don't always see eye to eye, but she's family and she ought to know.'

Frankie shrugged. 'I'll think about it.'

She scraped a thin covering of margarine on a slice of bread and took a bite. Chewing slowly, she turned her mind to the far more important problem that had been niggling away at her ever since she woke up.

'Are you going to tell me what the matter is, then?' her grandfather said, filling his cup from the teapot.

'It's Stanley. I know 'e's promised not to go off and try to join the Dead End Kids again, but I'm worried about 'im. It's not safe 'ere; he could get killed by a bomb even if 'e's in the shelter. I've seen it happen.'

Grandad nodded. 'I know, but if we evacuate 'im it could turn out like last time. Remember how upset he was. I don't want to put 'im through that again.'

'But it might not be like that. Some children are happy and well looked after when they're evacuated. Stanley was just unlucky.'

'There's always a risk, whatever we do, ain't there? Do we keep 'im 'ere where there's the danger of bombs, or send him off to where he might be ill treated?'

Frankie shrugged. 'I don't know.'

'Don't worry about 'im leaving the shelter. Ivy won't give him the chance to slip off again. I've spoken to 'er about it. She'll be stayin' put from now on till the all-clear goes.'

Frankie had heard them talking in their bedroom. There'd been no shouting like some husbands would do; that wasn't her grandfather's way. He was a gentle man, but when he did lay down the law, he meant it. He'd been very tolerant of Ivy up till now, but her neglect of Stanley had made him speak out, and she'd clearly taken it to heart, ostentatiously doing the jobs this morning that she usually shirked. How long that would last, Frankie didn't know; she suspected that Ivy would soon slip back into her old ways.

'In another few weeks I'll be working the day shift again, so at least I'll be 'ere at night,' Frankie said. 'Unless we can come up with some other way to get Stanley to safety, we have to 'ope there ain't a bomb with 'is name on it.'

'There's a letter for you,' Connie said as Bella walked into the kitchen. 'I've put it on the dresser. Would you like some porridge?'

'Yes please.' Bella was gradually getting used to the ways of the household. It had felt very strange at first to have someone like Connie making her a cup of tea or a meal, and she'd had to fight the ingrained idea that it was *she* who should be doing the serving. But Winnie's godmother was so friendly and unlike any other upper-class woman that Bella had come across that she had gradually relaxed and was enjoying living there.

Picking up the letter, she saw that it was from her mother and quickly opened it to find out if there was any news about Walter, who she'd only heard from once since his visit last month. After going to see their mother, he'd returned to the army, but she was still worried that he might change his mind and suddenly go AWOL. Scanning the letter quickly, she saw there was no mention of him; it was mostly about the new members of the household where her mother worked as a cook, two evacuees from Bethnal Green where Bella herself had lived until she'd been bombed out.

'Is everything all right?' Connie asked, spooning porridge into a bowl and putting it in front of Bella.

'Yes thank you. My mother's helping to look after two new evacuees, and seems to be enjoying having children about the place.' She laid the letter down on the table and took a sip of tea.

'You'll be able to meet them when you go home next week.' Connie sat down opposite Bella and poured them both a cup of tea. 'It'll be lovely to escape the constant raids. Imagine a whole night's uninterrupted sleep; what absolute bliss.'

'I feel guilty about going away while we're so busy,' Bella said, scooping up a spoonful of porridge. 'I did offer to postpone my leave, but Station Officer Steele insisted I take it, as we only get one week a year. She said it will do me good.'

'She's quite right, too. You do a difficult job, Bella, and you deserve your week away. The war will most likely still be here when you get back. She sounds like a jolly good egg, your station officer; looks after her people well and even does her best to keep Winnie in check, so I believe.'

'Did I hear my name?' Winnie said, coming in the door closely followed by Trixie.

'I was just saying how well Station Officer Steele does to try and keep you in check.' Connie got up from the table, took a clean cup from the dresser and poured a cup of tea for Winnie, who had opened the back door to let Trixie out into the garden.

'Luckily for me, I went my own way yesterday,' Winnie said, sitting down at the table.

'How are you?' Bella reached out and touched her hand.

Winnie smiled. 'I'm actually fine, thank you. I could have been blown to bits yesterday, which is rather a sobering thought, but it's made me realise that you've got to make the most of every day you have. There but for the grace of God and all that. I'm terribly sad that the darling Jones sisters are gone, and I wish with all my heart that it hadn't happened. They will be sorely missed; there'll be no more Gilbert and Sullivan songs to cheer us up while we prepare the ambulances.' She paused, looking down as she turned her cup of tea round and round in her hands. Then she looked up, moving her gaze first to Bella and then Connie. 'So now we've got to live well for both of them and not waste a single day being miserable. We've got to grab life and squeeze every ounce of living out of it.'

Trixie came running in through the back door and jumped her front paws up onto Winnie's lap, her tail wagging furiously. Winnie bent down and ruffled the little dog's ears. 'We've got to be like you, Trixie, enjoy every moment we have, eh?'

Bella caught Connie's eye and the older woman nodded and smiled at her.

'Wise words, Winnie, I think we can all learn from that.' Connie picked up her tea cup. 'A toast, then: to the Jones sisters, who gave their lives doing their duty, and to living life to the full in their memory.'

Bella and Winnie raised their own cups. 'To the Jones sisters, and to living life to the full,' they chorused.

As she took a sip of tea, Bella couldn't help marvelling at the way life twisted and turned. War seemed to speed it up, posing that unanswerable question over each day: was this your last? She made a promise to herself to try to do as Winnie had said, to enjoy every moment she had and live life to the full. She wouldn't feel guilty about taking her holiday any more; it was due to her and she would treasure every precious moment of it.

Chapter Eight

Sometimes Frankie hated the waiting. Not knowing when she'd be going out, where she'd be going and what she'd find when she got there would gnaw away at her while she sat waiting for her turn to come. Today was one of those days, because she'd rather be out and busy than sitting here worrying about Stanley. Was he at home in the shelter as he'd promised he would be, or had he run off again to join the Dead End Kids, or even just to try to rescue people on his own? He'd promised her that he'd stay put, but he'd told her that before and hadn't kept his word. He might not be so lucky next time.

Frankie sighed and stopped even trying to sketch the other crew members as they sat around the sides of the shelter, all ready to go with their steel helmets on, some occupying themselves with reading, playing cards or catching up on lost sleep. She wished she could drop off the way some of the crew could. At the far end of the shelter, Station Officer Steele was working her way through a pile of paperwork while she waited for the telephone to ring again.

'If you sigh one more time, I'm going to have to make you tell me what the matter is,' Bella hissed without looking up from the book she was reading.

'Nothing's wrong,' Frankie whispered back.

Bella snapped her book shut and looked at her from her seat opposite. 'I know when something's troubling you, so spit it out or I'll have to make you talk.'

Frankie couldn't see her friend's eyes clearly as they were in shadow beneath the rim of her steel helmet, but she knew from the tone of Bella's voice that they'd have that determined look about them that she got when she meant business.

'It's Stanley,' she admitted.

Bella got up and came across to sit on the bench beside her. 'Has he been hurt in a raid?'

'No, he's fine, but we've got to get 'im out of London. It's not safe 'ere for him with the bombs fallin' and him getting daft ideas into his head about joining the Dead End Kids.'

'But he's way too young to join them, isn't he?'

'Of course he is, but it didn't stop him trying yesterday... I thought he'd been killed.' Frankie's

250

voice cracked.

Bella tucked her arm through her friend's. 'What happened?'

Frankie told her about the frantic search for Stanley. 'I'm trying to persuade Grandad to evacuate 'im again, only he's worried about sending 'im off in case he ends up somewhere like last time where they don't want him and treat 'im badly. But if he stays here...' She swallowed hard. 'He could end up being hurt or worse. I'm frantic with worry.'

'I had a letter from my mother this morning telling me about the new evacuees who've come to stay at the place where she works. They've settled in well and are happy there.'

'They've been lucky, then.'

Bella nodded. 'Perhaps Stanley could go there as well. I could write and ask my mother. There's plenty of room for another one and he'd be well looked after.'

'But would they want another evacuee?' Frankie asked.

'It won't hurt to ask, and if the answer's yes, then I could take him with me when I go on leave next week, and I'd be able to make sure he settles in all right.'

'Would you?' Frankie felt a spark of hope. 'That would be the perfect answer. Yes please, write to your mother and ask, and I'll write too, tellin' her all about Stanley so she knows what 'e's like.' Frankie squeezed Bella's arm. 'Thank you, you're a good friend.'

Bella smiled. 'Likewise.'

The telephone jangled, making Frankie jump

and instantly putting everyone on alert, stopping what they were doing, all eyes trained on Station Officer Steele as she snatched up the receiver and answered in her crisp, efficient manner before starting to write out the chit for the incident.

'Frankie, Bella, you can take this one,' she called, putting the receiver down.

Frankie leapt up, glad that the waiting was over and she could get to work and forget her troubles for a while.

The all-clear had sounded a little after four o'clock in the morning while Winnie was driving back to Ambulance Station 75, and by the time she and Hooky drew into the cobbled space in front of the garages, the waiting crew members not out on call had deserted the cramped confines of the air-raid shelter and settled back in the comfort of the staffroom.

'If you're making tea, would you please pour me a cup while I sign in?' Winnie asked Hooky as they entered the common room, closely followed by Trixie. 'I'm absolutely parched.'

'All right,' Hooky said grudgingly.

Winnie patted her on the back. 'Thank you.' She was doing her best to be patient and tolerant of Hooky, who seemed to have abandoned her desire to work with another driver and had even stopped making snide comments about Trixie. Although her general mood and happiness left plenty of room for improvement, at least she wasn't sniping and snapping all the time. Winnie could live with that.

Winnie tapped on Station Officer Steele's open

door and went in ready to sign off the incident.

'Ah, Winnie, you're back.' Station Officer Steele handed her the paperwork to complete, then turned her attention to Trixie, who had gone into her usual rapturous delight at the sight of the boss, who always kept little titbits to feed her with, rapidly wagging her golden plume of a tail from side to side while she was made a fuss of.

Winnie filled in the required information to record what she'd done at the incident, then signed her name at the bottom. The final signing-off of a job back at the station always gave her a sense of satisfaction: a job well done and casualties safely delivered to the hospital. Working as an ambulance driver was a far cry from the life that had been expected of her as she'd grown up, and it gave her a great deal of pleasure to have thrown off those family expectations and be doing what she wanted to do. Her parents might have been lulled into thinking it was only temporary and that in time, even if they had to wait until the war was over, she'd comply and become the dutiful daughter they expected, marrying a suitable man and producing grandchildren for them. Winnie wasn't against marrying a suitable man, but *she* would be the one doing the choosing, and he would suit *her* and not her parents.

'There we are, all signed and delivered.' She handed back the paperwork.

'Thank you.' Station Officer Steele added it to a neat pile on her desk. 'Please take a seat, Winnie, I need to talk to you.' She stood up, indicating the empty chair in front of her desk, and quickly closed the office door before sitting down again in her own chair.

Winnie sat too, and Trixie immediately jumped up onto her lap and leaned her head back against her chest. An uneasy feeling settled over Winnie. As far as she knew, she hadn't done anything she shouldn't have. She and Station Officer Steele had come to an understanding since that terrible night when the Jones sisters had been killed, and strangely, she no longer felt that need to strain against the rules so much, although she would always go her own way if she thought it was the right thing to do. 'What's it about?'

'I had a telephone call from your father while you were out on call. I'm sorry to have to tell you that your brother Harry has been shot down and is missing.' She reached out and touched Winnie's arm, her face full of concern.

'Shot down?' Winnie asked, not quite believing her ears.

'I'm afraid so. Your father couldn't tell me any more than that.'

Winnie shook her head, trying to comprehend what she'd heard. She'd understood it but she didn't want to believe it. Not Harry. Her throat tightened and Trixie nudged at her hand, seeming to pick up on her distress. 'When?' Her voice sounded odd.

'Yesterday afternoon. I think it might be a good idea for you to go home,' Station Officer Steele suggested gently. 'It's a terrible shock for you.'

Winnie shook her head. 'I want to stay here and finish my shift, if you don't mind. Even if I go home, there's nothing I can do to help him. I'd rather be here and be useful.'

'I understand, but I don't want you driving. If you're needed at an incident, I'll pair you up with someone else as driver ... Mac, I think.'

'Thank you.'

'Now go and have some tea and put plenty of sugar in it.' Station Officer Steele raised her eyebrows and smiled kindly. 'That's an order, Winnie.'

Winnie picked Trixie up in her arms and stood up.

'If I can do anything to help, please don't hesitate to ask,' Station Officer Steele said, standing up herself and touching Winnie's shoulder. 'I mean that.'

Winnie nodded, unable to speak.

'Go on then, go and have that tea with sugar.' Station Officer Steele opened the door and ushered her out, then called, 'Mac, can I have a word, please?'

Winnie couldn't recall quite how she managed to get to one of the armchairs, but she must have, because she found herself sitting in one a few minutes later with Trixie on her lap and Hooky pressing a cup of hot tea into her hands.

'Has it got sugar in it?' Mac asked, coming over with the precious sugar bowl and a spoon.

'Course not,' Hooky said. 'Sugar's only for emergencies, you know that.'

'Well this is one of them.' Mac promptly added three teaspoons of sugar to Winnie's tea and stirred it briskly. 'Here, put this back in the cupboard, would you, Hooky?' He handed her the sugar bowl and sat down in the armchair opposite Winnie. 'Drink up, it'll do you good.'

255

Winnie took a sip and pulled a face. 'Not used to tea so sweet.'

'Call it medicinal, then.' He looked at her, his face full of concern. 'Are you all right? Do you want me to take you home? I'm sure the boss wouldn't mind.'

Winnie shook her head. 'Thank you, but no.' She sighed. 'I'd rather stay here. There's nothing I can do to help him, I just have to hope...' Her voice wavered and she took another sip of tea to compose herself. Part of her had been expecting this; being a pilot was risky and Harry had done well to survive this far. He'd been lucky up till now, but it appeared his luck had finally run out.

'If you're sure.' Mac smiled. 'You're coming out with me if we're needed. And Trixie, of course.' He reached out and ruffled the dog's ears. 'Stay right where you are and I'll let you know if we have to go out.'

'And I thought Hooky was bossy,' Winnie managed to joke.

'You ain't seen nothing yet.' Mac grinned and stood up. His kind blue eyes held hers for a moment. 'I'll leave you in peace for a bit. Try to rest.'

As luck would have it, or perhaps it was Station Officer Steele sparing her, Winnie didn't have to go out to another incident. She was glad when the time came for a change of shift and she and Bella could head home.

'Of course, yes, I'll tell her,' Connie's voice said from the hall upstairs.

Winnie froze on the stairs leading up from the

256

basement kitchen, with Bella and Trixie close behind her. They'd just got back from their shift and she felt tired and anxious, her nerves as taut as a violin string. Who was that speaking to Connie, and was there more news about Harry? And if there was, was it good or bad?

She waited as Connie said goodbye and replaced the receiver. 'Winnie, is that you?' her godmother called, and they could hear her footsteps tapping across the tiled floor of the hall towards the stairs.

Bella nudged Winnie in the back. 'Say something,' she hissed.

'We're home,' Winnie called shakily. She forced her legs to climb the remaining stairs to the ground floor, dreading what she was about to discover. By the time she reached the top, her heart was pounding, and it wasn't from the exertion of the climb.

'I'm glad you're back,' Connie said. 'That was your father on the telephone.'

Winnie felt Bella slip her arm through hers, and it seemed as if she was suddenly suspended in time as she waited to hear what Connie had to tell her. She was aware of the sound of voices out on the street and the ticking of the grandfather clock in the hall, but they all seemed distant as she focused on Connie's face, searching for any clue to prepare herself.

'Come through to the sitting room and we'll have a drink. I know I could do with one.' Connie led the way and went straight to her stash of medicinal brandy, pouring three glasses.

'Here.' She handed a glass each to Winnie and Bella and motioned them to the sofa, then sat opposite them in an armchair.

Winnie took a mouthful of brandy. The fiery liquid warmed her mouth and seemed to jerk her out of her dream-like state. 'Just tell me, Connie, for God's sake.'

Connie smiled at her. 'Harry's alive. He's alive. Apparently he managed to bail out. He came down in the sea and was picked up by a fishing boat.' She took a large mouthful of brandy. 'But I'm afraid he's been very badly burned.'

Winnie started to shake, her hand jerking so much that her remaining brandy sloshed about in the glass. Bella gently took it from her and put it on the little table by the side of the sofa.

'He's been taken to a hospital in Kent for the time being,' Connie continued. 'But he's alive, Winnie, and that's what matters.'

Winnie nodded, and great gulping sobs burst out of her. Trixie jumped onto her lap and licked her hand, and Bella wrapped her arms around her. Harry was alive, Winnie thought; his luck hadn't completely run out after all.

'The answer's "yes"! Stanley can go and live with Bella's mother. The lady she works for is happy to have another evacuee at the house.' Frankie sighed, feeling the weight of worry about Stanley slide off her shoulders, where it had been lying like a heavy cloak. The past few days since she'd written to Bella's mother had dragged by while she waited for a reply, but this morning's post had finally brought the answer. She handed the letter across the table to her grandfather. 'He'll be safe there.'

'That's a relief. So Bella will take 'im with her when she goes on leave?' her grandfather said after he'd read the letter himself.

'Yes, on Friday afternoon. We've got a few days to get 'im ready. I'll tell 'im before I go to work tonight.'

'Tell who what?' Ivy asked, coming into the kitchen. 'Whatcha talkin' about?'

Frankie hadn't breathed a word to Ivy about the possibility of Stanley being evacuated in case it didn't happen. There was no point in stirring up a wasps' nest if she didn't have to, but now the woman would have to be told.

'We're 'aving Stanley evacuated again,' Grandad said. 'Him running off to join the Dead End Kids was the last straw. It's not safe here for children.'

Ivy's face went red and Frankie noticed her fists bunched tightly at her sides. 'When did you decide this? No one asked me.' She humphed. ''Aven't I've been making sure he don't go out of the shelter any more? I'm doing my job.'

'I know you are, but he could still be 'urt in the Anderson if a bomb landed close enough. The best place for the boy is out of London altogether,' Grandad said, tapping his fingers on the table.

'But shelters are supposed to protect us,' Ivy whined. 'You've made enough fuss about us going in it.'

'You're better off there than in the 'ouse,' Frankie said. 'But nowhere is completely safe.'

'What if it turns out like last time?' Ivy asked. 'You said you'd never risk sending him to strangers again.'

'We're not,' Frankie said, and explained about

259

Stanley going to live with Bella's mother. 'He'll be safe and well cared for, and Bella's taking 'im there herself and will be with him for the first week. It's all sorted.'

Ivy's eyes darted from Frankie to her husband. 'He might not want to go.'

'Course he won't, you know Stanley, but 'e's got to and that's that.' Grandad stood up. 'I need to get going or I'll be late for work.' He bent down to kiss Ivy's cheek, but she turned her head so he missed. 'I'll see you later.'

He smiled and nodded at Frankie, and squeezed her shoulder as he passed by heading for the front door.

Frankie sat waiting for the explosion that she knew would come, and sure enough, the moment the door shut with a click, Ivy turned on her.

'This is your doing.' The older woman's eyes were full of hatred and her voice dripped venom. 'That boy should stay 'ere with 'is family where we can look after 'im properly.'

Frankie stood up and looked Ivy in the eye. 'Let's be honest for once, Ivy. You barely do anything for Stanley; it's more the other way around, ain't it? You're only worried about what will 'appen when he's not here any more.'

'I'll miss 'im, of course,' Ivy snapped, folding her arms tightly across her chest.

'Miss 'im queuing up for you more like, and doing all the other jobs you get him to do.' Frankie paused. 'Mind you, with Stanley gone, you'll have time to do something for the war effort. Ain't you always saying you can't join the WVS or the Red Cross because you need to be here for 'im? Well you won't have that burden on you any more. There's always a need for more helpers at the rest centres for those who have been bombed out, so you'll have plenty to fill your time.'

'But ... but...' Ivy's mouth was working liking a fish.

'Grandad will be delighted that you can 'elp out,' Frankie added as a parting shot. One problem dealt with and one to go, she thought as she went out of the front door to look for Stanley. As usual, he was out playing in the street with his friends. They had a game of marbles going on the pavement and were lying on their stomachs to get the best view.

Frankie crouched down beside Stanley. 'I need to talk to you.'

Stanley pushed himself up into a kneeling position. 'What about?'

'You'll soon find out. Can you leave this for a minute or two?'

Stanley nodded. 'Billy, take over mine for me, will yer?'

Billy nodded and the boys resumed their game as Stanley stood up and followed Frankie a few yards down the street.

'I've got something to tell you and you ain't goin' to like it.' She put her hands on his shoulders and looked him in the eye.

'Is Grandad all right?' Stanley looked worried.

'Of course 'e is; he just went to work. Didn't you see 'im?'

Stanley nodded. 'He threw a marble in for me before he left.'

Frankie took a deep breath. 'You know what it's

261

been like 'ere lately, Stanley, what with air raids every night... Well, we've decided the best thing for you is to evacuate you again...'

'No!' Stanley's eyes flooded with tears. 'You said I wouldn't 'ave to go again.'

Frankie squeezed his shoulders. 'I know we did, and we wouldn't do it if we didn't know where you were going and that the people you'll be staying with are good and kind. We've found you a place with my friend Bella's mother – remember I've told you about Bella at work?'

Stanley nodded, his face stained with tears and his mouth downturned.

'Well her mother and the lady she works for are both happy to give you an 'ome and Bella's going to take you there on Friday and will stay with you for your first week to make sure you settle in all right.'

'But what if it's 'orrible?'

'It won't be.' Frankie sighed. 'Look, Stanley, this war is dangerous. I've seen children hurt or killed in air raids, and I don't want it to 'appen to you. The only way we can protect you completely from the bombs is to evacuate you. We don't want you to go, we'll miss you really badly, but we want you to be safe and that's the most important thing.'

'Can I come 'ome if I 'ate it?'

Frankie wanted to cry. Putting Stanley through the worry again was awful, but the prospect of what could happen to him if he didn't go was worse. 'We've been really careful to find you a good 'ome this time, Stanley. There are other children already evacuated there and they're 'appy. I think you will be too.'

262

'But what if I'm not? Promise me you won't make me stay there,' Stanley pleaded.

'I promise, cross my 'eart.' She made the cross sign over her chest.

Satisfied, Stanley nodded. 'When am I going?'

'On Friday, in three days' time. We'll take you to the station to meet Bella and she'll be with you on the train. She's very kind and capable – she's my attendant, remember, and I wouldn't have just any old person working with me. She's the best there is and I completely trust her.'

'Can I go back to playing marbles now?' Stanley asked.

'Of course you can.' Frankie ruffled his hair and watched him run off down the street, his boots tapping against the cobbles, amazed at how he had accepted what she'd told him once he'd extracted the promise from her. She desperately hoped that this evacuation would work for him and she'd never have to honour that promise.

'There she is.' Frankie waved her free hand in the air to attract Bella's attention. The platform was busy with people waiting to board the train. There were uniformed soldiers, their kitbags piled up, and several sweethearts eking out their last precious moments together.

Bella's face broke into a broad smile, and as she hurried towards them, weaving in and out of the waiting passengers, Frankie thought how smart her friend looked in her green wool coat, a jaunty red knitted beret on her glossy dark brown curls. She was so used to seeing Bella in dungarees at work, she'd not recognised her at first.

Stanley's hand tightened its grip on Frankie's fingers and she gently squeezed his back to reassure him. 'Don't worry, Bella will take great care of you.' Stanley looked up at her, his blue eyes bright with tears. 'And that's a promise, otherwise we wouldn't be sending you with 'er.'

'And if I don't like it I can come back?' Stanley checked.

Frankie nodded. 'Yes, of course.' But despite her cheerful tone, all she wanted to do right now was run away from the platform and the hissing, steaming train waiting to carry him off, and whisk him back home to Matlock Street, where she could continue to see him every day. But there was a war on, and the prospect of what could happen if he didn't go was too awful to contemplate. What was a few months of missing him compared with knowing he was safe in the countryside and away from the dangers of the Blitz?

'Hello,' Bella said, smiling warmly as she reached them.

'Bella, this is my grandfather,' Frankie introduced them, 'and Stanley.'

Bella shook hands with both of them. 'Pleased to meet you. I'm looking forward to taking you home with me, Stanley. My mother and the two other evacuees are excited that you're going to stay with them.'

'It'll be good to 'ave other children to play with,' Grandad said, patting Stanley's shoulder. 'We're grateful to your mother and her employer for 'aving him to stay for a while.'

The guard blew his whistle at the far end of the train and started hurrying passengers on board

264

as he made his way down the platform towards them, slamming carriage doors as he went.

'We'd better climb aboard,' Bella said, pushing her case into the open door of the compartment beside them.

Stanley gripped Frankie's hand tighter.

'It's all right.' Frankie crouched down in front of him so she could look him straight in the eye. 'You have my promise, Stanley, remember.'

'A promise is a promise,' her grandfather said, ruffling Stanley's hair. 'You have my word that we'll stick to it should it be necessary.'

Stanley nodded, his bottom lip trembling as he did his best not to cry.

Frankie enveloped him in a big hug, squeezing him tightly, imprinting the feel of him in her arms and doing her best to swallow her own tears that threatened to escape. She needed to hold them back for Stanley's sake.

'All aboard, if you please,' the guard said as he passed by.

Frankie stood up. ''Ere, take Bella's 'and.' She passed Stanley over to her friend, who smiled at her sympathetically.

'Don't worry, I'll look after him. You'll keep an eye on Winnie while I'm away, won't you?'

'Course I will. Her brother's being transferred to the Masonic Hospital today, so she'll be able to go and see 'im soon, which will 'elp her.'

Frankie plastered a smile on her face and watched as Bella and Stanley climbed into the compartment and slammed the door shut behind them. Bella slid the window down and they both leaned out.

'We'll write to you tomorrow to let you know how we're getting on, won't we, Stanley?' Bella said, her hand on his shoulder.

Stanley reached out to Frankie and she took his hand as the guard blew his whistle at the far end of the train, waving his green flag in the air to signal to the driver. The train belched out great chuffs of smoke, which billowed up into the ornate roof of the station, then slowly the carriages started to move forward. Frankie walked along beside them, still holding Stanley's hand, but as the train picked up speed she fell back and had to let go, watching with tears streaming down her cheeks as he reached out into empty air until the train left the station and he was lost from sight, and all that remained was a sooty taint of coal in the air.

She stood rooted to the spot, staring down the track, until a firm hand gripped her shoulder.

'Come on, let's go and 'ave a cup o' tea,' Grandad said.

She nodded, not daring to speak. She was glad Grandad had been there with her to see Stanley off, because without him she might well have turned tail and run home before Bella arrived.

'We've done the right thing,' he said gently, steering her towards the station buffet.

Frankie sat down at one of the tables while he went to get the tea, glad of a few minutes to compose herself. She knew she'd been lucky to have her family together for so long when many others had been split apart by this damn war. So many husbands and wives were hundreds or even thousands of miles apart, not knowing when or even if they would see each other again, and children were living with strangers away from their own communities and everything they'd grown up knowing. Whole families separated and having to cope with whatever was thrown at them, be it by the Germans or their own government, with more and more restrictions in the name of the war effort.

'Here you are.' Grandad arrived bearing a tray with two cups of tea and two currant buns. 'This should perk you up a bit.'

Frankie smiled at the wonderful man who'd been there for her all her life as he sat down and placed her tea and bun in front of her.

'Thank you.'

'Eat up,' he said, picking up his own bun and taking a bite.

Frankie did as she was told and immediately felt better for having something to eat; she hadn't had the appetite for anything before they'd left home. Finishing the bun, she took a sip of tea and then leaned back in her chair.

'It was 'ard watching him go. I nearly bottled out and said he could stay,' she admitted.

Grandad laughed his deep, jolly laugh. 'So did I.' Frankie stared at him. 'But I knew I'd have you to answer to if I suggested it after you'd gone to all the trouble of finding 'im somewhere safe and persuadin' him to give it a try.'

'And I was thinking you'd be cross if I suggested it.' Frankie grinned. 'Just as well we both kept mum about what we were thinking, or Stanley would be on his way 'ome now and not out to safety in the countryside.'

'Right soft-'earted pair we are.' Grandad took a sip of his tea and sighed. 'It's a pity Ivy couldn't come and see him off.'

'Is it?' The words were out of Frankie's mouth before she had time to think, and she clamped her hand over her mouth, her cheeks growing hot. She knew there had been nothing wrong with Ivy when they'd left the house; she just couldn't be bothered to come to the station. Her headache was an excuse, and even her tears when they'd left were false, more for her loss of an errand boy than anything else.

Grandad raised his bushy eyebrows and looked at Frankie, meeting her eyes. 'You ain't very fond of Ivy, are you?'

Frankie considered what to say for a moment and then decided on honesty; it was what her grandparents had instilled in her growing up. 'No, I ain't.'

'Why's that?'

'Because she thinks of herself first and foremost now. She weren't like that to start with...'

Her grandfather nodded and took hold of his cup in both hands. 'I know.' He tipped the cup, watching as the liquid swirled around. 'She's changed from the woman I married.'

'Are you 'appy?' Frankie blurted out.

He met her eyes again and shrugged. 'She's my wife and I married her for better or worse, till death us do part.'

'I'd say it's mostly for the worse now.'

'This blasted war don't 'elp.' He quickly drained the last of his tea and put the cup down. 'At least with Stanley gone she won't have to worry about 'im during air raids any more; perhaps that'll cheer her up and we'll see the old Ivy again.'

Frankie wanted to shout at him that Ivy was selfish through and through and would no more change now than a leopard would lose its spots. He was such a good, kind man and deserved better than being saddled with her. He had as good as admitted that he wasn't happy with her, but his stubborn belief in the sanctity of marriage till the end, bitter though it might be, meant that he would stand by her no matter how demanding and uncaring she was. As long as he held onto that, Frankie had no choice but to stay living at Matlock Street to make sure that he had decent meals and act as a buffer for Ivy's failings and laziness.

'Are you 'appy with your job?' Grandad asked, changing the subject.

'Yes, it's hard sometimes, but I'd rather be driving ambulances than 'emming uniforms.'

'You will be careful, won't you?'

'I always am.' She smiled at him. 'The same goes for you.'

'Don't you worry. Old Hitler ain't going to get me. I've been walking the beat around Stepney for more years than I care to remember, and I ain't finished yet.'

Frankie nodded, hoping that he was right; no one could be certain of anything these days. At least she didn't have to worry about Stanley now that he was on his way to a new home in the countryside and away from the nightly bombing raids.

Bella loved to watch as the buildings gradually petered out and the countryside took over. Seeing so much greenery around her once more was like the gentle soothing of warm water when she lay back in the bath, and she felt herself relax. It happened every time she left London to return home for her annual holiday. It wasn't that she disliked London, but she'd been born and raised in the countryside and it instinctively felt right to her to be surrounded by the green of fields and woods rather than the buildings and streets of London.

Staring out at the passing fields, Bella remembered the first time she'd arrived in London, at the tender age of fifteen, uprooted from all she'd known, with her dreams of becoming a teacher shattered. She recalled her shock at the noise of so many people rushing here and there, and how closed in the buildings had made her feel. She'd been used to being able to see for miles, but in London her view was restricted to the other side of the street. It had taken some getting used to. Today would be the opposite for Stanley, going from the crowded streets of the East End to the open countryside of Buckinghamshire. He was sure to feel shocked and unnerved by the change.

She glanced across at him. He was staring out of the window, as he had been since they'd set off. She'd tried talking to him, but although his replies had been polite, the poor lad was clearly not in the mood for chatting, so she'd left him to his own thoughts for a while.

Now, pulling a small paper bag out of her coat pocket, she offered it to him. 'Would you like a humbug?' He looked at her uncertainly. 'Please have one, I'm going to.'

'Thank you.' Stanley delved into the bag, took out a sweet and popped it into his mouth.

'Are you all right?' Bella asked him.

Stanley nodded. 'Yes thank you.'

He did his best to smile, though Bella noticed it didn't quite reach his blue eyes, which looked wary and sad. Her heart squeezed for him; he must be terrified going off into the unknown again, away from the people he knew and loved and the streets he called home. Frankie had told her what had happened to him before, so she understood how worried he must be that it could all go wrong again. Only it wouldn't, because this time he was going to be looked after by her mother, and she would never be unkind to him or treat him badly.

Sucking on her own humbug, Bella leaned back against the springy train seat and thought about the coming week. Not only was she returning to see her mother, but she'd be going to meet James, taking him up on his invitation to have afternoon tea with him in Bletchley. It was going to be a wonderful week away from the bombing and the tiring shifts at Ambulance Station 75.

The first thing Bella noticed when the train pulled in to Little Claydon was that the large black and white sign was missing from the platform, removed to stop the enemy finding their way around too easily in case of invasion. Stepping down from the train, and holding out her hand to help Stanley, she also noticed that the flowers that had once brightened up the station were gone, cabbages and leeks growing in their place. The war had well and truly come to Little Claydon.

271

'This is it, Stanley.' Taking hold of his hand, she led him out through the booking hall and headed for Linden House, where her mother worked. It was a short way out of the village, past the school and the green, where ducks were dabbling away on the pond, completely oblivious to the war.

Bella was aware of Stanley looking around him, clearly feeling as out of place as she had when she first went to London. 'It's very different here from Stepney, I know, but I hope you'll settle in and grow to like it. Little Claydon's a lovely place and it's safer here for you.'

Stanley nodded, but didn't say anything.

They walked along in silence, leaving the main part of the village behind and heading along the lane that led to Linden House. Turning in through the high gate-posts with the stone eagles sitting proudly on top, Bella gasped at the transformation before her. The once colourful flower beds and sweeping expanse of immaculate lawns at the front of the house were gone, replaced by neat rows of vegetables. Her mother had described the changes in her letters but it hadn't quite prepared her for seeing the impact herself. Her mother's employer, Mrs Beaumont, was a staunch supporter of the war effort and had turned her home and gardens over to the production of food, creating a market garden and employing Land Girls to help with the work. They, like Bella's mother and the other evacuees, lived at Linden House alongside Mrs Beaumont.

'This is your new home, Stanley. What do you think?' Bella asked. 'It's quite a place.'

Stanley nodded but again didn't speak as he

stared at the impressive house built of warm red brick with tall windows looking out towards them. It wasn't a huge house compared with some upper-class houses but it was still much bigger than anything in Stepney, and beautiful to look at.

'This is where my mother works; remember I told you she's the cook here. She makes sure everyone gets well fed, Mrs Beaumont, the Land Girls and the other evacuees, and now you. She's a good cook.'

'I'm going to live 'ere?' Stanley asked, his eyes wide.

Bella smiled at him. 'You certainly are.'

The smell of carbolic soap hit Winnie the moment she and Mac walked in through the doors of the Masonic Hospital. She should be used to it now, as she took casualties into hospital on a daily basis, but that was work and she was here for something else – to see Harry. He'd been transferred here from the hospital in Kent yesterday, a week after he'd been shot down, and this would be the first time she'd seen him. Her parents had been to visit him in Kent and had been vague about how he was, giving very little away when she'd spoken to them on the telephone except to say that he was being well looked after. It was more what they didn't say that worried Winnie. She'd seen what fire could do to a person.

'Are you all right?' Mac's kind voice broke into her thoughts.

Winnie nodded and smiled at him. 'A bit nervous. I'm not sure how he'll be.'

'Then it's best to speak to a nurse first, find out

273

what to expect so you can prepare yourself.'

'I'm glad you're here; thank you for coming with me.' Winnie smiled at Mac. He'd been a great support in the past week.

'Any time.' He reached out and took hold of her hand, squeezing it gently. 'Let's go and find him and you can finally put your mind at rest.'

When Winnie entered her brother's darkened room ten minutes later, she was, for the first time in her life, utterly lost for words. The nurse had told her that Harry had third-degree burns to his hands, face and legs, but it hadn't prepared her for the sight that greeted her as her eyes adjusted to the dim light. A figure was suspended loosely on straps just clear of the bed, with his arms propped up in front of him, his fingers extended like claws. His face was covered in white gauze, with slits in it for his nostrils and a wider one for his mouth, through which his swollen lips protruded. The smell, acrid and unpleasant, made her want to turn tail and run; it was the smell of burnt flesh.

Swallowing hard, she forced herself to stay calm, holding her hands in tight fists as she approached the bed, willing her voice to come out normally and not betray her shock at her brother's appearance. 'Hello, Harry, it's me, Margot.'

He moved his head a fraction of an inch, then his lips opened and a harsh, rasping voice said, 'I knew you'd come.'

'How are you?' Winnie asked.

'Bloody sore! What do you expect?' Harry snapped. His chest rose and fell rapidly, and then he spoke again. 'Sorry, old girl, shouldn't have said that.'

'It's all right, I expect you're sick of people asking. Stupid question really; of course you're in pain. A lot of pain.'

'You alone?'

Winnie nodded, and then realised that Harry couldn't see as his eyes were covered by the gauze dressing. 'Yes, well, Mac from work came with me, but he's waiting outside. It's just me in here now. Do you want me to call a nurse?'

'No. They're in and out here all the time changing these blasted dressings, so don't disturb them now.'

'Can I get anything for you, bring you anything next time I come?' Winnie asked.

'You off already? Seen enough?' Harry's voice was bitter.

'No, though I'll go if you want me to,' Winnie snapped back.

Harry's mouth twitched. 'Thank God.'

'What's the matter?'

'At last someone's giving as good as they get.' He sighed. 'I'm glad you've come, and please be honest with me. Promise?'

'I promise.'

'How do I look?'

Winnie didn't know what to say. Did she tell him straight, as he'd asked, or should she try to soften the blow?

'You promised,' Harry reminded her. 'Can't bloody see for myself.'

'Well I can't see your face under the gauze, but your lips are swollen and red. One hand is bandaged so I can't see it properly, but the other one is black.'

'Tannic acid,' Harry said.

'What?'

'They told me they put it on my hands and it turns into a kind of black cement. They chipped it off one hand after I got here yesterday. The other one's next.'

'What happened? Why did you crash?'

'Because the bastards finally got me.' Harry fell silent for a few moments. 'I was chasing a Messerschmitt and another came up and hit me from behind. Poor old kite quivered like a wounded animal.' He paused and cleared his throat before going on. 'Cockpit was a mass of flames ... I knew I had to get out. Somehow I got the hood open, then I tipped the old girl upside down and fell out. I pulled the ripcord and floated down, and plopped into the old briny, where I floated till they fished me out.'

'We didn't know what had happened to you; they said you were missing in action, shot down, and we had no idea if you were still alive or...' Winnie's voice caught and she stopped talking.

'Steady on, old girl.' Harry sounded overbright. 'You weren't going to get rid of me that easily.'

Winnie put her hand tentatively on his shoulder.

'It's all right, that bit's not burnt.'

'I'm so glad you got out.' She gently stroked his shoulder. 'Where would I be without you to spar with?'

Harry laughed hoarsely. 'You could always try Mother.'

276

'Very funny. Now would you like me to read to you for a bit? You must get bored lying there.' She rummaged in her bag and brought out a book she'd taken from Connie's library, Harry's favourite as a boy. 'I've brought *Treasure Island.*'

Harry nodded, his swollen lips pulled into as much of a smile as he could manage. 'Please.'

Pulling up a chair beside his bed, Winnie sat down and started to read, glad that she could do something to take his mind off the pain and the darkness for a short while. It also, if she was honest, gave her time to deal with the enormity of what had happened to him. She'd reached the part where the Captain was threatening the doctor when a nurse came in.

'It's time to change your dressings, Harry.'

'Oh God, here we go again,' Harry moaned.

'Is he always this ungrateful?' Winnie asked.

'He's fine.' The nurse smiled. 'It's not easy for him.'

Winnie stood up and gently squeezed his shoulder. 'Behave yourself and I'll see you soon.'

'I'm glad you came,' Harry said. 'Thank you, Margot. I appreciate it even if I am a grumpy b–'

'Less of the language, if you don't mind,' a stern voice interrupted.

'Ah Matron, you've come along for the fun, have you?' Harry said with a note of challenge in his voice. 'Come to torture a poor soul in the name of changing a dressing.'

'What else?' Matron said, raising her eyebrows at Winnie and smiling warmly. 'This is your sister, I understand. She's a brave woman to come and spend time with you.'

'Not at all. Her tongue is nearly as sharp as yours,' Harry retorted.

Winnie smiled, glad to see that her brother's spirit wasn't defeated. His poor body might be burnt and his future uncertain, but he could still parry a good jibe given a suitable partner, and clearly Matron was well up for the role.

Stepping out into the corridor, Winnie's legs suddenly seemed to go all weak and shaky and stupid tears blurred her vision as she walked towards where Mac was waiting for her.

'Winnie!' He stood up and gently guided her to the chair where he'd been sitting, then crouched down in front of her. 'Are you all right? You've gone very pale.'

Winnie nodded. 'I'm shocked.' She took a deep breath to fight back the wave of tears that was threatening to spill out. 'I was fine in there, I had to be for Harry's sake... You should see him...'

Mac took hold of her hand as she told him about Harry's injuries. 'I don't know what's going to happen to him, whether he'll be able to see again or...'

'They're doing all they can to help him. He's alive, and that's what matters.'

'I know. I'm just being silly, that's all. He looks so different now.' Winnie sniffed, blinking away her tears. 'I'll come back and see him after our shift tomorrow. I started to read him *Treasure Island* and he liked that, and when that's finished there's *Robinson Crusoe* and then *The Lost World*, which he always loved. If I can take his mind off things, I'm sure it will help him.'

Mac laughed.

'What's so funny?'

'You.' He smiled warmly, his blue eyes meeting hers. 'You'll do your brother the world of good, Winnie, with your energy and determination. You're a force to be reckoned with, you know.'

'Perhaps I should give up working for the ambulance service and transfer to a hospital to help heal the wounded.'

Mac shook his head. 'There'd be too many rules for you. Stick to driving ambulances and focus on helping your brother.'

'I don't know whether to be flattered or insulted.' Winnie grinned.

'I mean it in the nicest possible way: I'd miss you if you left, Winnie.'

'Then I'd better not go, had I?'

Chapter Nine

'Do you want to come out and see the garden? There's chickens and a cow in the meadow,' Bertie, one of the other evacuees, asked Stanley, who'd just polished off a slice of carrot cake.

Stanley looked at Bella, his face unsure. She smiled at him. 'Go on, go and explore. I'll come out in a little while and you can show me what you've discovered.'

Before Stanley had a chance to say anything, Vera, Bertie's big sister, had taken Stanley by the hand and was leading him towards the door, closely followed by her brother. 'You've got to meet the Land Girls as well and we'll show you the...' Her voice was lost as they disappeared outside.

Bella went to the window and watched the three children head towards the walled garden.

'He'll be fine, don't you worry,' her mother said. 'How about another cup of tea?'

Bella nodded and returned to her seat at the large scrubbed wooden table in the middle of the kitchen. 'I promised Frankie I'd keep a good eye on him, make sure he's happy here.'

'He will be.' Bella's mother refilled their cups and added some milk. 'Vera's taken him under her wing and will look after him like a mother hen. No harm will come to him with her around.' She passed Bella's cup over to her. 'It must be hard for the mothers sending their children away. I don't know if I could have done the same with you and Walter.'

'They do it to protect the children. I don't think they want to; it's a question of keeping them safe because no one knows when or where the next bomb is going to fall.'

'I worry about you out in those air raids.' Bella's mother frowned. 'I hope you're careful.'

Bella smiled. 'We always are. We have our steel helmets on, and we all know that Station Officer Steele would give us what-for if we took stupid risks.'

'We never thought our children would have to go through a war, not after the last one.' Her mother fiddled with the edge of her crossover paisley print apron. 'Have you heard from Walter lately?'

Bella shook her head. 'You know he's not much of a letter-writer. I've only had one letter since he came to see me in London. He seemed to think that he'd be sent somewhere soon.'

'He wasn't quite... There was something bothering him when he was here. I tried talking to him about it, but he wouldn't answer my questions directly; you know how Walter can be.' Her mother sighed. 'Did he say anything to you?'

Bella stood up and started gathering the used plates from the table. 'He told me he'd probably be sent abroad again.' She couldn't tell her mother that he'd talked about going AWOL; that would upset and worry her unnecessarily.

'I hope he's wrong. If he's sent abroad, who knows when we'll next get to see him? It could be years.' Bella's mother stood up. 'Let's go and see what the children are up to, and I'll show you all the changes Mrs Beaumont's made. It's brought the place to life again and we feel like we're doing our bit for the war effort.'

Frankie didn't know which was worse: being out in an air raid ferrying casualties to hospital while the bombers droned overhead, or sitting here in the Anderson shelter with Ivy. This was supposed to be home and safe, but it felt more like being caged in with a hungry tiger.

'Bleedin' 'eck!' Ivy jumped as another loud bang and crump rocked the earth. 'Wish they'd bugger off and leave us alone. 'Aven't they thrown enough bombs at us?' She stood up and started pacing up and down the confined space between the bunk beds and the bench that Frankie's grandfather had

281

made. Reaching into her cardigan pocket, she brought out her cigarette packet and opened it, fumbling inside. 'Blast, it's empty.' She threw it down on the floor. 'I'm goin' in to get some more ciggies.'

Frankie stood up and blocked the doorway. 'No you ain't.'

'Get out of my way.' Ivy lunged for her.

Frankie grabbed the older woman's arms and pushed her down onto the bench. 'You promised you wouldn't go out in a raid, remember?'

Ivy's face was shadowed in the dim light from the Tilley lamp, but there was no mistaking the look of hatred. 'Who's to know if you don't say anythin'?' She pursed her lips. 'But you'd tell 'im, wouldn't yer? You and your precious grandfather, so bloody close. Makes me sick.'

There, she'd as good as said it. Frankie had known that Ivy was jealous of her relationship with Grandad and saw her as competition when there was none. She wanted to be number one in her husband's eyes, even though it was obvious that she didn't feel the same way about him. Ivy's number one priority was herself and it would never be any different.

Frankie shrugged and sat back down on the bottom bunk. 'Do as you please, Ivy. It's your life, you're old enough to know what you want. One thing, just in case you don't make it: where d'you want to be buried, that's if there's enough of you left to bury?'

Ivy folded her arms, staring at Frankie, ominously silent.

'Ain't you going out then?' Frankie asked.

'No I ain't,' Ivy snapped. 'I'll wait.'

Frankie smiled. 'Have you thought any more about joining the WVS or the Red Cross?'

'No I ain't.'

'They always need more help and would be glad to 'ave you, I'm sure.'

Ivy didn't respond except to glare at Frankie before shutting her eyes and leaning back against the corrugated metal wall of the Anderson.

Frankie lay down on the bunk and tried to relax. Ivy had lost some of her power now that Stanley had been evacuated again and Frankie no longer had to worry about him. The letter that had been waiting for her when she'd got home from work this afternoon had been like a balm to her nagging doubt over whether it had been the right thing to send Stanley away. His letter had been full of the things he'd seen and done. He'd even milked the house cow. Bella had put a letter in too, confirming that Stanley was settling in well and enjoying life in the countryside.

Another loud crump from nearby made the earth tremble, and Ivy's eyes snapped open. 'Bleedin' Jerries.' She shook her fist in the air. 'Can't even get a few minutes' sleep.'

'Why don't yer try lying down on a bunk? I'll move up to the top if yer'd rather have this one,' Frankie offered.

'I'll stay where I am,' Ivy snapped ungraciously.

Frankie closed her eyes as a wave of tiredness hit her. She knew from past experience that sleep was more likely to come lying down in one of the bunks than sitting there as taut as a wire like Ivy, but it was no use arguing with the woman.

Bella was early – her train wasn't due in for a good ten minutes yet – so she wandered up and down the platform watching as another train pulled into the station and halted with a hiss of steam. Carriage doors opened and a few passengers climbed out.

'Well this is a nice surprise. I wasn't expecting a welcome party.'

She spun around at the sound of the voice. 'Walter!' She flung her arms around him and hugged him tight. 'What are you doing here? You didn't let us know you were coming home.'

'Didn't know for sure until yesterday.' He sighed. 'I've got forty-eight hours' embarkation leave.' He swallowed hard. 'We're being sent abroad again.'

'Where?' Bella asked.

'You know I can't tell you that.' He picked up his kitbag, which he'd dropped in order to hug Bella. 'Come on, I don't want to waste any of this precious leave. Let's go home.'

'I'm supposed to be meeting a friend for tea in Bletchley.' Bella chewed on her bottom lip, torn between going with Walter and making the most of every second before he went away, and meeting James as they'd arranged. She'd been looking forward to it so much. 'That's why I'm here, to get the next train. What should I do?'

'Go and meet your friend, of course. I'll still be here when you get back.'

'I don't know...' Bella hesitated.

'It's all right, I really don't mind. I can't expect you to change your plans when I turn up out of the blue with no warning. I'll see you later.' He smiled at her and turned away. He'd only gone a few yards before he stopped and glanced back. 'Who is it you're meeting anyway?'

'Just a friend I met in London who works at Bletchley.' Bella's cheeks grew warm. She wasn't going to tell Walter about James or she'd never hear the end of it. He was just a friend after all, nothing more. *Though perhaps you'd like him to be,* a treacherous voice whispered in her mind.

'There's just one table left, over in the corner. It's a bit of a squash, I'm afraid,' the waitress said, leading Bella to a table on the far side of the tea room. 'We're busy this afternoon. Can I get you something now or do you want to wait till your companion arrives?'

'I'll wait, thank you, he shouldn't be long.' Bella sat down at the table and took her book out of her bag to read while she waited. It would help pass the time and take her mind off the meeting, because for some odd reason she was feeling slightly nervous.

She was quickly engrossed in the book and didn't realise that James had arrived until she heard her name. 'Bella, it's good to see you again. What are you reading?'

'James, hello. Um, it's *A Room with a View.*' She held up the book for him to see. 'It's the last one of the books you recommended. I'm hoping you'll suggest some more for me to read. I–'

A polite cough from behind James interrupted her.

James looked slightly flustered as he stepped to the side and ushered a young woman forward.

'This is Daphne. She's only just started at Bletchley; her mother's a friend of my mother's.'

'I'm afraid I've tagged along with James. I hope you don't mind.' Daphne didn't wait for Bella to reply; she pulled out the other chair at the table and sat down, leaving James standing.

Of course she minded, Bella thought, but it would seem churlish to say so. 'No, not at all.'

'Splendid.' Daphne picked up the menu and started to read it.

James caught Bella's eye and mouthed, 'Sorry,' then said, 'Right, I'll find myself another chair,' and went to find the waitress.

'James has been terribly good, showing me around and helping me settle in,' Daphne said, looking at Bella over the top of the menu. 'We go back a long way; our families have been friends forever. James's mother asked him to look after me, and he has done, so wonderfully well.'

Bella smiled. 'It helps to know someone already when you start a new job.'

They fell into an uneasy silence, Bella uncomfortably aware of the way Daphne was looking down her straight nose at her hair and clothes, which she knew were far less grand than the other girl's expensive outfit and immaculately coiffured hair.

'Haven't they got another chair?' Daphne asked when James arrived back with a tall stool.

'Not at the moment; they're completely full and no chairs to be had.'

'Oh I feel awfully guilty now. If I hadn't tagged along, you'd have been sitting here. Take my chair and I can perch on that.' Daphne made a play of getting up.

'No, it's fine.' James sat down on the stool. 'So, what are we having? Tea? Sandwiches? Currant buns if they have them?'

Once they'd decided, and their order had been taken, Bella asked, 'Would you mind recommending some more of Connie's books for me to read, please, James? She's got so many, it's hard to know where to start. I really enjoyed the ones you suggested. *A Study in Scarlet* kept me guessing until the end.'

'Of course.' James thought for a moment. 'Try *A Passage to India*.' He took a notebook and pen out of his jacket pocket and started writing a list.

'Oh, let's not talk about stuffy old books,' Daphne said, patting her blonde waves. 'Tell me, Bella, how do you know James?'

'I work with Winnie and live in the same house.' She took the list James handed her with a smile and put it safely in her bag. 'Thank you, I look forward to reading those.'

'Winnie?' Daphne's arched eyebrows rose higher.

'My sister Margot,' James said. 'She's known as Winnie at the ambulance station on account of our surname.'

'Oh, I see.' Daphne gave a trilling laugh that sounded oddly forced.

'We're all known by nicknames or our surnames; no one gets called by their first name,' Bella explained.

'How quaint. So do you have a nickname?' Daphne asked.

'Bella's my nickname; it comes from my surname, Belmont.'

'Ah, here's our tea.' James got up and stood to the side to allow the waitress to offload her tray more easily in the tight corner.

'Shall I pour?' Daphne asked once the cups and plates had been sorted out.

'Go ahead,' Bella said, doing her best to remain polite when all she wanted to do was tell Daphne to leave. She'd only spent a few minutes in her company and that was more than enough; this meeting with James that she'd been so looking forward to was turning into a disaster. Why had he let Daphne barge in? Because he was kind and too polite to say no, Bella thought, part of the reason why she liked him so much.

'James told me that you're visiting your mother,' Daphne said.

Bella chewed the mouthful of sandwich she'd just taken and swallowed. 'Yes, she lives at Little Claydon; it's not far from here. She's the cook at Linden House.'

'A cook! How lovely.' Daphne smiled and took a sip of tea. 'Mother's cook is such a dear, works wonders with the rations. I believe she's given some tips to your mother's cook too, James. Mother always says she doesn't know where she'd be without her.'

'How's Stanley settling in?' James turned to Bella, changing the subject.

'Very well. He seems happy, and the other evacuees have taken him under their wing. I think he'll be fine there.'

James smiled. 'That's good. It can't be easy for children to be uprooted from all they know and sent away to live with strangers.'

'I hope your evacuees aren't like the ones my mother had, full of lice and with no idea how to use a knife and fork,' Daphne said. 'They didn't last long and went back to London, thank goodness.'

'Stanley is perfectly clean and very well mannered,' Bella said.

They fell into an awkward silence for a few minutes, each of them concentrating on eating and drinking, until Daphne laid a hand on James's arm. 'Would you mind awfully going and asking the waitress if she's got any mustard to go in this sandwich? It needs a little something to lift the taste.'

'Of course.' James stood up and went to find the waitress.

Daphne checked over her shoulder to see where he was and then leaned across the table towards Bella. 'If you believe that James is interested in spending time with you and...' she paused, narrowing her icy blue eyes, 'maybe more, you are very much mistaken. He told me he didn't want to come and is just doing it as a favour to his sister. He asked me to tag along to help keep you at a distance.'

Bella felt as if a bucket of water had been thrown over her. 'But—'

Daphne held up a hand to silence her, smiling sweetly. 'You can't possibly imagine that someone like you would interest a man like James. He comes from a good family, while you ... your mother's a servant.'

Bella had heard enough. 'And *I* was a

289

housemaid before the war.'

'There we are then.' Daphne raised one perfect eyebrow. 'The fact remains that James only came today out of pity...' She left the word hanging in the air. 'He's far too kind and polite to let you down. As a fellow woman, I felt duty-bound to tell you.'

Grabbing her coat and bag, Bella stood up and, without saying another word, made for the door, weaving her way between the tables, biting on her bottom lip to hold back the tears that were stinging her eyes. She heard James call her name but didn't look back as she threw the door open and rushed out into the cold air, shrugging herself into her coat as she hurried towards the station. If that was the way James really thought, then she'd been a fool to think otherwise.

'You will write, won't you?' Bella asked, walking fast to keep up with her brother's long strides as they headed for the railway station.

Walter looked at her and grinned. 'Course I will. I always do, don't I?'

'Yes, but not as often as we'd like. Mother and I worry if we don't hear from you for a while.'

'Sometimes there's not much to say that the censor wouldn't cross out.'

'Well if you're going abroad there'll be new things to write about, different weather and food, for example.'

Walter laughed, shifting the heavy kitbag that he had balanced on his shoulder. 'Yes, miss, I'll try harder, miss. You really missed your calling. You're the classic bossy teacher.'

'Very funny.' Bella nudged him in the ribs. 'And I would have been if...' She paused, not wanting to go over old ground that neither of them could change and spoil what little time she had left with him. 'Stop a minute, I want to ask you something.'

Walter obliged and put his kitbag down on the ground, leaning it against his legs. 'What's the matter?'

'Are you all right now...' She hesitated. Was it better to just leave it and assume everything was fine again? She'd been waiting for him to say something while he was at Linden House, but he'd carried on as if he'd never told her about it back in London. The image of him that day flashed into her mind; he'd seemed so sad and broken. She had to know. 'I mean about being in the army and not going AWOL.'

His brown eyes met hers and he nodded. 'Yes. When I first came out of hospital I'd had enough and thought I had to get away, but then I realised that I need to see this through and do my bit to stop those...' He sighed. 'Look what they're doing to London now, we've got no choice but to keep fighting or they'll be marching through the streets of our cities in no time.'

Bella grabbed hold of his arm. 'You will be careful, won't you?'

Walter grinned. 'They didn't finish me off at Dunkirk and I shan't give them another chance. Don't worry, I'm older and wiser and have the scars to prove it. You need to be careful yourself.'

'I always am,' Bella said.

'Then we'll both be fine, won't we?' He looked

291

at her, his eyes meeting hers. 'Look, why don't we say goodbye here and you go back to the house? I know you hate farewells.'

'I'm coming with you.' Bella felt tears smart behind her eyes. 'So don't dally or we'll miss the train.' She marched off in the direction of the station to give herself time to compose herself. Walter was right: she did hate saying goodbye, and this one would be especially difficult, as she had no idea when she would see her brother again. But there was no way she was going to miss spending these last precious minutes with him.

'Yes, miss,' Walter said, catching up with her. 'I'm glad you're coming to wave me off.'

Bella smiled at him and linked her arm through his. 'Me too. It's been lovely having you home, Walter, I'm glad our leaves coincided for once.' Whatever the future held, she would treasure the memories of the past two days, spending precious time with her mother and her beloved brother.

'It's still warm.' Stanley held the egg out for Bella to touch.

'That's very freshly laid.' Bella stroked the speckled brown egg with her finger. It was her last day at Linden House and she would be returning to London on a late-afternoon train, ready to re-port back to work tomorrow at Ambulance Station 75, where she knew Frankie would be eager for news about how Stanley was settling in. She'd come out into the garden to help him with his new job of looking after the hens, something he'd done back home in Stepney and had happily taken on here.

'Frankie's going to ask me if you're happy here when I see her tomorrow. What should I tell her, Stanley?'

He looked down at the egg in his hand, turning it over and over for a moment, and then returned his gaze to Bella's face and smiled. 'Tell her I like it 'ere, I like it very much, and that I'm 'appy.' He sighed. 'I do miss her and Grandad a lot, but being evacuated 'ere is a lot better than last time.'

Bella smiled back at him. 'You're quite sure, you're not just saying it?'

'I am 'appy, honest I am. Cross my 'eart.' He sketched a sign over his chest. 'Tell her not to worry about me. I'm safe 'ere.' He frowned. 'It's 'er and Grandad that need to be careful in the air raids.'

'They'll be fine, don't worry. They both know what to do when Moaning Minnie starts to wail. Frankie's always with me when we're out in our ambulance – we look after each other.'

Stanley picked another egg out of the nest box and added it to the others in the basket. 'Wouldn't you rather stay here instead of going back to London, Bella? I would if I was you.'

'Course I would, but it's my job and I love it. There are lots of people who need help from the ambulance service, and I want to do my bit for the war effort.' Bella sighed. 'I do wish I could come here more often, but I only get one week's holiday a year.'

'You should be a school teacher, then you'd get a long summer holiday.'

'I wanted to be one,' Bella said.

'So why didn't you?'

293

'My father died and I had to get a job in service. I had to give up my dream of being a teacher for a while, but I'm going to train to become one when the war's over.'

'My father died when I was very small and my mother died when I was six,' Stanley said matter-of-factly as he closed the lid on the nest box and picked up the basket of eggs ready to take it back to the house.

Bella's heart squeezed at the thought of what that must have been like for the little boy. She reached out and put her arm around his shoulders as they headed back to the house, walking through the walled garden where the Land Girls were busy working in the large vegetable plots.

'Is that when you moved in with Frankie's family?'

Stanley nodded. 'Gran was alive then; she was really kind and happy all the time. I miss her.'

Bella squeezed his shoulder. 'I know Frankie misses her too. But you've still got Frankie and your grandfather,' Bella said. 'And Ivy.'

Stanley looked up at her and pulled a face. 'I don't like Ivy.'

'You don't miss her like Frankie and your grandad then?'

'No. She's not very nice.'

'Are you going to tell me what's wrong, or are Trixie and I going to have to make you talk with a jolly good tickling?' Winnie asked as she bicycled along beside Bella on their way home from work. 'I should warn you I'm a very good tickler; James and Harry could never hold out for long when we were young.'

'Nothing's wrong.' Bella pressed harder on the pedals and sped up, leaving Winnie behind.

'Then I'm the Queen of Sheba,' Winnie shouted, pedalling faster to catch up. 'You haven't been yourself since you got back from leave last week. Look, why don't we stop and talk for a while?'

'There's nothing to talk about,' Bella snapped, wishing Winnie would leave her alone. All she wanted to do was get home and lose herself in a book, because books didn't pretend they were something they weren't.

'Well I disagree. Come on, we can sit on the steps of St Paul's and you can tell me what's up-setting you.'

'There's–' Bella began.

'Don't be so bloody stubborn, Bella! I only want to help you.'

Bella sighed. 'Very well, let's stop for a minute.'

Once they were settled on the wide stone steps in front of St Paul's, Winnie started again. 'Did something happen while you were away that's upset you?'

'My brother was home on embarkation leave, I've told you that already, and it was awful saying goodbye not knowing when he'll be back.'

'But that's not all, is it? You've lost the spark in your eyes since you came back, and I don't think it's just because your brother's gone away.' Winnie's grey eyes narrowed as she scanned Bella's face, as if looking for clues.

Bella sighed and closed her eyes for a moment. Then, opening them, she smiled at her friend. 'You're wasted in the ambulance service. The government should be using you to interrogate spies; you'd wear them down until they were begging to confess all.'

'And you're avoiding answering my question.'

'Very well, but if I tell you, then we'll go home and that will be an end to it. Right?'

Winnie nodded.

'I met James like I told you, but it wasn't how I'd hoped. He didn't come alone, he brought Daphne with him – her mother is a friend of your mother's, and she's just started working at Bletchley too.'

'Not Daphne!' Winnie pulled a face. 'What on earth was she doing there?'

Bella explained how Daphne had invited herself along and had then taken over.

'Sounds like her, she's awfully self-centred, but surely that's not enough to upset you, is it?'

'It's what she told me when James wasn't there,' Bella admitted. As she told her exactly what Daphne had said, Winnie's face clouded and her mouth set in a furious line.

'Right, let's get this straight. I can completely, one hundred per cent assure you that James did not invite you to tea as a favour to me. My brother only does what he wants to do; he asked you because he wanted to and for no other reason. It had nothing to do with me.' Winnie stopped to take a deep breath. 'If I could lay my hands on that scheming Daphne right now, I'd shake the silly false smile off her face.' She put her hand on Bella's arm. 'I think the truth of the matter is she wants James for herself and was scaring you off. Did you ask him if it was true?'

Bella shook her head. 'I just left.'

'And played right into Daphne's hands. I think you should ask him yourself.'

'I can't.' Bella blinked back sudden tears. 'If he wanted to see me he'd have written to me again, but his letters have stopped; I haven't heard from him since.'

Winnie tilted her head to one side for a moment. 'Of course, the way you rushed out, he might think it's *you* who doesn't want to see *him* any more, so perhaps he's feeling sorry for himself too.'

'But I *do* like him,' Bella blurted out, her cheeks growing warm.

'I know you do.' Winnie grinned. 'And now that you've admitted it, I'm going to have to step in, because if I don't, there's a chance the awful Daphne might sink her claws into him.' She stood up and held out her hand to pull Bella up. 'I'm going to telephone my dear brother when we get home.'

'What if he's not there?' Bella said. 'He works shifts like us.'

'Then I'll leave a message. One way or another, I'm going to sort you two out.'

'Is that so?' Winnie smiled at Bella, who sat at the bottom of the stairs, her chin in her hand, elbows on her knees, watching her friend speaking on the telephone in the hall of Connie's house. 'And since when was it safe to believe every word that awful Daphne tells you? Remember how she always cheated at cards and every other game she played.'

Hearing only one side of a conversation was painful. Bella's stomach was scrunched into a knot

297

as her mind raced through the possibilities of what Winnie's words could mean. What had Daphne said to James? Winnie had spent the past five minutes interrogating him after she'd been lucky enough to catch him at his lodgings before he left for the late shift at work.

'Right, well I'll hand you over to Bella now and you can sort it out between you. Goodbye.' Winnie held out the receiver.

'What did he say?' Bella whispered, taking hold of it.

'Just talk to him.' Winnie patted her on the shoulder and disappeared down the stairs to the kitchen with Trixie trotting behind.

Bella took a deep breath and put the receiver to her ear. 'Hello.'

'Bella!' James's voice came down the line. 'I truly did want to have tea with you, otherwise I wouldn't have asked you. Daphne lied.'

'So why did you suddenly stop writing to me?' Bella asked.

'Because she lied to me as well. She told me the reason you'd rushed off was because you didn't want any more to do with me and said that I shouldn't contact you again.' He sighed. 'It seems we've both been victims of her scheming. So can we meet again next time I'm in London?'

Bella smiled as the weight of sorrow that she'd carried around for the past week melted away. 'I'd love to, as long as you promise not to bring Daphne with you.'

'Don't worry, she's going nowhere with me ever again. I'm avoiding her like the plague. Thankfully we're working different shifts, and if I do spot her, I shoot off in the opposite direction.'

Bella laughed. 'Just go and hide in the library, she'll never look in there.'

'Good idea. Look, I'm going to have to go, I'm due on shift soon. Write to me, won't you, and I promise I'll write too.'

'Of course I will,' Bella said. 'Goodbye.'

Putting the receiver down with a wide smile on her face, she turned and headed for the stairs, only to stop at the sight of Winnie and Trixie peeping around the kitchen door at her.

'I'm glad to see you smiling again,' Winnie said. 'Now do you believe that James genuinely wanted to see you?'

Bella nodded. 'Thank you for interfering and interrogating. If you hadn't, we'd both have gone on believing Daphne's lies.'

'And that would have been a terrible waste, because you understand James so well. You're a couple of bookworms and are made for each other.'

'And what about you?' Bella asked. 'Who's made for you?'

'Me?' Winnie shrugged. 'Who would put up with me, and more to the point, who could I put up with?'

'Are you sure you're warm enough?' Winnie could feel the icy fingers of the cold December air stroking the back of her neck where she hadn't tucked her scarf in properly.

'I'm absolutely fine. Will you stop fussing; you're like a mother hen,' Harry said. 'I assure you that I'll tell you when I need to go back.'

Winnie gave her brother a hard stare. 'You've been indoors for weeks and you're not used to being outside. It's especially cold today, so you're bound to feel the difference after the warmth of the hospital.'

'Stop fussing!' Harry snapped. 'I'm glad to be outside again, so please just let me enjoy it without you harping on as if I was some precious baby who needed wrapping up.'

Winnie grinned and brought a mittened hand up to her brow in a salute. 'Yes, sir, I've got the message, sir, loud and clear. So how does it feel to be outside again, sir?'

Harry smiled, the taut, shiny skin on his face stretching as far as it could. 'Absolutely bloody marvellous.' He stopped walking and breathed in slowly. 'Smell that air! It's so fresh, no carbolic here, and I can feel the wind on my face ... and hear the sparrows twittering.' He looked at her, but Winnie couldn't see his eyes behind the dark glasses that Matron had insisted he wore. 'I feel like I've stepped back into the real world again.'

'It's not the best world to come back into, with London still being blasted to bits day and night. Come on, let's keep going. I'm feeling the cold even if you aren't.' Winnie linked her hand gently through Harry's undamaged elbow, and they continued their stroll around Ravenscroft Park, which wasn't far from the hospital.

'It's a shock seeing the bomb damage,' Harry said. 'I've heard plenty of bombs screaming down during raids, but actually being out here and seeing what they've done for myself makes my blood boil.'

300

'You should see what they've done to the East End then; there's whole streets gone.'

'That's why we've got to keep bombing the blighters back.' He sighed. 'I wish I could get up there again and feel like I'm doing something.'

'Don't you think you've already done your share?'

'And I intend to do more when they let me go.'

'You want to fly again?'

'Of course!' Harry paused and turned to face Winnie. 'I need to ask you something. Don't go getting on your high horse, only I promised Mother I'd talk to you about it.'

Winnie instantly bristled. 'Ah, so she's starting a new strategy, is she, using you to try and get at me?'

'Look, she asked me to try and make you see sense and accept that driving job Father found for you. You'd still be doing something for the war effort but you'd be out of direct danger. She and Father have been through enough worrying with me.'

'What would you have done if they'd asked you to stop flying?' Winnie kept her voice calm; after all, Harry was just the messenger.

'Well, I'd have said no, of course.'

'Exactly! So why should it be any different for me? My job isn't as dangerous as yours; I don't go after the enemy in a little plane thousands of feet up in the air. I'm not...' She paused to take a breath and calm the rising tide of fury that was building up inside her. 'I don't want to argue with you, and I know you're only being a dutiful son and doing as Mother asked, but I am *not*

301

going to leave the ambulance service just because they want me to move to a safer job.'

Harry started to laugh. 'You should see your face. As a matter of fact, I think you're quite right to stick to your guns over this.'

'You do?'

'Of course. I needed to test your devotion to the job for myself and check you weren't refusing to leave just to annoy Mother.'

'Very funny. If you weren't recovering from injuries, I'd be tempted to give you a jolly hard whack.'

Two women passing by overheard her and gave Winnie a hard stare.

'Watch out, or they might report you to a policeman for threatening a wounded pilot,' Harry teased.

'You might be wounded, but there's nothing wrong with your mind or your tongue; they're just as sharp as they always were.'

'Why thank you, kind miss.' Harry bowed his head. Then, looking directly at her, he added, 'And thank you for being the same with me, for not pussyfooting around like some.'

'What did you expect? You know I'm not the most patient person in the world.' Winnie took hold of his elbow again. 'Thank you for understanding why I want to keep working as an ambulance driver. I just wish that Mother would finally accept my choice and leave me to get on with it.'

Chapter Ten

'Do you want me to set the table in the dining room?' Bella asked as she peeled potatoes beside Connie at the large sink in the kitchen.

'No, it's much nicer to eat down here, more cosy and comfortable, don't you think?' Connie said. 'We want to enjoy today and not be rushing up and down the stairs carrying food.'

'Shall I polish the silverware to use?'

Connie plopped the potato she'd just finished into the pan of cold water and looked at Bella, frowning. 'Do you *like* polishing silver?'

Bella shook her head. 'Hate it.'

'So do I, so why ever would we want to give ourselves that tedious job to do? My nanny used to send me down to help polish the silver when I'd been naughty, so I have no desire to do it at all. Our everyday knives and forks are perfectly acceptable.'

Bella laughed.

'What's the matter?'

'If you don't mind me saying, Connie, you are quite unique in ladies of your class. None of the others I've met would have dreamed of eating their Christmas dinner in the kitchen, or not using the best silverware and crystal with everything set out just so.'

'Precisely. I'm sure they've never had to do any of the work that goes into having it that way; if they did, they might change their minds and realise there are plenty of other things they'd rather do with their time.' Connie paused and smiled at Bella. 'I'm so glad you feel at home with us. You do, don't you?'

'Yes, I do. Thank you for letting me stay here. I wasn't sure at first because of ... well, I used to work in a house like this, but it only looks similar, it doesn't *feel* the same; you and Winnie aren't the same.'

'Winnie and I are, you could say, the black sheep of our family. We don't do what is considered the correct thing. Winnie's parents, on the other hand, do, and she has struggled terribly with them over what she wants and what they consider appropriate.'

'She doesn't give in, though.'

'No, she doesn't, and I'm proud of her.' Connie sniffed. 'Oh, that turkey smells delicious. I shall write to your mother this afternoon and thank her for her most generous gift. It's going to make our Christmas meal one to remember.'

'Food's not so hard to come by in the countryside, and they raised quite a few turkeys this year for Christmas.' Bella's mother had sent a hamper for them by train, with a turkey and vegetables, all raised and grown at Linden House, to enjoy for their Christmas meal.

'I was hoping James would be able to be here today; it would have been lovely for you too,' Connie said, deftly peeling another potato.

Bella's cheeks grew warm. 'He's got to work a shift so he couldn't come. He said in his last letter that he's hoping to get to London soon, though.'

'I'm glad the two of you are getting along so well. He's a lovely young man and deserves a sweet, kind girl like you rather than those monstrous types that his mother is always pushing at him – you know the sort I mean.'

'Oh yes.' Bella had told Connie all about the incident with Daphne at the tea room. 'We've sorted out that misunderstanding now. I do enjoy writing to him and getting his letters.'

'I'm happy for you both. I wish Winnie would find someone who is as good a match.'

'You mustn't try and push her into anything.'

'I wouldn't dream of it; knowing Winnie, she would do the opposite. She's like me.'

'So if her parents forbade her to like Charles Hulme... They've missed a trick there.' Bella plopped another peeled potato into the pan.

'I'm not sure about that. He's so awful, Winnie would never want to marry him, even if it was the opposite of her parents' wishes. It's funny, they only try to organise Winnie and James's lives, never Harry's.'

'Why's that?'

'He wouldn't stand for it.'

Bella hadn't yet met Harry, but she soon would, as he was coming to the house for Christmas dinner. Winnie had gone to the hospital to fetch him.

'Shall I cut your food up for you?' Bella asked.

'If you'd be so kind, that would be splendid.' Harry smiled at her as best he could; the reddened, shiny skin on his burnt face was like a mask, and didn't move in the same way as it would

305

once have done. 'I can manage to feed myself once it's chopped up.'

Bella had been shocked at first when Harry had arrived at the house. Although his face and hands had healed, the scarring was plain to see, and he looked so different from the handsome pilot in the photograph that stood on Connie's grand piano, with his features now blunted by fire and his grey eyes left vulnerable-looking where the eyelids had shrunk back.

She quickly cut up the turkey breast and vegetables for him, making sure they were bite-size pieces that he'd be able to spear with his fork. 'There we are.'

'Thank you very much.' Harry bowed his head to her and then tucked in.

'You've missed your calling, Bella, you should have been a nurse,' Winnie said, grinning at her from her place on the opposite side of the kitchen table.

'Which is something that could never be said about you, old girl,' Harry said.

'I know.' Winnie smiled at him. 'I simply wouldn't have the patience.'

'This is quite delicious,' Harry said. 'Best meal I've had in a long time. Thank you for inviting me here today, Connie. Mother would have had me go home to Oxford, but I didn't want to put up with her fussing over me.'

'Do you know when you're going to have your operation to give you some new eyelids?' Connie asked.

'Soon, I hope. It'll be wonderful to be able to close them again. We're just waiting for the skin to soften up around my eyes, and then I'll go to the hospital in East Grinstead ready for Mr McIndoe, the surgeon, to work his magic,' Harry explained. 'Sometime early in the new year, I hope.'

'Where are they going to get the new eyelids from?' Bella asked.

'From my arm, apparently.' Harry speared a piece of roast potato on his fork. 'Clever, eh?'

'Has the surgeon told you when you can fly again?' Winnie asked.

Harry put his fork down and stared down at his plate for a moment before looking up. 'I don't know if I will be able to with these hands.' He sighed. 'I did ask Mr McIndoe about it, and he said in the next war perhaps.'

'But you love flying, don't you?' Bella said, and then put her hand over her mouth. 'I'm sorry, I shouldn't have said that.'

Harry looked her straight in the eye. 'Course you should; it's the truth, so there's no use pussy-footing around it. I do love flying, Bella, but what's happened has changed things, and although I don't like it, I am very grateful to still be here, to be alive, because many of my friends didn't get that chance.' He smiled at her as best he could and nudged her arm with his elbow. 'I'm one of the lucky ones. I'm still here to celebrate Christmas, and many more to come, I hope.'

Connie held up her glass of wine. 'A toast then: to Christmas, and many more to come.'

Bella noticed that Harry was struggling to get a firm grip on his glass. Gently she covered his hand with hers, helping him to steady and raise it.

'To Christmas,' they chorused, clinking glasses.

Frankie stared at the empty chair across the table, wondering what Stanley was doing at that very moment. Was he eating his Christmas dinner? Perhaps he'd be wearing a hat made out of newspaper, and the table might be decorated with red-berried holly from the grounds of Linden House. She hoped he was having a good time.

'It don't feel right without 'im,' Grandad said, nodding towards Stanley's place as he speared a piece of homegrown carrot with his fork.

Frankie looked at him and shook her head. 'I know, but at least he's safe where he is.' She had sent Stanley a parcel with a pair of socks she'd knitted for him, some chocolate and a wooden toy aeroplane that Grandad had made. It wasn't the same as being with him, but it was the best she could do; there was no chance of going to see him today, as she was due back on duty at half past three this afternoon.

'Look at you, right miserable pair. Don't forget, you're the ones that sent 'im away,' Ivy said, her words slightly slurred. She'd been knocking back sherry from the bottle that Frankie's grandfather had given her as a gift. 'If it was up to me, 'e'd still be 'ere. The bombing might 'ave stopped now; there weren't any last night.'

'But that doesn't mean they won't come back,' Frankie said. 'Stanley's mother trusted us to look after her son, and that's why we 'ad to send 'im away, even if it means we miss 'im.'

'So stop moaning then; it ain't goin' to help,' Ivy said. 'Gawd, it's as if he'd died, the way you

308

two are carrying on.'

'Ivy!' Grandad said firmly. 'We miss the boy, that's all.'

Ivy looked at him, her eyes narrowed. 'Well you've still got me, 'aven't you? I ain't goin' nowhere.'

'I know. You'd never leave,' Grandad replied, his face unreadable.

Did he wish Ivy *would* leave? Frankie wondered as she cut up a piece of rabbit meat. But she knew he believed strongly in his wedding vows and would stick to them no matter how much of a disappointment his marriage might be proving to be. Ivy would never leave of her own accord. She was well settled in, clinging on like her namesake plant, knowing that she was on to a good thing: a nice home, a husband who earned a decent wage and who was tolerant of her.

She hadn't changed her ways since Stanley was evacuated. Her claims that she'd do some voluntary work to help the war effort had come to nothing. Every time Frankie or her grandfather suggested something, Ivy always managed to come up with an excuse, and so far had avoided doing anything. Even making the Christmas dinner. Frankie had done that, cooking the rabbit a friend of Grandad's had reared, along with home-grown veg from the garden. As Christmas dinners went, it wasn't too bad, but there was no plum pudding and custard for afters as there had been in previous years; no crackers, no fruit cake with icing. The war had changed Christmas, and not for the better.

'Oh Frankie! It's beautiful. Thank you so much.' Winnie enveloped Frankie in a tight hug. 'It must have taken you simply ages to embroider all the flowers. I shall be the talk of London wearing this.'

'You're welcome.' Frankie watched as Winnie fitted the cover that she'd made her over the brown cardboard gas-mask box and then slung the string over her shoulder and paraded up and down the staffroom like a fashion model.

'What do you think, Mac? Does it suit me?' Winnie called over to where he was standing on a chair stringing up some more paper chains that they'd made from newspaper the previous day.

Mac grinned at her. 'Absolutely.'

'Come on, Bella, get yours on too, and we can make a show of it,' Winnie said.

'Oh I don't know.' Bella had been just as delighted with the cover that Frankie had made for her, and had quickly fitted it, admiring the intricate embroidery, tracing the delicate work with her fingers. 'I don't have the same, umm...' she began.

'Show-offiness,' Sparky suggested from his armchair, where he sat with Trixie on his lap.

'Are you suggesting I'm a show-off, Sparky?' Winnie said, hands on hips, her pillar-box-red lips in a pout that quickly dissolved into a wide smile.

'Well I'd never class you as a shrinking violet, that's for sure,' Sparky retorted.

'Now, now, 'tis the season of goodwill to all men and women.' Station Officer Steele came over carrying a plate of fruit cake and offered it around.

310

'It's Christmas, and God willing the bombers will leave us alone again tonight. I made this cake as a present to you all, so eat up and then we'll have a good sing-song around the piano.'

'Do you really think they'll leave us alone?' Bella asked.

'Who knows? Maybe they do have some Christmas spirit after all, and they'll halt the fighting just for today, like they did in the trenches. We'll keep hoping and enjoying ourselves while we can.'

'This is very nice, thank you,' Sparky said, sampling a bite of the boss's cake. 'I didn't know you were such a good cook.'

'There's a lot you don't know about me,' Station Officer Steele said, smiling broadly. 'Cooking is just one of my many talents.'

'Watch out, or Sparky'll be suggesting you're showing off,' Mac said, perching on the arm of Bella's chair while he ate his slice of cake.

'Where'd you get all the fruit for this?' Winnie asked as she helped herself to a piece. 'It's not made with black market goods, is it?'

'Certainly not! I've been saving my rations for months. Any more remarks from any of you and I'll keep the rest for myself.' Station Officer Steele looked stern, and then her face broke into a smile. 'So who's for a sing-song?'

'Go on then.' Sparky stood up and put Trixie back down on the chair, then followed the boss over to the piano in the corner of the room. 'Do you know "Leaning on a Lamp-post"?'

'I certainly do, it's one of my brother's favourites.' Station Officer Steele sat down at the piano, and everyone turned their attention to her and Sparky as they launched into the song. Frankie was surprised to hear that Sparky had a good strong voice that could easily have graced the stage in the West End.

Working a shift on Christmas Day was turning out to be much more fun than Frankie had expected. The staffroom had been decked out and looked very festive. Sparky had managed to find a Christmas tree from somewhere, and Station Officer Steele had brought in decorations from home, saying that no one else but her would see them if she put them up in her flat, so the tree glinted prettily with glass baubles and dainty wooden figures. The crews had got into the Christmas spirit and made decorations out of newspaper; snowflakes had been cut out and stuck on the windows with flour-and-water paste, paper chains and Chinese lanterns made, and a whole army of paper dolls strung up hand in hand around the room. Everyone had made good use of the extra time when Christmas Eve had produced no air raids and there'd been no incidents to attend.

As soon as Sparky's voice faded at the end of the song, the room erupted with loud applause and cheers in appreciation of his singing. Looking slightly flushed, he bowed deeply and extended his hand to include Station Officer Steele, who stood and curtsied, her cheeks flushing pink.

'Encore!' Mac shouted, standing up and moving closer to the piano. The rest of them followed and stood around in a semicircle listening as Sparky began to sing 'When I'm Cleaning Windows'.

Frankie stood arm in arm with Winnie and

Bella, swaying gently to the music and enjoying every moment. She was pleased that her dear friends had been delighted with the covers she'd sewn for their gas-mask boxes. There was so little in the shops these days that making a gift was the best option. She'd made covers for Alistair and Mac as well, only she'd left theirs plain and un-embroidered. Bella had been busy too, and had given her and Winnie a pair of knitted mittens and a scarf each, while Winnie had presented her friends with lipsticks. Frankie was going to ration hers carefully, because there was no knowing when she'd be able to get another one.

'Come on, join in,' Sparky shouted.

Everyone did as they were told, singing the words they knew and humming along to any bits they didn't. After that, they moved on to carols, until their throats were parched and some tea was needed to revive them. All the while, the air-raid siren was silent, the telephone didn't ring and Christmas Day remained a time of peace and quiet with no bombs raining down out of the sky.

Bella leaned back in the armchair and closed her eyes, letting the images in her mind grow as she listened to the voices coming out of the wireless. The Ghost of Christmas Present was urging Scrooge to change his grasping ways, and she could picture his face as he fought against his natural miserly instinct. She was as entranced by the story tonight as the first time she'd heard it, when her father had read it to her as a child, but this dramatisation of the Victorian tale seemed all the more poignant now, with the country at war.

She opened her eyes and glanced around the room, where everyone was listening quietly. It didn't matter that *A Christmas Carol* was being broadcast to the nation on the Children's Hour programme of the Home Service; the story was suitable for any age. Some people were knitting or sewing as they listened; others just sat drinking tea. Even Sparky had sat down, and looked relaxed and quiet for once.

There was an air of contentment in the room, Bella was glad to be here among people she liked and trusted, people she'd been through hard times with, people who had supported her and who she in turn had supported. Working here had brought her a sense that she was doing something important, far more worthwhile than being a housemaid. She had made friends and found a new home. The war might still be raging on, but for these few hours it felt as if Station 75 and all those in it were cocooned in a safe, comfortable bubble, with time to rest and enjoy the pleasures of Christmas.

Frankie pulled her ambulance service cap down lower over her ears as she stepped outside into the cold, crisp air, ready to take her turn at picket duty. Christmas Day or not, they still had to keep up a continuous guard during the hours of darkness to stop anyone pilfering petrol from the open garages, where the ambulances stood ready to go to emergency call-outs.

'The cold's woken me up,' Winnie said behind her. 'I was getting a bit sleepy up there in the warmth.'

'We're not used to sitting about on duty these days,' Frankie said. 'Are you sure you want to come out here when it's not your turn?'

'I needed some fresh air and Trixie can have a run around.' Winnie linked her arm through Frankie's as the little dog darted about sniffing at smells. 'I can keep you company too.'

'At last,' Hooky's voice called from within the garage. 'I'd begun to think no one was coming to take over.'

Winnie shone the faint beam of her torch inside the garage and saw Hooky sitting huddled up in one of the deckchairs.

'I'm not late,' Frankie said. 'It's exactly 'alf past seven.'

Hooky struggled out of the deckchair and stood up. 'I'm freezing out here.'

'If you kept moving around rather than sitting down, you wouldn't get so cold,' Winnie said.

'I hate picket duty,' Hooky grumbled, walking past them.

'Well we all have to do our bit,' Winnie said crisply. 'In you go and have a cup of hot cocoa, that'll soon warm you up.'

'It'll take more than a cup of cocoa...' Hooky threw back over her shoulder as she opened the door and went in, letting it slam shut behind her.

'She's tip-top and full to the brim of Christmas cheer.' Winnie giggled. 'I shouldn't say that, but she rubs me up the wrong way sometimes.'

'Takes all sorts to crew an ambulance station,' Frankie said. 'You know, I'd never met anyone like you before I came 'ere.'

'Was I so awful? I still feel terribly guilty about

315

squirting you with water that first day.' Winnie burst into laughter. 'Your face was such a picture.'

'I didn't expect to get a soaking, did I? And you looked a sight too; you went white with shock.' Frankie started to laugh as well. 'And the boss must 'ave been watching what you were up to; remember how she gave you a right old telling-off?'

When she'd managed to stop laughing, Winnie asked, 'Are you glad you came here, Frankie? Are you happy?'

'Yes, I am. I love it – being with everyone and doing a job that 'elps people. It beats sewing uniforms any day.'

'I love it too. It scares me sometimes being out in air raids, but there's nothing else I'd rather do.' Winnie squeezed Frankie's arm. 'How was Christmas at your house?'

'Not the same without Stanley. We muddled through. Ivy had too much sherry and let her tongue run away with her. I was glad to come to work, if I'm honest.'

'Hopefully Stanley will be home next Christmas.'

'As long as he's safe, that's what matters. We ain't the only ones who missed someone this Christmas, so it's no good feeling sorry for ourselves. There are plenty of people worse off than us.'

'You are good and kind, Frankie. I'm afraid I was glad that some of my family weren't there today. Luckily my parents stayed at home, so I didn't have to mind my ps and qs. Aren't I awful?'

Frankie nudged her. 'No, just honest.'

Trixie suddenly started to bark, making them both jump.

'Trixie, what's the matter?' Winnie asked.

'Call your dog off, we come in peace,' a Scottish voice shouted.

Winnie shone her torch outside the garage and saw two familiar figures walking towards them. Trixie launched herself at them, jumping up and down and wagging her tail.

'Alistair!' Frankie said, rushing to meet him. 'What are you doing here?'

'I've come to see you. Merry Christmas, Frankie!' He flung his arms around her and lifted her off her feet, swinging her round.

'I'm not going to do that to you, Winnie. I'd probably put my back out,' the other man said.

'Very funny, James,' Winnie replied. 'I thought you were working today?'

James bent down and stroked Trixie's head. 'I was, but I decided to get the train into London after I'd finished. Thought I'd come here to see you ... and Bella.'

'Ah, Bella more than your darling sister, I suspect.' Winnie linked her arm in his. 'Come on, I'll take you to her; she'll be delighted to see you. Will you be all right out here, Frankie?'

Frankie laughed. 'Perfectly, Winnie, thank you. I think this picket duty is goin' to be one of the nicest I've done.'

'So,' Alistair said when Winnie had led James inside, 'have you had a good Christmas Day?'

'Not bad, and it just got much better, actually.' Frankie leaned her head against his chest. 'Aren't you tired after your shift?'

'A bit, but being with you makes me feel a whole lot better.'

317

'Did you know James was coming 'ere?'

Alistair shook his head. 'No, we happened to meet outside in the street. I've got something for you… Wait there a moment.'

Frankie waited while Alistair went towards the archway that led to the street, returning a few moments later pushing his bicycle.

'Merry Christmas.' He rang the bicycle bell. 'I hope this makes getting around easier for you, and when the spring comes, we can go on long rides out to the countryside, find some bracken to show you.'

'Are you giving me your bicycle?' Frankie asked.

'No. I've bought you one of your own.'

'For me?'

'Yes, for you.'

Frankie was stunned. 'I… Thank you, thank you, Alistair. It's such a generous present.'

'My pleasure. I'm glad you like it.'

'I do, but there's just one thing. I don't know how to ride a bicycle; I've never 'ad one, you see.'

'Well now you have, and I'm sure you'll easily learn. I'll help you.'

'Now?'

'It's a bit dark; you really need to see where you're going. We could practise tomorrow before your shift. I've got the day off.'

'It's a date then.' Frankie threw her arms around him and kissed him.

'There's Orion.' Bella pointed to the constellation hanging in the inky blackness high up over London. She and James were lying on their backs, well wrapped up in coats, scarves and hats, on the flat roof of Station 75.

'And Ursa Major and Minor,' James joined in.

'One good thing about the war is you can now see the stars over London. I really missed seeing them properly when I moved here; it was as if they'd been snuffed out.'

'Do you think the bombers will come tonight?' James asked.

'I hope not. They're usually here by now if they do come. It wouldn't be right to go and bomb people today, would it?'

'No, but I'm not sure that would stop them if they really wanted to.'

'Let's not talk about that now; we should make the most of this time,' Bella said. 'I'm really glad you came tonight.'

James reached out for Bella's mittened hand and squeezed it. 'Me too. I didn't know if I'd be able to get away, so I didn't write and tell you beforehand just in case I couldn't. I was on early shift and managed to get a train into London after that, and came straight here.'

'Weren't there any celebrations going on at your work?' Bella asked.

'Some, but I didn't want to join in. I wanted to come and see you more.'

'Didn't the delightful Daphne want you to be with her?'

'Oh don't,' James groaned. 'If I see her coming, I go the opposite way. Luckily she seems to be working a different shift pattern, so I've hardly seen her since she barged her way into our afternoon tea. Hopefully she's sunk her claws into

319

someone else now.'

'She certainly has a way about her, doesn't she?' Bella said. 'She should be trained up as a secret agent and used against the Nazis.'

'I think they'd send her back pretty quick.' James sat up and pulled Bella up with him, putting his arm around her shoulders. 'Let's not talk about her and waste this precious time we've got together.'

Bella leaned her head against his shoulder. 'You coming to see me is the best Christmas present I could have had.'

'You won't want this then?' James said, pulling something out of his pocket and putting it in Bella's hand.

'What is it? It's too dark to see,' Bella said, patting it with her mittened hands. 'Ah, it feels book-shaped to me.'

'Sherlock Holmes has nothing on you,' James said. 'It is indeed a book.'

'Which one?'

'I've just given you a clue; work it out.'

'One of Arthur Conan Doyle's Sherlock Holmes stories?' Bella suggested.

'Perhaps.' James laughed. 'I hope you enjoy it.'

'Thank you.' Bella kissed his cheek. 'I will love it all the more because you bought it for me.'

'Likewise my scarf and mittens, because you made them for me,' James said.

Bella nudged him and laughed, glad that he'd liked the woollen comforts she'd made and posted to him. 'Merry Christmas, James.'

'Penny for them?' Winnie looked up at Mac, who

stood in front of her holding out a cup of cocoa. 'You looked like you had the cares of the world on your shoulders.'

Winnie smiled at him and took the cup. 'No, just a niggling problem.'

Mac sat down in the armchair next to hers. 'Anything I can help with?'

Winnie took a sip of cocoa and looked around at the other crew members in the common room. Some had migrated over to the piano and were having another sing-song; others were involved in a rowdy game of cards, playing for matchsticks. There was no one nearby to hear her if she did confess what was weighing on her mind, and Mac was kind, always a good person to talk to. It might help her to see things more clearly.

'I ... I'm wondering if I should leave the ambulance service.' She looked down at Trixie, curled up asleep on her lap, and ran her fingers over her silky smooth ears.

'Leave? But why?' Mac asked quietly.

'Because of what happened to Harry. It's been a struggle for my parents, and as much as I've fought against doing what they want me to, perhaps it's time I did do something less in the firing line. For their sakes, not mine. If it was just me to take into consideration, then I'd be here till the bitter end, however that turns out.'

Mac frowned. 'That's a hard choice.'

'They played their trump card getting Harry to ask me. I said no the first time, but he asked again today because my mother's been badgering him about it, and it's getting harder to say no. I wonder if I'm just digging my heels in to be stubborn and

321

I should do the right thing to stop them worrying so much.'

'If it's any help, I have doubts about whether I should be here, too.'

'Because of being a CO, you mean?'

'No, I wonder if I should be doing more. I'm thinking about joining the Royal Army Medical Corps; doing something at the front line but not actually fighting.'

'No!' Winnie's stomach lurched at the thought of Mac leaving. 'You can't.'

Mac raised his eyebrows. 'Why not?'

Winnie's face grew warm. 'Because I'd miss you. I don't want you to leave, Mac.'

His eyes held hers for a moment. 'I'd miss you too, Winnie, but it gnaws away at me sometimes that I'm not doing enough.'

'I'd call going out in the middle of a raid doing plenty; you risk your life every time you go out. We never know for sure that we're going to come back.'

'I know, but–'

'And there's a need for you here as much as in the army. You're helping ordinary people who're being injured. They need people like you.'

Mac grinned. 'And you too.'

Winnie sighed. 'That's just it, Mac. We're doing an important job and it's not easy for any of us. It's as scary as hell sometimes and we see awful things, people blown to bits and children made orphans. We've got to keep on, we mustn't give up.'

'Then don't,' Mac said. 'If you're as passionate about this job as you sound, then don't even think about giving it up to suit anyone other than your-self. Parents always worry about their children; it goes with the job. Yours should be proud of you.'

Sudden tears smarted in Winnie's eyes and she blinked them away. 'I'm not sure proud is a word that my parents would ever use about me. I've always been too loud, too silly, too naughty for them.'

'Sounds like they want the impossible. You are who you are, Winnie, and I know you do a brilliant job. You're a good driver and a great member of this ambulance station. Station Officer Steele certainly thinks so.'

'Does she?'

'Of course she does. Promise me you'll talk to me again before you decide anything.'

'Only if you do the same,' Winnie said.

Mac considered for a moment. 'Very well then.' He held up his mug of cocoa and bumped it gently against Winnie's. 'We have a deal.'

'Keep looking ahead and pedalling – not too fast, mind.' Alistair stood behind Frankie holding on to the back of her bicycle saddle. 'I'll hold on and run after you.'

'Don't let go,' Frankie said, her foot poised ready to press down on the raised pedal.

They'd come to Tower Gardens, a short distance from Ambulance Station 75, so that Frankie could learn to ride the bicycle Alistair had bought her for Christmas. She'd felt very wobbly to begin with and had kept putting her foot down to stop herself falling, even though Alistair was holding her up. But she was gradually getting better, growing in confidence and keeping more upright.

'Ready, one, two, three.' She pushed off against the ground with one foot at the same time as pressing down on the raised pedal. 'Keep holding me.'

'Don't worry, I am.'

She gripped tightly to the handlebars, conscious of keeping her legs going round and round on the pedals and all the while trying to balance on two thin wheels.

'You're doing well,' Alistair called, running behind her. 'Keep going. Go a bit faster; it's easier to keep your balance than if you're going slowly.'

Frankie pressed harder and started to enjoy herself. It was different from driving. She had more control of the motion, she was the one making the bicycle move; it wasn't just pressing down on a pedal as she did in an ambulance to fire more fuel into the engine. She liked the feeling of bowling along with the cold winter air nipping at her ears. Her legs were pumping a rhythm and it felt good.

Coming to the end of the path, she braked and stopped, putting her foot down and turning to speak to Alistair, but he wasn't there. He was further down the path, walking towards her with a huge smile on his face.

'You did it, Frankie!' he called.

'You said you wouldn't let go.'

'Well you didn't need me to hold on any longer. You can ride a bike now; you don't need me running along behind. When we go out bicycling together from now on, I'll be riding beside you. Try it again on your own.'

Frankie turned the bicycle around and took a

deep breath. She could do this. As she pushed off again, she was aware that Alistair wasn't holding on, but then he hadn't been before and she had done it on her own. She picked up speed, a sense of exhilaration filling her. This was going to make so much difference to her life. She could bicycle into work and wouldn't have to rely on delayed or cancelled buses any more.

Chapter Eleven

'Where are we going?' Winnie asked as Mac climbed into the passenger seat.

'Queen Victoria Street.' Mac slammed the ambulance door shut and settled Trixie on his lap as Winnie put the ambulance into gear and pulled away, carefully steering around Sparky, who was efficiently dealing with yet another incendiary bomb that had landed in the courtyard in front of Station 75, smothering it with a bucket of sand. The small bombs, with their menacing potential to start destructive fires, had been raining out of the sky tonight, and Station Officer Steele's strict adherence to having fire watchers on duty had no doubt saved the station from catching light.

Hooky had a shoulder injury, preventing her from carrying stretchers, so she'd been put on fire-watch duty up on the flat roof of the station, and Mac had been drafted in as Winnie's partner for the shift, which she was quite happy about. On a night like this, having a decent partner by your side made life so much easier.

Out on the road, Winnie had to keep alert, ready to swerve around any incendiary bombs landing in front of her. They would burst into flame, burning brightly with a green magnesium fire and clouds of white smoke.

'There's more fire hose up ahead,' Mac warned her, pointing to a tangle of intestine-like hose wriggling across the road.

'At least we can see where we're going for once; it's nearly as bright as day.' Winnie slowed the ambulance and bumped it over the hose. So many fires were alight in the City of London that the blackout was pointless; the streets were lit up from burning buildings and the clouds above reflected the flames in a rose-pink glow.

A loud explosion from the next street made them both wince. 'I'll never get used to this,' Winnie said.

'Do you want me to drive?' Mac asked.

'Certainly not! I can manage perfectly well, thank you very much.' She glanced at him quickly before returning her attention to the road. 'I'm sorry, I didn't mean to snap. Bombs exploding nearby unnerve me sometimes. It's been quite a shift so far.' This was their third call-out since the air-raid siren had gone a little after six o'clock.

'There's nothing to forgive. We all get jumpy at times. Anyone who says they've never been scared out in a raid is a liar.'

The journey along Cannon Street down into Queen Victoria Street was difficult, as Winnie had to weave the ambulance past several large fires raging in the warehouses lining the street, squeezing around fire engines while smoke and embers swirled in the air.

'There they are.' Mac pointed to a policeman waving to them from further down the street, signalling where they should stop. But before they could reach him, a small river of liquid from a burning warehouse escaped and poured out across the street in front of them. It was caught by an ember and quickly went up in a sheet of flame, blocking their way. Winnie braked hard.

'Bloody hell! What's that?' She slumped back against her seat.

'I don't know, but it burns well whatever it is.'

'Now what do we do?'

'Could we go round by Upper Thames Street?' Mac suggested.

'That'll take ages, and it could be blocked anyway.' Winnie chewed on her bottom lip. 'Or we could go through it; it's not far.' She looked at Mac. 'What do you think?'

'If we're quick, we'd be through in a moment. I say go for it, if you're willing.'

Winnie nodded. 'Hold on tight to Trixie.' She put the ambulance in reverse and went backwards for a few yards to give them time to pick up speed. 'Ready?' She reached across and stroked Trixie's head, then looked at Mac.

He nodded.

Taking a deep breath, Winnie hovered her foot over the accelerator. As she did so, an image of her brother lying in his hospital bed, burnt and in pain, came into her head. No, she told herself, this isn't like what happened to Harry. They'd be through it in a moment and it would be fine. She hoped.

'Hold on.' She pressed her foot to the accelerator and they shot forward, the yards between them and the sheet of flame eaten up in seconds, until there was no room for doubt or changing her mind. Then they were on it, and through.

Pressing the brake pedal and coming to a halt near the astonished-looking policeman, Winnie suddenly started to laugh as the tension of the last few minutes erupted out of her. 'Don't tell Station Officer Steele we did that. I don't think she'd approve somehow.'

'What the eye doesn't see...' Mac raised his eyebrows, smiling at her. 'You're a brave woman driving through fire to get to casualties, Winnie.'

Winnie shrugged. 'Enough of that sort of talk; we're just doing our job, like everyone else out here tonight.'

With three casualties labelled and loaded into the ambulance on stretchers, Winnie closed the back doors, leaving Mac inside to take care of them on the journey to hospital. Walking around to the driver's door, she glanced up at the sky and gasped. It was terrifying and horrific and yet extraordinarily beautiful, glowing yellow, green and red as great billows of smoke whirled across it. Towering above the burning buildings, blackly silhouetted against the colourful smoke, was the dome of St Paul's, its golden orb and cross shining out brightly, reflecting the flames raging all around it. The sight of the great cathedral still standing firm and proud, looking as if it was floating above a sea of fire and smoke, filled Winnie with a sudden surge of hope. Perhaps not all would be lost tonight. Could her beloved St Paul's survive? She desperately hoped so.

Frankie knew something was wrong the instant she opened the back doors of the ambulance and saw Bella's stricken face.

'Two have gone.' Bella bit hard on her bottom lip, trying hard not to cry. 'There was nothing I could do.'

Frankie swallowed, fighting back a sickening feeling. She and Bella had never lost a casualty on the way to hospital – until now. 'They were too badly injured,' she said gently. 'Even if they'd survived the journey, there might have been nothing the doctors could have done for them.'

Bella nodded. 'I know, but...' She shrugged.

'We need to get the other one out quickly, get him to people who can hopefully help him.'

Together she and Bella swiftly and smoothly unloaded the injured fireman, who was still unconscious, and carried him into the busy casualty department, hoping that at least he would survive. Then they returned to the ambulance and took the stretchers bearing the bodies of the two brave men who had died to the mortuary.

'Are you all right, Bella?' Frankie asked when they were back in the ambulance cab and heading back to Station 75.

'A bit shocked and upset,' Bella said. 'I felt so useless. There was nothing I could do to help them.'

'You're not a doctor, and even if you were, there

might have been nothin' you could have done to 'elp. You're not to blame in any way, you 'ear.' Frankie glanced at Bella, then reached out and squeezed her arm. 'It's this bloomin' war.'

'I know, I just... We've never lost anyone before.'

'We've been lucky; a lot of the other crews have. It had to 'appen sometime and tonight's raid is one hell of a big one. I–' Frankie swerved to avoid an incendiary bomb that had just landed in the road.

'And it's not over yet,' Bella said.

Back in the shelter at Station 75, Frankie signed in and reported the number of casualties taken to hospital to Station Officer Steele, who was mounting her usual guard over the telephone. The incidents were coming in thick and fast tonight.

'Hopefully our next call-out won't be so bad,' Frankie said as Bella passed her a much-needed cup of tea and they sat down to wait.

'It can't get much worse than that, can it?' Bella stared mournfully into her tea.

Frankie put her arm around her friend and squeezed her shoulders. 'Chin up, Bella. We'll be all right, just you wait and see.'

Frankie and Bella carefully picked their way over the tangled fire hoses to where an ARP warden was waiting with casualties. They carried an empty stretcher between them, keeping their heads bowed to protect their faces from the hot swirling embers that clattered down on their steel helmets and pricked at any skin they touched.

A hose suddenly jumped off the ground, nearly tripping Frankie over as a surge of water pulsed through it.

'Watch out!' a fireman shouted from further down the street, where the nozzle end of the same hose lashed from side to side with the sudden force of the water pushing through it, almost knocking the men holding it off their feet. Lack of water was proving to be as much of an enemy tonight as the bombs raining down. The River Thames was at a very low ebb, and fractured water mains meant that the firemen simply didn't have enough water to battle the flames that had spread rapidly through the City's narrow streets and warehouses.

'Are you all right?' Bella said.

'Yes, I'm fine. Make sure you tread carefully,' Frankie called back over her shoulder. She could feel beads of sweat trickling down her back. She and Bella weren't as close to the burning buildings as the firemen were, their silhouetted shapes standing out against the orange flames, but the heat was intense and the air acrid with smoke, making the backs of their throats sting.

Reaching the four casualties, who were laid on the ground, their faces and uniforms caked with dust and dirt, Frankie and Bella quickly got to work, crouching down by the injured men and examining them to assess their injuries.

'They got caught when a wall came down,' the ARP warden explained. 'They ran for it and nearly got away.'

Frankie knew the routine well, and it helped that the first man she assessed was conscious and could tell her what his name was and where he had pain. She quickly filled in a label for him and tied it to one of the buttons on the front of his tunic.

'We'll soon get you into the ambulance and on your way to hospital,' she said, patting his hand gently.

'You're like angels coming to our rescue,' the fireman said, smiling at her. Frankie smiled back, amazed at how upbeat and cheerful casualties often were. They usually had a spirit of defiance about them, remaining positive if they could, as though they weren't going to let the war beat them.

'I won't be long. I just need to assess your colleague here.' Frankie stood up and walked the few short steps to where the next casualty lay.

'He ain't a fireman,' the first man called over. 'He's a policeman, come down with us on our pump from Stepney.'

A prickle of unease ran through Frankie. Was it someone she knew, one of her grandfather's friends in the force? Crouching down by the still form, her heartbeat seemed to stutter inside her as she recognised the man lying beside her. It was Grandad. Gently brushing brick dust and dirt off his face, she struggled to keep calm as her whole body started to shake.

'What was he doing here?' She turned and looked at the fireman. 'He should have been at home, off duty.'

'Do you know him?' the fireman asked.

Frankie nodded. 'He's my grandfather.'

'Frankie!' Bella came rushing over and crouched down beside her. 'Let me check him.'

'No, no, I can do it.'

'I'll do it; you find out what the heck he was doing here,' Bella ordered. 'Then we can get them into the ambulance and to hospital.'

Frankie turned back to the fireman, who shrugged. "E just turned up at our station, said he wanted to 'elp. The more 'elp we 'ad the better tonight.'

'How is he?' Frankie glanced at Bella, who was writing out a label.

'Unconscious, broken leg, cuts, bruises; that's as much as I can say at the moment.' Bella quickly threaded the label around a button on the front of Grandad's police tunic. 'Best thing we can do for him is get him to hospital.'

Loading the four stretchers into the ambulance seemed to Frankie to take forever, even with the help of the ARP warden, who had insisted on taking her place carrying Grandad's stretcher. She'd been glad to accept his offer; she was shaking so much she was afraid she might drop him.

'All set,' Bella said, climbing into the back of the ambulance to watch over the men on the journey to hospital.

Frankie had her hands on the doors ready to close them, but she stopped. 'I need to stay with him,' she blurted out, her eyes blurring with tears. 'I can't drive, Bella.'

'You have to, Frankie. Who else is going to do it?' Bella grabbed Frankie's hands and squeezed them. 'It's your job, you must do it.'

'Look at me, I'm shaking...' Frankie couldn't stop tears from rolling down her cheeks. 'If he dies, I have to be with him. He needs me there.'

'He's not going to die,' Bella said. 'He'll be fine, you'll see.'

'Those firemen weren't.'

Bella sighed. 'Who's going to drive if you can't?'

'You.'

Bella's eyes widened and she stared at Frankie. 'I can't. I haven't passed my test.'

'You *can* drive, Bella. You're good, Mac says so. Please, I wouldn't ask if I really couldn't do it myself. I need to be near him. You understand, don't you? He's all I've got left of my family.'

Bella nodded slowly, squeezing Frankie's hands again. 'All right, I'll do it, I'll try my best.'

'Thank you.' Frankie threw her arms around her friend and hugged her tightly. 'Get us to the hospital, Bella. You can do it, I know you can.'

Bella sat motionless in the driver's seat, her heart thumping so hard it was as if it was trying to beat its way out. She ran her tongue over her dry lips. She couldn't believe what she'd just agreed to do. Not only was it madness; it was against the rules. Station Officer Steele would have a fit if she knew, because the simple fact was, Bella wasn't qualified to do the job. She'd never driven an ambulance before, let alone one full of badly injured people who needed to get to hospital. She hadn't even passed her test in a car.

She sighed, feeling herself shake with fear. What she'd agreed to do was wrong in so many ways, but she didn't have a choice. She had to do it, because Frankie couldn't. It was up to her to get Frankie's grandfather and the other casualties to hospital. If she didn't, then they might die and

334

she'd have as good as killed them herself. Frankie would lose the man who had been a father to her, and Bella knew how terrible that felt.

Images of her own father suddenly collapsing and dying in the garden where he'd been working flashed into her mind. Bella had been there with him, seen him clutch at his chest, the colour drain from his face as he'd slowly keeled over into the vegetable bed he'd been weeding. His life had been snuffed out in seconds. He was gone far too soon and the pain that followed was terrible, heartbreaking; it had changed her life forever.

Dashing away the tears that rolled down her cheeks, she reached for the ignition. She had to do everything in her power to stop that from happening to dear Frankie, whom she had grown to love like a sister. She had to do it now.

'You can do this,' she said through clenched teeth as she started the engine.

Putting the ambulance into gear, she pulled away jerkily and crawled along, painfully aware of the size and load of the vehicle, its unwieldy bulk behind her like a heavy shell on the back of a snail. Sitting in the driver's seat, she felt tiny, the length of the bonnet stretching out in front of her while she perched at the wheel, manoeuvring and pressing the pedals and telling herself constantly that she could do it. All she had to do was get up to sixteen miles an hour, that was all; she could manage that. She could, she would. She must.

She'd done so much better on the practice drives she'd had with Mac, although they'd been few and far between. Mac had always been encouraging and had helped her confidence to grow instead of battering it down like Sparky had. But those drives had been in a car, not an ambulance.

Gripping the steering wheel so tightly that her knuckles stood out white, Bella did her best to keep breathing slowly and steadily, focusing hard on the road ahead, concentrating on what she was doing, on every movement she made with her hands or feet, telling herself that every yard she drove was that bit nearer to help. She felt cocooned in the cab, vaguely aware of the chaos going on outside, the sky lit up with the glow of London burning while firemen battled to save buildings. Her job was to keep going, keep driving and get Frankie's grandfather to hospital.

By the time she turned the ambulance in through the gates of the hospital, she felt exhausted, her whole body aching with tension and her head throbbing from concentrating so hard. As she drew up behind another ambulance, the engine stalled and she pulled on the handbrake with relief. Closing her eyes, she sent up a silent prayer of thanks before flinging the door open and racing around to the back.

'How is he?'

Frankie looked ghastly, her dirt-smudged face streaked with telltale tear tracks. 'He's still breathing,' she said, jumping out.

Together they gently manoeuvred the stretcher out of the ambulance and carried Frankie's still unconscious grandfather into the casualty department, which was overrun with people hurt in the raid. Bella recognised a familiar figure in a white coat who was examining another patient brought in on a stretcher.

'Alistair,' she said.

At the sound of his name, he looked around and saw them. He quickly gave instructions to some hospital orderlies to take the patient he'd been looking at through to the treatment rooms and then came over.

'Are you all right?' he asked, concerned.

'It's my grandfather...' Frankie's voice wobbled.

Alistair looked at him quickly. 'Bring him through.'

He led the way and they followed. As the orderlies transferred Frankie's grandfather onto a bed, Alistair looked at the label attached to his tunic.

'What happened?' he asked.

'He...' Frankie began.

'He was hit by a building coming down, found unconscious.' Bella took hold of Frankie's hand.

Alistair nodded. 'Listen, Frankie, I'll do my very best for him, I promise.' He reached out and gripped her other hand.

Frankie nodded, sniffing back tears.

'We've got other casualties to bring in,' Bella reminded her.

'But...' Frankie hesitated, and then nodded.

'There's nothing you can do to help me. I will look after him,' Alistair said. 'Go and bring in the others.'

'Thank you, I'm glad it's you...' Frankie's voice broke.

'Come on, we need to let Alistair do his job.' Bella linked her arm through Frankie's and led her away, leaving her friend's grandfather in Alistair's capable hands, hoping with all her heart that he would be able to save him.

Chapter Twelve

'Not this time, Trixie.' Winnie braced herself not to weaken at the sight of her dog's pleading liquid-brown eyes. 'You've got to stay here.'

'I'll look after her; she'll be quite safe here with me.' Station Officer Steele bent down and scooped Trixie up into her arms. 'But it doesn't mean I agree with what you're doing.' Her shrewd eyes held Winnie's. 'You're not on duty so I can't order you not to go...' She smiled. 'But even if I did, that would be no guarantee that you'd do as you were told, would it?'

Winnie shrugged and smiled back. 'Of course not. I know you have my best interests at heart, but I've got to go and find out for myself.'

'Whatever's happened, there's nothing you can do to change it, you know that.' Station Officer Steele reached out and touched Winnie's arm. 'Promise me you'll be careful and wear your steel helmet.'

'I will. Thank you for minding Trixie for me. It's no place for her.' She stroked the dog's golden head. 'Don't worry, I'll be back in time for my shift.'

'Go on then.' Station Officer Steele smiled ruefully. 'And mind you keep your helmet on.'

Outside, the smattering of snowflakes drifting down were like frozen tears weeping for London, Winnie thought, as she made her way westwards along unrecognisable streets, picking her way over rubble, her boots crunching on broken glass. The bleak December day, with its icy wind sending freezing fingers needling through her clothes, reflected the sad weariness in the eyes of everyone she passed. Exhausted firemen, their eyes red-rimmed in their smoke-blackened faces, were rolling up hoses, leaving some fires to burn themselves out. There was nothing more they could do.

It was unbearable to see that so much of the London she'd grown to love had been destroyed. The narrow streets full of old buildings, where workshops, warehouses and Victorian offices had stood cheek by jowl with banks, had been reduced to piles of rubble or hollow-eyed smoking ruins. Hundreds of years of tradition and history were gone forever, destroyed in just a few vicious hours.

Had St Paul's suffered the same fate? When she'd last seen it, it was still standing, but what chance did it have when so many incendiary bombs had rained down and with fires burning so fiercely around it, the flames and hot cinders spreading in the strong wind?

The sight of the great building had never failed to raise her spirits every time she bicycled past it. She loved the way it seemed to spring up amongst the huddle of buildings crowded around it, its dome soaring heavenwards, with the glinting golden orb and cross perched at the very top. If it was gone, then the heart would have been ripped out of the City.

St Paul's had been the first thing she'd thought of when she'd woken this morning after snatching a few hours' sleep on one of the mattresses in the women's rest room at Station 75. She'd stayed there for the remainder of the night instead of trying to negotiate the hellish inferno that lay between her and Bloomsbury. Others had done the same. Bella and Frankie were still sleeping when Winnie had tiptoed out of the room, carrying Trixie in her arms to stop her from going over and waking them. On her way across the staffroom she'd run straight into Station Officer Steele, who'd wanted to know where she was going.

She'd been determined to find out what had happened to her beloved St Paul's. Was it still standing? Was it damaged at all? Her last view of it, with its dome silhouetted against the blood-red sky and the orb and cross reflecting the flames, was burned into her memory. Was that the last time she'd ever see the great cathedral soaring up into the sky?

Ignoring the ropes cordoning off the damaged street, Winnie slipped underneath them unchallenged and picked her way over rubble and past the shells of buildings. She was glad that Station Officer Steele had insisted she wear her helmet, as it helped her blend in with the other emergency crew members around.

Passing Cannon Street station, she winced at the bare iron skeleton that was all that was left now. Was that how St Paul's would look? She kept on going, taking care not to trip on the tangled skeins of fire hoses that twisted over the dust and debris strewn across the street, the fear of what she might find lodged in a solid lump in her chest. And then she saw it. The dome rearing skywards, standing tall, defiant and proud. A sob caught in her throat and she let hot tears slip unchecked down her cheeks.

'Thank God,' she whispered, her voice hoarse with emotion.

A surge of adrenalin propelled her onward towards St Paul's. She still needed to make sure it was undamaged.

'Winnie!' Hearing her name, she stopped and turned around.

'Mac! What are you doing here?'

'Checking you're not getting yourself into trouble.' He looked worried. 'Are you all right?'

'Perfectly.' Winnie wiped her face with the back of her hand.

Mac fished a clean, ironed handkerchief out of his pocket. 'Here, let me. You've made it even dirtier.' He gently wiped her face clean.

'Thank you.' Winnie took a deep breath. 'Did Station Officer Steele send you?'

Mac shrugged. 'Maybe she did, but I'd have come anyway if I'd known what you were doing. She came and woke me up, said you'd gone out on some wild goose chase.'

'It's not a wild goose chase to me!' Winnie snapped. 'I needed to check if St Paul's had survived, and it has, at least as far as I can see from here. I'm now going to find out if there's any damage. So you can tell the boss I'm perfectly fine, thank you very much, and I'll be back for duty on time.'

Mac held up his hands. 'Whoa. I came in peace, Winnie. Do you mind if I come with you. I rather like the old cathedral myself, you know.'

Winnie nodded and smiled. 'I'm sorry. Yes, of course you can come.'

As she gazed up at St Paul's, standing whole and relatively unscathed after the horrors of the previous night, Winnie felt the tension and worry melt away. London had burned, but not the cathedral. Even the Christmas trees outside the west door had miraculously survived after a night of flames.

She flung her arms around Mac and danced him in a circle. 'It's a miracle!' she sang. She beamed at him and planted a kiss on his lips before turning back to gaze once more at the building soaring above them, looking stronger and even more beautiful in contrast with the smouldering wrecks surrounding it. The air might have been rank with the odour of burnt timber and steaming rubble, and some of the surrounding wood-paved streets were still burning, but St Paul's had survived.

'I can't believe it.' Winnie shook her head. 'I thought it would have been blown to bits or been reduced to a burnt-out shell after last night, but it's still here, and I'm so glad I–' She noticed the shocked expression on Mac's face. 'Oh my, I'm so sorry.' She put a hand to her mouth. 'I got a bit carried away. I hope I didn't upset you with that kiss?'

Mac shook his head and suddenly grinned. 'I was rather hoping you might do it again. I've been wanting to kiss you myself, actually.'

Winnie looked him straight in the eye. 'Then why don't you?'

'I've got to tell her,' Bella whispered.

'You don't. I ain't going to say anything and there's no one else who knows.' Frankie gulped the last of her tea and stood up. 'I've got to get to the 'ospital.'

Bella reached out and squeezed Frankie's arm. 'I know you'd never breathe a word of what happened, but my conscience is pricking and I have to be honest with her. She's been very good to me.'

Frankie shrugged. 'Good luck then.'

'I hope your grandfather's all right.' Bella stood up and hugged Frankie tightly. 'I'll come straight to the hospital as soon as I've told her. I'll be there soon after you, I promise.'

Frankie nodded. 'Thank you.'

Taking their empty mugs over to the kitchen area, Bella wondered if she was doing the right thing. Should she tell Station Officer Steele what she'd done last night? She didn't have to; everything had thankfully turned out well and the job was done. Winnie would have advised her to keep mum, but Winnie wasn't here, and the secret weighed heavily on Bella's conscience. There was nothing for it but to own up and face the consequences, whatever they might be.

Knocking on the boss's door, she felt her heart banging hard in her chest.

'Come in,' Station Officer Steele called.

As soon as Bella opened the door, Trixie jumped up from where she'd been sleeping on a folded blanket and rushed over to greet her, her golden plume of a tail wagging furiously.

'Hello, Trixie.' Bella bent down and made a fuss of her.

'Did you manage to get some sleep?' Station Officer Steele asked.

'Yes thank you. I was so tired, I was out like a light. Frankie's just gone to the hospital to see how her grandfather is.'

'Yes, a nasty business. I can imagine it was quite a shock for her to discover that he was one of the casualties.'

Bella nodded. 'Yes, she was very upset. In fact...' She paused, and took a deep breath to steady herself. 'That's what I've come to talk to you about. You see, Frankie wanted to stay with her grandfather in the back of the ambulance. She was worried he might not survive and wanted to be there with him just in case... So you see, she couldn't drive the ambulance.'

Station Officer Steele motioned for Bella to sit down on the empty chair by her desk. 'Please go on.'

Bella was relieved to take the weight off her shaking legs. 'And ... and so I drove it. There wasn't anyone else and I had to get Frankie's grandfather and the other casualties to hospital.'

'You drove an ambulance full of casualties to hospital last night?' Station Officer Steele looked at Bella, her eyebrows arched.

Bella nodded and looked down at her hands tightly clasped in her lap, bracing herself for what came next.

'Sparky was wrong about your driving abilities, then, wasn't he? Mac said you were very good.'

Bella looked up and saw that Station Officer Steele was smiling at her. 'But I shouldn't have driven the ambulance, should I? Not officially. I

344

haven't even passed my test in a car yet. I broke all the rules.'

'Indeed you did, Bella. But you know, in some circumstances rules just have to be broken. Who knows what might have happened if Frankie had driven in that state; she might have been so upset that she had an accident. You obviously got them to hospital safely and in one piece.' She smiled. 'I admire you for telling me; you didn't have to, and I might never have heard about it otherwise.'

'I couldn't *not* tell you,' Bella said. 'It wouldn't have been right. Are you going to sack me?'

'Do you think I should?'

'I hope you don't.'

'Then you'll be happy to know that I don't intend to. In fact I think it's time you took your driving test and became an official ambulance driver, don't you?'

'Do you think I could do it?'

'My dear Bella,' Station Officer Steele reached over and patted Bella's arm, 'you already have, and in the middle of one of the fiercest raids of the Blitz, with a full load of casualties in the back. That was a far tougher test of your driving skills than any the others have done.'

Bella smiled. 'I was terrified, though.'

'That doesn't matter; a bit of fear can help, keeps you on your toes and makes sure you do well.'

'Thank you.' Bella stood up. 'I must get to the hospital to be with Frankie. I hope her grandfather will pull through, but if he doesn't, she'll need someone there with her.'

'Stay with her as long as you need to,' Station

Officer Steele said. 'We'll cover for you both if we need to.'

'Aye, aye, what 'ave we got 'ere then? Two young lovebirds?' Sparky's voice called from the interior of one of the garages as Winnie and Mac walked past hand in hand. 'Glad to see you've both seen sense at last. Made for each other, you two are.'

Winnie peered into the gloom. 'You on sentry duty now, Sparky?' He was sitting in one of the deckchairs, well wrapped up in his thick coat, hat, scarf and gloves, cradling a steaming mug of tea.

'More like keepin' out of the way.' He grimaced.

'What's the matter?' Mac asked.

'I'll tell you in a minute,' Sparky said. 'So did you find it in one piece then?'

'Yes thank you, we did.' Winnie smiled happily. 'St Paul's is still standing in spite of the hell that was released on the City last night, though most of the buildings around it are burnt out. It's a miracle it survived.'

'You can put that down to the fire service,' Sparky said. 'I 'eard from a fireman this morning that Churchill told them to make sure it was saved, because it's too important to lose.'

'Good old Winston, I love him more than ever now,' Winnie said.

'So why *are* you out here then?' Mac asked. 'Has something happened?'

'You tell me.' Sparky pulled a face. 'The boss is on the warpath over something and she wants to see you two as soon as you get back. What 'ave

346

you done this time?'

Winnie looked at Mac and shrugged.

'Come on, let's go and get it over with,' Mac said, squeezing her hand. 'It won't be the first time you've had to face her over something.'

But it might be the last time, Winnie thought. She'd been warned before about taking risks, after the incident when she'd driven past a burning building to get a woman in labour to hospital. Station Officer Steele had given her another chance, but perhaps this time she'd gone too far and the boss would have no option but to sack her. The joy of finding St Paul's still standing quickly evaporated as she and Mac made their way upstairs.

Trixie's delighted cavorting welcome contrasted sharply with the boss's stony expression as she let Winnie and Mac into her office and shut the door behind them. She didn't invite them to sit. A terrible sense of déjà vu settled over Winnie. How many times had she been in this situation before, bracing herself for a reprimand for some flouted rule or order?

Station Officer Steele sat down at her desk and drew in a sharp breath. 'I suppose you thought I wouldn't get to know, what with all the chaos going on last night.'

'Know what?' Winnie asked.

'Don't play games with me, Winnie. I'm too tired and I haven't the patience. What you did was bloody irresponsible, foolish, dangerous and...' She paused for breath and looked at them, her eyes suddenly bright with tears. 'You could have been killed ... and damaged an ambulance.'

'How did you know?' Mac asked calmly.

'I had a telephone call from a policeman to congratulate me on the bravery of one of my ambulance crews, who, he says...' she picked up a piece of paper from her desk and read from it, '"drove through a sheet of flame blocking the road to get to casualties".'

'There were lots of ambulances out last night; it could have been any one of them,' Winnie suggested.

Station Officer Steele raised her eyebrows and looked Winnie straight in the eye. 'Only one with our station number on the side, and a dog among the crew.'

Winnie looked down at her feet, bracing herself for the end of her career as an ambulance driver.

'Of all the stupid, foolish and ... brave things to do.' Station Officer Steele reached out and took hold of Winnie's hand. Winnie looked up and saw that her boss was smiling. 'I was scared witless at the thought of what you did, because it could so easily have gone horribly, horribly wrong. The ambulance might have caught fire, the petrol tank blown up ... but thankfully it didn't, and your bravery saved the lives of three firemen. That's why you're both being put forward to receive a medal in recognition of your devotion to duty.'

'But–' Winnie began.

Station Officer Steele put her hand up to silence her. 'I admire your bravery immensely, but please don't make a habit of driving through fire. My ambulance and my nerves couldn't stand it.'

'I thought you were finally going to give me my marching orders,' Winnie admitted.

'What, and lose one of my finest drivers?' Station Officer Steele smiled. 'You're both needed more than ever, because if last night was anything to go by, the enemy hasn't finished with us yet. I fear there's more to come.'

Frankie perched on the edge of her seat, jumping at every movement in the corridor, every sound of a door opening and closing. Her whole body was as taut as the strings in the old piano back in the staffroom at Station 75; even her fingertips tingled with fear. Was her grandfather going to be all right? The nurse she'd asked had gone to find out, and all Frankie could do was sit and wait. And hope.

She'd wanted to come straight back here after her shift, but Station Officer Steele had insisted that she rest first, because she'd have been no good to anyone the state she was in. Under pressure from the boss and Bella, Frankie had given in and agreed to lie down for a while. She'd been adamant that she wouldn't sleep, but her body had had other ideas, and the next thing she'd known it had been eight o'clock in the morning.

Springing to her feet, she started to pace up and down the corridor. It was taking all her self-control not to burst in through the double doors leading to the ward and go in search of Grandad herself. It was only the thought of disturbing the injured men inside that stopped her. Even the smell of the hospital was making her anxious. She should be used to it by now, coming into hospitals as often as she did to bring in casualties, but this was different. Having someone in here that you loved put a whole new slant on the place; it was scarier and a great deal more personal.

'Frankie!' She turned to see Bella hurrying towards her, and the sight of the familiar figure suddenly released a great sob from deep within her. 'Oh Frankie!' Bella wrapped her arms around her and held her tightly. 'Have you heard anything?'

Frankie shook her head and dashed her tears away with the back of her hand. 'The nurse has gone to find out for me.'

'Come and sit down.' Bella led her back to the seat she'd been waiting on before and gently pushed her down onto it, then plonked herself down beside her, linking her arm through Frankie's and leaning against her.

'All I know is he's on this ward, so he's alive, but I don't know anything else, if he's going to be all right or if...' Frankie couldn't bring herself to say the words, although they were charging around her thoughts.

'It's good that he's got through the night,' Bella said.

'He could still die!' Frankie snapped, and immediately regretted her harsh tone as she felt Bella stiffen. 'I'm sorry.'

'It's all right, Frankie, you're worried. I would be too. You can shout at me some more if it will help.'

Frankie smiled at her dear friend. 'I couldn't do that to you, Bella. Now Ivy I could...' She suddenly realised that her step-grandmother probably didn't know what had happened. There had been such chaos last night, and Grandad hadn't officially been on duty, so word wouldn't have got through as quickly as if he'd been injured at work.

'Is she here?' Bella asked.

'No, and I don't know if she's even been told yet. I'll have to go 'ome when I know more.'

'Miss Franklin?' The nurse had returned.

Frankie leapt to her feet, glad that she had Bella beside her, giving her much-needed support as she prepared herself for the news, be it good or bad.

'How is he?' Her voice sounded odd.

The nurse smiled kindly. 'He's comfortable, and if you'd like, I can take you to see him for a few minutes.'

'Is he going to be all right?' Frankie asked.

'Yes, I believe he will be, given time to mend his broken bones and plenty of rest. He's been lucky. We'll be moving him out to one of our sector hospitals in Kent this afternoon to recover.'

Frankie nodded, biting down on her bottom lip to stop herself from crying with relief.

'If you'd like to come this way.' The nurse held out her arm. 'Your friend too, if you like.'

'Do you want me to?' Bella asked.

'Please,' Frankie said. She could do with someone by her side.

Bella kept a firm hold on Frankie's arm as they walked into the ward.

'Third bed along on the right.' The nurse pointed it out. 'Five minutes and no more; he needs to rest. He'll be pleased to see you,' she added kindly.

The sight of Grandad, his head swathed in bandages, his face bruised and scratched and one of his legs in plaster, was a shock. He seemed

351

somehow smaller, his large frame shrunk as he lay on the pristine white sheet.

'Grandad,' Frankie said, pasting on a smile even though her insides were quivering and tears were stabbing at her eyes. She took a deep breath and pushed down her emotions. She needed to help him, not upset him. 'How are you?'

He tried to smile, and then winced, putting a hand to his head. 'Feel like I've done ten rounds in a boxing ring.'

Frankie reached out and held his hand. 'More like with a brick wall, you mean. We brought you in.'

'What, in your ambulance?'

Frankie nodded. 'Gave me one 'eck of a shock, finding you like that. What were you doing there?'

'I 'ad to do something, couldn't just sit there when it was such a bad raid, so I went to the nearest fire station and volunteered to 'elp.'

'And got caught when a wall came down.'

'I don't know... Last thing I remember was a fireman shouting at me to run. I just felt useless sitting in the shelter with Ivy...' He paused and looked around. 'Is she 'ere?'

'I don't know if she even knows you're hurt,' Frankie said. 'I'll go 'ome and tell her.'

'They're going to move me – let 'er know, will yer?'

'Of course.'

'Time's up,' said the nurse, bustling over and taking hold of Grandad's wrist to check his pulse.

'You take care now, and I'll come and see you as soon as I can.' Frankie bent down and kissed his cheek.

'Don't you worry about me,' Grandad said, reaching out and grabbing her hand. 'You're the one driving an ambulance around in the middle of air raids. You will be careful, won't yer?'

'Of course, we always are.' Frankie smiled at him and squeezed his hand. 'I'll be seeing you soon.' She turned away and strode towards the ward doors without looking back. She didn't want him to see the tears streaming down her cheeks.

'Frankie.' Bella came hurrying along behind her and grabbed her arm. 'Are you all right?'

Frankie nodded. 'Yes, just a bit shocked, that's all. Hard to see him looking like that.' She sniffed. 'He ain't lost any of his spark, though.'

'It's good they're going to evacuate him out to a safer hospital,' Bella said. 'You won't have to worry about him during air raids any more.'

'Looks like all my family are going to the countryside.' Frankie managed a smile. 'Just me and Ivy left now.' She sighed. 'I need to go 'ome and tell her.'

'Do you want me to come with you?' Bella asked.

'No, but thank you for offering. She's not the kind of person I'd inflict on my friends.' Frankie sighed. 'It's no good putting it off. If I go straight there, she'll still have time to come and see Grandad before he's sent to the countryside.'

Bicycling back into Matlock Street, Frankie was grateful for Alistair's thoughtful and generous gift. It made getting around so much quicker and easier. She hoped they'd be able to take some trips out of London together when the weather got better, as he had suggested.

Letting herself into number 25, she heard the sound of the wireless coming from the kitchen. She wheeled her bicycle into the hall, leaning it against the wall, and prepared herself to face her step-grandmother.

'You're back then,' Ivy sneered the moment Frankie walked through the door. She was sitting in her usual place in the armchair by the fire, a cup of tea by her side, *Picture Post* on her lap and a cigarette in her fingers spiralling smoke into the air. 'I've bin 'ere all on my own for hours now. Your bleedin' grandfather went off in the middle of a raid. We were in the shelter but 'e wouldn't settle, said he 'ad to go and 'elp out even though it wasn't 'is shift. Didn't care that 'e was leaving me alone.' She paused for breath and then went on. ''E's still not back and I ain't got a clue where he is.'

Frankie pulled out a chair, sat down at the table and placed her head in her hands.

'What's the matter wiv you?' Ivy spat. 'You've got a face on yer like a wet dishcloth.'

Closing her eyes, Frankie took several deep breaths to calm herself. Her heart was beating a rapid tattoo and she wanted to throttle this vile, selfish woman who thought of no one but herself. When she was ready, she sat up straight and looked Ivy square in the eyes.

'I know where Grandad is.'

Ivy narrowed her eyes and took a long puff on her cigarette. 'Where?'

'In 'ospital.'

The colour drained from Ivy's face and her mouth opened and shut like a fish for a few moments before she managed to form any words. 'What's happened to 'im?' Her voice came out shrill and fast.

'He got a lift with a fire crew last night into the City, and was caught when a wall collapsed. I was sent to the incident to pick him up.'

Ivy sat silently for a moment. 'What the bloody 'ell was he doin' getting involved with a raid in the City?' she spat. 'That ain't his beat.'

'No, but he still wanted to 'elp. It was hell out there last night.'

'What happened to 'im?'

'He's lucky to be alive. He was unconscious when we took him in; 'e's cut and bruised and has a broken leg.' Frankie got up from the table and went to stand at the window that looked out over the back garden. 'He's at the London now, but they're moving him out to another hospital in the countryside this afternoon. You've still got time to visit if you want.'

'How am I supposed to cope wiv 'im in hospital out in the country?' Ivy said.

Frankie turned back and looked at her. Ivy had surpassed herself with her lack of consideration. Her first thought always was for herself, and she didn't seem to care that her husband had been injured. Would she even bother going to see him before he was evacuated out to Kent?

'I'm going to wash and change,' Frankie said. She wasn't going to even try and persuade Ivy to do the right thing, because she'd be wasting her breath. All that mattered to her right now was that

355

her grandfather was alive and would recover with time. The heavy weight of exhaustion was creeping through her body, the events of the past few hours catching up with her, and the thought of some deep, dreamless sleep was wonderful. 'Then I'm going to sleep for a bit before I go back on shift.'

'What a magnificent picture,' Winnie said, staring at the front page of the newspaper that lay on the table in the staffroom of Station 75. Under the banner 'War's Greatest Picture: St Paul's stands unharmed in the midst of the burning city' was a photograph of the dome of St Paul's wreathed in thick plumes of smoke. 'I love it. Look how it's standing there looking so proud and defiant while everything around it is burning.'

Frankie took her eyes away from the milk she was warming up in a saucepan on the cooker and smiled at her friend. Winnie was more thrilled with today's copy of the *Daily Mail*, which Sparky had handed her at the end of the shift, than if she'd been given a diamond necklace. 'It was quite a night all round.' And one she wouldn't forget in a hurry, she thought. 'Nearly done here; are you ready to go upstairs?'

Winnie nodded. 'Yes, yes, of course. Welcoming in the new year up on the roof is going to be such fun.'

Frankie was glad they'd decided to stay on at Station 75 after the end of their shift to welcome in the new year together. She couldn't have faced returning to Matlock Street, where it would have been just her and Ivy. It was so much better to be with her dear friends.

'Have you ever toasted it with cocoa before?' She poured the hot milk into three mugs and stirred them well to mix in the cocoa powder. 'You're probably more used to champagne.'

'Champagne perhaps, but never in such good company as I'll have tonight. Cocoa and good friends is the perfect combination.' Winnie smiled.

'It's nearly time,' Bella said, bustling into the room with her arms full of coats, hats, scarves and mittens. 'Is the cocoa ready?'

'Hot and ready to drink.' Frankie took her coat and put it on, followed by her ambulance service cap. She added the scarf Bella had knitted for her, and then her new mittens. 'Grab yourself a mug and let's go.'

With only a few minutes until midnight, Frankie stood on the flat roof of Station 75 looking out over a blacked-out London. There was just the thinnest crescent moon hanging in the star-pricked inky heavens above them, and it was too dark to see anything other than black smudges, but she could feel the city around her and knew exactly where each well-loved landmark lay. Close by was the Tower of London, which had seen in countless new years, standing solid and firm, un-damaged apart from the White Tower, which had been hit two nights ago. She hoped that the rest of it would survive the war and still be there for generations to come to love as much as she did.

'Well here we are,' Winnie said. 'A new year is almost upon us. Let's hope it's the year when this bloody war comes to an end.'

'Hear, hear,' Bella said.

'A toast, then: to 1941 and safer times.' Winnie suddenly laughed. 'I can't see your mugs to bump against.'

'Here.' Bella switched on her small torch, and its faint glow illuminated their faces in a weak pool of light.

'To safer times.' Winnie held up her mug of cocoa and bumped it against Frankie and Bella's, their eyes meeting as they smiled at each other before Bella switched off her torch, plunging them back into darkness.

'To safer times,' they chorused back.

As Frankie took a sip of cocoa, enjoying the liquid warmth running down within her, loud cheers went up from somewhere out in the nearby streets.

'Must be midnight,' Bella said. 'Happy new year! It seems odd not to hear the church bells ringing out across London to welcome it in.'

'Let's hope the next time they ring it'll mean it's all over, and not the other ... that we've been invaded,' Winnie said.

'Oh don't talk about that,' Bella said. 'Come on, let's sing "Auld Lang Syne".'

Putting their mugs down safely by their feet, the three friends joined hands and sang out, their voices clear in the cold, frosty air.

It took Frankie back to the last time she'd sung the song, a year ago in the kitchen at Matlock Street, joining in with Grandad, Stanley and Ivy. How things had changed since then. Her grandfather was in hospital in Kent, Stanley evacuated, and she herself was working as an ambulance driver. She wished that most of the changes had never happened – that Grandad hadn't been hurt and that there'd been no need to send Stanley away – but she would never regret becoming an ambulance driver, even though it was hard and frightening at times. It had brought her so much: two dear friends in Winnie and Bella, and Alistair too, of course. How different things would have been if she'd stayed sewing uniforms.

They fell silent for a few moments at the end of the song, their hands still clasped together. Frankie was so glad that she was here, up on the rooftop in the middle of the blackout. The air almost seemed to crackle with the hope and possibility of a new year, a new beginning.

'Nineteen forty-one. That will take some getting used to,' Winnie said, breaking the silence. 'What's it going to bring us, I wonder?'

'What do you hope for?' Frankie asked.

'For the war to end,' Winnie said.

'Do you think it will?' Bella asked.

'I don't know. If I'm honest, I think we've got a long way to go yet...' Winnie paused. 'But we won't give up.'

'Never,' Frankie said. She squeezed both her friends' hands. 'Whatever happens, we're in this together, we'll look out for each other. Friends till the end.'

Acknowledgements

A huge and heartfelt thank you to the Romantic Novelists' Association, without whom this book would never have been written. Their annual conferences give writers a chance to have one-to-one appointments with agents and editors, and in 2015 I was fortunate to get one of these precious opportunities – thank you, Elaine Everest. My appointment with Felicity Trew, who is now my wonderful agent, was where this book grew from. Thank you, Felicity, for all your encouragement, care and support, and for helping my dream come true.

Thanks to my fabulous editor, Manpreet Grewal, and all the excellent team at Sphere, who have been so warmly welcoming. It is truly a delight to be working with you all.

An historical book like this needs a lot of research – thank you to the Imperial War Museum and London Metropolitan Archives for access to your fascinating archives.

I was lucky to make contact with the family of a real London Auxiliary Ambulance Driver, Violet Sturt, who shared photos and answered questions for me – thank you to Violet, Margot and Philip Sturt, and also to Leslie Trott for putting me in touch with them.

My writing friends have been a constant source of encouragement and support – thank you to my dear Dreamcatcher friends, Angela Pickering, Biddy Fraser, Jo Fox and Rosie Edser. Pam Brooks and Heidi-Jo Swain – thank you for being there and holding my hand, especially through those dark days – and Pam, I am so glad that you can say 'I told you so!' Thanks also to the lovely ladies of the RNA's Norfolk chapter, who are such a fun and supportive group.

Thank you to my parents for never tiring of answering my many questions about life in the Second World War. My dad sparked my interest in this period; his tales of life as a boy watching the country at war were endlessly fascinating and entertaining. It is a great sadness to me that he is no longer here to see this book and read it for himself– he would have been so pleased.

And last, but by no means least, thank you to my family – my husband, David, who has supported my writing every step of the way, knowing and understanding the need to write and helping make it possible; and to my children who put up with scattered piles of paper and research books.

This Large Print Book for the partially sighted, who cannot read normal print, is published under the auspices of

THE ULVERSCROFT FOUNDATION

THE ULVERSCROFT FOUNDATION

... we hope that you have enjoyed this Large Print Book. Please think for a moment about those people who have worse eyesight problems than you ... and are unable to even read or enjoy Large Print, without great difficulty.

You can help them by sending a donation, large or small to:

The Ulverscroft Foundation,
1, The Green, Bradgate Road,
Anstey, Leicestershire, LE7 7FU,
England.
or request a copy of our brochure for more details.

The Foundation will use all your help to assist those people who are handicapped by various sight problems and need special attention.

Thank you very much for your help.